HOSTAGE POLICY
The Third Jerrod Gold Novel

James C. Gray

HOSTAGE POLICY
The Third Jerrod Gold Novel

OTHER BOOKS BY JAMES C. GRAY

CRUSH THE WICKED
The First Jerrod Gold Novel

CROSS EXAMINATION
The Second Jerrod Gold Novel

Available in Trade Paperback and
Kindle through Amazon.com

Desert Enigma Publishing, LLC
P.O. Box 2555
Dayton, NV 89403
D.E.Publishing1@gmail.com

HOSTAGE POLICY
The Third Jerrod Gold Novel

Cover Art by: Travis Miles
www.ProBookCovers.com

Printed by: Kindle Direct Publishing,
An Amazon.com company

Also available in Kindle eBook on Amazon.com

ISBN-13: 978-0-9863595-4-5

DEDICATION

Gregory H. "Gregg" Williams
Badge 178
1947-1998

I Will Never Forget Who Trained Me.
Rest In Peace, Partner.

-- Badge 202

ACKNOWLEDGMENTS

To my law enforcement brothers and sisters who,
despite the criticism, continue performing the necessary
tasks our communities demand knowing someone will be there
when they call 9-1-1.

To Cindy. Who continues to encourage me building these
stories and tolerates my time away from her when I do.
You get the first completed draft and I get my first honest review.
Thank you. I love you.

To Christy. First time seeing a work-in-progress.
Your observations and insight helped bring it all together.
Thank you. I love you.

"Let your plans be dark and as impenetrable as night,
and when you move, fall like a thunderbolt."

-- Sun Tzu
The Art of War

CHAPTER 1

SEPTEMBER 1991 -- Wednesday -- Noon

The front door didn't have a lock.

Mesa County Sheriff's Detective Sergeant Jerrod Gold had pulled open the front door to Sophie's Diner over two hundred times in the last five years. But, on that day, he reached for the handle, paused, and noticed for the first time there was no lock.

The twenty-four-hour family-friendly restaurant -- with its central location in affluent Willowmere, quick access to the Pacific Coast Highway, strong coffee, tasty food, friendly staff, and clean restrooms -- made Sophie's the office-away-from-the-office for local and state law enforcement.

As he sauntered into the diner, Jerrod was unaware the restaurant would be shuttered six months later and -- after the building had been demolished to make way for a new Starbucks Coffee -- that location would forever be haunted as the scene of the horrific event that would occur there.

All because of him.

"Two for lunch, Mr. Gold?"

"Four today, soon-to-be Mrs. Gold," Jerrod replied to his fiancée and restaurant manager, Nicole "Nikki" Verdugo. "The others'll be right in."

"Hot Tub?" she suggested as she directed them to the large horseshoe-shaped booth with a "Reserved" card placed on the table.

Jerrod nodded.

Nikki said, "Iced tea for you. I know already. How about you, Zippy?"

"Coke, please," Detective Bryce "Zippy" Zippich said. "Lots of ice."

"Okay."

A minute later, Detectives Nathan "Nate" Boxley and Marshall "Beach" Sutton walked into the restaurant.

"Hello boys," Nikki said. "Drinks?"

"Coke, please," Nate said.

"Diet Coke for me," Beach said.

She nodded. "Go join your partners-in-crime."

"Partners-in-crime-busting, ma'am," Beach countered. "Gonna catch us some mini-storage burglars today."

"Whatever, Beach." Nikki shooed him away. "Go. Sit."

Nate and Beach sat down with Jerrod and Zippy. The four investigators talked among themselves as Nikki brought their drinks and placed menus on the table.

"Lunch specials are on the board," she said.

As Nikki walked away, Beach turned to Jerrod. "Lucky dog."

"Indeed," Jerrod said as he perused a menu. "I was sitting right where you are now the first time I saw her."

"And you knew right then," Nate said.

"It was love at first sight," Zippy said.

Nate added, "And the rest is history."

"It was more like 'lust at first sight,'" Jerrod added. "But we're definitely in love now and are planning a long history together."

"Ahhh," Beach said. He pushed a mock tear from the corner of his eye.

"When's the wedding, again?" Zippy asked.

"February... uh... something... a Saturday," Jerrod said. "We're still working out the details. You were all invited."

"Food and an open bar. We'll be there," Beach said.

"What are you guy's doing this weekend? Jerrod asked.

"Softball tournament in Stockton," said Nate -- the lanky former standout high school and college baseball player.

"Sleep in late and go to bed early. Drink beer in between," said Beach -- the overweight senior detective nicknamed after the one-speed fat-tired "beach cruiser" bicycle.

"What are you doing, Zippy?" Nate asked.

Zippy smirked, looked at Jerrod, and turned back to Nate. "Playing golf with my dad -- and the Sarge -- at the Willowmere Country Club."

Nate glanced at Beach, and they said in mocking sing-song unison, "Golf with the Sarge at Willowmere."

"Nice," Nate added.

Zippy said, "My brothers are busy, and my dad invited him to play with us."

Beach glared at Zippy, curled his hand into a fist, and placed the thumb portion to his lips -- the universal sign for "ass-kisser."

Zippy glared back. "Screw you, Beach."

Jerrod's cell phone rang and he looked at the display. "It's Zaff. I'd better take this."

"Zaff" was Detective Lieutenant Benjamin "Ben" Zaff -- commander of the Mesa Sheriff's Investigation Division.

"What's up, L-T?" Jerrod said into the phone.

"Where are you?" the lieutenant asked. There was urgency in his voice.

"Just sat down at Sophie's with Zippy, Nate, and Beach. Why?"

"There's been a shooting at the Willowmere City Hall," the lieutenant said. "A man with a handgun. One person's shot inside and a hostage has been taken. Shooter's still in the building."

Jerrod stood up and looked at the three other investigators. "Where do you want us? We're just a couple minutes away."

"Willowmere PD is asking for SWAT. Get down to the scene and help however you can."

"We're heading there now," Jerrod said.

His detectives were out of their seats awaiting instructions as Jerrod tossed a five-dollar bill on the table. "Shooting at Willowmere City Hall."

"What the hell?" Nikki asked as the four men rushed to the door.

Jerrod yelled to Zippy. "Be right out."

Jerrod turned to Nikki. "There's... uh... a thing happening at city hall. Probably be over before we get there. I'll call you as soon as I know something."

"Kiss me before you leave," Nikki demanded.

Jerrod gave her a hurried kiss. "I love you. Nothing will go wrong. I'll see you tonight."

She blinked back tears as she watched him run out the door.

Jerrod had ridden to the restaurant with Zippy in his unmarked Ford sedan.

"All my gear is in my car... back at the office," Jerrod said as they ran into the restaurant parking lot.

"I have my raid jacket and ballistic vest. And a shotgun," Zippy said.

"You take the jacket and vest. I'm taking the shotgun," Jerrod said.

The police radio traffic was frantic as Zippy drove the single mile from the restaurant to city hall in under three minutes. Nate followed with Beach in his Chevrolet sedan.

Jerrod loaded four twelve-gauge rounds of buckshot into the magazine tube of the Remington Model 870 police shotgun. The fifth round was a cartridge containing a rifled lead slug. He opened the shotgun breach, dropped the cartridge into the opening, and pushed the slide forward to chamber the round. He insured the "safety" was on with his thumb.

He took the seven-point gold badge in its belt clip and secured it to the front of his short-sleeve shirt.

Jerrod saw Willowmere Fire Department trucks and two ambulances staged a half-block from city hall. A few seconds later Zippy screeched his car to a stop in the roadway behind a Willowmere PD blue-and-white patrol car blocking the street in front of the city hall building.

Uniformed officers pointed handguns across the hoods of patrol cars at the front of the building. A Willowmere PD sergeant yelled to Jerrod and Zippy as they got out of their cars: "Cover the rear."

Nate and Beach ran with Jerrod and Zippy behind the two-story building. The structure was L-shaped and formed two sides of a small, triangular parking lot just big enough for five or six cars. There were no cars in the lot and only one heavy fire door giving access to the building.

The four investigators took cover positions across the parking lot from the building. Nate, Beach, and Zippy crouched behind a concrete retaining wall. Jerrod stood behind a thick power pole and trained the shotgun at the door.

Nate had his portable radio on and Jerrod heard Mesa Comm announce the Sheriff's Office SWAT was enroute to take-over the scene.

"We'll just hold things down until SWAT gets here," Jerrod yelled to his detectives. "No heroes today. I promised Nikki I was coming home."

One minute became five. Five then became fifteen as they waited for SWAT to arrive. There had been no movement at the back of the building and no noise from inside.

The detectives were joined by a uniformed sheriff's patrol deputy -- Scott Jackson. Scott was also carrying a Remington shotgun.

Jerrod and Scott had a history together: Both had been the first responders to the ghastly scene of the family homicide-suicide on Cardinal Lane a year-and-a-half earlier.

"Scott," Jerrod yelled. "We're covering the rear of the building until SWAT shows up. No one comes in or gets out of the area."

Scott gave him a thumbs-up and took a cover position at the corner of the city hall building to the far right of the door.

Twenty minutes elapsed and SWAT hadn't arrived.

Jerrod saw the door being opened slowly. He aimed the muzzle of the shotgun and pressed the safety button into the "fire" position with his forefinger. He rested his finger along the trigger guard.

A flash of color -- light blue -- peeked from the door. It was the pleated skirt of a woman's dress. A pale leg followed. Then the arm and torso and face of a thirty-year old woman became exposed. It was followed by a sixty-year-old man -- wild white hair and a red plaid long-sleeve shirt -- appearing behind her.

The left arm of the man was around her neck. His right hand held a long-barreled black revolver with the muzzle pressed against the terrified woman's head.

CHAPTER 2

Jerrod was eighty feet from the door. The man held the woman in front of him and Jerrod could only see his face. The door slammed shut with a loud thud.

"Just put the gun down," Jerrod yelled to the man. "No one needs to get hurt here."

"Fuck you," the man yelled back. "I'm just going to walk away... and you're not going to stop me."

"The hell you are," Beach yelled as he pointed his Glock 9mm auto-pistol at the man. Beach was ten feet to the left of Jerrod. Nate and Zippy -- both in green MCSO raid jackets -- were just to the left of Beach. Their handguns were trained on the man as well.

Jerrod heard Nate talk into his portable radio, "Male suspect just came out the back door. White hair, red long-sleeve shirt. He has a female hostage. Handgun to her head."

"Hey, hey, hey," Jerrod yelled at the man. "Talk to me. Just let the lady go and we can end this without any more problems."

The man scanned the area and saw the muzzles of five law enforcement firearms pointed at him. "No. No. No. No. I'm going back inside," he yelled.

Jerrod watched the man shuffle the woman back toward the door and peek over his shoulder. He let go of the woman's neck and reached for the door handle. The revolver stayed to the back of the woman's head. He pulled at the handle and realized the fire door had securely locked behind him.

"Lock yourself out, dipshit," Beach yelled at the man.

"Beach!" Jerrod yelled. "Shut up."

Beach glared back.

"Nobody's going anywhere," Jerrod yelled to the man. "What's your name?"

"I'll kill her," the man yelled back as he grabbed the woman around the waist. "I swear I'll kill her."

"No one is going to kill anyone," Jerrod yelled.

No words were exchanged for the next few seconds. The man, now frantic, scoured the area for an escape route. His finger stayed on the trigger of the gun pressed to the head of his hostage.

"The lady has nothing to do with this," Jerrod yelled to the man. "We can all put these stupid guns down and talk."

"All I wanted was a building variance," the man yelled. "And all I heard from the city was: 'You need to submit this,' 'That will be another two hundred dollars,' 'You need to change the plans.' I'm sick of this shit."

"We can work all that out," Jerrod said. "I can help you. But we all just need to end this without anyone getting hurt."

The man didn't speak. He stood motionless for nearly twenty seconds. He then moved the handgun from the woman's head and to his own temple.

"Just let her go," Jerrod yelled.

The man relaxed his grip from her waist. The woman took a half-step away from the man.

"Don't run," Jerrod yelled to the woman. "Just walk to the uniformed deputy on your left. Now we're getting somewhere. You're going to be okay."

As the woman made her first full step away from the man, two dark-blue uniformed Willowmere PD officers with handguns drawn ran around the corner of the building past Scott Jackson.

"What the hell?" Jerrod yelled at the officers. "Get back. Get back."

The two officers stopped fifteen feet short of the man and pointed their guns at him.

The man ran to the woman, grabbed her around the waist, and again placed the gun to her head. The woman wailed.

As the Willowmere officers ran at him, the man had turned to his left -- now placing the hostage between himself and the officers. Scott Jackson moved from his cover position and followed the officers along the wall. He raised his shotgun and stood -- now fully exposed -- behind them.

The right side of the man's head was clearly visible to Jerrod. He sighted down the length of the shotgun barrel and bracketed the small brass "BB" front sight directly on the man's ear.

Jerrod lost all conscious thought at that moment. Time slowed. Vision narrowed. Sound muted. The training from his firearms instructors over the previous eleven years -- especially that of Valle Verde Police Sergeant Mark "Marko" Otero -- had instilled a muscle-memory which made his actions automatic.

7

Jerrod pulled the rubber pad of the wooden shotgun stock securely against his shoulder as his finger moved to the trigger. His left forearm rested against the power pole to stabilize his aim.

The Willowmere officers yelled at the man as he pulled the terrified hostage closer to him. The revolver still to her head. The man yelled back as he moved the revolver from the woman's head and pushed the muzzle toward the officers.

Jerrod paused his breath and smoothly applied pressure to the shotgun trigger. As the spring tension of the firing pin was released, the primer of the twelve-gauge shell was impacted, the powder charge ignited, and a half-inch wide lead projectile raced down the eighteen-inch shotgun barrel at 1,560 feet-per-second.

The one-ounce lead slug nicked the top of the man's right ear and sped through his brain before anyone in the area had heard the boom from the shotgun. Unlike in the movies, the man wasn't blown back by the impact of the slug. His legs simply crumpled, and gravity pulled him straight down. As he fell, a pattern of splattered blood became visible on the wall behind him.

The woman was dragged down with the dead man as the revolver clattered to the concrete. The two Willowmere officers rushed in and pulled the screaming woman away from the motionless man.

"Scott!" Zippy yelled.

Jerrod looked to the right and saw Scott Jackson down on his right knee and leaning against the wall. His shotgun lay on the ground. He was holding his chest and bright red blood stained the left side of his khaki-tan short-sleeve uniform shirt.

Nate keyed the microphone of his portable radio and screamed, "Shots fired. Suspect down. And... my God... deputy down. Rear of the city hall. We need an ambulance. Code Three."

Jerrod, Beach, Nate, and Zippy ran to Scott. They eased him to the walkway and had him lay on his back. The entire left side of his torso was stained with blood.

"I can't... get my... breath," Scott gasped. "I can't... breathe."

Zippy pulled the front of Scott's shirt open and the buttons broke away. He tugged at the Velcro elastic straps of Scott's ballistic vest and threw the blood-stained front panel to the side.

Scott's t-shirt was soaked red. He coughed and spit out foamy-pink sputum. Nate ripped open the t-shirt and exposed a small hole near Scott's left armpit. Blood dribbled from the wound. A bullet had found the arm hole of his vest and entered his chest. Air could be heard being pulled into the wound when Scott inhaled.

Jerrod looked at Nate. "Put your hand over that wound and hold pressure on it. Let air out, but no air goes into his chest. Time it with his breaths."

Nate hesitated for a beat and then placed his bare hand over the wound. The blood trickle slowed, and no air passed the seal.

"Roll him over," Jerrod ordered.

They rolled Scott to his right side and looked at his back. The bullet had not exited.

Jerrod laid next to the downed deputy's head and talked directly into Scott's ear. "Listen to me. You've been hit in the lung. The bullet's still in there. Just breathe. Take in as much air as you can. Slow and steady. An ambulance is right around the corner and they're going to get you to the ER in no time."

Scott coughed-up more pinkish foam. His breathing became rapid, and he panted as he tried to capture air in his lungs.

A siren could be heard nearby.

"Breathe. Breathe," Jerrod said. "You're going to get through this."

Scott nodded and slowed his breathing.

"Scott," Jerrod whispered. "Does it hurt?"

Nate looked at Jerrod with bewilderment.

"Yeah." Scott coughed. His eyes narrowed. "It... fucking... hurts."

"Good," Jerrod said. "Embrace that pain. Savor that pain."

"Sarge. Stop. Please," Zippy pleaded.

"Scott," Jerrod continued, undeterred. "That pain means you're still alive. That pain means you're not paralyzed. That pain means you're going to survive this. They're going to give you some strong drugs at the hospital and take that pain away, but until then -- thank God you can feel it."

"I don't want to die, Sarge," Scott whispered.

"You're not going to die, Scott. Not today."

Seconds later, more uniformed Willowmere PD officers, SO deputies, firefighters and, finally, an ambulance poured into the small parking lot behind the city hall building. Two paramedics with large plastic aid boxes rushed to Scott.

Nate kept pressure on the wound with his right hand and held Scott's hand with his left.

"You're going to make it, brother," Nate whispered. "We're staying with you."

Scott nodded.

"He has an '*open pneumo,*'" one of the paramedics yelled to the other.

"Pneumo," short for a *pneumothorax,* or a "sucking chest wound," occurs when the chest wall is punctured, and air is pulled into the wound causing the lung to collapse.

The paramedics had Nate lift his right hand off Scott's chest as an adhesive foil-backed bandage was slipped over the wound. A clear plastic mask was secured over Scott's nose and mouth. A thin tube ran to the valve of a small green tank of pure oxygen.

"Breathe. Breathe," Jerrod whispered.

Scott looked at Jerrod through moist eyes and moved his lips under the fogged mask. Jerrod couldn't make out what he said.

Two firefighters pulled a gurney from the ambulance and rolled it next to Scott. He was lifted onto the gurney and loaded into the nearby ambulance. Nate stayed at his side.

"Nate," Jerrod directed. "Don't leave him until he's wheeled into surgery."

Nate nodded and jumped through the open rear door of the ambulance. A path had been cleared and the ambulance sped towards Saint Michael's Hospital and the competent emergency room personnel there.

Jerrod picked his shotgun up from the walkway and looked around the chaotic scene. Uniformed officers had already hung yellow CRIME SCENE DO NOT ENTER tape all around the congested parking lot. Local media sound trucks were arriving. Reporters stood impatiently behind the yellow ribbons, microphones in hand. News cameras were being lugged to the scene perimeter.

A familiar voice yelled from behind the tape. "Jerrod. Jerrod. Sergeant Gold."

Jerrod glanced over and saw Bruce Witt -- the former *Valle Verde Sun* crime-beat news reporter and current independent videographer -- trying to get his attention.

Jerrod ignored Bruce, and the large camera perched on his shoulder, as he scanned the scene. He focused first on Scott's bloody clothing on the walkway and then at the two Willowmere officers comforting the still sobbing hostage as she sat with her back against the wall. Her hands covered her face. Specks of blood dotted her hair and neck and the light blue dress.

Beyond the young lady was the cooling body of the man who had held her hostage a few minutes earlier. A six-foot pool of clotting blood covered the walkway. The revolver lay in the creeping red mess.

"Come with me," Jerrod said to Beach and Zippy.

They walked toward the Willowmere officers. Jerrod stopped near the closest one. Mid-twenties. No stripes on his sleeves or bars on his collars. A junior patrolman.

The officer looked at Jerrod and down at the "Sheriff's Sergeant" badge hanging from the front of his shirt. "Your guy gonna be okay, Sarge?" the officer asked.

"I sure hope so. I need to talk to you and your partner for a second."

Jerrod turned to Beach and Zippy. "Help the young lady."

Beach told the second officer Jerrod wished a word with him as Zippy squatted down by the woman. Beach crouched down on the other side of the woman as the second officer stood up.

The second patrolman -- mid-forties, overweight, dark mustache, four five-year service stripes on his left sleeve -- stood up and walked toward Jerrod.

"Are you guys okay?" Jerrod asked.

"Yeah. No problem," the second officer said.

Jerrod looked around the scene. "They're going to separate us in a few minutes for interviews. I may not get to talk to either of you two again, so I'm going to say it right now. In private."

"What's that?" the first officer asked.

"That gallant little move you two idiots made just got one of our guys shot. We had that man ready to give up and our deputy was still behind cover until you two charged in. He's headed to the ER right now with a bullet in his chest and that man over there is dead because you two assholes fucked up."

"Who do you think you are?" the second officer said. "You're in our city and we don't have to take this shit from you."

Jerrod held the shotgun across the front of his body and made sure the safety was on. "How long have you been with the PD?" Jerrod asked.

"I have twenty-years here," the second officer said.

"So, if you've been a Willowmere cop for twenty-years," Jerrod said as he slid his right foot back to brace himself, "that actually means you've got about one-year of experience -- twenty times."

The second officer chewed on Jerrod's words for a few seconds. He clenched his fists and raised them to waist-level before moving a couple steps toward Jerrod. "You wanna go right now, smart-mouth."

Jerrod used his right hand to slam the stock of the shotgun as hard as he could into the Kevlar ballistic vest covering the officer's doughy belly. The officer screeched as he grabbed his gut and dropped to his knees.

"Still 'wanna go,' dickhead?" Jerrod said as he cocked the shotgun back to make another blow.

"Sergeant Gold. That's enough," a baritone voice yelled from behind him.

Jerrod didn't need to turn around to know the voice was that of Sheriff Wayne B. Osborn.

CHAPTER 3

"Here we are again, Jerrod," Mesa County District Attorney Inspector Stanley "Stan" Walsh said in his deep Texas drawl.

They sat alone together in an interview room. A portable cassette tape recorder sat on the tabletop but was not recording at that moment. Jerrod had been transported back to the Sheriff's Office building on Beach Boulevard. It was his turn to be interviewed about his involvement in the fatal officer-involved shooting.

"Any word on Scott?" Jerrod asked.

"He made it into surgery," Stan said. "Don't know after that."

"How about the hostage lady?"

"She's okay."

"How about the people inside city hall?"

"One male inside. DOA."

"How about the shooter?"

"He's still dead," Stan said.

Jerrod shook his head. "Very funny. No, do we know anything about him?"

"Not really," Stan said. "Did you call Nikki?"

"I called her from the scene. She knows I'm alright. I asked her not to let the girls watch the news tonight. They wouldn't understand what happened there."

Stan said, "As you're aware, the DA's Office will be conducting the criminal investigation into this incident and will determine what, if any, criminal charges will be filed from it."

"I know the drill."

Stan paused as he bent over and pulled up the sock under a western-cut boot. "Mr. Harlan asked me to question you about striking that Willowmere officer."

Jerrod nodded.

"Mr. Harlan" was the Mesa County District Attorney -- Lawrence Harlan.

"Do you want a lawyer or a union rep or someone with you during the interview?"

"Nope," Jerrod said. "Let's just do it."

"Because this is a criminal investigation, I have to read you the *Miranda* admonition. Alright?"

"I'm familiar with the 'California Peace Officer Bill of Rights,' *Professor*. Do what you need to do."

Stan pressed the "record" button on the recorder. "The following is a tape-recorded interview with Mesa County Sheriff's Sergeant Jerrod Gold. Today's date is..."

This was the second time in six years Stan had interviewed Jerrod after he had fatally shot someone. The first had been in 1985 after he, then a Valle Verde PD detective, had struggled for a gun with Armando Mendoza.

Jerrod answered Stan's questions and recounted the sequence of events leading up to, during, and following, the shooting.

During a brief pause in the interview, Jerrod noticed for the first time he hadn't suffered any of the physical post-stress symptoms he had experienced before: His leg had no uncontrollable shaking, he hadn't felt excessively warm, and he hadn't felt the usual fatigue after adrenaline had coursed through his system -- if adrenaline had even been released. Other than his concern for Scott Jackson and some residual anger at the two Willowmere officers -- he just felt normal.

And that worried him.

Stan wrapped-up the forty-minute interview and turned off the recorder.

"Jerrod, I don't see any problems with the shooting. Same as last time. However, butt-stroking that officer... I don't know where that's going. It's already been on the TV news, and it might get political."

"Stan. If either of those officers walked in this room right now-" Jerrod glanced at the recorder to make sure it was off, "You would have to pull me off them. Scott got shot and that man's dead because of those assholes."

Stan nodded.

"We were deescalating that situation and the hostage was being released until they came charging around the corner. I know it and they do too."

"The sheriff's put you on two days paid administrative leave, Jerrod," Lieutenant Ben Zaff said from behind his Investigations Division desk. "Take tomorrow and Friday off and then your normal weekend. Come back in on Monday... unless I call you."

Jerrod nodded. "How's Scott doing?"

"Out of surgery. He'll probably be okay... physically anyway."

"Good. He may need some help recovering from this... on the mental health side."

"We've contacted a counselor," the lieutenant said, "and are setting up a formal debriefing for anyone who wants to come in and talk about the incident."

"Good. How about my guys -- Beach and Nate and Zippy?"

"All have been interviewed and sent home on admin-leave too. They'll be back on Monday as well. Any property crimes that come in can wait until then."

"Thanks, L-T."

"Get some rest and enjoy the days off."

As Jerrod left the lieutenant's office, he reached his hand out and touched an eight-inch diameter clear resin ball attached to the wall near the doorway.

The ball -- placed under a framed photograph of Detective Sergeant Brent Rozman -- contained a coffee-stained white ceramic cup bearing the logo of the 1989 World Series Champion Oakland Athletics.

Saint Michael's Hospital -- Intensive Care Unit

"I can't let anyone in, Sarge," Deputy Tyler Baumann said. The uniformed deputy stood guard in the hallway of Scott Collins' hospital room.

Tyler had been the third deputy to ascend the ladder at the Cardinal Lane murder-suicide scene in 1990.

"No problem," Jerrod said. "How's he doing?"

"He's alive. Looked okay the last time I peeked in." Tyler shrugged. "He hasn't regained consciousness since surgery. Doctors and nurses have been in and out of the room, but they aren't saying anything."

"I understand your orders, but I'd appreciate a minute with Scott," Jerrod said. "The three of us have a history and I'd like to see him before I take my days-off."

"Suspended?" Tyler asked with a grin. "I heard you smacked a Willowmere officer with a shotgun."

"Admin-leave -- paid -- for now. I'm just going to accept whatever the sheriff gives me when this all shakes out."

Tyler looked up and down the hallway. "One minute."

Jerrod pushed the door open and found Scott propped up in his hospital bed. He was bare-chested and took in full breaths without the assistance of a respirator. Clear fluid from a hanging bag fed an IV in his right hand. Another clear tube leaking pink fluid protruded from the left side of his chest and was held in placed by two thick black sutures. A red-stained gauze pad was taped to his chest under his left arm.

"How you doing, pal?" Jerrod whispered to the unconscious man. "Looks like we're going need to schedule another session with Dewey."

Charles "Dewey" Mazurek was the US Army veteran who had met with Jerrod, Scott, and Tyler and helped them deal with the aftermath of the Cardinal Lane incident.

"Sorry I didn't press the trigger a second earlier," Jerrod whispered as he tucked-in a loose corner of the bed sheet. "If I had, neither one of us would be in this room right now."

"Thank you, Tyler. Looks like he's resting okay."

"No problem, Sarge. Go home and get some rest yourself."

CHAPTER 4

Jerrod got to his Valle Verde home and found Nikki and her two daughters snuggled on the sofa. They were watching the movie *Dirty Dancing* from a VHS cassette.

"Hello, ladies," Jerrod said with as much faux enthusiasm he could muster.

The oldest daughter -- Lilly, eleven -- smiled and waved.

"You're late," scolded Marty -- the nine-year-old. "Marty" was short for her first name: Martina.

"I *am* late, and I apologize," Jerrod said. "I had a very long day."

Nikki walked to him and gave him a long hug. She whispered in his ear, "I saw the news. The girls don't know anything."

"Good," he said as he kissed her.

"Kissing," Marty said. "Yuck."

"Get you something to eat?" Nikki asked.

"Sure. Missed lunch... and dinner."

"Beer?"

"No, thank you. Not tonight."

Jerrod was now fully aware his body had not yet reacted to the fact he had taken a man's life that day. He didn't even feel numb about it. He feared one beer would lead him to every beer in the refrigerator and whatever else he had to drink in the house. He simply could not take that chance.

"How's the deputy who got shot?" Nikki asked. They sat together at the kitchen table.

"Out of surgery." Jerrod covered his mouth as he both chewed and spoke. "Resting okay in ICU. I don't know. He was with me on that Cardinal Lane... thing. That messed us both up a little. We'll see what this does."

"I know that officer... the one you hit, Jerrod," she said. "He's been a regular at Sophie's as long as I've been there. Believe it or not, he's actually a real nice guy."

"I'm sure he is," Jerrod said "I totally messed up today. I can't explain why I hit him. I was so angry."

"No need to explain," she said. "Finish dinner while I get the girls into bed."

Jerrod pushed the pasta around his plate as the events of the Willowmere City Hall played over and over in his head. His anger peaked each time he watched the two officers ran past Scott and ignited the bloody sequence that followed.

"We had that guy," he muttered to himself. "Those assholes."

"What was that?" Nikki asked from the living room.

"Nothing. Sorry. Talking to myself."

"Go see the girls," she directed.

The bedroom door creaked as he opened it. Lilly and Marty shared a queen-size bed in the cluttered room.

"Goodnight ladies."

"Goodnight," the girls said.

"Get some sleep."

"Okay."

Jerrod joined Nikki in the living room and flopped into his leather La-Z-Boy recliner. He rocked the chair as they spoke.

"The girls are outgrowing that room," Jerrod said. "They're probably going to want their own rooms at some point."

"They're fine, really."

Jerrod stared at the TV and didn't answer.

"Look at me," Nikki insisted.

"What?"

"I was scared today. When you and the guys tore out of the restaurant."

"You've seen me do that a hundred times before."

"While you were in Patrol, yeah. It was different then."

"I'm sorry. We did kiss before I left. Just in case." He tried to lighten the mood.

"Just in case you didn't come back. Great."

"I not finding the right words today. You talk, please."

Nikki hesitated. "I don't know what to do right now. How to act or what to say." Her eyes started to tear. "I didn't know you the last time... *this* happened, and I know you had some problems with it after."

"Does 'this,' mean killing someone in the performance of my duties."

"Yes, exactly." She leaned toward him. "I don't know if I should hug you, or leave you alone, or pack the kids up and go stay at my mom's for a few days."

Jerrod leaned forward and touched her leg. "You don't have to do anything. I just have to deal with this. The good news is I *have* been through this before and I know exactly what *not* to do."

"Okay," she said. "Normal life. Just your average long weekend. Play with the kids. Take a bike ride. Mow the lawns. Wash the cars."

"Exactly.

"Fine," she said -- effectively ending the conversation.

They watched Patrick Swayze and Jennifer Grey dance the final scene of *Dirty Dancing* just before Fox News came on at nine o'clock.

The lead story was a recap of the Willowmere City Hall incident. The names of the building department official killed and the woman hostage were not released.

The news rolled video of Scott Jackson being loaded into the ambulance and of Jerrod confronting the two Willowmere officers. The red mess and the body of the shooter were intentionally blurred. The video showed Jerrod striking the officer and the officer falling to his knees.

Jerrod shook his head. "I can't believe I did that."

The segment cut to a soundless archived video clip of Jerrod giving a news briefing. "Sgt. Jerrod Gold, Mesa County Sheriff's Office" was captioned.

"Clever. That clip's from the Walter Jelinski homicide last year," Jerrod said.

The segment shifted to what looked like a DMV photo of the shooter.

Nikki sat up. "I know him. They didn't show this earlier. That's Nelson. He comes into the restaurant with his son a few times a week. They were in yesterday."

The caption under the photograph gave the name: "Nelson LaMahieu."

The news quickly moved on to a segment about a forest fire in Big Sur.

Jerrod said, "I'm sorry you knew the man I shot today."

Nikki looked at him with an odd expression and he paused to process his own words. It had sounded like he was saying he shot someone every day.

"That didn't come out right, again," he added.

"No, it didn't."

Jerrod stood up. "Looks like the world, as we know it, revolves around the people who come and go from Sophie's Diner." He didn't wait for a response. "I'm going to bed."

As Jerrod showered and then slipped into bed, the Willowmere City Hall was front and center in his mind. But before Nikki lay beside him ten minutes later, he had fallen into a deep sleep and stayed that way for nearly nine dreamless hours.

CHAPTER 5

Kirk LaMahieu sat on the living room couch in the house he had, until that afternoon, shared with his father.

He had answered the door when uniformed and raid-jacketed officers descended on the modest Willowmere home, notified him of his father's death, and served him with a warrant to search the house. He was questioned at length about his father -- Nelson LaMahieu -- and their ongoing battle with the City of Willowmere over some repairs and modifications they wanted to make on the house and his mental condition and any violent history and comments he may have made prior to going to city hall.

He had sat meekly as the officers thoroughly searched the house -- *his house* -- and carried out bags and boxes of whatever it was they found interesting. He had gracefully accepted the officer's condolences and managed a weak smile as they shook his hand.

Kirk LaMahieu watched the Fox News coverage of the Willowmere City Hall shooting and recorded it onto a VHS tape.

As he viewed the news segment for the eighth time since it aired, he paused the grainy tape during a portion of Sergeant Jerrod Gold's soundless interview.

Snap. Snap. Snap. Snap. Snap. Snap.

With a firm two-handed grip and perfect sight alignment, Kirk LaMahieu aimed the muzzle of his unloaded chrome Smith and Wesson Model 629 .44 Magnum revolver at the image on the screen and smoothly pulled the trigger.

CHAPTER 6

Four Months Earlier -- MAY 1991

"Sergeant Gold," he answered into the receiver of his desk phone.

"This is Eric Blanchard."

"Hello... Chief."

"Can you come by my office? Right away?"

"Sure. Be right there."

"Close the door and have a seat," the chief deputy directed. Both his suntanned face and voice were serious.

Jerrod sat.

"This is all getting posted on Friday morning, but you no doubt heard about Mitchell Sullivan's demotion to sergeant and his transfer to the Detention Bureau."

"Yes, sir. He told me about it. In person. Last night."

"I have some questions for you. Whatever we talk about will never leave this room. I need to know the truth. Understand?"

"Yes, sir."

"When this whole thing about Sullivan and Darrell Regner and the video and the newspaper article came up regarding Brent Rozman's death -- coincidentally while Mitchell was away from the office -- I suspected you were somehow involved."

Jerrod nodded.

"And when I saw your name on that video tape envelope, I knew you were behind it."

"Yes, sir."

Is that 'yes, sir,' as-in you were, for lack of a better term, behind it? Or are you just being a smart-ass?"

"Sir, I have a question for you. You talked to Bruce Witt and asked him not to write that article exposing Brent's death as a suicide. Correct?"

"Yes. How did you know that?"

"Did Bruce put up much of a fight? Argue about the freedom of press or government oppression or the public's right to know?"

"He put up a fuss." The chief paused to think. "But he eventually agreed not to print the article to save Brent's family from any more trauma."

"That, sir, assumes there was ever going to be an article."

"You little bastard." The chief leaned back in his chair for a few moments. "Okay. Let me do the math here."

"Sure."

"You found out about the video tape and used it to leverage Regner into going to the sheriff with the truth about the, well, accident, to save his own ass."

Jerrod nodded.

"Regner took the bait, and you knew Sullivan would have to fall on his sword to save his career -- what's left of his career -- when he got called in."

"Sir, do you remember a conversation we had shortly after the Cardinal Lane murder-suicide?"

"Yes."

"You told me you wanted people 'who could think on their feet, take charge, and get results.'"

"I knew it. Unbelievable."

Jerrod asked. "What's going to happen to Regner?"

"He's getting a forty-hour suspension for his part."

"No demotion or reassignment?"

"No. He's staying where he is. The sheriff appreciated Regner coming to him with the truth. Sullivan took the big hit."

"Good. Who's replacing Sullivan?"

"Ben Zaff is coming back as the Investigations Division Commander."

"He's perfect. Thank you, sir."

The chief scoffed. "I can't believe you set this whole thing up."

"I just played the cards that were dealt, sir."

"Jerrod. Do you have any idea how difficult this whole mess has been on the sheriff?"

"No, sir."

"Burying one of his sergeants, disciplining another, and demoting the son of one of his closest friends for covering-up the details about Brent's death?"

"I understand, sir."

The chief deputy put his elbows on his cluttered desk, peeked at the closed door, and spoke in a hushed tone. "What I'm about to tell you *is not* going to be posted on Friday morning. Understand?"

"Yes."

"Sheriff Osborn told me he is not going to run for reelection next year. Five terms -- twenty years -- is going to be enough for him."

"Yes, sir."

"But he's not going to retire early and appoint a successor. He's going to finish his term and wants the next sheriff to be elected. Are you following?"

"Yes, sir."

"There may be a lot of interest in that position. If I decide to run, I'm going to need people around me I can trust. Can I count on you when the time comes?"

"Yes, sir. Of course."

"Glad to hear that," the chief said with a shake of his head. "With what I've just learned about you today, I'd sure hate to find out you were helping someone else."

Friday Morning

At precisely 8:00 AM, the bulletin boards throughout the Mesa County Sheriff's Office had notices attached formally announcing the comings and goings of department personnel.

Jerrod Gold scanned the memo and, as expected, former lieutenant Mitchell Sullivan had been demoted to sergeant and transferred to the Detention Bureau -- Main Jail. Lieutenant Ben Zaff was transferred from Patrol Division to lead the Investigations Division.

CHAPTER 7

Nikki Verdugo poured a glass of wine and curled on the sofa to take a few moments alone in the unusually quiet house.

She pined every day for her first love, husband, and father of her children. A few days before Christmas in 1985, Blake Verdugo said he had a headache, kissed her, told her he loved her, went into the bedroom for nap, and never woke up. Trying to explain to her daughters -- Lilly was six and Marty was only three -- that their father would never be with them again was the most difficult task she had ever had. And watching those same children open the Christmas gifts Blake had carefully purchased and wrapped himself caused tears to stream down her face anytime she thought about it.

Her mother -- Bernice -- had been her savior. She had lost her husband a few years earlier, understood grief, and knew how to navigate the slow and painful recovery from it. Second by second. Minute by minute. Hour by hour. Day by day.

Nikki grew stronger and independent as she poured attention into her daughters. She did everything in her power to make up for the loss of Blake.

The sheriff's deputies, Willowmere cops, CHP officers, and regular customers who frequented Sophie's Diner all knew what had happened and joined together to help and protect her in the months after Blake's death. A meet for ice cream or a movie date with the girls. Help with a project or repair around her home. All done from a respectful distance and never with a hint of romance.

Then they drifted away.

Nikki had started to wonder if men were still attracted to her. She worried she would never feel the warm embrace of a man who loved her as much as she loved him. "Too soon," Bernice had warned. "Wait at least a year to make any big decisions or get into another relationship."

Then, on Independence Day 1986, Jerrod Gold -- brought there by his field training officer on his first day with the sheriff's office -- walked through the front door of Sophie's Diner.

Jerrod was tall and slim. Chestnut brown hair. Deep blue eyes. Requisite cop mustache. No wedding ring. An outsider who had no clue about her or her past, but who she knew in that magical instant would at some point become her true love and soul mate.

He was quiet. Reserved. Shy even. He spoke in hushed tones and with a slight mumble which caused her to strain a bit to hear each word he uttered during a series of brief conversations in the restaurant. Conversations that were always about her. He gave little insight into himself. Never boastful. Never self-promoting. Never revealing. Always guarded.

She watched him for disqualifying features and found none. He was polite. Had good table manners. Was friendly and open to other restaurant customers who interrupted his hurried meals to ask questions. Was a decent tipper, but not overly generous. And he was apologetic when a radio call took him away from a half-eaten meal and he'd run out the door.

But he never asked her out. Never hinted he wanted to see her away from Sophie's. Maybe, she thought, he already had a girlfriend. Maybe he had just gotten out of a bad relationship. Maybe he didn't like kids. Or, maybe, he just didn't care to be with women.

She took a chance and asked him to come to a remembrance for Blake a year after he died. He surprised her by showing up and was the last guest to leave -- the following morning. Their relationship took baby-steps from there: A disastrous meal with the girls. A wonderful walk to the beach. Regular visits to her condo. Taking her and the girls to meet his mother and stepfather. An invitation to move into his house. And, eventually, a proposal of marriage.

He was totally committed to her but asked nothing from her. He ate any meal she prepared -- steak or peanut butter -- without comment or complaint. He would wash his own clothes and sew on a button even after she offered to do it. He played with the girls and loved them as if they were his own. Lilly had asked Jerrod bluntly if he was their "new dad" since theirs was dead. He told her Blake was alive in her heart and was with her all the time.

She learned that Jerrod's placid exterior was a thin veneer covering a conflicted man. He was like a pot set to simmer at all times, and it came out occasionally in the pointed sarcasm he used. He had mastered the art of making statements which could be taken as either a joke or as biting criticism. She had mastered the art of interpreting which was which.

She soothed him on his often restless, and occasionally sleepless, nights. She held him as he awoke from the nightmares of which he would rarely share the details. And she keenly got close to him when he needed her and kept her distance when he did not.

Jerrod eked the details of his life before she met him. She had never once caught him in a lie, but he famously withheld information in a perceived need to protect her from his thoughts and experiences. She knew there was much about the often brooding and complicated man she would never fully understand.

His actions were all planned and performed according to script and schedule. His script and his schedule. When he became laser-focused on a task -- big or small -- he had little patience for detour or spontaneity. She learned to recognize and not take personal his ability to close his mind to the outside world while thinking about an investigation, working on a project, watching a television program, or while immersed in a book. "Refrigerator noise" he had once described it to her. While on a mission, he had once said, all outside influences had the mostly non-existent sound of the motor on a refrigerator. Anything she had to say could wait until he resolved his thoughts, and she had his full attention.

That is, most of the time.

CHAPTER 8

JUNE 1991 -- Wednesday Evening

"I guess we should start planning a wedding," Nikki asked. The tone of her voice made the question rhetorical.

Jerrod held the place on the newspaper he was reading with his finger. "Sure, honey. Whatever you want."

"Please note the 'we' part of what I just said. 'We' should start planning... now."

Jerrod dropped the paper to his lap. "Okay. Give me a list of things to do and where and when I should show-up."

"Like, just make an appearance at your own wedding. You don't seem too committed."

"Plan the wedding the way you want it. I don't--" He cut himself off.

"You don't... *care?*" Nikki looked away and stared out the living room window.

"I do care. I'm just flexible on the whole thing," Jerrod said as she looked back at him. "Church wedding. Civil thing. Run to Nevada. I don't care how it's done as long as it gets done."

"Who asked who to get married?" she asked.

"You did," he glanced at the TV. "Something about 'not going to my retirement party as just my girlfriend.'"

"No," she scoffed. "Couple weeks ago. A Tuesday night, I believe. Your old-man-killer-guy had just been convicted and that lieutenant you didn't like got demoted. You tucked the girls in and came back out into the living room and said, 'let's do it' and you were 'all-in' and you asked me to marry you."

"Shit. Does your mind record everything I say?"

"Just the important things." She chuckled. "Most of what you say goes in one and out the other."

Jerrod folded the newspaper. "Let's plan a wedding."

"What's that term you cops use all the time?" Nikki smiled. "'Copy that.'"

CHAPTER 9

Mesa County Sheriff's Office -- Investigations Division

There had been no significant changes since former-Lieutenant Mitchell Sullivan had been demoted and sent to the Main Jail. The division of duties Sullivan had initiated the previous December were left intact. Sullivan had been right -- having two groups of detectives specializing in either crimes against persons or property led to more accountability and consistency.

Jerrod and the three detectives working with him -- Nathan "Nate" Boxley, Marshall "Beach" Sutton, and Bryce "Zippy" Zippich -- had formed a tight bond. Although first thinking they were being punished by the realignments Sullivan had made, they soon learned Property Crimes was the place to work. They took their responsibilities seriously and jealously protected their assigned areas. Arrests for property-related crimes increased as they found themselves less occupied by the unpredictable priorities created by violent crimes.

Jerrod and Darrell Regner had worked out any differences they may have once had. Regner continued supervising two detectives -- "Father Jeff" Moreno and Calvin Yee.

Jerrod and his crew often worked with Regner's team on new major crimes -- homicides, robberies, and major assaults -- but just for the first few days or so of the investigation.

Sergeant Ted Lindsey still supervised the combined Coroner/Crime Scene Unit with Detective Raymond "Shroom" Mingus.

The Staff Sergeant/Special Investigations position remained open, but unfilled.

Lastly, and most importantly, Division Secretary Linda Westphal continued to be the hub of the group -- the sole adult among a group of unruly children -- and the gatekeeper of the office supply closet known as "Fort Knox."

CHAPTER 10

Saturday Morning

"You asked for a list," Nikki said. "Well, mister, here's your list."

Jerrod had just settled into his leather recliner to read a hardback novel -- *Dead Irish* by John Lescroart. "This book is awesome. It's set in San Francisco. Twisty plot. Great characters. Dismas Hardy and Abe Glitsky. Just brilliant. There's even a scene at Candlestick Park. You need to read it when I'm done."

"Like I have any time to read. Put your book down. I need you to focus."

He placed the bookmark between the pages. "Yes, dear."

"Perfect response."

"I am trainable. Don't believe anyone who says I'm not," Jerrod said as he scanned the handwritten list of bullet-pointed tasks:

* Select wedding date
* Find venue
* Find an official to perform the ceremony
* Make guest list
* Designate the best man and groomsmen (3)
* Order invitations
* Mail invitations
* Purchase a fabulous wedding ring set for the bride...and something nice for the groom.
* Arrange food and beverage
* Order wedding cake
* Hire Photographer
* Hire DJ
* Arrange rehearsal dinner
* Thank-you gifts for groomsmen
* Plan honeymoon
* Show up on time for your own damn wedding

"Easy peasy. Lemon squeezy," Jerrod said as he put down the list and reached for the novel. "I'll have all that done by next weekend. Back to the story. I'm at a real good part."

"We start planning now," Nikki scolded. "Pick a date. After the holidays. January or February."

"How about around Valentine's Day?" He put his hand over his heart. "That'll be so romantic."

"Good start," she said as she thumbed a 1992 calendar. "Valentine's Day is on a Friday. I bet a lot of people will get married that weekend."

"How about the weekend before?"

"Saturday or Sunday?" she asked.

"Saturday."

"Saturday is on February 8th,"

"Perfect date. Outstanding. Making progress already," Jerrod said as he creeped his hand toward the novel.

"Do not touch that book," she said. "Now we need a venue," she said.

"Okay," he sighed. "Church? Hall? Nevada? What?"

"You're not a church guy and I already had my 'white wedding' with Blake." She paused for a moment. "It's a definite 'no' on Nevada. I want it to be here. So how about a hall of some sort?"

"I know a place out in the hills just north of town. Cute. Has a kitchen area. Okay parking. They do weddings and other events there."

"Let's go see it," she said.

"Sure," Jerrod said as he again reached for the book.

"Now."

"Right now?" Jerrod rolled his eyes so hard he gave himself a headache.

"Right now."

Jerrod, Nikki, Lilly, and Marty piled into his silver Ford F-150 truck and headed out to the redwoods.

Lilly yawned as loud as humanly possible as he pointed out the schools he had attended and the fields he once played baseball and the orchards he explored by bicycle as a child.

He spared them from describing the dozens of other locations they passed that once the served as the scenes of horrific traffic collisions; urine-soaked drunks; drug overdoses; bloody fights, stabbings, shootings; abused children; battered spouses; and violent deaths he responded to and investigated over the last eleven years.

Silently, and from the deepest recesses of his mind, the sights and sounds and smells from each of those scenes reemerged, in vivid detail, as he relived them all one by one.

The Redwood Center was a single-story wood-sided building with a weathered shake roof. There was a broad lawn separated from the large gravel parking area by a sturdy split-rail fence. The entire property was surrounded and protected by towering old-growth redwood trees.

A pickup with a mismatched-color front fender sat in the lot and a man in his mid-sixties was busy pushing a gas mower over the lush lawn. Jerrod parked and they walked to the wood fence hoping to get the man's attention. The man made one more pass and stopped the noisy mower.

"Can I help you folks?" the man said as he swiped a sweaty temple with his sleeve. "Getting ready for a *quinceañera* here tonight."

"We're getting married," Jerrod said. "We live here in Valle Verde and are looking for a local venue for the wedding."

"Would you know if this place is available in February?" Nikki added.

The man looked back at how much lawn he still had to mow. "My wife handles all that stuff. Come on in and look around. I'll take a break and give her a call. Hope you're not looking for a Saturday. They get rented out quickest."

What's a 'queen's arena?'" Marty asked.

"'*Quinceañera,*'" Jerrod enunciated. "It's a coming-out party for girls when they reach fifteen."

Marty smiled. "I want one of those."

Jerrod looked to Nikki. "Why not?"

Nikki interjected. "Honey, your fifteenth birthday is going to be very special."

They followed the man into the hall and peeked into the main room. It was long and narrow with a raised platform at the far end and a majestic river rock fireplace forming the entire back wall. The girls spotted a rope swing strung between two huge redwoods behind the building and ran out to play on it.

"This is nice," Nikki said. "Fingers crossed it's available."

The man had detoured to the kitchen and could be heard talking on the phone. "February. Yeah. Next year. 1992 for Pete's sake."

"Not looking too promising," Jerrod whispered.

"What date in February?" the man asked.

"Saturday the 8th," Nikki replied. "But we're flexible."

"Saturdays. I don't know," the man said before putting the receiver back to his ear.

Jerrod nudged Nikki with his elbow and whispered again into her ear. "You were pretty 'flexible' last night. Been doing yoga or something?"

Her reaction was the look of shock followed by a smirk and then a suppressed laugh. "Yeah, right. I have time for yoga. You animal."

The man lowered the receiver. "You're in luck. Had a cancellation for February 8th. Here, you talk to her, I got a lawn to mow."

Nikki took the receiver and booked the official date and location for their wedding.

"That's two things off the list in a couple hours," Nikki said.

"I propose we get some lunch to celebrate," Jerrod said, "and then I can get back to my book."

"Lunch. Yes," Nikki said. "Book. No. We still have to make a guest list and you need to select your groomsmen."

Oh, fuck me, was the first response to pop into his head. "Yes, dear" is what came out of his mouth.

Three weeks later -- Sunday Afternoon

"Jerrod," Nikki said -- getting no response from the man sitting cross-legged in his recliner with eyes locked onto the pages of a novel.

"I just bought a necklace on sale for two thousand dollars. It's gorgeous. Thank you."

"Wait... what?" Jerrod said as he looked up.

"No necklace. Just messing with you. But since I have your full attention now, I need to know who your groomsmen are going to be."

"I've been thinking about that."

"Give me names," she said as she took pen to paper.

"Craig Wallace. Willie Gonzalez. And, uh, how about Marko Otero."

"Have you talked to them yet?"

"Not yet," Jerrod said. "Question for you. Just an FYI so I can be a better husband someday."

Nikki's hand moved to her hip.

"Is reminding me to do something every week technically considered 'nagging?'"

"Do you want me to call those guys?"

"No."

"Our wedding. Your task."

"Yes, dear."

"Hello," the female voice on the telephone receiver said.

"Sandi?" Jerrod asked.

"Were you expecting some other woman to answer?" Sandi Wallace said.

"No. Sorry. Of course. This is Jerrod."

"Jerrod," she said. "Got the invitation. We'll be there. RSVP'd a week or so ago."

"Excellent. We're looking forward to seeing you. Is Craig home?"

"He's on the property somewhere. Hang on."

He heard the receiver being placed down and Sandi's voice yelling for Craig from a distance.

Craig Wallace -- his former VVPD detective partner -- was on the phone a minute or so later. "She's finally going to make an honest man out of you."

"She is. Indeed. I have a favor to ask."

"Sure."

"I'd like you to... uh... be in the wedding. One of my groomsmen."

"Tuxedo and shit?" Craig asked.

"Yeah."

"You have to make a request like that in-person," Craig said. "Pretty sure that's the proper etiquette."

"I'm learning all about that." Jerrod paused. "Lots of rules. 'In-person?' Really?"

"If that gets you to come visit for a couple days." Craig paused. "Yeah. *Really.*"

Jerrod looked at a calendar. "How about the Fourth of July. It falls on a Thursday and I can take Friday off. We've got a thing to go to Saturday, so it'll be a quick trip."

"Sounds good," Craig said.

"What's the name of that town you live in?"

"Cahoots, Nevada."

"Okay, then. Give me some directions."

CHAPTER 11

Investigation Division -- Property Crimes Unit

"Who's the guy in the photo, Sarge?" Zippy asked. "Your dad?"

Jerrod had just hung a framed five-by-seven-inch black-and-white photo over his desk. He had found the photo in a magazine ad, and it had given him an idea.

"That guy," Beach said, "is Jack Webb. He played Los Angeles PD Detective Sergeant Joe Friday in the old TV series -- *Dragnet.*

"I've never heard of him... or it," Zippy said.

"Where have you been all your life?" Nate asked. "Everyone knows Joe Friday. 'Just the facts, ma'am.' He's iconic."

Beach added, "The 'real' LAPD retired Joe Friday's badge -- 714 -- after Jack Webb died."

"'714, '" Nate added, "is the number of home runs Babe Ruth hit in his career. Coincidence? I think not."

"So why is *his* picture up there, Sarge?" Zippy asked.

"He's going to be the Property Crimes 'muse,'" Jerrod said.

"What's a 'muse?'" Beach asked.

"It means: A motivator, or an inspirational person," Zippy said.

"Exactly," Jerrod said. "Sergeant Joe Friday is our new muse. If we get stuck on a case, we can look up at the picture and ask: 'What would Joe Friday do?' Then we cut through the crap and take care of business."

"WWJFD?" Nate chuckled.

Jerrod smiled. "'WWJFD.'"

CHAPTER 12

Saturday Morning

Jerrod had trimmed the edges of his front lawn and used a hand-push reel mower to form a perfect diamond-shaped pattern -- just like the outfield grass at the home field of the San Francisco Giants at Candlestick Park.

He peeked up and saw Nikki standing at the threshold of the open front door. She was holding the portable telephone.

"What's up?" Jerrod asked as he finished a strip.

"There's a man on the phone asking for you."

"From work?"

"I don't know. He just asked for you."

"Ask him his name."

Nikki spoke into the phone.

"His name is 'Jerry.'"

As he walked toward to door, Jerrod searched his mind for someone he knew named "Jerry."

Nikki pushed the phone toward him. "He says he's your father."

"This is Jerrod."

The voice on the other end was unmistakable. "Hello, son. This is your dad."

Jerrod paused for a second. "How you been, Jerry?"

"That's still how it's going to be?"

Jerrod didn't answer.

"Are you still there?"

"What do you need?" Jerrod asked. "Another ride to rehab?"

"I don't drink anymore. Been clean for over a year."

"I'll believe that when I see it. What do you want?"

Jerry said, "I just talked to your aunt and your grandmother. They told me you're getting married in February and they got invitations to the wedding."

"That's right."

"I haven't received an invitation yet."

"I figured you'd be busy with your... how many now... third or fourth wife?"

"Third. But we're not together anymore."

"Shame. I didn't get to meet any of my stepmothers."

"You're not funny."

Jerrod swiped at a persistent black fly. "I didn't get invitations to the last two of yours, so I figured that's just the way we're going to handle things now."

"I'm your father and I should be at your wedding."

Jerrod paused. "I'll think about that and get back to you."

Jerrod answered the next six questions from Jerry with one-word answers.

"I'm sorry I called," Jerry said.

"Me too," Jerrod replied.

"Goodbye, son."

"Later," Jerrod said as he pressed the "off" button.

"Mom, I'm going to ride my bike to Grama Laura's house," Lilly announced.

"Grama Laura" was Jerrod's mother -- Laura Renaud. She lived about seven blocks away in the exclusive "Rochester" neighborhood with Jerrod's stepfather -- Don Renaud.

"That's fine, honey," Nikki said. "Keep an eye out for your sister."

Marty had gone to a neighbor's house to play.

Nikki brought Jerrod a Heineken and they sat together on the front stoop.

"The kids are growing up fast," Jerrod said.

Nikki didn't respond.

After a longer than necessary silence, Jerrod asked, "What?"

"You really shouldn't talk to your father that way."

Jerrod had just felt his heart rate start to settle from the call. It started to rise again. "If you knew him, you wouldn't want to talk to him at all."

"We should invite him to the wedding. I'd like to meet him."

"I don't think that would be a good idea." Jerrod took a drink. "But I'll consider it."

She took his beer from his hand and took a long pull. "After I lost my dad and my husband." She paused. "I have wished every single day I could talk to both of them again. Just for an hour... or a minute... or a second."

Jerrod scanned his lawn for any stray blades of grass.

Nikki added, "You don't get to pick your relatives and you could lose him tomorrow." She touched his chin and pulled his gaze to hers. "Do you want that phone conversation to be the last words you ever had with him."

CHAPTER 13

JULY 1991 -- Thursday Morning

"Happy birthday to you," Jerrod sang in the privacy of his truck. "Happy birthday to you. Happy birthday, dear America. Happy birthday to you."

He was on the road at dawn -- the morning sun slamming into the windshield as he headed due east on the Fourth of July.

The San Luis Reservoir near Santa Nella looked nearly empty after a five-year drought stifled the water coming into it. Northbound Interstate 5 was clear and fast through the Central Valley -- as fast as he dared after seeing a few California Highway Patrol units strategically positioned to chase down speeders intent on pushing it. The strident officers of the CHP tended to not really care that you were a sheriff's sergeant from Mesa County when they decided to make a stop and issue a citation.

Highway 4 in Stockton took him to Highway 99 north and through minimal holiday traffic in Sacramento. When he got onto Interstate 50 it was clear sailing. After a pit-stop in Placerville for a fresh cup of coffee and a full tank of gas, he was headed over the Sierra Nevada non-stop to Cahoots. The winding highway took him to Echo Summit and then the sharp decent to South Lake Tahoe. He passed between the tall towers of Harrah's and Harvey's Hotel and Casino which signaled his entry into The Great State of Nevada.

Following the directions given to him, Jerrod cruised north along the deep blue water of Lake Tahoe and headed east again over Spooner Summit before the drop into Carson City. He drove through a quaint downtown and past the expansive grounds and silver dome of the state capitol building. Interstate 50 headed due east again and out of the city.

Five miles later, he noticed signs advertising the legal brothels which dotted the area and, finally, a sign which read: "Cahoots -- 3 Miles."

A sign at the edge of town read: "Welcome. You're now in Cahoots." Jerrod craned his neck and caught the writing on the sign from opposite side: "Thanks for visiting. You're no longer in Cahoots."

Per the directions, he turned right at the town's only streetlight, crossed a river bridge, and onto a county road. He admired the tan-colored mountain range soaring to his right and the tall, green-topped trees straddling the riverbed on his left. He rolled-down the window and filled the truck with crisp clean high desert air.

Jerrod found the address, drove past an open gate, and parked in front of a modest single-story house. As he got out, he heard a familiar male voice from the front porch: "About damn time. Sandi's not here. Let's go eat."

Craig Wallace sported a full beard and was a little thinner and grayer than Jerrod expected. He ambled down the porch steps with the support of a cane in his right hand. He walked with an awkward limp across the gravel driveway as two dogs -- a small black one and another larger one with red hair – strode beside him. Before shaking his hand, Craig said, "Welcome to God's Country, Jerrod. We'll take my Jeep."

"Let me lock the truck," Jerrod said.

"Don't worry about it," Craig scoffed. "No one's gonna mess with it here. Dogs'll make sure of that. Let's go."

Craig's Jeep was vintage: A rusty yellow Wrangler YJ. Big knobby tires. No doors. Manual transmission. Black bimini top stretched over the roll cage.

Jerrod jumped into the passenger seat as the engine roared to life.

"Got a V-8 in this one," Craig said with a smile. "No damn smog controls either," he added as he punched the gas and flung a tail of gravel behind them.

Back on the county road, Craig pointed to his left toward the mountain range and yelled over the wind howling around them, "Those hills are all Bureau of Land Management out there as far as you can see. Open to everyone... and we have wild horses."

Jerrod pointed toward the river. "Those trees are beautiful. What are they?"

"Cottonwoods," Craig said. "Should see 'em in the fall. Leaves turn to brilliant yellow. We get all four seasons here."

The Sagebrush was a tiny local's breakfast and lunch restaurant half a block from the streetlight. Craig slid to a stop in the gravel lot and left the keys in the ignition.

"Morning, Craig," a stocky middle-aged waitress yelled from across the tiny restaurant. "You boys sit anywhere you want. Coffee?"

They had just settled in a booth when two tall cups of coffee and one menu arrived.

"'Craig Special?" the waitress asked.

"Sure," he said.

"What's the 'Craig Special?'" Jerrod asked.

"Double burger, Swiss cheese, grilled onions... and Tater Tots," the waitress offered.

"Make it two. Hold the menu," Jerrod said.

The waitress smiled. "Your friend is gorgeous, Craig. Is he married?"

"No," Craig said. "You're married, dear. He's engaged. This is Jerrod Gold."

"That's a shame," she said as she touched Jerrod's shoulder. "We could make some pretty cute kids together."

Jerrod felt his face getting warm.

"Or maybe just pretend to being making kids," she added with a raised eyebrow.

Craig laughed.

"Gold... Jerrod Gold," the waitress said as she danced away from the table.

Craig laughed harder.

The waitress yelled to her husband in the kitchen, "Two 'Craig Specials' for table three."

Craig sipped his coffee. "They never touch me."

"Who?" Jerrod asked as he added half-and-half to his cup.

"Waitresses. I've seen it happen a couple dozen times. 'Oh, Jerrod,' and then they touch you. They never touch me."

"Guess I hadn't noticed."

"You will from now on."

Craig took a small snap case from his shirt pocket and shook two white pills into his hand.

"Headache?" Jerrod asked.

"Knee ache," Craig said after swallowing the pills with a sip of coffee.

"Vicodin?" Jerrod asked.

"Perks. 10ers," Craig answered. "Only thing that helps these days."

"I'm sorry about the knee. My plan went way wrong."

Craig scoffed. "It was a good plan. Would have been a great plan if that bullet had missed."

"Was the juice worth the squeeze, partner?"

Craig smiled. "Sure."

"I'll always owe you," Jerrod said as the waitress arrived with two heaping plates containing about 3,000 calories each.

Craig shook out his paper napkin. "Yes. Yes, you do."

Jerrod patted his belly as they walked back to the Jeep. "Best burger... ever."

"That it is. Love that place," Craig said as he fired up the Jeep. "Want to see some horses?"

"Sure."

Craig yelled over the rushing wind, "Remember the movie, *The Misfits*. Early 60s. Last movie both Clark Gable and Marilyn Monroe made."

"Of course. Classic."

"They filmed a lot of that movie around Cahoots and Reno and up at Pyramid Lake."

"Very cool."

"The mustangs that live here are wild... or feral... depending on who you talk to. Just beautiful free-roaming unowned creatures."

"Can't wait to see them."

"Need to stop by the house first."

Craig pulled in front of the house and yelled to his dogs. "Get in."

The dogs sprinted to the Jeep, jumped in on the driver's side, and settled in the seat-less rear cargo area.

"Impressive," Jerrod said.

"They like it in the hills. Cottontails and jack rabbits running everywhere. They know better than to mess with the mustangs."

Craig limped to the porch without his cane and picked up a plastic cooler. He returned, placed the cooler near the dogs, and pulled out two frosty Heinekens.

"Road soda?" Craig asked.

"Of course."

At the end of the paved road, a heavy metal gate gave access to the vast BLM land behind it.

"The gate isn't locked," Craig said. "Just a chain. Close it behind us."

Jerrod jumped out of the Jeep.

"And watch where you put your hands and feet," Craig warned. "It can get a little snakey out here."

"Rattlesnakey?"

"Yeah."

"Fuck me," Jerrod murmured as he watched the ground around his feet.

Past the gate, they ascended along a bumpy gravel road and Craig said, "Remember the cottonwoods down by the river?"

"Sure."

"There are natural springs that pop-up all over these hills and the cottonwoods only grow near the springs."

Jerrod saw dots of foliage on the trees along the hillside.

"The springs are where the mustangs get their water. Can usually find 'em there."

Two dusty miles up the road, they crested a rise and Craig eased to a stop. "There you go."

A herd of nearly twenty majestic horses stood on and around the road near a tall cottonwood. Most were chestnut with black manes, a few were dapple grey, and there was one yellow buckskin. Two white-socked dun foals stuck close to their mothers. Nearly all had their heads down grazing the dried grass. A few stood in the water and drank from the spring. A couple peeked up to see who was visiting them. One muscular blue stallion stood guard.

"Beautiful," Jerrod said.

"They are," Craig said as he creeped the Jeep towards the herd.

"Will they move?"

"At their own pace," Craig replied.

The horses parted like the sea. Jerrod reached out to brush his hand along the flank of a dun mare.

"I don't see a lot of ribs showing on these horses," Jerrod observed.

"All they do is eat and drink... and make little horses."

Another five bumpy miles up the road, they wound through a sparse forest of stocky pinyon pines and came to a rocky bluff with a panoramic view of the entire Cahoots Valley.

"Grab a fresh beer and check this out," Craig said.

As the dogs chased rabbits, Jerrod and Craig walked out to the bluff and took in the view. A second herd of horses grazed in the distance.

"That movie we talked about," Craig said. "*The Misfits.*"

"Yeah."

They play it at the Old Opera House every year or so. Part of the movie was about rounding up these horses and selling them for slaughter."

"It's been a while since I last saw it," Jerrod said. "But I recall Marilyn saves a horse or something like that at the end."

"Yeah... kind of. Anyway, Montgomery Clift cuts some horses loose, but Clark Gable catches the stallion. Clark then gets dragged behind the horse and almost stomped by it. Clark finally gets the stallion down, but then just lets it go. He says something like he didn't want anyone making up his mind for him. The movie ends with Clark and Marilyn driving off together."

They watched the distant herd wander off in a tight line.

Jerrod said. "The guy who shot you -- Armando Mendoza -- sort of looked like Clark Gable."

"I only saw him for a few seconds before he blew my knee up. I'll have to take your word for it."

"Well... he did... sort of." Jerrod searched for something to change the subject. "'God's Country,' you said when I first got here. It sure is."

Craig took a few beats to respond. "Glad you got to see it... finally."

"'Finally?'" Jerrod asked.

"Yep," Craig took another sip. "You're the first visitor we've had from anyone at the PD in over three years."

Jerrod didn't have an immediate response.

"Right after I got shot," Craig continued. "People came by all the time. You. Pete Hanson. Willie Sanchez. Marko Otero. Rusty Browne. Dave Yamamoto and AJ Jenkins. The Kevins. A few others."

"Of course," Jerrod said.

"Then it slowed down to just Sandi and me and the doctors and the surgeries and infections and dealing with the city and workers' comp and all the bullshit."

45

"I'm sorry," Jerrod said. "I don't have an excuse for not coming up to see you."

"Wasn't looking for an excuse, Jerrod." Craig took a long pull from his beer. "This is going to sound weird but--" Craig stopped himself.

"'Weird but' what?" Jerrod asked.

"Never mind. Not important right now."

"You'll tell me when it *is* important, right?"

"Sure."

The exhausted dogs jumped into the Jeep, and they descended the rutted gravel road back to the gate.

"I'm not sure what to say," Jerrod offered after a long awkward silence.

Craig thought for a few seconds. "I'm sorry about what I said back there. I should have kept it to myself."

"I'm glad you told me," Jerrod said as he turned away. "It was all my fault."

"For the last goddamn time. It wasn't your fault. It just happened. Let it go."

Jerrod let the Jeep out the gate and secured the chain -- pleased no reptiles of any sort were there to greet him.

Near the house, Craig said, "Sandi's home." He turned to Jerrod. "Please don't mention what I said up there. Between you and me only."

"Not a word," Jerrod replied.

Sandi Wallace could have been a fashion model or a movie star. Mid-forties. Slim. Blond hair in a ponytail. Brilliant hazel eyes. She put down a paperback and hopped down the porch steps to meet them. "Been a while, Jerrod," she said as they hugged. "We haven't seen too many guys from the PD since we moved here."

"That's gonna change," Jerrod said.

The house interior had a welcoming country feel to it. Lots of leather and wood. A picture window opened the main room to a spectacular view of the mountain range the mustangs called home. A stone fireplace stood in the corner.

Sandi said, "Sorry I missed you when you arrived, Jerrod. Had to run into Carson to get supplies. We don't have a supermarket out here... yet."

"'Carson' is Carson City? Jerrod asked.

"Everyone here just calls it 'Carson,'" Craig added.

"Okay."

"I picked up a nice tri-tip for dinner," Sandi said. "Got it marinating in the 'fridge already."

"Love tri-tip," Jerrod said.

"It's funny," she continued, "the butchers here didn't know what a 'tri-tip' was. I brought them a picture from a cookbook. They looked it up and found it was also called a 'Santa Maria' steak.' Whatever the name, it's the same great meat."

"Now, boys," Sandi said as she stood up. "We've got nothing planned for tomorrow. So, you two just get caught up and I'll see you in the morning. Thank you for doing the dishes. I'm going to bed. Got a good book going."

She kissed Craig on the cheek and touched Jerrod's shoulder.

"Good night, Sandi." Jerrod said. "Some meal. Thank you for everything."

After the master bedroom door closed, Craig said, "See. Just like I said at the restaurant. She touched you."

Jerrod laughed. "Touched me; but kissed you. If it had been the other way around, you might have a point."

"Guess so," Craig said. "Like bourbon?"

"Not really," Jerrod said. "I used to steal bourbon from Don's cabinet when I was in high school. I'd get hammered before going to Friday night football games. Pretty nasty stuff, actually."

"Not this bottle. You'll like it. I'll add a little ice to dilute it."

Craig went to his bar and poured a couple fingers of bourbon over large cubes.

"That's what I did to Don's bourbon -- diluted it with water to replace what I had taken."

"You wouldn't be the first kid," Craig said as he delivered the highball glass to Jerrod. "Let the ice melt a little. Breathe in the fumes through your mouth -- not through your nose like wine -- the alcohol won't sting so bad. Tell me what you smell."

Jerrod swirled the ice in the amber liquid and smelled it as instructed. He picked up notes of oak and pepper and maybe some honey.

"Now sip and let it cover your tongue."

His first sip was more pleasant than he expected. Jerrod said, "Oh, I could get used to this."

Craig pressed his glass forward and Jerrod clinked it with his.

"Cheers, Grasshopper." Craig smiled. "The master still has many things to teach you."

"Just like old times, partner."

Craig put down his glass and braced himself for a hacking cough. His eyes were wet when he stopped.

"Noticed you don't smoke anymore," Jerrod commented.

"Gave 'em up when we moved here," Craig said. "It's the altitude -- 4,400 feet here. Pretty rough on these old sea-level lungs."

"Okay," Jerrod said. "Just been weird seeing you without a cigarette after all these years. Was expecting you to fire one up at any time."

Craig nodded. "Another taste?" he asked as he started to stand and winced at the pain in his knee.

"I'll get it, Old Man. Sit your ass down."

Jerrod added ice and poured more of the distilled nectar into the glasses.

"Craig, you started to tell me something today. While we were up on that bluff. What was it?"

Craig leaned back in his chair and massaged his knee for a few seconds. "Oh, yeah. That scene in *The Misfits* with the stallion and shit was filmed about twelve miles east of here in a *playa* -- a dry lakebed -- off Highway 50. They renamed that playa 'Misfits Flat.'"

"That's a wonderful piece of trivia and may come in handy someday. But that's not what you were talking about."

Craig studied the contents of his glass and glanced over to the closed master bedroom door. "You can't repeat this, Jerrod. I need your word."

"You have it."

"Back when we chased Armando Mendoza and that lucky bullet -- make it that the unlucky bullet -- fucked my knee up, I still had a lot of good years to go as a cop. I liked being a detective. Maybe could have made sergeant... or even higher. Then I would retire when the time was right. When I wanted to."

"All true," Jerrod said.

"But instead, I got told I was being retired. I got told I couldn't be a cop anymore. I got told my knee was never going to be right. I got told I'd just have to deal with that. Kind of like Clark Gable and that stallion, I didn't want anyone else making up my mind. But, ultimately, I didn't get to decide any of those things."

Jerrod nodded.

"My point -- what I couldn't tell you earlier -- is that I sometimes wish Mendoza's bullet had hit me right between the eyes. Killed me dead. Ended it. Done. Over. Fuck it."

"You don't mean that."

"I *do* mean that," Craig snapped. "There would have been a big cop funeral. Officers from all over the state would come and pay respects. The mayor and the chief would say nice things about me about duty and honor and sacrifice. There'd be bagpipes and shit. And maybe my picture would even hang the squad room... until the older guys stopped noticing it and the newer ones stopped asking who it was."

Jerrod listened.

Craig's voice broke. "Instead, Sandi had to sit with me. Get me things. Drive me around. Help get me to the fucking toilet. And now we both live on my disability retirement at half of my pay -- tax-free -- but still just half. We moved here because we couldn't afford to live in Valle Verde anymore."

Jerrod shifted in his seat.

Craig finished his drink. "If that bullet had killed me, then Sandi -- my angel -- could have kept the flag from my casket on the mantle, collected half-a-million in life insurance, and been able to start a whole new life without having to be the unpaid full-time caretaker of a gimpy used-to-be cop like me."

Jerrod was exhausted, but still had a restless night. The day filled with beer, wine, great food -- and that wonderful bourbon -- didn't help. He felt like he hadn't slept, but knew he had because of the disturbing dreams that woke him up all night.

Morning came with the distinctive smell of frying bacon. Jerrod felt the tinge of hangover as he sat on the side of the bed. He wandered into the main room and sensed the added aroma of fresh brewed coffee.

"Cup, Jerrod?" Sandi asked.

"Absolutely. Little creamer."

Jerrod cradled the warm mug. "Craig sleeping in?"

"He said he has a headache." She smiled. "Can't imagine why?"

"I know why." He laughed. "Hey, I noticed Craig doesn't smoke anymore. But he's got a real bad cough."

Sandi thought for a second. "Yeah. He quit not long after we moved to Nevada. He's allergic to pretty much everything that grows out here. He gets a break during the cooler months."

"Okay," Jerrod said. "He once told me he started smoking in Vietnam. That was a while ago."

"What was a while ago?"' Craig asked as he limped into the room.

"Your 'lucky' cigarette habit," Jerrod said.

"Yeah." He said as he poured himself a cup. "I especially miss it right now. Coffee and a smoke. What a great way to start the day. Need to get your chemicals *just* right."

Sandi and Jerrod both laughed.

"Bacon and eggs and toast," Sandi said. "Hope that works for you gentlemen."

"Works just fine," Jerrod said.

"Got the wedding all planned?" Sandi asked.

Jerrod smiled. "I get my orders and complete them to the best of my ability."

"Looking forward to it," Craig said. "Can I wear western boots with that tuxedo?"

"Of course," Jerrod hesitated. "And, Craig, I'd like you to be my best man. If that's okay?"

Craig paused as he pondered the question. "It would be my honor."

CHAPTER 14

"Well, hello, Jerrod," the records clerk said through the safety glass in the Valle Verde PD public lobby. "How's life at the SO?"

"And how are you?" he said. "It's okay. Not the same as here. I miss the PD from time to time."

She nodded. "What brings you in?"

"I'm here to see Willie... if he's around today."

"I saw him a little while ago. Hang on."

The clerk went to a desk and punched a few numbers on the phone.

"He's in his office. I'll buzz you in."

"Thank you."

Detective Sergeant Guillermo "Willie" Sanchez was seated in his office off the main Detective Bureau bullpen.

"My brother from another mother," Willie said as he walked up, pushed aside Jerrod's extended hand, and gave him a hug.

"How've you been, Willie?"

Willie sat back down, leaned back, and spread his arms wide. "Just living the privileged life of a public servant."

"Come a long way," Jerrod said. "They had four of us crammed into an office this size at the old PD."

Willie had gained a few pounds and shaved off his thin mustache.

"Yes, sir. You look to be on-duty right now," Willie observed. "So, what brings you here? Business or pleasure."

"I'm getting married in February."

"I gathered that from the wedding invitation," Willie said. "I have also deduced that 'Nicole' must the same as the 'Nikki' I met last year."

"And your deductions are confirmed."

"Knock her up, or something?" Willie smiled as he hung his left arm and rattled the heavy chain on his metal watch.

"No. No. We're not having kids. She has two daughters."

"Cool. Doing the stepdad thing? Is the real dad causing any problems?"

"No. He died just before I met Nikki. Sudden brain-bleed thing."

"That sucks." Willie said. "Anyway, I'll be at the wedding."

"Willie. I want you to be *in* my wedding. Be one of my groom... uh... guys."

"'Groomsmen,'" Willie corrected as he leaned back again. "Yeah. Sure. Why not?"

"Craig's going to be in it too. And Marko... but I haven't asked him yet."

"He's working today. I'll call him to meet you."

"Very good. Thank you," Jerrod said. "Getting the crew together one more time. Lot of history there."

"Just tell me when and where, brother," Willie said. "And I'll be there... with bells on."

"Two 'without' and a coffee, please," Jerrod said to the man wearing a white apron standing inside The Corner Hot Dog Stand.

"Two chili dogs. No onions. And a coffee," the man said. He looked to the uniformed officer next to Jerrod. "You, sir."

"Coffee only, please," said Valle Verde PD Sergeant Mark "Marko" Otero.

"Oh, in that case," Jerrod said, "this one's on me."

"You're so generous. I knew I liked something about you."

"So," Marko started, "Willie calls and says to 'meet the plainclothes officer at The Corner.' I wasn't expecting it to be you."

"I got a big favor to ask," Jerrod said as he paid for the order.

"You already owe me about fifty favors. And I'm gonna collect someday. What is it?"

"You got the wedding invitation for February, right?"

"I got it. Haven't RSVP'd just yet. Pretty sure I'll be there."

Jerrod paused. "I wondered if you would be one of my groomsmen."

"Who else is going to be in it?"

"Craig and Willie."

"Craig's coming down from the high desert?" Marko pondered.

"Yep. I spent a couple days with him and Sandi. They'll both be there."

Marko scratched his chin. "Me and Craig and Willie. I'll have to think about that."

"Okaaaay?"

"Of course, you idiot. I'd be honored to stand with you?"

"Great. Thank you."

"Sure."

"I've got this cousin I'd like you to meet." Jerrod leaned in. "She's about your age. Got divorced a year or so ago. Cute little son."

"I'm okay on that, Jerrod. No need to set me up."

"I just thought--"

"Don't think," Marko interrupted. "That's why you're in trouble all the time. Walk with me."

Marko moved into the nearly vacant parking lot and put his Styrofoam cup on the hood of his patrol car. Jerrod did the same.

"How long have we known each other?" Marko asked.

"I don't know. Since I was a police cadet. Fourteen. Fifteen years."

"Have you ever seen me with a woman? Ever talk about women? Ever get stupid around women like most guys?"

Jerrod thought back for a few moments as he unwrapped the first chili dog. "Never thought about it. So, I guess not."

"Then you don't know?"

"Know what?" Jerrod asked just before sticking the chili dog into his mouth.

"That I'm gay, man."

Jerrod stopped chewing as he studied Marko and waited for him to break a smile. No smile appeared.

"Chew completely. Then swallow," Marko warned. "Don't you dare choke right here. My CPR card is expired."

Jerrod struggled to swallow. "But... no... uh... you're not serious?"

"Serious as AIDS, my friend."

Jerrod cocked his head. "Wait... what... since when?"

"Since... gosh, let me think... *forever*," Marko replied. "People don't 'turn' gay. Sometimes you're just not very bright."

Jerrod chuckled. "I... uh... had no idea. I guess I don't have much experience with... um... gayness."

"Gayness?" Marko laughed. "Haven't heard that one before."

"Sorry."

"Just 'gay.' Marko shook his head. "Do you still want me in your wedding?"

"Can I get back to you on that?" Jerrod asked. "I need some time to process this."

Marko scoffed.

"I'm just messing with you. I don't care *what* you are because I already know *who* you are."

Marko nodded.

"We've been friends a long time." Jerrod paused. "Willie called me his 'brother from another mother.' I feel the same about you. You saved my life. I absolutely want you to be next to me at my wedding."

"Done then. I'll be there."

Their hug sealed the deal.

"Can I bring a date?" Marko asked. "It'll be a dude."

"Sure. If you want," Jerrod smirked. "But I do have this other cousin. He's a professional chef..."

CHAPTER 15

SEPTEMBER 1991 -- Investigations Morning Meeting

"I trust everyone had a refreshing weekend," Lieutenant Ben Zaff said to start the meeting. "No major call-outs and the incoming reports are minimal."

"We're all caught-up on sleep," Darrell Regner said.

"There is one odd case that came in," Ben said as he held up an incident report. "Not really either a persons or a property crime."

"Intriguing," Jeff Moreno said.

Ben continued, "A woman reported her husband has been cashing his paycheck and spending it like crazy."

Darrell Regner asked, "Booze? Dope?"

"Nope," Ben continued, "Massages. He been visiting a massage parlor near the Valle Verde airport -- just outside the city limits -- so it's our problem. He's been going there more and more often recently."

Beach Sutton leaned back in his chair. "Must be the old 'Rub and Tug.'"

Beach's comment got a sharp glance from Linda Westphal.

"Well, that's what the wife thinks too," Ben said. "She was suspicious and followed him to this parlor," he glanced at the report, 'The Happy Orchid."

Beach snickered. "Should be named, 'The Happy Ending."

Linda glared at Beach, "You're a pig."

"Oink," Beach replied.

"The wife wants this parlor investigated for prostitution," Ben added, "and since Detective Sutton has so much background on the subject... and I'm afraid to know exactly how." He paused for effect and got the desired laughter before sliding the report across his desk to Jerrod. "I think Property Crimes is the place for this case too... *come* to some resolution."

In the office of Property Crimes, Jerrod said, "Nice one, Beach. Just had to open your trap. 'Rub and Tug.' Seriously."

"What?" Beach responded.

Nate chimed in. "Beach, you sure seem to know a lot about the massage industry."

"Rumors only," Beach said. "And I'm very 'well read.'"

"What now, Sarge? Zippy asked.

"WWJFD?" Jerrod said.

"What Would Joe Friday Do?" Nate asked. "Joe Friday would be working the day shift in something other than the Vice Unit. His partner would be Bill Gannon. And he wouldn't waste any time on this petty shit."

Jerrod said, "I'll try to pry some cash out of the Investigations Fund and let's just go see if this massage parlor is legit or not. Someone's going to have to go in undercover."

"I nominate Beach," Nate said.

"I second that motion," Zippy said.

"Hey, wait," Beach said.

"I have a nomination and a second," Jerrod said. "All in favor."

"Aye," Nate said.

"Aye," Zippy said.

"Hold-on a fucking minute," Beach said.

"Aye," Jerrod said. "The 'ayes' have it." He looked at Beach. "Through democratic process, you have been duly elected. You, sir, are our new UC -- Under Cover. Congratulations."

Nate started a slow clap.

"Zippy," Jerrod said. "What the hell are the elements we need to prove for prostitution anyway? 647-something?"

"Penal Code 647-parentheses-b.'" Nate added.

"Nate just said 'penal,'" Beach said.

Jerrod looked at Beach. "You're a child."

"What?" Beach said.

Zippy opened a paperback edition of the California Penal Code and thumbed the pages to 647(b). "It is a crime to solicit, or agree to engage in, or actually engage in, any act of prostitution in exchange for compensation."

"That's pretty general," Nate said.

Zippy continued, "The solicitation, agreement, or act must be for intercourse or a lewd act." Zippy read further. "A lewd act involves the touching of the genitals, buttock, or female breast for sexual arousal or gratification."

Beach leaned back. "Read that part about 'sexual arousal or gratification' again, please."

"Oh, there's more," Zippy said. "The suspect has to do something to further the commission of an act of prostitution."

"The 'overt act,'" Nate said.

"Okay," Beach said. "What if the massage...uh... massager asks me if I'm 5-o?

"'Masseuse,'" Zippy corrected.

"If she asks if you are the police; you can lie right through your teeth," Nate said.

Jerrod added. "That is an old and very false belief. We can legally deny we're cops right up to the point the 'cuffs go on."

"We need to be careful not entrap anyone," Zippy said. "I just looked that up too."

"Please continue," Beach said.

Zippy read: "Entrapment is when a normal, law-abiding citizen is induced into committing a criminal act they would not otherwise have committed because of overbearing harassment, fraud, or threats made by the police."

"Okay," Jerrod said, "'no harassment, fraud, or threats.'" He turned to Beach. "You can still ask for something... extra... and see where that goes. But if the masseuse says 'no'... then it's a 'no.'"

Jerrod looked at Nate. "Would you get hold of Narcotics and see if we can borrow a 'wire' for the day so we can record Beach on his mission."

"Will do," Nate said.

Jerrod looked at his detectives. "We're sure putting an awful lot of effort into this misdemeanor investigation."

Zippy nodded.

Jerrod continued, "I propose we grab some lunch and then head down to The Happy Orchid."

"I used to come here all the time," Jerrod said. "Best burritos on the Central Coast."

Jerrod and the detective sat around a table inside Garcia's Mexican Food in Valle Verde.

Garcia's had changed little since Jerrod had started going there over ten years earlier. The original owner -- Salvador "Sal" Garcia -- had taken ill and the business was being run by his eldest son -- Ernesto.

"Hello, Jerrod," Ernesto said. "Brought the whole posse with you, I see."

"Indeed," Jerrod said, "Need to fuel up for a big operation this afternoon."

"Huge operation," Beach added.

"Came to the right place," Ernesto said.

The detectives later devoured their massive burritos filled with meat, rice, beans, onion, and cilantro.

"This is incredible," Beach said just before taking another bite from the juicy burrito of *birria* – steamed beef.

"This place should franchise," Nate said as he wiped his chin with a napkin of his *pollo* -- chicken -- burrito. "It would kill."

Zippy just nodded and smiled as juice from his *carnitas* – braised pork -- burrito dribbled down his wrist.

Jerrod put down his *carne asada* – grilled beef -- burrito and held up his right hand. He pointed to the horseshoe-shaped scar on the back of it. "The events that led to this scar all started right here and involved some of these burritos."

Jerrod recounted having stopped into Garcia's for a to-go order while still a Valle Verde PD detective. He pointed to the screen front door and described the push-pull tussle he had with the bear-like man -- Oso. That encounter eventually led to the drug operation headed by Armando Mendoza, the deaths of Hector Medina and Valdemar Reyes, the vehicle pursuit of Oso and Mendoza, Craig Wallace being shot in the knee, and the fatal shooting of Mendoza with his own gun.

Jerrod left out the part about Captain Andrew Wheaton and the protection payoffs he had been taking from Mendoza.

"I had no idea," Beach said.

"That's how it all started," Jerrod said. "Just minding my own business and getting some lunch."

"We need a 'bust' signal for Beach," Zippy said. "You know, when the crime is complete, and we need to rush in and save him."

Beach started, "'Gee, little lady. You sure have cold hands.'"

Nate laughed. "How about, 'A little faster, please.'"

"I've got one," Zippy chimed in. "'This has never happened before.'"

Jerrod chuckled. "Very clever, gentlemen. But this is all going to be recorded. I propose, 'It's getting hot in here.'"

"Perfect," Zippy said.

Jerrod had joined Zippy in his unmarked car. They did a drive-by through the small strip mall in which The Happy Orchid was located to pinpoint its location. They then searched for a spot where they could watch the front of the business from their car.

Beach had been Nate's passenger and the four detectives met in a parking lot near the Valle Verde airport. Nate had borrowed a "wire" from the County Narcotics Team.

A "wire," also known more accurately as a "body wire," was a portable listening device with a small microphone attached to a battery-powered transmitter. Undercover officers could easily hide the device under their clothing or in a backpack. The transmitter shared a frequency with a receiver which allowed back-up officers to both monitor and tape record any conversation between the UC and the targets of their investigation.

Jerrod started. "We found a place near the business where we can set-up and, hopefully, listen to everything happening with Beach."

"'Hopefully?'" Beach asked.

Nate turned to Beach. "How about you just put the wire in your jacket pocket. I don't see a need to actually wear it on you."

"Good idea," Jerrod said. "Just keep the jacket near you. We should be fine."

"'Should be?'" Beach asked.

"Okay," Jerrod said. "I got one hundred dollars cash out of the Investigations Fund for this. Five twenties. The L-T wants the money back, so I made photocopies of the bills to record the serial numbers."

"I'm pretty sure you just committed a federal crime there, Sarge," Beach said.

"Call the Secret Service and see if they give a shit," Nate said.

"Good point," Beach said.

Jerrod handed the bills to Beach. "I have no idea what this place charges. Forty? Sixty? All hundred?" Jerrod paused. "Use it all, if you need to, but please keep an eye on where the bills go."

"Copy that," Beach said.

"Remember, " Zippy said, "we need to prove the masseuse solicits, agrees to engage, or actually engages in an act... in exchange for compensation."

"Check," Beach said.

"But no 'actually engages'... in anything, Beach," Jerrod warned.

"Yes, sir." Beach said.

"And we need an overt act," Zippy added.

"Would accepting the cash be an overt act?" Beach asked.

Nate and Zippy nodded.

"Why not?" Jerrod said. "Taking cash for sex is pretty overt. We'll go with that."

"What's the bust signal?" Nate quizzed.

"'It's getting hot in here,'" Beach said.

"We are good-to-go," Jerrod said. "Saddle up."

The four detectives drove to a trailer park just in-sight of the massage parlor. Jerrod sat in the passenger seat of Zippy's car and held the portable receiver and recorder on his lap. Nate and Beach stood outside the car.

"UC ready," Jerrod asked.

"Ready," Beach said.

"Comm check," Zippy said.

Beached walked a short distance from the cars and counted slowly, "1... 2... 3... 4... 5... 5... 4... 3... 2... 1."

"Five-by-five," Jerrod said -- meaning they could hear him clearly.

"We'll start recording just before you go inside," Jerrod said. "Peek at your watch and say the time out-loud before you open the door. We'll toot the horn if we can hear you. Keep the jacket near you at all times."

"Okay, Mom," Beach said. "How about we get this thing going?"

Beach stopped at the massage parlor door, announced the time, and listened for the confirming horn honk before entering.

"Welcome to The Happy Orchid," the woman with a bright red wig at the reception counter said with a flat accented tone. She glanced away from a fashion magazine. "You want massage?"

"Yeah... uh... I guess... yeah," Beach stammered. "My... uh... back is sore."

"Stage fright," Nate commented as they monitored the wire.

"He's not getting an Oscar nod for this performance," Zippy added.

"Stay on script, Beach," Jerrod encouraged. "Just stay on script."

"Forty dollars," the receptionist said now without glancing away from the magazine. "Cash only."

Beach peeled off two twenties and handed them to her.

She placed the bills into a gray locking cash box behind the counter. "You have seat. I go get Sapphire."

"What if I want a 'special' massage?" he asked.

"You talk to Sapphire," she said before pushing through a curtain made from strings of colored beads and out of sight into the back of the business.

"Forty bucks," Jerrod commented. "Bargain price."

"'Sapphire,'" Nate repeated. "Very exotic."

"Think she's what: Russian? Hungarian? Romanian?" Zippy asked. "She's definitely not Croatian."

"Oh, you a big man," Sapphire said after she parted the bead curtain and slinked toward Beach.

"Yeah. Uh. You're Sapphire" he said to the masseuse dressed in a short red silk robe. "Very pretty."

"Thank you," she said as she stood over him and held out her hand to him. "You come with me."

"Bet she says that to all the guys," Nate said with a toothy grin.

"Promises. Promises," Zippy added.

Nate asked, "Do you know what it's called when one cow spies on another cow?"

"No. What?" Zippy asked.

"A steak-out."

"Focus, gentlemen. Focus," Jerrod said.

Beach was led by the hand through the hanging beads and into a tidy room with a massage table in the center. A single chair sat in a corner and a small table nearby held an assortment of lotions and a folded white towel.

Sapphire closed the door quietly. "Back rub. Fifteen minutes for forty dollars. Take off your clothes. Leave underwear on."

Beach took off his coat and hung it on the chair. "What if I want to take off my underwear?" he asked.

"I just got a visual I won't be able to erase from my brain," Zippy said.

Nate and Jerrod tried to stifle their laughter. It didn't work.

Sapphire smiled. "That is forty dollars more."

"What do I get?"

"You have forty?" she asked.

Beach reached into his pocket and slapped two twenties on the table.

"Are you police?" she asked.

"Do I look like a cop?" he countered as he patted his huge belly. "They probably don't make uniforms big enough for guys like me."

"They do make them that big," Jerrod said. "But I am very impressed by Beach's level of self-awareness."

"Nice improv, my man," Nate said.

"Rethinking that Oscar nomination," Zippy said.

"Take off your clothes," she directed. "Make sure you're not police."

"Fine," Beach said as he picked up the twenties and put them back in his pocket. "A back rub is just fine. Forget the other part."

Sapphire admonished. "Mr. Fenris say must take clothes off first. Make sure not police."

"'Mr. Fenris?'" Nate repeated.

"This is getting interesting," Jerrod added.

Beach sat in the chair and took off his shoes. He stood up to unbutton his shirt. "Nah. Never mind. Just the back rub."

"I rub your front too," Sapphire blurted.

"What do I get?" Beach demanded.

"I make you hard. I make you feel good."

"What do I get?"

"I give you hand job. Make you relax and feel real good."

"Hand job for forty dollars?" Beach asked.

"For forty. Yes," Sapphire said.

"Deal," Beach said as he took the bills from his pants pocket and dropped them back on the table. "It's getting hot in here."

"There's the signal. Crime complete," Zippy said.

"Let's go save our boy," Jerrod directed.

Nate was already headed to his car.

"It is nice and warm in here," Sapphire said as she slowly peeled open the robe and exposed a pale body and firm breasts. "And you're very sexy man."

Beach watched her slink cat-like toward him. He thought he actually heard her purr.

"It's really hot in here," Beach said.

She took the two twenty-dollar bills and slipped them into the elastic of her skimpy panties. "You are only thing hot in here," she said as she inched closer to him.

The two unmarked detective cars pulled into the lot and parked near the parlor entrance. Nate and Zippy stood near the open car window and listened to the wire with Jerrod.

Beach stepped back and found he was against the wall. She moved close and he felt himself getting aroused. She pressed against him and moved her hand down to his placed her palm on his massive chest. She had a pleasant scent. "Oh, please," he said, "it's so hot in here."

"Want us to take 'em now, Sarge?" Nate asked.

Jerrod smiled. "Not... just... yet."

Zippy and Nate both doubled over in laughter.

Sapphire unfastened his belt buckle and started moving her hand down his zipper.

"Please, I beg you," Beach cried. "It's too hot in here."

"Go get him," Jerrod directed.

Nate and Zippy ran into the business as they shouted, "Sheriff's Office. No one move."

Sapphire pulled her robe closed and pulled away from Beach as she heard the commotion.

"Thank God," Beach sighed as he fastened his belt.

Zippy stayed in the reception area as Nate ran through the hanging beads.

"Beach?" Nate yelled. "Beach? Which room?"

"Back here," Beach shouted as he pushed past Sapphire and opened the door.

"We were just talking," Sapphire said as Nate walked into the doorway.

"I know you were," Nate said as he took out his handcuffs. "And now you're under arrest."

"She... uh... just a heads-up... doesn't have any weapons on her," Beach said with a chuckle.

Nate secured Sapphire's hands behind her back. Beach pulled open a portion of her robe and took the two bills from her panty strap.

"That's mine," she protested.

"That's evidence," Beach retorted. "I'm the police too."

"You too fat to be police," she said.

"I prefer the term 'big boned, '" Beach said.

Nate and Beach escorted Sapphire to the reception area where Jerrod had joined Zippy.

Jerrod looked to Beach. "Nicely done, Detective."

"You guys sure took your sweet-ass time getting in here."

"The wire was breaking up a little," Jerrod shrugged.

"We weren't sure you said 'hot' or 'not,'" Nate said. "It was difficult to make out."

"Beach. Where are the four twenties?" Jerrod asked.

"I've got the forty back from Sapphire," Beach said as he pointed to the reception counter. "The other forty is in that lock box."

Jerrod walked over to the counter and found the red-wigged woman in a frantic conversation on the telephone. He lifted the cash box, tried to open it, and found it to be locked.

"Open it," he told the woman.

She shook her head and held the receiver out toward Jerrod. "Mr. Fenris want to talk to you."

Jerrod took the receiver. "This is Sergeant Gold. Mesa County Sheriff's Office. Who are you?"

"My name is Fenris Cernv, and I own The Happy Orchid. I run a duly licensed and legitimate business. There must be some sort of misunderstanding here?"

"No misunderstanding," Jerrod replied. "One of your masseuses solicited an act of prostitution to an undercover detective."

"That can't be true," Cernv said.

"It was all recorded on tape," Jerrod said. "And Sapphire'll be going to the Mesa County Jail in a few minutes."

"I'm sure we can come to some type of arrangement," Cernv suggested.

"The only arrangement I'm interested in his getting our bait money back from this cashbox," Jerrod said. "Red here won't open it for me, so I'm seizing the whole damn thing."

"That won't be necessary," Cernv said. "I'll have her open the box."

"Too late," Jerrod said. "We'll take our marked bills out and you can explain to a judge why the rest should be returned to you."

There was a long pause before Fenris Cernv spoke again. "You're making a huge mistake, Sergeant."

Jerrod chuckled. "Sir. That would hardly be the first time."

Friday Afternoon

"Do you golf, Sarge?" Zippy asked Jerrod.

They were alone in the Property Crimes Section. Nate and Beach were out together on some follow-up.

"Uh, no," Jerrod said. "Never got into golfing. Was told I can't swing the club right."

"It's a lot of fun," Zippy said. "My dad's very good. I do okay. "

"Maybe when I retire and have nothing better to do."

Zippy said, "We're gonna play at that par three course north of Valle Verde on Sunday. Nine holes. Be done in an hour or so. My dad's a good teacher. Why don't you join us?"

"Sunday," Jerrod said. "Sure."

CHAPTER 16

"Glad you two could join us," Laura Renaud said as Jerrod and Nikki walked into the foyer of her Rochester Avenue home.

"Thanks for having us, Mom," Jerrod said as he kissed her cheek. "Your invitation sounded... important."

"Well, it is important," Laura said. "We have an announcement to make."

"You're finally leaving Don. Thank God." Jerrod smirked. "Divorcing him will be the best decision of your whole life."

Laura laughed. "Don and I aren't getting divorced. You can relax. It's something else."

Jerrod and Nikki followed Laura through the formal dining room -- with its large table intimately set for four -- into the spacious kitchen.

Laura looked at Jerrod. "You know where the beer is, honey. Help yourself." She turned to Nikki. "I've opened a very nice Napa Valley pinot noir for us."

Jerrod went to an adjacent laundry room -- which was bigger than an average bedroom -- to a well-stocked refrigerator and grabbed a Heineken.

"Where's Don?" Jerrod asked as he pulled open a kitchen drawer and found a bottle opener.

"He's out back. He picked up a few beautiful steaks. Go talk to him."

Jerrod went through the family room and into the backyard. Lush and private. The manicured landscape surrounded him. The sweet smoke of sizzling steaks on a charcoal grill led him to directly to his stepfather -- Don Renaud.

"How are you, Don?" Jerrod watched as Don carefully flipped four beautiful filet mignons on the grill.

"Hello, Jerrod," Don said an unusually chipper tone. "What temperature do you like your steak?"

"Uh, medium-ish for me."

"How about Nikki?"

"She likes her's more on the well-done side."

Don glanced over his shoulder. "No can do. I'd just as soon throw it away."

"She won't eat it unless it's at least medium-well. I'm serious."

"I'll burn it a little for her." Don smiled. "But If I see her head to the microwave with it -- you're both getting kicked out of the house."

Jerrod nodded. "So, Don, what exactly is the announcement this meeting has been called for?"

"We'll explain everything it at dinner."

Don pulled the steaks off the grill and placed them on a wood cutting board. "We'll let these rest a few minutes and then dig in."

A green salad with bay shrimp and a potato dish had been placed on the dining table. Don selected and served steaks to each plate.

Laura reached her arm out and took Don and Nikki's hands in hers. "Don, will you please say grace."

Jerrod took Nikki and Don's hands to complete the circle. They bowed their heads.

"Dear Lord. Thank you for this fine meal we are about to consume. May it nourish both our bodies and our souls. Thank you for the company of Jerrod and Nikki on this special occasion. Please look over their beautiful children. And Lord, please keep us mindful of the needs of others."

"Amen," the four said in unison.

Nikki poked her fork at the tender steak and a trickle of red juice appeared on her plate. She glanced at Jerrod. Her disgust was palpable.

Jerrod mouthed, "Just eat the edges."

She nodded her head.

"Okay, " Jerrod said. "What's the big announcement?"

Laura looked at Don -- who took longer than necessary to finish chewing a bite of the prime beef. He dabbed the corners of his mouth with a white linen napkin.

"Your mother and I are retiring."

"Congratulations," Nikki said.

"Excellent news," Jerrod said.

Laura looked at Jerrod and then Nikki. "And we're moving to Arizona."

Jerrod forced down the bite of salad he was chewing. "'Arizona? What... the hell."

"We just got back from there," Don said. "We bought a house in Lake Kiowa City -- Home of The London Bridge -- right on the Colorado River."

"When... what?" Jerrod asked.

"We're moving in February," Laura said. "Right after the wedding."

"I'm shocked, honestly," Jerrod said. "Why Arizona?"

Don took a bite of potato before answering. "I just turned seventy-two. I've been working for over sixty years -- with forty-five years just in real estate. I'm ready to stop working."

"And these wet winters here," Laura added, "are tough on Don's bursitis. He feels much better in the drier desert air."

"The girls will miss you," Nikki said. "They're going to be sad."

"They can come visit, dear," Laura said. "We'll have a swimming pool."

"I'm speechless," Jerrod said. "But it sounds like a great plan. I'm sure this house will sell in no-time."

"We're not going to list the house," Don looked at Laura then back to Jerrod. "We want you and Nikki and the girls to live here."

Jerrod was dumbfounded. "Here? In 'The Rochester?' You can't be serious."

"I've worked out all the details," Don said. "We'll act as the bank. We set up a mortgage and you make payments to us. We'll make it affordable for you. And, besides that, it'll give us a tax advantage as well."

"I don't know," Jerrod said. "The property taxes alone on this place--"

"That's taken care of as well," Don interrupted.

Nikki glanced at Jerrod. He knew the look. She wanted that house.

"We're serious," Laura said. "We want the girls to grow up here like you and your--" She cut herself off.

Don dropped his fork to his plate. Nikki had no idea what had just happened.

Jerrod asked, "'...and your' what, Mom? Were you going to say, 'your brother?' Tommy?"

"I'm sorry, Jerrod," Laura said.

Don glared at Jerrod.

Jerrod met his eyes and said, "Tommy just loved living here and that sure worked out well. Didn't it."

Laura dabbed her eyes with her napkin.

"Apologize to your mother," Don demanded.

"Fuck you, Don."

Nikki cleared her throat. "Don. Laura. Your offer is very generous, but..." She looked at Jerrod.

Jerrod threw his napkin on the table. "There's no way we'd want this house, and we couldn't afford it if we did."

"Jerrod. What the hell just happened back there?"

Jerrod and Nikki had just pulled out of the driveway and headed home. He chirped the tires as he sped away.

"I don't want to talk about it. It's family business."

"I'm your family."

Jerrod poured a double gin over ice and tossed the bottle cap on the counter. "Tommy was my brother."

"Honey. Sit down. Tell me about him," Nikki pleaded.

They moved to the living room sofa.

"Tommy was about two years younger than me." Jerrod sipped the gin. "We weren't that close. I did my thing and he did his."

"Like what?" Nikki asked.

"I played baseball. That's all I wanted to do. Tommy liked to draw. Landscapes. Bugs. Animals. Flowers. Anything. He was so talented."

"So, what happened?"

"My folks divorced." Jerrod took another sip. "Jerry moved to Las Vegas. Mom married Don. It was all too much for him... and me too."

"You never told me you had a brother."

"I don't *have* a brother."

"I don't understand."

"He disappeared. He's missing. Alive or dead. I don't know."

"Jerrod. I'm so lost. We're going to be married. I need to know. Please explain."

Jerrod leaned back on the sofa. He sipped again and paused for a long moment. "Okay. Here's the short version: My father -- Jerry Gold -- liked to drink. Mom got tired of it. She gave him an ultimatum: stop drinking or get divorced. He stayed sober for a while. We had fun as a family. San Francisco. Hearst Castle. Sequoias. Yosemite. Disneyland. Giants and A's games. You name it. Then he started drinking again. There was another ultimatum. And then another."

Jerrod's stared at the glass in his hand. "Then Mom started going to real estate classes. Got her agent's license. I didn't understand until later, but she was getting ready to leave Jerry. That process dragged out for over a year."

"Keep going," she said.

Jerrod shook his head. "He came home drunk one night. Me and Mom and Jerry sat around the dining room table. She told him it was over. That they were done. She had already talked to an attorney and would be filing for a divorce the next day." Jerrod started to sob. "It was fucking terrible. Worst day of my life. Rug just pulled out."

Nikki held him. Tears poured out of Jerrod's eyes.

"Where was Tommy when this happened?" she asked.

Jerrod wiped his face with his sleeve. "In his room. Drawing something. He didn't get involved it that stuff."

"How did Tommy disappear?"

"Well, the house we were living in got sold. Me, Mom, and Tommy moved into a little rental place here in Valle Verde... not far from here."

"How about your dad? Jerry?"

"He bounced around town for six months or so. Then he got a job in Las Vegas and moved there."

"What about Tommy?"

"I was getting to that." Jerrod finished the last of the gin and rattled the ice cubes. "Mom met Don on some weekly real estate tour thing where they visit houses just listed for sale."

"I've heard of that," she said.

"Well, they hit it off. A few months later they were engaged and got married a short time after that. Then we all moved into Don's house in The Rochester. That damn house."

"Again. What about Tommy?"

"Tommy didn't like school. He didn't like sports. He just wanted to draw stuff. He was a natural. But Don would have none of it. He harped on Tommy over and over and over that he had to finish high school. He had to go to college. He had to make something of himself. That drawing alone wasn't going to pay the bills. I heard all the same bullshit from him."

"Then what?"

"After school let out in 1974, Tommy asked Mom if he could spend the summer with Jerry in Las Vegas."

71

"And he went?"

"Yeah. He went. But he told me before he left that he intended to stay in Vegas and not come home. He couldn't stand living with Don."

"How old was he then?

"Thirteen."

"How did he 'disappear?'"

"One day, Jerry went to work. Tommy stayed home. Jerry came home later and Tommy was gone. Gone gone. No note. Didn't take any clothes. Didn't take any of his drawing stuff. Just fucking disappeared."

Nikki covered her mouth with her hand. "Oh, my God."

"The police were called." Jerrod rubbed his eyes. "They took a report, I guess. But we haven't heard anything since."

"I can't believe you've never mentioned this to me."

Jerrod glared at her. "Why would I ever bring it up?"

CHAPTER 17

Sunday Morning

The Foothill Golf Course was pretty basic and just as described -- an "executive course" with nine par-three holes.

"Sergeant Jerrod Gold," Zippy said. "This is my father, Charles Zippich."

The men shook hands. "'Jerrod' is just fine, sir."

"And everyone just calls me "Chick,' Mr. Zippich said through a thick Croatian accent. "Glad you could join us."

"I have never played, sir," Jerrod said. "I've swung a club, but not very well. Some mini golf. You know, windmills and stuff."

"Let's go to the driving range and take a look," Chick said. "I brought you a set of clubs and got us a couple buckets of balls."

At the range, Chick set Jerrod's feet as he addressed the ball, adjusted his grip, and coached him on taking an easy swing. Most of the balls "sliced" right after he struck them. On one swing, the ball clunked against the club and shot off at a sharp angle to the right.

"What the hell was that?" Jerrod asked.

"'S-word,'" Zippy said.

"It was 'shitty' alright," Jerrod said.

"No," Chick said. "You 'shanked' it. Hit the ball with the rounded hosel of the club instead the face. We can fix that too."

"You are a patient man, Chick," Jerrod said.

"This game is all about patience."

After a few more weak attempts and more adjustments, Chick asked, "Jerrod, did you play baseball at some point?"

"Yes, sir. Played for years. Little League through high school and Colt League."

"That explains things," he said. "Hitting a pitched baseball is probably the most difficult skill to master in sports. The best players in the game fail to hit safely seven out of ten times."

Jerrod nodded.

"But hitting a little white golf ball sitting perfectly still on a tee right in front of you is, by far, the most humbling skill."

Jerrod and Zippy laughed.

Chick continued, "The shifting of your weight is more of a pivot. Let's try something. Address the ball as normal and drop the club on to the ground."

"Okay," Jerrod said as he took his stance.

Chick placed a golf ball in Jerrod's right hand. "Now toss the ball, underhand, down range."

Jerrod tossed the ball as instructed.

"Feel that?" Chick said as he handed him another ball. "It's a pivot. Do it again."

Jerrod tossed the ball. And did it a third and fourth time.

"Now pick up the club," Chick said, "and swing it with that same pivot."

Jerrod addressed the ball and hit a perfect drive down range.

"Excellent,' Chick said. "Let's leave on a good note. Now we play."

The course was simple to understand. Hit the evil white ball from tee box to green. Then make two putts into the cup and you have par. Fewer strokes are good; more strokes are bad. Jerrod found it was much easier said than done. He got more instruction on golf rules and etiquette and technique around the greens and in bunkers -- which he had mistakenly called "sand traps" -- as they walked the course.

"I think you're getting the hang of this game, Sarge," Zippy said.

"Practice makes perfect," Jerrod said.

"Perfect practice makes perfect," Chick corrected. "You're doing fine."

After the ninth hole, the men shook hands. "That was fun," Jerrod said.

"Care to join us next Saturday," Chick said. "My son and I are playing eighteen holes at the Willowmere Country Club. I'm a member there. Beautiful course and they have golf carts. My other sons aren't available, and we could use a 'third.' What do you say?"

"Saturday?" Jerrod pondered as he thought about the list of wedding tasks he still had to complete. "I'd love to join you."

"How was golf?" Nikki asked as Jerrod walked in the house.

"Humbling. Where are the girls?"

"Out. Neighbors' houses."

"Okay."

"I visited with your mom while you were gone," Nikki said.

His shoulders slumped. "Why?"

"She's sad and I wanted to see if I could help her."

"Get it all worked out? Is she feeling better now? Back to normal?"

"Don't use that tone."

"I'm sorry." Jerrod said. "This whole subject -- as you may have observed -- is still a little raw."

"I've never seen her this depressed," she said.

"I have."

"I think she may have taken some medication or something."

"Not the first time."

"She took me into Tommy's room." She sighed. "His drawing are still on the walls. He was very skilled."

He stared at nothing. "I haven't been in that room for fifteen years."

"Laura said Marty likes to sleep in that room. She calls it 'The Picture Room.' She thinks those drawing are photographs."

Jerrod nodded. "He drew stuff from memory. We'd go someplace and a day or so later he'd have a sketch done. It would look like a photograph. He just drew what he had captured in his mind."

Nikki took a long pause. "She said something very interesting. You may not like it."

"I'm listening."

"She said she has wondered for years why you, her only remaining son, the 'skilled detective' -- her words, not mine -- has never looked into his own brother's disappearance. No questions for her about it. Not a single telephone call to the Las Vegas police. Nothing."

"She said that?"

"She did." Nikki peered deep into his eyes. "Is it true?"

Jerrod didn't answer.

It was a school night. Lilly and Marty had gone to bed and Jerrod fought off sleep as he tried to watch the nine o'clock news.

"Don and your mom still want us to buy their house," Nikki said.

He didn't look away from the TV. "I don't think it's a good idea. That's too much house. I like it right here. It's cozy."

"Sure. Because this is *your* house. Me and the girls just live in it. Right? At some point, I'd like to be in a house that's *ours*. Don and Laura have offered it to us."

"This is just as much your house as it is mine."

"Do you remember saying that the girls were growing up and would want their own rooms at some point."

"Do you, literally, record everything I say?

She smiled. "Yes. Yes, I do."

"There needs to be a statute-of-limitations on that, or I should be more careful in what I say."

"How about you just live up to what you say."

Jerrod was fully awake at this point. "Let's say I agree? Let's say we go ahead and buy that house?"

"That sounds like a 'yes.'

He shook his head. "It was posed as a hypothetical."

She smiled. "Still sounds like a 'yes."

"I'm not going to win this one. Am I?"

"Silly. It'll be win-win for everyone."

"I'll talk to them tomorrow."

"Duly recorded."

"I have no doubt."

"Come in," Laura Renaud said after answering the door. Hair down. No make-up. She shuffled to the kitchen. A bottle of wine and a glass were on the counter where she sat.

"Mom. I am so sorry about what I said the other night. I was out-of-line."

She held a long pause. "Do you know how many times I have blamed myself for what happened to Tommy? Her chin quivered for a moment. "The guilt I have carried. The 'what-ifs' I ask myself every single day."

"Mom, I knew Tommy was going to stay with Jerry. He planned all along to not come back."

Her lips pursed. "You knew?"

"I promised him I wouldn't say anything... and I didn't. To be honest, I didn't have a problem with him staying there."

"It was that bad here?"

"It was."

She started to speak but stopped and stared out the window.

"I'm going to Las Vegas," Jerrod said to break the silence.

"That's nice. You and Nikki could use a little vacation."

"No vacation. I'm going to look for Tommy."

"She told you. She told you what I said to her."

"She did. Please don't be mad. I'm going to look into it. Stir the pot, as it were. See if I can find out anything and where that goes. It may not be the outcome we hope for, but I'll try to get some answers."

Laura chuckled. "I remember the day you came home from high school and announced you wanted to be a Valle Verde police officer."

Jerrod sat next to her.

"I was petrified. No mother wants to send her son to war, and no mother would want her son to be in police-work either."

He scoffed. "It's not like war, Mom."

"Except that time those men shot out the front window of your house. And you and Natalie got cut with all that glass. And then there was the man -- who lived right down the street from here -- who stomped on your hand and left that scar and tried to kill you. Do I need to go on? It *is* like going to war, son."

Jerrod nodded.

Laura thought for several seconds. "I've never told a soul about this, and you have to give me your word you'll not share this with anyone."

"I promise."

Laura held his hand. "Remember that little boy over in Merced who was kidnapped and held for years by a pedophile before escaping."

"Sure," Jerrod said. "Steven Stayner."

"In my grief-sick mind..." She swallowed hard and shook her head before continuing. "I, at one point, wished Tommy had been like that poor boy. That he had been abducted and was being kept somewhere but would return to us at some point."

"I understand."

"Thank you for looking into this, son. I'm proud of you and I have faith in you."

"You're welcome, Mom. Can I take a peek in Tommy's room?"

"Stay in there as long as you'd like."

"Mom?" Marty asked. "Why did we have to get dressed up and come to this restaurant?"

Marty sat with Lilly, Nikki, and Jerrod at a table inside the upscale Tomei's Restaurant on the Willowmere Wharf.

"Because this is a special occasion," Nikki answered.

"I propose a toast," Jerrod said as he raised his martini.

Nikki lifted her glass of wine, and the girls raised their Shirley Temples.

"To our new marriage," Jerrod continued. "To our new family and to our new house. We move-in right after the wedding."

They clinked glasses.

"You," Nikki said to the girls, "are both getting your own rooms."

"Can I have the room with the desk and two windows?" Lilly asked.

"Can I have the one with all the pictures?" Marty asked.

"Yes," Nikki said. "And yes."

As Nikki and her daughters chatted, Jerrod tuned out their voices and sipped his cocktail as he looked out the picture window down onto the ocean and beach nearby. A solo surfer sat on his board, studied the water, let a few waves pass, then paddled hard to catch a perfect one, launched to his feet, and enjoyed the last long ride of the day.

Calm. Peaceful. Satisfying.

He looked at the reflection in the glass of himself and his family.

Together. Happy. Celebrating.

Their lives were good. Very good.

CHAPTER 18

Wednesday Morning -- Property Crimes Unit

"You heard the L-T," Jerrod said. "Four mini-storage 'burgs' last night. Mid and south county. Locks on the units were sheared with bolt-cutters, but the fences weren't touched. Have to be the same suspects. This is now our problem, and it will not repeat tonight." He looked at his detectives. "Ideas?"

"You mean, 'What Would Joe Friday Do?'" Zippy asked.

Jerrod nodded.

"We can call the storage offices," Nate said, "and get a list of renters who were in the last couple days. Since the fences weren't cut, they could have just used a pass code to get through the gate."

"Good," Jerrod said.

"Get some names," Beach suggested. "Call the Probation Department and see if any of them have a search clause on their probation. Go knock on some doors."

"More," Jerrod encouraged.

"And ask 'em if there is any video," Zippy added. "I didn't see any mention in the crime reports about video."

"Maybe look into employees with access afterhours," Nate said.

"I propose," Jerrod started, "the four of us. Together. As the cohesive team we are, head south, do what we do, arrest the assholes responsible, and recover all of that stolen property... right after lunch."

"Sushi," Nate suggested.

"Wendy's is fine with me," Beach chimed in.

"I was thinking something more... sit down," Zippy said. "Where you need to use a fork to eat."

"Settled then," Jerrod proclaimed. "We're going to lunch at Sophie's Diner."

CHAPTER 19

One day after the Willowmere City Hall shooting

"Bruce Witt," the voice on the telephone answered.

"Fuck you."

"Who is this?"

"Jerrod Gold."

"Oh... shit... Jerrod," Bruce stammered. "You must be home on leave or something."

"Yeah. Paid leave for a couple days. Hope you made a boat-load of cash off that video."

"Hey, that's how I make a living, dude. Sorry."

"Don't be. I know that's what you do and I'm just messing with you."

"Thank God," Bruce sighed.

"That was very clever you recycling the video clip from the Jelinski murder scene."

"I know, right." Bruce chuckled. "Want to know how much I sold the exclusive video of the shooting and you hitting the Willowmere cop and that old clip for?"

"No."

"Well, it was a lot. A DA investigator called today for a copy of the raw video. Stan Walsh. I told him to get a court order. "

"That's great, Bruce. Feel free to give it to Stan. Don't make him jump hoops. He's a good guy. What happened happened."

"Okay."

"My only problem with the whole thing, is that I didn't get a chance to warn my folks first. They found out on the news because you released my name before the sheriff did."

"I... uh... yeah... shit... didn't think of that."

"What made you go to the back of city hall when all the action was happening out front?"

"You showed up," Bruce said without hesitation. "You and your guys went to the rear of the building, and I decided to follow. I figured if something was gonna to go down -- you'd be in the middle of it. And I was right."

"You owe me, Bruce."

"I can make a copy of the raw video for you too."

"That's fine. But you still owe me."

CHAPTER 20

For twelve years, the same four men had a standing nine o'clock tee-time every Saturday morning at the Willowmere Country Club. All were serious and competent and impatient golfers.

The course scheduler would often hold-back other groups of players he deemed may impede the nine o'clock group. Two golf carts were detailed to a high gloss each Friday afternoon and reserved for the foursome.

The staff and every other member of the exclusive golf club knew who they were and stayed out of their way. "Yes, sir" was the only acceptable response to any of their requests.

The four single-digit handicapped players had their own brand of "skins-game" each Saturday morning. They strictly enforced the *USGA Rules of Golf* and there were no "gimmes" on the greens -- even a two-inch putt had to be sunk into the cup.

Each hole was worth one hundred dollars. The golfer with the fewest strokes on a particular hole won the "skin" and was paid one hundred dollars by each of the other players. If two or more players tied for the low stroke total at a particular hole, there was "no blood" and the "skin" rolled over to the next hole -- which became worth two hundred dollars. Future ties would compound the "skin" for the next hole until a player won the hole outright.

Several thousand dollars in crisp US currency would exchange hands each Saturday morning.

The player with the highest score for the entire round was obligated to pay for lunch and drinks for the three others. That bill could easily reach two to three hundred dollars at the extravagant club restaurant and bar.

One of the club golf pros -- since fired from the course and having moved from Mesa County -- had made the grave mistake of repeating the nickname he had overheard one of the golfers refer to their foursome.

That nickname was: "The Tetrad."

CHAPTER 21

Saturday Morning -- Willowmere Golf and Country Club

"We tee-off at 8:36," Charles "Chick" Zippich said. "Let's hit a few balls at the range and make some putts at the practice green before we head out."

"You're going to like this course, Sarge," Bryce "Zippy" Zippich said. "Way different than that 'pitch-and-putt' we played last weekend."

"Zippy. You can just call me 'Jerrod' out here. Okay?"

"Yeah. Sure."

They each hit a couple dozen clean white practice golf balls at the range and putted on the velvet green near the clubhouse. Jerrod rehearsed the ball-toss pivot Chick had shown him the previous weekend.

"Zippich three-some. On-deck," the course starter announced on a PA system.

"Good morning, Chick," the pink-cheeked man at the starter's shack said. "Hey, Zippy. Who's your 'third?'"

"Jerrod Gold," Chick said. "Friend of my son's. Friend of mine."

The starter looked at Jerrod's feet and noticed he was wearing running shoes instead of golf spikes. "Play much?"

"Just started. That obvious already?"

He shook his head and looked at Chick. "There's a group playing behind you." He looked around. "They're pretty intense players. If they happen to catch you, just finish the hole you're on and let them play-through. Please. I beg you."

"No problem, Chick said.

"You're up," the starter said. "Have a great round."

Chick, Zippy, and Jerrod stepped onto the first tee-box. A straight downhill par-four. Chick striped his drive down the center of the fairway. Zippy hit his ball with a nice draw to the left fairway. Jerrod's drive sliced right and out of view.

"It's open to the right over there. You're probably okay," Chick said.

Chick and Zippy shared a golf cart. Jerrod followed behind in his own cart.

Chick "birdied" the hole and Zippy pared. Jerrod found his ball, pitched it onto the green, but then three-putted to score a "bogey" five.

The next few holes went the same. Chick played great. Zippy played good. Jerrod struggled.

"What are these bottles for?" Jerrod asked as he pulled an odd-shaped plastic bottle from a rack on his golf cart.

"It has sand and grass seed in it," Zippy said. "Use it to fill any pivots you leave on the fairways. Just sprinkle it in the pivot and smooth it with your foot."

"Okay. Thanks."

Jerrod hit a ball into a small pond on one hole and lost a couple more balls in some tall grass along the fairways.

Chick said, "We need to step-up our pace to stay ahead of that group behind us."

On the fairway of the sixth hole, Jerrod looked back and saw the group arriving at the tee box behind them.

Jerrod drove his cart over a small hill and out of sight from the tee. Chick and Zippy were already close to the green and had driven ahead. Jerrod estimated the green to be around 135 yards away, so he selected an eight-iron and addressed his ball.

A golf ball flew over the hill, bounced once, and struck him on the right thigh before rolling a few feet away.

The group between had "hit into" him and no one had yelled "fore" to warm him the ball was headed his way. Both were serious violations of golf etiquette.

Jerrod swung his club, misjudged the slope, hit the turf behind his ball, and dug a deep divot. His ball skidded across the turf ankle-high toward the green.

He went to the golf cart and took out the bottle of seed and sand to fill his divot. He looked back at the hill and saw no one coming. He kicked the offending golf ball that had just struck his leg into the pivot and stomped it with the heel of his shoe -- firmly planting it into the supple fairway turf. He filled the indentation -- and ball -- before driving off to the green.

As Jerrod waited his turn to putt, he watched the four golfers drive over the hill. One of the players -- physically big, mid-sixties -- looked exasperated as he scoured the fairway for his ball.

"Good luck finding that one, dick," Jerrod said to himself.

After they finished the hole, Chick suggested they wait near the adjacent tee-box to the next hole and let the group play-through.

Jerrod watched the four players chip onto the green and putt. The face of the big player who had been looking for his ball was beat-red.

"Nice putt, 'General,'" another player -- mid-sixties, Filipino -- said to the red-faced man. "But that lost ball cost you two-strokes." He looked around at the other players. "That'll be three-hundred each, please."

"The General" and the two others each pulled thick wads of cash from their pockets, peeled off three bills, and handed then to the Filipino player

"Pretty serious game," Chick whispered.

"Feel free to play-through, gentlemen," Chick said to the group as they drove up to the tee-box.

The General asked, "Did any of you see a ball come over the hill behind you on the last hole? I 'nutted' one and I'm sure it was in the fairway."

Chick and Zippy shook their heads.

"I heard something land over there," Jerrod said as he pointed to a line of trees and brambles along the fairway.

The General selected the one-wood "driver" from his golf bag and walked to within a few feet of Jerrod.

"Bullshit," the General said. "I play this course every week and that ball was in the fairway."

"Are you accusing me of something... *friend*?" Jerrod asked.

"Forget it," the Filipino player said to Jerrod. "He's just a hot-head."

The General looked Jerrod up and down. "You're not a member here, are you?"

"No, sir. Just a guest."

"Well, enjoy the only round you'll ever play on this course... *friend*."

"I'm finding this round to be extremely satisfying, sir," Jerrod said as he rubbed the welt building on his right thigh. "More than you'll ever know."

The General glared for a few seconds. "You look familiar. Have we met before?"

"Pretty sure we haven't," Jerrod said.

"Let's go," the third player -- also mid-sixties Eastern European -- said to The General.

85

"My 'honor,'" the Filipino player announced as he stepped onto the tee box to be the first to drive the next hole.

"You're last, General," The fourth player -- mid-sixties Spanish-accented -- snickered.

Jerrod and The General locked eyes of a few seconds more until he moved to the tee box.

After all four players hit strong drives from the tee, The General glanced back and again made eye contact with Jerrod. He turned away and placed his driver into his golf bag -- custom-made of fine black-leather with gold piping -- strapped to the back of the cart.

The gold-embroidered name on the bag read:

BG Michael T. Sullivan
US Army (Ret.)

A single silver star had been embroidered below his name

Jerrod thought: *"Sullivan?" Could that be former-MCSO Lieutenant Mitchell T. Sullivan's father. He was a retired Army general. I need to do some checking.*

Jerrod, Zippy, and Chick holed-out on the 18th green and shook hands.

"That was quite a treat," Jerrod said to Chick. "I'll never be able to thank you enough."

"It was my pleasure," Chick said.

They pulled the carts to the clubhouse and were greeted by three college-aged men. The young men unloaded the golf bags and wiped down the faces of their clubs with WCC-logo towels before moving the bags to a rack for pickup.

Jerrod handed the young man helping him a five-dollar bill. His weak smile didn't mask his disappointment.

"Lunch is on me," Jerrod announced.

"And just how do you intend on financing that, Jerrod?" Chick said as a broad smile stretched across his face.

"How bad could it be?" Jerrod asked.

"You're gonna find out," Zippy answered.

They were seated under a huge umbrella on the large clubhouse patio. Jerrod scanned the crowd of mostly male players. One table held a foursome of women. The players represented a variety of races and ethnicities, but the WCC staff was entirely white.

"Twelve dollars for a BLT?" Jerrod said as he scanned the WCC menu. "Six for a Heineken. Three for an iced tea. I'm in the wrong neighborhood."

"You were warned," Chick said.

"I think I'll take the 'on-call detective' pager for a week just to catch up on what this is going to cost," Jerrod said.

After they had ordered their lunch, Jerrod raised his bottle of beer, "Chick. Zippy. I can't thank you two enough for this treat. A great round on a beautiful day with two incredible people."

"You're welcome, Jerrod," Chick said. "The pleasure was ours."

Zippy nodded. "Glad you came out too Sarge... Jerrod... I'll just stick to 'Sarge.'"

Chick smiled. "I'm surprised either of you wanted to play today after... you know... that situation at city hall the other day."

"I thought about canceling, to be honest." Jerrod took a drink from his beer. "But I'd just be moping around the house thinking about that... thing. This has been a very nice distraction. I'm going to just roll with it and try to stay as normal as I can. Thank you again."

Jerrod found the table containing the four serious players they had met on the course. The General had his back to him. The Filipino player noticed Jerrod and said something. The General turned around and glared for a few seconds.

Chick noticed the situation. "I don't think he likes you much."

"I pretty sure it's mutual," Jerrod replied.

"Do you know what happened to that golf ball he was looking for on the sixth hole?" Chick asked.

Jerrod paused for a few seconds. "Let me say... hypothetically... that if that ball had been an acorn, in a few years there'd be a mighty oak right in the middle of that fairway."

Zippy laughed so hard he snorted.

"I just figured out who that guy is, "The General -- Michael Sullivan -- said as he turned back to the table.

"Who?" the Hispanic player -- Gaspar De Perras -- asked.

"He's that sheriff's sergeant who hit the Willowmere officer with a shotgun a few days ago," Sullivan said. "It was on the TV news and in the Mesa paper."

"Right after he blew a bad-guy's brains out with that shotgun," the Romanian player -- Fenris Cernv -- said.

"'Gerald' or something like that," the Filipino player -- Pirro Espiritu -- added.

"'Gold,'" Sullivan said. "'Jerrod Gold.' I know exactly who that little fucker is now. My son has talked about him. He told me he's an insubordinate smart-ass."

Cernv looked at Jerrod. "That's the bastard who arrested Sapphire and took my cash box. I'm still trying to get that back."

"Speaking of the sheriff's office and your son," the Espiritu said. "Sheriff Osborn has announced his retirement and won't be endorsing anyone to replace him."

"He wants 'the voters to decide,'" Cernv mocked.

De Perras said, "Who are we going to find that we can trust now that Mitchell is--"

"Mitchell is *what*?" Sullivan interrupted.

"Uh... unavailable...," De Perras said.

"'Disgraced,' you mean?" Sullivan shot back. "I've known Wayne Osborn for nearly fifty years. I called him and asked him for the simple favor of just putting a letter in Mitchell's file and leaving it at that. I can't believe he demoted my son."

"What the hell are you talking about," Espiritu said. "He wanted to fire Mitchell for lying to him. He let him keep his job *as a favor* to you."

"Demoted my son," Sullivan said, "Just as he decides to retire and open up that spot for the first time in twenty years. Mitchell was prime to be the next sheriff."

"Osborn's never really helped us," Espiritu said. "He's as straight as they come."

De Perras nodded.

"Eric Blanchard's going to run," Cernv said.

"He got that chief deputy position Mitchell wanted. He's going to run, for sure," Espiritu said.

"'Blanchard,'" Sullivan scoffed. "Navy guy. Fucking surfer too. Can you imagine a surfer as our next sheriff?"

"*Dude*," Cernv said -- catching glances from the other three.

"We need to approach Blanchard," Espititu said, "and see if we can... uh... shall we say... help him help us."

"Or find someone who can run against him... and win," De Perras suggested.

Sullivan leaned in and placed his elbows on the table. "Or eliminate Eric Blanchard all together."

Lilly peaked out the living room window. "Mom. Jerrod's home."

"Thank you, honey," Nikki yelled back from the kitchen. "You and your sister get washed for dinner."

Jerrod was tackled by two little girls as soon as he walked into the house. "Have you two been good today?"

"We're always good today," Marty said.

"Where have you been? Lilly asked.

"I was golfing with some friends."

"What's 'golfing?'" Marty asked.

"It's kind of a show-me thing. But I brought you both a present."

"Yea," Marty said. She jumped up and down. "What is it? What is it?

Jerrod reached into a pocket and pulled out two bright red golf pencils. "They've got the name of the golf course on them. See."

Marty held the pencil to her chest. "Thanks, Jerrod."

Lilly studied the pencil. "The eraser isn't even used. Cool. Thanks. We have to get ready for dinner."

"Go, child. Get clean."

Jerrod walked into the kitchen and found Nikki at the sink. He grabbed her around the waist and smelled her hair. She turned and kissed his lips.

"Have fun golfing?"

"'Fun. Yeah. I've got some more practice to do before I join the PGA."

"Doesn't the 'PGA' stand for 'Police Guzzling Alcohol?'"

Jerrod thought for a beat. "I'm sure I already belong to that club. Which reminds me... I think I'll have a beer."

Jerrod took a Heineken from the fridge and looked around for an opener.

"And screw you, by the way," Nikki said. Hands on hips.

Jerrod opened a drawer. "What?"

"I max-out my credit cards at Christmas and on birthdays to get gifts for the girls that they forget about in about two days."

"That, dear, is a well-established and stipulated fact." He looked in another drawer.

"And you, Super Jerrod, hand the kids mini pencils -- probably stolen from the course -- that instantly become family heirlooms."

"With unused erasers," Jerrod added. "Know why they're unused?"

"Because you make no mistakes?"

He looked her in the eyes. "You got it." He smiled. "Now, honey, I love you, and I love what you've done organizing this kitchen--"

"But?" she asked.

Jerrod laughed. "But if I were a bottle opener, where would I be... this week?"

She punched him in the arm.

Jerrod leaned back in his chair. "That was a fine meal. Thank you."

Nikki started collecting the plates.

"I'll do the dishes," Jerrod offered. "But I need to run next door and talk to The Colonel before it gets too late."

"Go talk to The Colonel. I've got the dishes."

Jerrod took two Heinekens from the refrigerator and the opener from its most recent hiding spot.

Jerrod walked through the mutual open yards to the back steps of retired Army Lieutenant Colonel Charles Horvath's home and knocked on the door.

The Colonel unlocked the door. "Is everything okay?"

"Just fine, sir. Got some questions for you." Jerrod held up the two bottles. "Beer?"

"Don't mind if I do. Come on in."

"I met a man at the golf course today," Jerrod started as they settled in the living room. "A very unpleasant man."

"And?" the Colonel asked. His white hair was still in a military cut, but his close-cropped beard was not regulation.

"The other players called him "General." His bag had embroidered on it a solitary star and 'BG Michael T. Sullivan US Army (Ret.).'"

The Colonel sipped his beer. "What's your question?"

90

"I want to find out more about him," Jerrod said. "Like, what's a 'BG?'"

"'BG' is short for Brigadier General. The first rank of general officer in the Army. Therefore, the one star. His pay scale would be 'O-7.'"

"But does he still have some 'juice' in the Army?" Jerrod asked.

"All generals have 'juice,'" The Colonel chuckled. "He would have commanded an entire brigade. That's four battalions of 1,000 soldiers each. 'Full-bird' colonels would report to him. He had juice alright. I was two ranks below that as an 'O-5' and had a lot of juice... in my day."

"How do I find out more about him? His time in service. Where he was stationed. Citations received. When and why he was discharged?"

"Why the interest, Jerrod? Don't you have official access to records?"

"Sure. DMV and criminal history stuff. And I'll run those. But I need more. Trust me on this."

"Be careful where you poke your nose," The Colonel cautioned. "Retired generals don't just fade away. They tend to get into politics and onto the boards of big corporations. They keep their influence long after they leave the service."

Jerrod nodded.

"Besides, those military records are confidential. They're all retained at a facility in St. Louis and are difficult to get."

Jerrod leaned forward. "Unless you know how, sir. Wouldn't you like to know how much juice you still have... *these days*?"

CHAPTER 22

Sheriff's Investigations -- Monday Morning Meeting

"It's nice to have the entire Property Crimes Section back to work," Lieutenant Ben Zaff said to start the eight o'clock meeting. He looked at Nate Boxley and Zippy Zippich sitting in their usual spots under the whiteboard and Beach Sutton by the window. Jerrod sat at his usual seat at the table forming a "T" with the lieutenant's desk.

"Thank you, sir," Jerrod said.

Linda Westphal -- the Investigations Secretary -- sat across the table and nodded to him. Detective Sergeant Darrell Regner -- the cube-headed supervisor of the Person's Crimes Section -- sat next to Linda.

The lieutenant said, "We have some very good news: Scott Jackson was discharged from the hospital yesterday and is recovering at home. It looks like he should make a full recovery."

Physically, at least, Jerrod thought to himself.

"Many kudos came in for Ted and Shroom," the lieutenant continued, "for all their work Thursday and Friday helping the Willowmere PD process the multiple crime scenes at the city hall. Thank you both for your hard work."

Detective Sergeant Ted Lindsey and Detective Raymond "Shroom" Mingus gave meek waves as the others in the room looked over at them.

"The DA's Office has done all the interviews and are compiling the reports for the criminal portion of the incident." The lieutenant chose his words carefully. "Any criminal... uh... charges will be determined... hopefully by the end of the week."

Since the city hall shooter /hostage taker was dead -- the only possible "criminal charges" would be directed at Jerrod for the shooting and, far more likely, for striking the Willowmere officer.

As the meeting concluded, Jerrod collected the stack of weekend property crime reports and stood to leave the room. He watched each person -- including Darrell Regner -- touch the clear resin ball under the picture of Brent Rozman as they filed out of the room.

Monday Evening

"Thank you for coming over, Jerrod," Samantha "Sam" Jackson said at the doorway. "Scott was hoping you would come see him."

Jerrod scanned the interior of the modest Mesa home. "No problem, Sam. How are you doing?"

"He's not sleeping well. He doesn't like the pain pills, so he's pretty sore. Cops. Stubborn. Typical. You know."

"I'm sure that's all true. But I asked how *you* were doing?"

Her chin quivered and she covered her mouth with her hand. Tears filled her eyes.

"Let it go," he whispered.

"I don't know how you guys do it," she said. "Leave the house. Put on the gear. And it's like... let's just see what the shift brings you."

Jerrod nodded.

"Maybe take a couple reports," she continued, "or write a speeding ticket...or arrest a shoplifter... or climb a ladder and find a room full of dead bodies... or get shot in the chest by a madman."

"That's what we do, Sam."

"That's not normal," her sadness turned to anger. "That's not right. Nobody should have to..." Her words trailed off.

Jerrod hugged her as tears poured out. Her whole body pulsed with her sobs.

"Every day...," she said as she stepped back and pushed tears from her face. "Every day, I see that sweet man walk out our front door to go to work. And twice now a completely different man has walked back in." She held Jerrod's hands with hers. "I'm not sure I can handle a third time."

"Can I see him?" Jerrod asked.

"Sure. This way. Something to drink?"

"Sure. Coke?"

"You got it. Thanks, Jerrod. I needed a good cry."

"Don't we all."

Sam led Jerrod to the master bedroom. Scott Jackson was seated upright in the bed and was wearing a white t-shirt.

"Hi, Sarge," Scott said. His color was good, and his eyes were clear.

"How you doing, pal?"

"Okay... I guess. Breathing better now. Still hurts like hell and I'm going to have an awesome battle scar on my chest. Want to see?" Scott started pulling his t-shirt up from the waist.

"I'll take your word for it," Jerrod said.

Scott smiled and dropped the shirt. He adjusted himself on the bed and winced as he moved.

Sam walked in and handed Jerrod an iced Coke in a glass.

"Thank you," Jerrod said.

Sam nodded and walked out of the room.

Scott said, "Tyler told me you came by the ICU the night of the... you know."

"I did." Jerrod sipped the Coke. "You were unconscious, so I had to do all the talking."

"I had a dream that you were there. In the dream you said something about us having to go see Dewey again -- like after the Cardinal Lane thing."

"I did say something about seeing Dewey. Glad I didn't confess all of my sins."

Scott didn't smile. His face became dour and his eyes got moist. "I've been thinking about what you said to me after I got shot. 'Feel the pain. Embrace the pain.' Or something like that."

Jerrod nodded.

"Sarge, I'll be honest, I was so fucking mad at you when you said that. And I kept thinking about it in the ambulance and at the ER. I couldn't breathe right, and the pain was terrible," Scott paused for a long moment. "But I knew, somehow, I was going to be okay."

Jerrod took another sip. "Scott. You looked at me and said something right before they loaded you into the ambulance. It was noisy and the oxygen mask was all fogged up, so I couldn't make out the words."

Scott looked away and thought for a few seconds.

"I remember what I said." Scott turned his attention back to Jerrod. "It was: 'I didn't sign up for this shit.'"

CHAPTER 23

Tuesday Evening

Jerrod Gold chuckled to himself when he parked his truck in front of the psychologist's office. It was located three doors to the right of The CrowBar cocktail lounge in an east-side Valle Verde strip mall. He could spend a few sessions just talking about the things that had happened in that bar.

The unoccupied waiting room was decorated with a love seat along one wall and three matching wooden chairs along the opposite wall. A small credenza sat under the only window in the room and held a supply of paper cups, packets of instant coffee, and a selection of tea. A water dispenser, with spigots for both chilled and hot water, stood next to the table. An assortment of magazines spread across a worn coffee table in the center of the room.

Jerrod picked up a months-old *People* magazine with a photo of late-night TV host Johnny Carson on the cover and sat on one of the chairs as he waited for his six o'clock appointment.

At five minutes to six, he heard hushed conversation between a man and a woman and the shuffle of footsteps in the hallway outside the waiting room door.

"See you next week," the male voice said.

"Next week. Thank you, Doctor," the female voice responded as the front door opened and closed.

Ten seconds later, the door opened, and a man stepped inside the waiting room.

"Mr. Gold?" he asked.

"Yes, sir."

"I'm Sidney and I'll be back to get you in a few minutes," he said. "I need to make a few notes from my last session. Please help yourself to a beverage."

"Thank you, sir. I'll do that."

Five minutes later, at precisely six, Sidney reentered the room. "Please follow me," he said with a smile and a subtle wave of his hand.

Jerrod followed Sidney -- late-fifties, average height and weight, short-cropped black hair, opened-collar dress shirt and slacks -- into an office across the hallway. He held the door open as Jerrod walked in. The sign on the door read: Sidney Yamamoto, PsyD -- Clinical Psychology.

A blue sofa was to the left and a single wooden chair sat in the middle of the room. A digital clock with a large display sat on the table to the right of the sofa.

"Please have a seat." Sidney pointed to the sofa.

Small throw-pillows stood along the arms of the sofa, so Jerrod sunk into the middle of the three cushions. Sidney sat in the chair and pulled in close, so their knees were within six inches of each other. His head was a few inches higher than Jerrod's.

"My name is Sidney Yamamoto. What brings you to my office today?"

"Your office is near my house and you're on my health insurance list."

"No," Sidney laughed, "what issues are you having that caused you to come here today?"

"Oh... uh... sorry. I was involved in a shooting a couple weeks ago. A man died and a deputy was shot."

"And you hit another policeman. I saw that on TV."

"Well... that too."

"My son's a policeman. Here in Valle Verde. His name is David. I'm certain you know him."

"Of course. I've known Dave since high school."

Sidney paused. "Have you been experiencing restless sleep, nightmares, flashbacks, or loss of sexual function? Those can all be indicators of Post-Traumatic Stress Disorder. Are you familiar?"

"'PTSD,' sure." Jerrod crossed his legs. "I've known it pretty well. My problem is the opposite. I haven't had any of those. I sleep fine, barely think about the shooting, and... the other thing... is okay too."

Sidney touched his chin. "Then how can I help you?"

"I'm not sure. I, in the most literal sense, blew a man's brains out with a shotgun." Jerrod paused. "And it doesn't seem to bother me. I haven't felt any reaction. Nothing. But it *should* bother me. I'm just normal about the whole thing... and that scares the shit out of me."

"Our sessions run about fifty minutes," Sidney said. "We'll get to know each other today and see where we are."

"How do you like to be addressed. Do you prefer 'doctor?'" I heard the last... lady say that."

"I have a doctorate in psychology, so 'doctor' is appropriate. However, I prefer to keep things informal and just go by my first name."

"Okay. That's easy."

Sidney continued, "The things we talk about here are privileged and confidential. Unless you tell me you're planning to commit some sort of violent crime, or to hurt yourself, nothing we talk about will be shared outside of this office."

Jerrod nodded. "I understand."

"Have you been to any sort of therapy or counseling before, Jerrod?"

"Not really. Some...kind of... informal debriefings. Through the SO... the Sheriff's Office."

"This will be pretty structured," he said. "Tell me about yourself."

Jerrod gave a brief overview of his life: childhood, school, sports, love life, and his law enforcement career.

"Are your parents still alive?"

"Yeah, they're still alive. They divorced when I was about fifteen. My mom is still here in Valle Verde and my father lives in Las Vegas."

Sidney made a few notes on a yellow pad. "Are you estranged from your father? I noticed you called your mother 'mom,' but you just called him your 'father.'"

"'Father.' 'Dad.' I don't know. We're not estranged... we just don't talk very often."

"Siblings?"

"A brother."

"Are you married?" Sidney asked.

"Not married. Engaged to be married. Next February."

"Congratulations."

"Thank you."

"Any children?"

"She has two daughters."

"How about yourself? Any children?"

"Probably," Jerrod said.

Sidney stifled a laugh. "Are you always this... flip?"

"Only when I'm anxious, sir."

"We'll have to stop soon," Sidney said. "I think I have a decent idea of where we are and some things we can discuss."

"Sounds good. How often do I need to come?"

"I'd say every other week should do it. Tuesdays at six work for you?"

"Sure."

"Jerrod, I have some homework for you for our next session."

"Okay,"

"I'd like you to answer two questions. The first is: What do you feel your strongest personal asset or skill is?"

"And the second?"

"What is your worst personal flaw?"

"That's pretty deep," Jerrod said.

"Sort of. But please think about those questions and come up with serious answers."

"I will."

Sidney leaned forward. "I think you just might learn some things about yourself."

CHAPTER 24

Parking lot.

City Hall.

Shotgun.

Power pole.

Opening door.

Leg.

Light blue dress.

Woman.

Man.

Wild white hair.

Dark revolver.

Talk to me.

Let her go.

Door locked.

Hey, dipshit.

Another two hundred dollars.

Walk to the deputy.

Two officers.

Stand-off.

Gun to her head.

Gunshot.

Blood.

"No. No. Noooooooooo!" Jerrod screamed as he bolted upright in bed.

"Honey," Nikki soothed as she hugged him. "You were having a bad dream. It's alright, baby. I'm with you. You're okay."

"It was just a dream." Jerrod gasped for breath.

"You're fine, baby. You scared me."

"At city hall. The woman died."

"Honey, the woman lived. You saved her."

"In the dream..." Jerrod started. "In the dream she died... and *you* were the woman."

CHAPTER 25

After the girls were in bed, Jerrod and Nikki snuggled on the sofa. A nature documentary was on the TV.

At a commercial, Nikki said, "He was in the restaurant again today."

"Who was?"

"The son, Kirk. The son of the guy... you know... at city hall."

"That's nice." Jerrod sat up. "Does he know you and I are... together?"

"I don't think he does. He hasn't said anything."

"Let's keep it that way. Okay."

"Fine. But I think he's harmless. Just sad. You know."

"I still think it's better--"

Nikki cut him off. "You should talk to him."

"Sure. First thing tomorrow. Set it up."

"Don't get snippy. I just think you should clear the air with him. You know, tell him how *you* feel."

"What's his name again?"

"'Kirk.'"

"Let me rehearse that a little. 'Hey, Kirk. I'm Jerrod. Glad we could get together. Hey, bro, I'm really, really sorry I had to dump your father. Line-of-duty thing. Hope you understand. Gotta go.'"

"You had to 'dump' him?" Her faced twisted in disgust. "I don't even know who the hell you are right now."

"It's not going to happen, honey. Sorry." Jerrod looked toward the TV. "The show's back on."

CHAPTER 26

Property Crimes Unit

"Kirk LaMahieu," Jerrod typed into the dedicated computer terminal connecting the sheriff's office with the CLETS -- the California Law Enforcement Telecommunications System. He listed "Willowmere" as LaMahieu's city of residence and got an instant reply from the California Department of Motor Vehicles date base:

Kirk Franklin LaMahieu.
Valid Class 3 Operator License.
Birth date in 1955. 36 years old.
Five-foot-eight. 165 pounds.
Blond hair. Hazel eyes.
No traffic convictions.
No reported collisions.
No license suspensions.

Jerrod typed LaMahieu's full name and date of birth into the terminal and searched for a criminal history. He got no match.

"Clean as a whistle," Jerrod muttered.

"What was that Sarge? Zippy asked.

"Nothing. Just talking to myself. Sorry."

CHAPTER 27

Friday Evening

"I went to the funeral today," Nikki said.

"Who's funeral?" Jerrod asked.

"Nelson's."

"Are you fucking kidding me?"

"He was a friend. I liked him. I like his son. He needed someone to be with him."

"Why would you?" he said. "Let me ponder that for a second. Oh, yeah. He killed a man. He took a hostage. He shot a deputy. He made me shoot him. Other than that, I can't think of anything."

"I don't care what you think," Nikki shook her head. "It was the right thing to do."

For the first time in a long time, Jerrod could find no words to respond.

Tuesday Evening

"Andrew Wheaton died," Jerrod said. He was reading the *Valle Verde Sun* in his La-Z-Boy.

"Who was that?" Nikki asked.

"Andrew Wheaton was a captain at the Valle Verde PD when I worked there."

"That's sad," she said. "Were you two close?"

"I wouldn't characterize it as 'close.' He was the speaker at the 'career day' back in high school that got me interested in police work. I haven't seen him since he retired."

"How old was he?" she asked.

"The obituary says he was sixty?"

"That's pretty young. How did he die?"

Before answering, Jerrod traveled back -- in a flash of memories -- to the series of events in 1985 which led to the murder of Hector Medina, the jail "suicide" of Valdemar Reyes, and, at his hands, the shooting death of Armando Mendoza. To Craig Wallace getting the career-ending gunshot wound to his knee. To the violation of Wheaton's solemn oath to protect and serve the public when he was first handed his badge. To the surrender of that badge when he was forced into a sudden retirement after the payoffs he had taken from Mendoza were exposed. To the cover-up on his behalf by the city to contain the embarrassment of the scandal. And to the close brush with death Jerrod had and the horseshoe-shaped daily reminder he had received on the back of his own right hand.

"Guilt, honey," Jerrod said. "That man died from guilt."

CHAPTER 28

"I've been doing this for a while... but this is a first," Sheriff Wayne Osborn said from behind the large wood desk in his second-floor corner office.

Sergeant Jerrod Gold sat in a chair across from the desk. He peeked out the large plate glass window behind the sheriff which allowed a brilliant view of the Mesa River. The flags of United States and State of California, draped on poles, framed either side.

"Next to one of our deputies being killed or seriously injured in the line-of-duty," he continued, "seeing one of my people having to take a human life has been my next greatest fear as sheriff."

"Yes, sir."

"Sergeant, you have created a dilemma for me," the big man said as he took a deep sigh and glanced at two official memos sitting side-by-side on his desktop. "I've never issued both a commendation and a notice of disciplinary action to the same deputy for the same incident."

Jerrod shifted uncomfortably in his chair. The sheriff's use of the term "deputy" could have been used as a generic term for any sworn member of the SO... or for a sergeant about to be demoted back to "deputy" status.

"Your shooting of that man at the Willowmere City Hall was entirely justified. The DA's office has cleared you of criminal charges... for that... and the shooting was completely within our Use of Force policy."

The sheriff handed Jerrod a Letter of Commendation. "As far I'm concerned, that matter is closed"

"Thank you, sir."

The sheriff said, "The other... issue... is you striking that Willowmere officer." He shook his head. "I came around the corner of that building just in time to see you hit him. Although I didn't really *need* to be there -- anyone with a television got to see it on the news."

"Yes, sir."

"In the days right after the shooting," the sheriff continued, "I had some difficult conversations with the Willowmere police chief and, I'll be honest, she wanted to see your head on a pike. She insisted you be terminated and criminally prosecuted for that unjustifiably stupid and unprofessional stunt."

The sheriff leaned back in his chair.

"I've read all of the reports and interview transcripts from the incident. The Willowmere chief and DA Harlan have read them all as well. We then met and came to a mutually agreeable decision about what would happen to you."

Jerrod felt his heart start to race.

"There will be no criminal charges filed against you for striking that officer... and I'll tell you why."

"Please."

"From the information in the reports, it became abundantly clear that you and your detectives were deescalating the situation. Those two officers who ran into a scene and incited the man to fire his handgun -- which, in turn, wounded Deputy Jackson and caused you to have to shoot the man -- were sent back there by the Willowmere chief herself."

"Interesting. Thank you, sir."

"Don't thank me yet," the sheriff snapped back. "The 'no-filing' wasn't done for your benefit. There's a sad reality that a criminal charge could lead to a trial, which could lead to full public disclosure about the Willowmere PD's foolish actions, which would lead, most certainly, to considerable embarrassment for the department. "The 'politics,' if you will, of this situation worked squarely in your favor."

"Yes, sir."

"As far as in-house discipline goes," the sheriff said as he picked up the second document from his desktop. "I struggled with this one. No one in my command is allowed to strike anyone, under any circumstance, unless they are effecting an arrest and that person is physically resisting. Is that understood?"

"Yes, sir," Jerrod said as he mentally braced himself.

"Chief Deputy Blanchard has weighed in. He pointed out your past outstanding performance and your lack of any prior disciplinary action. In fact, you haven't even dented a patrol car."

Jerrod wiped his sweating palms on his pants.

"You will not be demoted. I was going to let you fight to get your 'stripes' back but decided against it. You will, however, receive a forty-hour suspension for your conduct."

"I truly regret what I did and take full responsibility for my actions. I came in here ready to accept whatever you decided. Forty-hours is very reasonable, sir."

"Cut the crap, Sergeant. You sound like Eddie Haskell in *Leave It to Beaver*. I'm not done with you yet."

"Sorry, sir."

"You're also being transferred. In a few weeks, you will be working the night shift next door at the Mesa County Main Jail. Out of sight and out of -- at least -- the public's mind. Some other sergeant there will be pleased to get... let's call it an 'early release'... from his duties there when you take his place."

Jerrod felt his stomach start to ache.

"A year or two in jail should give you some time to think about how you'll handle yourself the next time you feel your emotions get the best of you."

Jerrod's head was full of thoughts, and he barely heard what the sheriff said next.

"Eugene Luttrell -- former Chief Deputy Luttrell -- called and reminded me 'you owe jail time.' Now is the time to pay that debt."

CHAPTER 29

"Anything change since our last session?" Sidney Yamamoto asked.

"Yeah, actually. Couple significant things."

"Such as?"

"The night after we talked last, I had a bad dream... about the shooting."

"Tell me about it."

"The dream was just the way it played out: The guy came out with the lady hostage, we yelled back and forth, he started to let her go, but then he shot her in the head."

"But, as I recall from the news, the hostage survived."

"Yeah, in real life. But in my dream, the woman dies... and that woman was my fiancée, Nikki."

"Very disturbing."

"No shit disturbing." Jerrod caught himself. "Sorry about that, I get smart-ass and use profanity when I'm anxious."

"No problem. What's the other issue?"

"I met with Sheriff Osborn about the shooting and hitting that Willowmere officer."

"How'd that go?"

"I was cleared on the shooting."

"Good."

"And I was given five days 'on-the-beach' and reassigned to the jail for the other... thing. No criminal charges."

"What's the 'beach' thing? Do you have to go pick up cigarette butts or something?"

"No. No," Jerrod laughed. "Days-on-the-beach" is a cop term. For being suspended without pay."

"I don't get it."

"Well, the thinking is this: If you can't work for five days, then you might as well do something fun -- like go to the beach."

"Very clever. I'll be sure to bring that term up in some future conversation with my son. David will appreciate the nuance."

Sidney got serious. "Do you have answers to the two questions I asked you to think about last time we met?"

"Yes, sir. I had to do a little soul searching on those."

"Good. That's the idea. Once you're able to look inward, you can start to understand yourself."

"That's a little too 'herbal' for me, sir," Jerrod said, "But okay."

"What did you come up with as being your greatest asset or skill?"

"Well. I had a couple options, and this may sound odd and not very honorable--"

"I'll remind you; all our discussions stay in this room."

"Okay, I get that," Jerrod said. "My greatest skill is the ability to talk people into doing things they wouldn't otherwise do."

"That's not so bad. That's what salesmen -- and politicians, for that matter -- do every day."

"If you think about it, sir, it *is* sales." Jerrod paused. "Look, I sit down with people who have done terrible things. Robbed a store. Killed their spouse. Molested a child. And then I become their new best friend. I talk calmly. I don't judge. We banter. I get them some coffee or a Coke. I build a little rapport. We become pals. I throw in a little complement. I use the same words they use. I create a bond. I find the cracks in their armor. I exploit their weaknesses. And then, little by little, I get them to tell me, their new buddy, the things that *they know* will put them in prison for years... or for the rest of their whole damn lives."

"But that's what detectives do. That's an excellent skill to have."

"That's the problem."

"I don't follow."

Jerrod pulled one of the sofa pillows onto is lap and squeezed it. "The answer to the first question is also the answer to the second."

"I'm lost," Sidney said. "Help me out."

Jerrod paused to find the words. "I don't know how to explain. I use my 'greatest skill' all the time. With everyone. I make stuff up. I fib when I don't have to. I massage. I manipulate. I act. I plot. I scheme. I play with emotion. All the time. All the fucking time. To get what I want. The prize. The possession. The assignment. To be liked. To be adulated. Or just for fun. It's like a sport to me. It's like a big chess match. I make strategic moves, but with real people." His voice cracked. "I get other people -- including my closest friends and my family -- to do things, for me, that they wouldn't otherwise do."

Sidney took a long pause before speaking. "So, your blessing is also your curse."

"You can put it that way."

"Are you playing me right now, Jerrod?"

"No... maybe. I don't know. I don't know that I don't know. But what I just told you is all true. It's become part of my... my... nature."

"Interesting." Sidney's finger tapped his chin. "I've been doing this a long time and have a pretty good BS detector."

Jerrod was straight-faced. "Am I BS-ing you right now?"

"I don't know."

Jerrod broke into a smile. Sidney smiled back.

"How about now?" Jerrod asked

"I still don't know."

"See what I mean?"

"Have you ever been called-out on your... curse?"

"Nikki has a pretty good sense for my bullshit. She calls me out all the time. Mostly innocent stuff like made-up stories to the kids. But she'll say something about it later. I'm more careful in what I say around her."

"She's a good balance for you."

"Indeed."

Sidney snickered. "You kind of remind me of the Matthew Broderick character in *Ferris Bueller's Day Off.*"

"I guess so." Jerrod's mood lightened. "The other day, the sheriff said I sounded like Eddie Haskell. He has a good BS detector too."

Sidney paused. "Give me an example of a... to use your term... a 'fib,' you've told in the recent past."

Jerrod thought for a few seconds and glanced at the back of his right hand. "Here." He held up the hand and showed Sidney the horseshoe-shaped scar on it.

"That's some scar," Sidney said. "I had intended to ask you about that."

"I've told people at least a hundred different versions of how I got this scar. Smashed by a car engine. In a motorcycle accident. Bitten by an eel. Burned on a camp stove. And on and on."

"How did it really happen?"

"A man crushed my hand with the heel of his boot in a fight for my gun. His name was Armando Mendoza."

"And you later killed him while struggling for a gun," Sidney recalled. "My son had talked about that incident."

"Now you know."

"Jerrod. We're going to work on those things."

"Thank you, sir."

Friday Morning

Jerrod wasn't there to see it, but at precisely 8:00 AM, the notice listing intra-office transfers were posted throughout the Mesa County Sheriff's Office.

Jerrod was being transferred to the Main Jail on the twelve-hour 7:00 PM to 7:00 AM "graveyard" shift.

This position in the Property Crimes Unit was to be filled by his former field training officer and beat-partner and poker-buddy and close friend -- Sergeant Roger Collins.

CHAPTER 30

Monday Morning

Jerrod's unpaid week-long suspension had officially begun. But instead of a "week-on-the-beach," he had decided to take a couple days in the desert.

The morning flight from San Jose to Las Vegas was uneventful. Jerrod had considered flying as a "LEO" -- Law Enforcement Officer -- a simple enough process which allowed credentialed fill-time cops to bypass security and board the plane early. However, he decided to just blend with the crowd of giddy passengers anxious to drink to excess and leave their paychecks in "Sin City."

This trip was personal, and Jerrod had much different priorities.

At McCarran International, Jerrod selected a choice treat for a rental car: a new Ford Mustang GT 5.0 convertible. With its gleaming black body and tan leather interior, it reminded him of the replica Ferrari Daytona Spyder made famous as Sonny Crockett's ride in the first couple seasons of *Miami Vice*.

He laid the Mustang's soft-top back and tossed his bag in the backseat. The early October desert air was still warm, but the brutal heat of summer had clearly passed -- making it the perfect time to cruise with the top down. The powerful V-8 motor created its unique deep rumble as he drove past both the classic and new casinos and hotels lining Las Vegas Boulevard -- The Strip -- and headed downtown on his mission.

As he reached the edge of downtown, he noticed the area becoming seedier. Less glitz and glam. More grime and grunge. The streets were lined with pawn shops, instant loan offices, bail bonds signs, cheap hotels, and instant wedding chapels. Tourists were replaced by homeless. Desire was replaced by despair.

The industrial area of the city was no improvement from downtown. Jerrod guided the Mustang to the litter-filled curb in front of the address he sought. The sign on the building read: "Jerry's Automotive." It was his father's shop.

The business looked more like a detention facility than an auto repair shop: designed not to keep the inmates in, but more to keep the uninvited out. High chain-link fences surrounded the property. Barbed wire lined the fence tops. Welded rebar grids covered the windows. Cars and trucks and motorcycles in various states of repair dotted the yard.

Jerrod moved his bag to the safety of the trunk, walked past the open swinging gate, and up an oil-stained concrete drive.

Out of the shadow of a repair bay, a man -- late-fifties, tall, average weight, ball cap -- walked out wiping his hands on a red shop towel. His eyes squinted as they adjusted to the daylight and he asked, "Nice Mustang, sir. What can I help you with?"

"Fuck the Mustang," Jerrod answered. "I'm here to find Tommy."

"Jerrod. Son," Jerry Gold said. "You should have called. I didn't know you were coming."

"I've been to Vegas three other times," Jerrod said, "and didn't call then either."

Jerry studied Jerrod but said nothing as he pulled a red and white soft pack of Marlboro cigarettes from his breast pocket. The cellophane had been removed and a corner torn from the pack's bottom. Jerry snapped the pack against the side of his other hand and pulled a single smoke out -- leaving a smear of grease from his fingers on the tobacco end. He popped the clean filter into his mouth and lit it with a worn Zippo lighter.

Jerry took a long drag and spoke as he exhaled. "Nice to see you too, son."

They sat together in the shop's cramped office. "Still work on your own cars, Jerrod?"

"Nope," Jerrod said. "Take 'em to a shop."

"Guess you're not here to talk about cars?"

"You would be correct. I'm here to learn more about my brother. And I'm starting with you."

"I can't tell you more than you probably already know. This happened seventeen years ago. I haven't learned anything new."

"We'll see. Just tell me everything."

Jerry confirmed he knew Tommy and Don hadn't been getting along and that Tommy had planned to stay in Las Vegas past the school summer vacation. He hadn't told Laura of the plan thinking she simply wouldn't let Tommy leave at all.

Jerry asked, "When was the last time you saw your brother?"

Jerrod thought for a second. "I knew you were coming to get him, but I was playing baseball up in the Bay Area that Saturday. I didn't see you and I didn't get to say goodbye to Tommy."

"He was a sweet kid," Jerry said as he pulled out another Marlboro. "Quiet. Respectful. Kept to himself. I've still got some of the drawings he did on the wall. And he loved you, Jerrod. In fact, he idolized you."

"What happened the day he disappeared?" Jerrod asked.

"Same as most days back then." Jerry brushed some ashes off the desk. "I was living in a condo east of downtown. Just me. I hadn't remarried at that time. I was working at the dealership then and went to work that morning. Seven or so. We had plans to go to dinner that night. It was a Friday and Nixon had announced he was going to resign that day. I didn't much care for Nixon, so I wanted to celebrate."

"What happened when you got home?"

Jerry rubbed his unshaven chin. "Uh...parked in my usual spot. About six o'clock. Went up to the condo. Door was unlocked. No Tommy."

"Then what?"

I looked around the condo. Bedrooms. Bathroom. Then I thought he may have gone on a walk. Maybe down to the little corner market... or something. I waited for an hour or so. Took a shower and got cleaned up to go out. Still no Tommy. His clothes were all in his room. Art stuff too."

Jerrod nodded.

"I started to worry," Jerry said as he struggled with his emotions. "Actually, son, I started to panic."

"Keep going," Jerrod encouraged.

"I drove around the neighborhood. Checked the store and asked some people on the sidewalks. I didn't even know what he had been wearing. People just shrugged at me."

"When did you call the police?"

"It was already past dark at this point. I called and the fucking cops, sorry, I mean police officers, took their sweet-ass time getting here."

"It's okay," Jerrod said. "Go on."

"Anyways," Jerry continued, "I told the cops Tommy had disappeared."

They kept asking if he was a runaway. I told him he had kind-of runaway from his home in Valle Verde to come stay here. That's all they needed to hear. They said they'd make a report, but to just call the station when Tommy came home. They got a job or something, you know, on their radio--"

"A radio call?" Jerrod interrupted.

"Yeah. A radio call. They hurried off to their car and tore out of the parking lot."

Jerrod was putting the pieces together in his head. "Do you still live in the same condo?

"Yeah."

"Is Tommy's stuff still there?"

"I packed it up. The box -- he didn't have much -- is in his closet."

"I need to see it."

I can close early," Jerry said. "I don't have any urgent jobs right now."

"Okay. I need to get something to eat," Jerrod said.

"It's eleven-thirty right now," Jerry said. "Go grab some lunch and be back here about two. You can follow me home from here."

"Sounds like a plan."

"Glad you're here, son."

Jerrod nodded. "See you at two."

Jerrod's fast-food lunch wasn't sitting well when he returned to Jerry's Automotive. Maybe it was the food. Maybe it was the stress. Regardless, he decided to ignore the cause and get back to his mission.

Jerry was just locking the gate with what might have been the largest chain he had seen that wasn't securing a large ship's anchor. A ten-year-old rusty blue Chrysler sedan was idling at the curb. Jerry made a "follow me" gesture and got into the sedan.

Jerrod followed him along the surface streets back into downtown Las Vegas and east from there. After ten minutes of turns and short-cuts, they arrived at the parking lot of a dreary two-story condo complex. Jerry pulled the sedan into a numbered parking slot under a carport and motioned for Jerrod to park a nearby "Visitors Only" spot.

"Might want to put that top up, son," Jerry yelled. "And lock it tight."

"Great neighborhood," Jerrod muttered to himself.

Jerry's two bedroom and one bathroom condo sat on the second floor and looked out over the carport roof. The interior was tidy for a single guy, but it appeared the furniture had come with the place when he moved there in the 70s. It became instantly obvious Jerry had no problem smoking inside the condo.

"I can open a few windows," Jerry said. "It can get stuffy in here."

"Sure," Jerrod said -- not really thinking about the question or the answer.

Jerrod studied a framed pencil drawing of a cat which was hanging on a hallway wall. The drawing so life-like he expected the cat to move at any moment. The initials "TG" in simple block letters were on the lower right-hand corner.

"Did you see Tommy the day he disappeared? Jerrod asked.

"Yes. He came out of his room. We talked for a few minutes while I had coffee. Then I left for work."

"You said the door was unlocked when you got home?"

"Yes."

"Did Tommy have a key to the door?"

Jerry thought. "I'm not... yes. Yes, he did. Kept it on a string. A red string. He was going to start school in a couple weeks. He needed a key to get in after school."

"Did you find the key after he disappeared?"

Jerry searched his memory. "No. I'm pretty sure I never found the key."

"I don't suppose the same lockset is on the door now?"

"No," Jerry said without hesitation. "I had the locks changed after...." He paused when he realized how the sentence would end. "Both my wives left."

Jerrod nodded. "I need to see Tommy's stuff."

Jerry led him to a tiny bedroom. A twin-size bed was in the far corner. A cheap dresser in another. A small wooden desk with a chair sat in a third corner. Two more of Tommy's sketches -- a butterfly and a landscape -- hung on the wall over the bed.

Jerry opened the sliding mirror door of the closet and pulled out a cardboard banker's box. "He didn't have a lot of things."

"When's the last time you looked in here?" Jerrod asked.

"I don't know... ten years."

"Give me a few minutes... alone... okay," Jerrod asked.

"Sure. Yeah, I'll go get cleaned up. Alright, son."

"Thanks, Dad," Jerrod said without thinking.

He didn't look at his father but felt him pause for a few beats before leaving the doorway.

"Not much at all," Jerrod said to himself as he pulled the cover off the box.

Neatly folded were a single pair of 28 waist Levi 501 jeans, three colored t-shirts, a few pairs of boxer shorts, and some white tube socks. A spiral-bound sketch pad and a few artist's pencils were on the bottom of the box.

Jerrod carefully laid the jeans and t-shirts out on the bed. That was all he could remember Tommy ever wearing: jeans and t-shirts. That's what he wore to Don and his mother's wedding. You would have had to hold him down to get a suit and tie on him.

Jerrod picked up one of the t-shirts and pressed it to his face. He took a deep inhale but was disappointed to smell only decades-old cotton.

He heard the shower start in the adjacent bathroom as he sat at the desk and looked through the sketch pad. Some of the drawings were completed and others were not. All had a unique flair to them. Calming. Peaceful. Quiet. Most of the drawing were of animals. A dog. A snake. A deer. Some had multiple drawing on the page. There was a scene from a forested area. Another of a creek or river.

Jerrod thumbed and took in each sketch and stopped on the only one depicting a human being. It was the face of a woman. Twenties. Long wavy hair. Full lips. Deep-set intense eyes.

There was no house key on a red string in the box.

Jerrod was seated at the small kitchen table and had cleared a spot on the table from the stacks of both opened and unopened mail, all addressed to "Jerrod Gold," his father's formal name. They didn't share the same middle names -- intentionally done so Jerrod would never be referred to as "Junior."

Jerrod had found a six-pack of Coors Banquet in the refrigerator and helped himself to one.

Jerry came out of the shower with only a towel wrapped around his waist. He noted his 'ol man still looked to be in pretty good shape for his age. "Found the beer...good...uh... I keep it for guests. Help yourself."

"I have a few more questions. I'll still be here when you get dressed."

"Yeah... okay, son," Jerry said as he headed for the master bedroom.

Jerrod studied the drawing of the woman. There was something in Tommy's style that pulled the viewer into the woman's soul. She didn't look at all like their mother -- Laura -- or any of the aunts in their family. She had to be local. From somewhere in Las Vegas.

Jerry came out of the bedroom. Black golf shirt. Tan slacks. No cap. Clean shaven. Hair combed.

"Who's this woman?" Jerrod asked.

Jerry looked at the drawing and sat down at the table. "Wanda."

"Wanda?"

"Yep. Waitress at a restaurant up on Las Vegas Blvd. The Peppermill. You probably drove by it coming from the airport."

"Remember her last name?"

Jerry took a long moment. "No. That was just the name on her uniform... thing."

"Name tag?"

"Yeah. She really liked your brother. Would refill his Coke as many times as he wanted."

"Is she still there?"

"No. She left right after... you know. She was real upset that Tommy had gone."

"Interesting," Jerrod said. "Do you have any photos of Tommy while he was staying here?"

"Yes," Jerry said as he stood and walked to a cabinet in the living room. He rummaged through a drawer and returned with a paper envelope from a film processor with 35mm color prints and negatives inside.

Tommy looked just like he had remembered him: Straight dark collar-length hair parted down the middle. Serious expression contrasting with gentle deep-blue eyes. No smile. Jeans and t-shirt. Black Converse All-star sneakers.

Jerrod held up a photo. "Where was this one taken?"

"Circus Circus."

"This one?"

"Mount Charleston. We went fishing up there."

"Grand Canyon. Lake Mead. The Hoover Dam," Jerrod said. "Where is this? This bridge here."

"That's The London Bridge. In Lake Kiowa City. That's in Arizona."

"Small fucking world," Jerrod muttered.

"What, son?"

"Never mind."

Jerry said. "I mentioned earlier I still worked at the dealership then. Had weekends and holidays off. So, me and Tommy drove all over the place together."

Jerrod sorted the photos and took only the ones with Tommy in them. He returned to the bedroom and compared the photos with the clothing Tommy had left behind.

He found Tommy wearing each of the three colored t-shirts in several of the photos. A couple other photos showed Tommy wearing a navy-blue t-shirt with a pocket on the left breast. That shirt was not among the three shirts on the bed.

"Can I keep these photos?" Jerrod asked.

"I don't know about that," Jerrod replied instantly.

"How about just the negatives. I'll get my own prints made."

"Deal."

Jerrod followed his father to the living room cabinet as he searched for an envelope. He noticed a chess board set up on top of it. The pieces had been advanced from their starting positions.

"Still play?" Jerrod asked.

"Play what, son?"

"Chess. Looks like you have a game going."

Jerry stopped his search. He placed his palms flat on the cabinet as he leaned over the chess board. Tears splashed onto the board.

Jerrod said nothing. Two minutes passed until his father spoke again.

"I was teaching your brother to play. He was getting pretty good. We played every morning. That day, I had to leave for work, so we were going to finish the game... later... when I got home."

Jerry stared at the board and pulled a hand up to wipe his eyes.

"That's how we left the board. I haven't touched it since."

"But now you're waiting for *him* to come home."

"Yep."

"Dad. I'm gonna do what I can to make that happen."

"Want to stay here tonight?" Jerry asked.

"Thanks. No. I have a reservation at a hotel. Downtown."

"What hotel?"

"Four Queens."

"That place is okay. Older, you know. Not as flashy as all the new clubs out on The Strip."

"I'm fine with that."

"They have a real nice restaurant there. Downstairs. Hugo's Cellar."

"Want to join me for dinner?"

"Sure."

"How about we meet at the restaurant," Jerrod suggested. "At six."

"Okay."

"That'll give me time to drop these negatives off for overnight prints, check-in, get settled, make some calls, and freshen up."

"That place is pretty swanky," Jerry said. "But the slacks and the shirt you're wearing are fine."

"No t-shirts? No jeans?"

Jerry caught the irony. "Yep."

"See you then."

"See you then."

The Mustang's motor roared to life and Jerrod peeked up at his father's condo as he drove by. Jerry stood on the landing -- one hand on the railing and the other in a meek wave -- knowing full-well he would see him again in a couple hours.

It occurred to Jerrod that broken man had never been given the opportunity to say goodbye to his other son.

CHAPTER 31

Jerry was seated near the entrance to Hugo's Cellar when Jerrod arrived at six o'clock.

They stood behind a couple waiting for their table and watched the *maître d'* hand the lady a single long-stemmed red rose.

"Classy," Jerrod whispered.

Jerry nodded.

"Mr. Gold. Party of two," the maître d' announced.

"Yes," both Jerrod and Jerry said simultaneously.

That got a chuckle from the black tuxedoed man. "Together... I certainly hope. Please follow me."

They were led to a white linen-topped table for two in the middle of the restaurant.

Jerrod moved ahead of Jerry to commandeer the "cop seat." The one with the best view of the entrance and greatest peripheral perspective of the entire room.

The maître d' said, "Your server with be by with menus and take your drink orders. I hope you enjoy your meal."

"Thank you," Jerry said.

"If I may?" the maître d asked. "Father and son? Special occasion?"

"'Father and son.' Yes," Jerry said.

"'Special occasion.' Yes," Jerrod followed.

"Excellent," the maître d said before leaving to greet more guests.

"Busy for a Monday night," Jerrod said.

"Busy every night," Jerry said. "We may not have been able to get a table at all on the weekend."

"Quite the place. Dark. Cozy. Love the brick ceiling," Jerrod said.

"Frank Sinatra and The Rat Pack were regulars here," Jerry said. "So, I've heard."

A waiter in a gold tuxedo jacket came to the table. "My name is Eugene, and I will be your server tonight. Make I take your drink orders." He looked to Jerrod first.

"Sure. Tanqueray martini. Rocks. Perfect. Three olives. Please."

"Very good, sir." Eugene turned to Jerry. "And you, sir."

"Tonic lime, please."

Eugene nodded. "I will be right back with your drinks and to take your order."

"Tonic and lime?" Seriously," Jerrod asked. "If you're gonna drink... just drink."

"I told you I haven't had a drink in a year," Jerry said. "And what's a 'perfect' martini?'"

"Gin with equal parts dry and sweet vermouth. The olives give it a nice little hint of salty too."

"Enjoy."

"Oh, I will."

Eugene returned with their drinks and Jerrod knocked his fork to the floor making room for his cocktail.

"Oh, crap. Sorry about that," Jerrod said. "Clumsy."

Eugene picked up the fork. "I'll bring you another, sir. Your orders, gentlemen?"

Jerry ordered the ten-ounce New York Strip steak. Medium rare.

"Same for me," Jerrod said. "Medium-ish."

Jerrod stirred his drink with the olives and tasted it. "Now that's a perfect 'perfect.'" Want a sip?"

"No, I'm fine. I told you I don't drink anymore."

"But you don't drink any less either. Am I right?"

Jerry looked around the room for a moment thinking about how he was going to respond. He pulled apart a soft bun and smeared butter on it. "You've always been a clumsy kid," obviously referring to the errant fork. "I remember when you could walk right into a doorway and trip yourself on pretty much anything."

"I'm still not very graceful. Some things don't change."

"'Graceful' is a term I would never use to describe you," Jerry chuckled. "In fact, if there was one lump of dogshit on an entire golf course... you'd step in it."

Jerry's comment got a sideways glance from a lady in the adjacent table.

"You're hilarious," Jerrod said. "Speaking of golf... I started playing a couple weeks ago."

"Your grandfather was a good golfer. Loved to play. I never picked it up."

Jerrod added, "Gramps tried to teach me how to hit a golf ball. He said I was hopeless because I had a 'baseball swing' and they didn't work the same. I still do, I guess. I 'slice' everything right."

"Gonna keep golfing?"

"I don't think it's my sport and it's pretty expensive. We'll see."

Eugene returned with a rolling cart stocked with a large, chilled bowl of lettuce and more than a dozen toppings. He announced the salads would be prepared table side. Jerry made his selections and Jerrod followed.

"This is nice," Jerrod said as he dug into the heaping salad.

"Careful, son. Save room for that steak."

"No," Jerrod said. "I'm gonna walk out of here stuffed to the gills."

As Jerry picked at his salad, his face grew serious. "Sorry about the little meltdown over the chess board today. This has happened so fast. It's coming back all at once."

"It's okay. We're going to get to the bottom of this."

"Before you showed up today, I'd could go almost a half-hour without thinking about Tommy. Wondering where he went or what happened..."

"We'll find some answers. Okay."

"Okay. My son... the detective."

"Your son... period."

Eugene brought a tray containing two tiny ice cream cones filled with raspberry sherbet "to cleanse one's palette" before the entree would arrive.

Jerrod licked the rich frozen dessert and gave an approving nod.

"I was a bad father," Jerry said after tasting the sherbet.

Jerrod watched him for a few moments. "You weren't a bad father. You were a bad husband."

Jerry's expression was of mixed reactions. "I admit to that. Three marriages. Three divorces."

"You do understand you can love a woman and not be married to her."

"No," Jerry paused. "I don't quite see it that way. But I'll always love your mother the most. I really blew that one."

Jerrod nodded.

"Do you play chess anymore?" Jerry asked to change the subject.

"No. Don't even have a board. Haven't played... well... since you moved here to Vegas."

"Know who taught me how to play chess?" Jerry asked.

"Gramps, I'd assume."

"Nope. Your grandmother."

"Gram?" Jerrod chuckled. "I've played games with her a thousand time. Yahtzee. Cribbage. Card games. But never chess."

"She was a brilliant player in her day," Jerry said. "Could have been a grandmaster, or something... if she wasn't a woman."

"I had no idea."

Eugene returned with a wheeled cart and two plates covered by silver domes. He uncovered two perfectly seared steaks. "These are prime twenty-eight-day dry-aged steaks," Eugene said as he expertly placed the plates on to the table. "Medium rare and medium, with potatoes au gratin and roasted garden vegetables. Enjoy."

Jerrod took a moment to admire the plate. "If I had a camera, I'd take a picture of this... this... piece of art... and share it with all my friends."

"Share the steak... or the picture?" Jerry asked as he sliced a bite from the tender beef.

"The photo," Jerrod said as he placed his hand and forearm around the plate. "This steak is all mine."

The two hungry men attacked their plates. Nods and smiles and primal grunts of approval came from each of them.

"I have never had a steak this good," Jerrod said. "Never. Ever."

Jerry wiped the corners of his mouth with a napkin. "Are you and Nikki going to have kids?

"I don't see that happening. We have no plans to add to the family."

"So, it looks like our branch of the family tree is going to end with you?"

"It appears so. I'll let you know if that changes."

Jerry didn't have to speak. His disappointment was plain to see.

Jerrod placed his fork and knife on the empty plate and pushed it away. "My God, that was good."

Jerry had eaten about half his steak. "I'm taking the rest home so I can relive this experience tomorrow."

Eugene returned and took the plates. He came back a few minutes later with a silver tray containing an assortment of chocolate-dipped strawberries and other fruit.

"Got any room left for that?" Jerry asked.

"I don't think so," Jerrod replied. He picked up a strawberry. "Probably grown in Valle Verde."

"Probably so," Jerry said as he took an apricot. "If we touch it, we have to eat it."

"Agreed."

Eugene returned with Jerry's steak in a foil-lined to-go bag and black folder. "It was my pleasure serving you, gentlemen. You may now fight over the check."

"Thank you, Eugene," Jerrod said. "Best meal in about... pretty much forever."

"Thank you, Eugene," Jerry added.

"My treat, Dad," Jerrod said as he grabbed the check.

"Let's split it," Jerry suggested.

"I've got this," Jerrod said as he placed a credit card in the folder slot. He intentionally did not look at the total on the check. He would leave a twenty-five percent tip for the outstanding service.

"Thank you, Son."

"You're welcome, Dad. What do you think about traveling to Valle Verde next February? Your oldest boy is getting married."

"I'll be there."

Jerrod and Jerry walked along the table games on the casino floor of the Four Queens. Lights and bells and coins landing on metal from slot machines filled the background. A holler came from an animated group circling a craps table.

"Someone hit their number," Jerrod said.

"The club will get it back in a minute or two," Jerry replied. "The club always gets it back."

"I guess they don't keep building these places because they hand out a lot of money."

"Indeed," Jerry said.

Jerrod stopped. "I enjoyed spending this time with you."

"I did too."

"I've got a three o'clock flight tomorrow," Jerrod said. "How about I swing by the shop before I head to the airport."

"I'd like that," Jerry said as he stuck out this right hand.

Jerrod moved the hand away and hugged his father.

"See you tomorrow," Jerry said as his eyes began to well.

"See you tomorrow."

CHAPTER 32

Jerrod was up at six o'clock. He had showered and shaved, checked-out of the Four Queens and was driving the Mustang up Las Vegas Boulevard by seven. He glanced over to the passenger seat at Tommy's sketch pad with the drawing of "Wanda" in it.

The Peppermill Restaurant and Lounge was easy to locate. The large purple neon sign on the facade could probably be seen from outer space.

"Just one," Jerrod said to the young woman near the entrance. Her name tag read: "Pamela."

"Booth? Table? And the counter is available if you'd like," Pamela asked.

Jerrod scanned the half-full restaurant. "Booth, please."

"Right this way."

Pamela led him to a four-top booth and placed a menu on the side of the table with its back to the door.

Jerrod slid in on the opposite side of the table.

Pamela, confused, moved the menu. "Something to drink, sir?"

"Thank you. Coffee, please."

A minute later, a late-thirties male server came to the table with a logo mug filled with coffee. His name tag read: "Ron."

"Something to eat, sir,"

"I'm going to keep it light," Jerrod said. "Had a huge meal last night. Hugo's Cellar. Downtown."

"I've heard of it," Ron said. "Never been."

"Bring an appetite when you finally go?"

"I will. Your order, sir."

"Couple eggs over medium. Toast. Sourdough. No meat. Please."

"Coming right up, sir."

As Jerrod sipped the coffee, he scanned the restaurant. The purple theme from the exterior continued indoors. The upholstery was crimson red and, if you were looking for the old Las Vegas feel, you had found it there. The customers there were mostly men. Mostly white. Mostly blue-collar. A few wore suits. And there were a handful those who appeared to be tourists.

But no cops.

Unlike Sophie's Diner with its all-day and all-night rotation of law enforcement; there were no uniformed officers in the place. They must have their own version of Sophie's somewhere in the continuously growing city.

Jerrod's picked at his food. He wasn't very hungry but knew the day would be crazy and he wouldn't get another chance to eat until late that night. He finished most of the eggs and one piece of toast before pushing the plate aside.

"Was everything alright, sir?" Ron asked as she filled his coffee mug and picked up the plate.

"Everything was just fine. Is there a manager on-duty this morning?"

Ron froze for a moment. "Uh. I can get you more eggs if they weren't prepared the way you wanted. I can't get in any more trouble with this manager. Please."

"You're not in trouble. The eggs were fine. You were fine. Please send the manager over and I promise I'll say wonderful things about you."

"Thank you, sir," he said. "Thank you."

"No, Ron. Thank you."

A portly man with "Peter" on his name tag came to the table. "You asked to see a manager, sir. Was your food and service to your liking?"

"Pamela and Ron were top notch. Efficient and friendly. The food was very good. I have no complaints."

Peter nodded.

"Can you sit for a moment. I have a couple questions?"

"Uh... sure... we're kind of busy."

Jerrod looked around the room. "You're not that busy. Please sit. I won't take long."

Peter sat across in the opposite seat. His level of anxiety was obvious, and Jerrod added to it.

"My name is Jerrod Gold. I am a detective sergeant with the sheriff's office in Mesa, California. Do you need to see my credentials?"

"No, sir. I believe you."

"I'm investigating a missing persons case. A teen-aged boy from my jurisdiction went missing here in Las Vegas."

"Recently?" Peter asked.

"No. In 1974. He was a regular customer in this restaurant. He came in often with his father."

Peter paused. "Sir, I was about five years old in 1974. I don't think I can help you."

Jerrod pushed. "I'm specifically looking a server who worked here at that time. Her name was 'Wanda.' She left shortly after my...," Jerrod feigned a cough, "... excuse me, the teen vanished. I think she may be helpful to this investigation. Do you keep personnel records from that far back?"

"Sir. I don't know. I've only been a manager for about six weeks. I'll have to check."

"How about anyone on duty this morning who was working here at the time?"

Peter took a moment to answer. "We have one server who's been here a long time. But I don't know if she's been here that long. Her name is Elizabeth. She's working in a different section right now."

Jerrod poured it on. "Two parents have not known if their son is alive or dead for eighteen years. Can you spare her for a few minutes to see if she has any information I can use?

Peter relaxed as he realized the focus of the questioning was about to be transferred to someone else. "Sure. I'll send her right over."

A large-hipped woman aged about sixty walked up to Jerrod's table. "Elizabeth" was on her name tag. "You're a cop? And want to talk to me? Something about a kid?"

Jerrod realized she was not going to be a pushover like her manager. He tried a different approach.

"I need some assistance on a missing persons case. Please have a seat. I won't keep you long."

Elizabeth slid into the booth. Her dour expression didn't change.

"Do you have children?" Jerrod asked.

"That's none of your damn business," she replied.

"You're correct, ma'am. It is not."

"Get to your point. I have food coming out any second."

"Brass tacks. Okay. Were you working here in 1974?"

"Here? At The Peppermill?" she asked before looking off to the ceiling. "I started here the year before that. Raised three kids by myself on what I made here. Not that that somehow just became any of your business."

"My mom raised my brother and me alone after the divorce," Jerrod said. He paused, swallowed, and looked away for effect. "My wife-to-be raised her two daughters after her husband's sudden death on what she made serving tables. You have all my respect."

Elizabeth thawed a little.

"I am looking for a server who worked here in 1974 when a young man disappeared. He was a regular in this place with his father and this server took a liking to him. I suspect he had a little crush on her too."

"There has been a thousand servers come-and-go since I started. If they weren't here for at least a month, I didn't even try to remember their names. Does this server -- they called us 'waitresses' back then -- have a name?"

"Yes. 'Wanda.'"

Elizabeth looked at the ceiling again. "'Wanda.' 'Wanda,'" she repeated. "Nah. Doesn't ring a bell."

"The young man that's missing was a talented artist. He drew sketches. The only sketch of a person that his father could find was of 'Wanda.' Would you like to see it?"

"Yeah. Okay."

Jerrod opened the sketch pad to the page and handed it to Elizabeth.

"I remember her," she said instantly. She was a hippy chick. Was here about that time."

"Anything else you remember about her? Last name? Where she came here from? Where she went after?"

"I'm not sure her name *was* 'Wanda." Could have been. But this sketch is life-like. I know that face."

"Anything you can remember. Any little detail might help."

"She came here from up north."

"Northern Nevada?"

"Yeah. Some little town. I have no idea where she went after she quit this place or got fired or whatever."

"Any idea what town?"

Elizabeth gave the ceiling another glance. "It has an unusual name, but I can't think of it now."

"You've been a great help. Thank you. I owe you one."

"Leave your server a nice tip." She made a coy grin. "That'll be thanks enough."

Peter walked to the table as Elizabeth returned to her section. He placed Jerrod's check on the table and made no attempt to sit down.

"Any luck with the records?" Jerrod asked.

"I checked with the owner, and he said we do not keep personnel records from that far back. The IRS only requires us to retain them for three years. All records past then have been destroyed."

"Thank you, Peter," Jerrod said as he stood and peeked at the check. "I appreciate your help. I will be back to visit your fine restaurant on my next trip."

Jerrod left a twenty-dollar bill on the table for a six-dollar check.

CHAPTER 33

Las Vegas Metropolitan Police Department

"I'm here to see Sergeant Bloomstrom," Jerrod told the uniformed officer at the reception desk at Las Vegas Metro. "I have an appointment with him."

"Your name, sir?"

"Gold. Sergeant Jerrod Gold. Mesa County SO. That's in California."

"Have some ID?"

Jerrod fished out his departmental ID and slid it across the counter.

The officer punched some numbers on his desk phone. "Sergeant Gold here to see you." He listened for a few seconds. "Okay, Sarge."

The officer handed the ID back to Jerrod. "He's sending 'Kid' to escort you up. It'll be a minute or so."

Jerrod nodded and took a seat in the lobby.

A young man -- late teens and thin -- wearing a khaki uniform came into the lobby and held the door open. "Sergeant Gold?"

Jerrod walked toward the door.

"Welcome to Las Vegas Metro. You're here to see Pez?" he asked.

"Sergeant Bloomstrom."

"Yeah, that's Pez."

"Why do you call him that?"

"You'll see."

In the elevator, Jerrod looked at the young man's uniform. He had an under-sized gold Police Cadet badge and the name tag read: "P. Bentley."

Jerrod asked, "Why do they call you 'Kid?'"

"My name is 'Paul.' My dad was a cop here." He paused. "He was a 'Paul' too. 'Paul's Kid' just became 'Kid,' I guess. I kind of grew up here at Metro."

"I started as police cadet too. I was about sixteen or so. Little department in California. Had a badge just like yours."

Kid laughed. "Cool. I'll get a real badge someday. Right here at Metro... when I'm old enough."

The elevator opened to a large room containing a maze of cubicles. Uniformed and plainclothes officers moved about the space. There was a constant clamor of telephones ringing, keyboards clacking, and voices talking.

Kid walked Jerrod through the maze and landed at the cubicle of Sergeant Roy Bloomstrom.

"Told you," Kid said.

"You did. Thank you."

Kid walked off and Jerrod looked at how the cubicle was decorated. There were at least fifty PEZ candy dispensers on every flat surface. They were a colorful display of Disney characters, superheroes, Smurfs, Ninja Turtles, and many others.

Roy stood and extended his hand. "Everyone just calls me Pez. Have a seat." He picked up Sleeping Beauty and pulled back her head to expose a candy. "Peppermint... I think."

"I'm glad you called ahead before coming here," Pez started. "We had to dig for the report in one of our warehouses. Anyways. I have the file."

"Let's get to it," Jerrod suggested.

Pez lifted a manila folding file which was surprisingly thin. "Not much here I'm afraid. This won't take very long. I hope you have something else to do here in Vegas."

"What else is there to do here?" Jerrod panned.

Pez snickered as he opened the file. "Reported: August 9, 1974. R/P: Father -- Jerry Gold. Missing: Thomas Wesley Gold. Age: Thirteen. Father left for work. Thomas was home alone."

"'Tommy,'" Jerrod said. "We called him 'Tommy.'"

Pez nodded. "Tommy was home alone. Father came home from work. His clothing was there, but no Tommy."

"Tommy left all of his drawing stuff too," Jerrod added. "He was a talented artist. Drew all the time. He wouldn't have gone anywhere, on his own, without it."

Pez scanned the brief report. "No mention of that here."

"Was there any follow-up done? Area canvas? Neighbors interviewed?"

Pez looked at the report again. "Other than some dental records submitted later by... Laura Renaud."

"That's my mother."

"Pez continued, "The report was taken as a simple runaway." He flipped a few pages. "Doesn't look like any follow-up was done."

"Is there a photo of Tommy in that file?

Pez thumbed the pages again but didn't find one.

"Want one now?" Jerrod tossed a photo of Tommy wearing the blue t-shirt on the desk. "I picked these prints up on the way here. My Dad has had these the whole fucking time. Tommy was wearing that exact blue shirt, blue Levi 501 jeans, and black low-top Converse All-Stars when he... left."

"Well... uh..." Pez said.

"Pretty stellar police work here, *Sergeant*," Jerrod said. He didn't try to hide the sarcasm. "Handle all your cases like this?"

Pez leaned back in his chair. "Hang on a second. You 'buzz' your way in here on what is obviously a personal matter. Okay. Ask us to open our files. Okay. Then you have the balls to criticize the way we do business? Fuck you."

"Buzz" is a cop term for using one's law enforcement influence to gain advantage or favor. The badge is often called a "buzzer."

"I did. I did that too. And I am criticizing how this investigation was handled," Jerrod replied. "Do you have any idea of what it feels like to lose a brother?"

Pez scoffed. "I've got a question for you, *Sergeant*." His patience had instantly worn thin. "How many square miles are there in your county? What's your service population?"

"That's two questions, Pez." Jerrod could see where this was going but answered anyway. "About 450 square miles. Couple hundred thousand."

Pez had his response prepared. "Clark County has about 8,000 square miles. We cover from Indian Springs to the west to Mesquite in the east and all the way down to Laughlin in the south." His volume increased. "We'll be at one million residents in a year or so... and that doesn't even count the several million more idiots who show up every weekend from who-knows-where AND THINK THERE ARE NO FUCKING RULES HERE."

A bull-necked detective from the adjacent cubicle stood up and glared at Jerrod. "Everything cool here, Pez?"

"Everything's fine," Pez said as he pushed his palms down in a calming motion. "It's okay. We're okay." He took in a deep breath. "This guy here is one of us."

Pez grabbed a dispenser from his desk and flipped it to the detective. "Here. Wile E. Coyote. Tropical fruit... I think."

"Alright," the detective said as he sank back down in his cubicle.

"Sorry about that," Jerrod said.

Pez held up his hand. "Don't worry. That's been brewing for, what, almost twenty years. The apology should come from me."

"Again. I'm sorry."

Pez was silent for a long moment. "Tell you what I'll do. I'll get a hold of the officers that took this report -- if their still alive -- and see if they kept notes or remember anything else that wasn't in the report."

"That's a long shot," Jerrod said.

"Maybe so. But I'll do what I can to find out something about your brother."

Pez read off the telephone numbers on the report for both Jerry and Laura.

"Those are still good numbers," Jerrod said. "Let me give you mine as well... just in case."

Jerrod took out a MCSO business card which listed his Investigations telephone number. "This is my desk number, but I'll write my home number on the back... since this *is* a personal matter.".

"Touché?" Pez panned. "I'll keep the card but put a note in the file."

"Thank you. Can I get a copy of that report?"

"I don't know about that," Pez said.

Jerrod said nothing.

Pez shook his head. "Do you always leave with what you came for?"

Jerrod gave a subtle nod.

Pez stood up and yelled across the room. "Send Kid over."

Kid jogged to the cubicle. "Yeah, Pez. What do you need?"

"Make a copy of this report for the sergeant here."

"Everything?"

"Every page. Go."

As Kid headed to the copy machine, Jerrod said, "Thanks. I was hoping to get a few more answers, but I appreciate what you are doing. I owe you one."

"Sure. Any questions?" Pez asked.

Jerrod hesitated. "Kid mentioned his father *was* a Metro officer. Retired... I hope."

"Nope," Pez dropped his gaze to the coffee-stained carpet between their chairs. "Paul Bentley's picture is on the wall in the lobby. He was killed on duty in 1980. Stabbed in the chest by some doper. I really miss that guy. I loved that man like--" He stopped as his eyes got glassy.

Jerrod waited to again make eye contact. "Loved him like... *a brother?*"

CHAPTER 34

"Learn anything? Jerry asked as he stepped from under a mid-eighties Chevrolet sedan on a lift.

"Yes and no," Jerrod replied. "Not a whole lot of investigation went into Tommy's case. They considered him a runaway and assumed he'd turn up at some point. I'm still looking into it."

"Get something to eat?" Jerry grinned. "Go to The Peppermill this morning, by chance?

"How'd you know that?"

"I figured you would. Find any 'clues' there? That's what detectives call 'em right, 'clues.'"

Jerrod chuckled. "Sure, if you're Sherlock Holmes in one of Arthur Conan-Doyle's novels."

"What's the correct term then, smart-ass?"

"We call those 'leads.' As in 'one thing *leads* to another.'"

"Well?"

"The restaurant only keeps personnel records for about three years, so that 'lead' is a dead end."

"Anyone there remember Wanda?"

"Was just getting to that. I spoke to a server named Elizabeth and showed her Tommy's drawing. She didn't remember Wanda by name but recognized her face. Described her as being a 'hippy chick.'"

"'Hippy chick,'" Jerry repeated as pulled the pack of Marlboros out of his shirt pocket.

"Elizabeth said Wanda moved to Vegas from a small town in Northern Nevada. An unusually named town. Any ideas?"

Jerry lit a smoke and watched cars drive by the shop as he thought. At a glance, he could name the year, make, and model of each of them as they passed. "1981 Ford LTD. 1988 Toyota Celica. 1977 Buick Skylark. 1985 Mercury Topaz."

Jerrod had no doubt his father's identifications were correct. He watched a large recreational vehicle lumber by.

"Winnemucca," Jerry said.

"I think you mean, 'Winnebago?'"

"Not the RV, "Jerry said. "Yes, that was a Winnebago, but I'm talking about a little town up north. Somewhere between Reno and who-fucking-knows. I remember her telling us that -- me and Tommy. Wanda was originally from Winnemucca, Nevada."

"My dad... the detective."

"Your dad... period."

The flight from Las Vegas was on the same airline and followed the same route. But there was a stark contrast about the passengers on board. There was no cheer. There was no energy. All were spent -- along with the rent and car payment -- on their visit to "Sin City."

Jerrod was no exception. His mind raced as he recounted the events of the last two days and the revelations he had learned. He pulled out the photo prints of Tommy and tried to image what he would look like today... if he was still alive. Would he even recognize him? Maybe? Maybe not? He had a detective's intuition -- a deep feeling somewhere between the belly and the brain -- that the waitress depicted in Tommy's drawing, was, in some way, involved in his disappearance.

He planned the next move: Search for Wanda by starting in Winnemucca, Nevada -- "somewhere between Reno and who-fucking-knows."

"Hello," Nikki answered the phone at their home.

"It's Jerrod. Just landed in San Jose. How are you?"

"Missing my guy. Hoping you didn't find some new girl in Las Vegas."

"There was this one gal, her name is Elizabeth... you want details."

"No."

"I have my session with Sidney at six. With the traffic from here, I'm going to have to go straight there to make it on time."

"You go see Sidney before you see me," her sarcasm was clear. "I'm getting used to that. Have a good session."

"I love you."

"I love you, too."

"How was your week?" Sidney Yamamoto asked.

"I went to Las Vegas and visited my father," then Jerrod corrected. "Uh... my dad."

"How did that go?"

"Good visit. Talked a lot. Ate damn well. Learned a few things about my brother."

"You told me on your first visit that you had a brother, but we have never discussed him."

"He's missing. Since 1974. Just disappeared in Las Vegas."

"Missing?"

"Vanished. Home in the morning. Gone in the afternoon. Not a trace since."

"How do you feel about that?"

Jerrod kept straight-faced. "I never really liked him. He stabbed me in the arm with a pencil once, so I don't care that he's missing."

"You're not serious?"

"That's correct. I'm not serious. I loved my brother."

"And you went to look for him?"

"Yes."

"And your father has, more or less, now become a witness in your investigation. You needed something from him."

"Yes. No. I guess so. Lighten up, Sidney."

"Then tell me what you learned," Sidney asked.

Jerrod gave him all the details of Tommy's disappearance and the new "leads" he had developed.

"Are you always 'working?'" Sidney asked.

"I suppose so."

"Do you think that's healthy, Jerrod?"

"Probably not."

"We'll come back to this." Sidney jotted a few words down. "I was checking my notes before you came in tonight. Something occurred to me."

"What's that?" Jerrod asked.

On a previous visit, you described your greatest strengths and weakness. You said they were the same thing."

"Yes?"

"Do you have any knowledge of ancient Japanese history? I'm talking about feudal Japan. 13th century into the 17th."

"Not really, sir."

"I'll break it down a little," Sidney said. "During these feudal years, large clans controlled huge estates throughout Japan. All the power within the country was controlled by these clans. To keep their power, the clans hired skilled warriors and master swordsmen -- the *samurai* -- to protect the estates."

"I've heard of the samurai, of course," Jerrod said.

"The samurai lived by a strict moral code -- called *bushido* -- which controlled their actions. The lived pure lifestyles and honed their fighting skills for battle."

Jerrod chuckled. "I don't think I would qualify under any sort of strict moral code."

"Well, the samurai took their code so seriously, that they would choose death over defeat or dishonor. In fact, many samurai committed ritual suicide -- known best as *hara-kiri,* but more accurately as *seppuku* -- by disemboweling themselves. Japanese pilots in World War II used a form of seppuku when they would intentionally fly their bomb-laden planes into enemy ships."

"The *kamikaze,*" Jerrod added.

"Exactly,"

"What's this all got to do with my... issues?" Jerrod asked.

"My next point is just that," Sidney said. "During the days of the samurai, there was another group of Japanese warriors who were less honorable. In fact, they were the opposite of that: covert, sneaky, masters of disguise and manipulation, skilled at espionage, sabotage, and assassination. They fought dirty, but effectively. They were despised by the samurai because they lived by no code and, therefore, had no honor. These warriors were known as the *ninja.*"

"You're saying I'm more like the ninja than samurai? No honor? No code?" Jerrod scoffed. "I've killed, sir. Twice. But I'm no assassin."

"I'm not saying that at all. The ninja had their place at the time. What I'm getting at is that your skills of persuasion and manipulation has its place now as it did then. Covert operators have great value. When it's channeled. When it's for a positive result. When it's not used for personal gain or advantage."

"That's a lot to take in, sir."

"Yes, it is." Sidney leaned forward. "Me must start somewhere."

"Greetings from Las Vegas. I am bearing gifts," Jerrod announced as he burst through the front door and stood, arms open, in the living room.

Lilly and Marty ran from their bedroom and hugged Jerrod. Nikki walked out of the kitchen and waited her turn.

"I have just returned from the land of wasted dreams and financial ruin," he said. "You. Older one. What's your name again?"

"You know my name is 'Lilly.'"

"Yes, of course, 'Lilly.' You get a 'Welcome to Las Vegas' snow globe. It is very rare for it to snow in Las Vegas, but my dad told me it has happened."

"Thank you, Jerrod."

Now for you, younger one. "Name, please?

"I'm 'Marty.'"

"Yes. Yes. Yes. 'Marty.' I had to search far and wide to find this item with you, and only you, in mind.

"What is it?' the bouncing ten-year old asked.

"Are you ready?' Jerrod said as he pulled a delicate white ceramic bell from his bag. It had "Las Vegas" and a pair of rolling dice stenciled on it.

Marty rang the bell. "I love it. Thank you."

"You're welcome, girls. Now leave me. Go away. I have business with your mother."

Nikki gave Jerrod a tight hug. "Do you remember my name?"

"Your name is, let me think, 'The Most Beautiful Woman in The Entire Universe.'"

"Good one," she said. "So, you searched 'far and wide' for those gifts. Probably in the airport gift shop?"

"It was a big gift shop.' Jerrod laughed. "Think of those trinkets more as future family heirlooms."

"I'm sure they will be," she said. "Hungry?"

"Sure."

"How's your father?"

"Good," he said between bites of a delicious pasta dish. "Actually, not good. He's a sad and tired man. He lives day to day blaming himself for losing Tommy." Jerrod felt a wave of emotion.

Nikki kissed him on the cheek. "And my detective husband-to-be will sort it all out and give that poor man some relief."

"I will." He looked her through moist eyes. "If it's the last thing I do."

CHAPTER 35

Her fine hair was snow white and her face bore the deep wrinkles from a lifetime of worry and wear and struggle and sacrifice.

She was a woman whose father who died when she was a teen. A woman whose mother raised her and her three sisters alone. A woman who married and produced four children of her own during the worst of The Great Depression. A woman who moved with the ripening crops throughout California as "fruit tramps" -- straight from a John Steinbeck novel -- taking any meager job that would earn enough to feed her kids. A woman who watched her husband board a Navy ship to fight in the South Pacific, and, ten years later, watched her eldest son do the same as he headed to Korea. And a woman who welcomed and loved and nurtured those two damaged men when they returned from war.

Jenne Gold was rarely seen without a KOOL cigarette in her hand. A pack of "king-sized" menthols was always nearby. An abalone shell cover over a disposable BIC lighter stood guard nearby. She liked her cigarettes and had so for seventy-four of her eighty-six years on this planet. Her doctor had told her she should stop smoking. But when he was met with her trademark gaze of disapproval, quickly reversed course, and told her to do whatever she wanted.

"Hi, Gram," Jerrod said as he sat down with her in the dining room. He placed a brown paper bag next to his chair.

She studied him for a moment. She was calm and perceptive. Frail outside. Tough inside. Fit and stable. Smart and often painfully direct.

"Hello, Jerrod," she said. "How was the visit with your father?"

He knew that she knew the details already. "Good. He's coming to the wedding."

"I'm glad you invited him," she said. "I haven't seen him since...," she thought for a second, "... my eightieth birthday."

Jerrod nodded.

"Learn anything new about Tommy?"

"Not really. There wasn't much of an investigation done. They wrote it up as a simple runaway. But I came up with a few new tidbits and am looking into them."

She paused and bowed her head. He bowed as well. No words needed to be exchanged.

"What's in the bag, Jerrod?" she said as she took a long drag from her KOOL.

"Board game."

"Which game?" She asked as she blew a puff of smoke at an errant tuft of hair on her cheek. "Monopoly? Life?"

"Chess."

Jenne Gold scoffed. "I haven't played chess in years. I've probably forgotten how by now."

He smiled. "The rules haven't changed in about five hundred years, Gram. But I'll take it easy on you. Just this one time."

Jenne chuckled and they locked eyes. "Set 'em up, child. You take 'white.'"

Jenne studied the board. "Switch your queen and king."

"How about you play your pieces and I'll play mine. I'm pretty sure that's still one of the rules."

"I would if you set them correctly. See a problem?"

Jerrod scanned the board. "No problem here."

"Your queen -- the white queen -- always starts on the white square," she said. "Just remember: 'The queen's shoes always match her dress.'"

Jerrod switched the pieces.

"And *you* were going to take it easy on *me*."

Jerrod made the first move, two spaces forward, with his queen's pawn.

Jenne countered by moving her queen's pawn two spaces to match.

Eleven moves later, Jerrod tipped the white king over with his forefinger. "I resign."

"That was fun," she snarked. "I was hoping for a bit of a challenge. The good news is you can only improve from that performance."

"Want to make this a regular thing, Gram? Teach me how to play. To play well."

She lit another cigarette. "Sure. I taught your father and your uncles. Every man should know how to play chess. Life is a game of chess. Relishing the good moves. Recovering from blunders. Being able to see the whole board. Strong opening. Smart middle. Solid endgame. Attack. Skewer. Pin. Trade. Defend. But we'll get into that down the road."

"Who taught you?"

"My father -- your great-grandfather. He was named 'Jerrod.' So was his father -- along with all other first-born males -- going way back to our family roots in England. All of them, so I've been told, played chess."

Jerrod paused. "You had a brother, correct?"

"Yes." She took a long moment. "He was a 'Jerrod,' too. But he died young and never learned to play the game. My father taught me instead."

"I had always wondered where my first name came from," Jerrod mused. "How long has Dad gone by 'Jerry?'"

Jenne said, "He kept getting called 'Gerald' or 'Gerard' in high school, so, when he enlisted in the Navy, he went as 'Jerry' and has stayed with that since."

"Fascinating," he said.

"Did you know your first name has a meaning behind it?" she asked.

"No. I had no idea."

She stamped out a cigarette and reached for another. "The name 'Jerrod' -- spelled that particular way -- means: 'Rules by The Spear.'"

CHAPTER 36

Monday Morning

"Sergeant Gold. Property Crimes," he answered his desk phone.

"Roy Bloomstrom. Las Vegas Metro," the voice on the receiver said.

"Pez," Jerrod said. "Was just thinking about you."

"No, you weren't," he replied, "but here I am anyway."

"So. Good news, I hope?"

"I tracked down the two patrol officers who took the original missing person report on your brother. Both had retired awhile back. One of them died about five years ago. The second moved down to Lake Kiowa City, Arizona."

"What is it with Lake Kiowa City?" Jerrod asked.

"The London Bridge is there," Pez said.

"But it's just a fucking bridge," Jerrod replied. "Does it have mystical powers or something?"

"I don't know about that," Pez said, "but I do know that this officer didn't remember taking the report. "Just one of many,' was his response."

"Notes?" Jerrod asked.

"Tossed 'em. Sorry. I'm afraid this aspect has come to a dead-end."

"It sure has," Jerrod said. "Call me if something comes up, Pez?"

"I will. Take care."

"Kirk LaMahieu was in the restaurant again today," Nikki said.

Jerrod was reading the novel, *Dead Irish,* and didn't look up. "That's nice. Hope you sent my best."

"He knows were together," she said. "He heard another customer talking about it."

"Great," he said as he marked his spot and put the book down. "Did you give him an invitation to the wedding?"

"You're not funny. He congratulated us. He seemed happy about it."

"Not trying to be funny. Honey, I killed his father and I suspect he might be a touch upset about that. Do you see a potential for some... conflict?"

"No. I don't. He's a nice guy. Same as before... city hall."

"Okay," he said. "Fine."

"You don't get to use 'fine,'" she scolded, "that's my word."

"Okay," Jerrod chuckled. "We need to have a serious talk. Please sit down."

She sat on the sofa.

"The paperwork on the new house is ready," he said. "We can sign for the house once we're officially married and move in as soon as Mom and Don leave for Arizona."

"This is exciting, Jerrod. Our house."

"Yes. And *our* mortgage. Plus, the mortgage on this place while I rent it out. We're going to have to be frugal for a while. Or increase our income. It's going to be tight."

"What are you saying?"

He shifted in the La-Z-Boy. "I'm saying maybe you could find a new profession. You know, get out of the restaurant business. Do something you've always wanted to do. Something that pays better than the tips you bring home."

"Just quit?" she asked. "A big part of my life has been at that restaurant. The girls have been going there, well, since before they were born."

"I understand," he said. "Please just think about it. Okay?"

"Fine."

CHAPTER 37

"What has been your greatest accomplishment, Jerrod?" Sidney Yamamoto asked. "Something you've earned?"

"Personal or professional? Jerrod asked.

"First thing that comes to mind."

Jerrod thought for a long moment. "I guess that would be finding the perfect woman to marry."

"You feel that strongly about Nikki?"

"Of course. She's perfect for me. I'm pretty lucky."

"Okay," Sidney said. "How about your greatest failure?"

"That one's easy," Jerrod said. "Hector."

"Tell me about Hector?'"

Jerrod pulled a side pillow onto his lap. "He was a street kid I knew as he grew up. He got into some trouble, and I couldn't save him."

"*Couldn't* or *didn't?*"

"Both are true, I suppose. We were friends. I knew that kid before he could speak English. The dispatchers would just buzz him into the old PD when he came to see me. I'd send him out to get me chili dogs and coffee."

"What went wrong?" Sidney asked.

"Everything. I've seen it dozens of times. No father in the picture. Mom works her ass off to feed her kids. A set of bad peers. A mentality that they'll be in prison or dead before they turn twenty. Live for today. Don't worry about tomorrow. Drink. Smoke dope. Have fun. Be reckless."

"What happened?"

"When he was a teen, I found out he was getting mixed up in the wrong crowd. I reached out to him and a few days later, I was notifying his mother and sister he'd been murdered."

Sidney nodded and took a few notes.

"Ever have to make a death notification, Sidney? Family member, maybe?

"Never have. How is it done? Is there a procedure?"

"Yeah. Depends on the circumstances. Patrol is different from how detectives do it because we need to interview after the notification."

"Patrol, then? How do you handle it?

146

"Okay. You get a radio call to telephone dispatch. If it's for an outside agency, dispatch has an official teletype with the details and who to contact at that agency. You don't make notifications based on telephone calls from other agencies. These things tend to happen in the middle of the night."

"Okay," Sidney said.

"So, you get the particulars of who had died and who needs to be notified and where you should be able to find them and who they need to call."

Sidney nodded.

"You drive to the house or condo or trailer or whatever. But before you get there, maybe down the block, you stop and write the contact information for the family to call on the back of a business card. You double and triple check the info before you go to the door because you don't want to be writing stuff at the door."

"Keep going."

"You shut down the patrol car. Black it out and turn the radio down. Knock on the door and ask for the relative listed and give them the news. You tell them... uh... insert deceased family member's name here... has 'died.' You never say 'passed' or 'gone' or any soft words to describe why you're there. Then you wait for a reaction, give them the card, ask if they want you to help them make the call, and then stay with them until... you know... they don't need you."

"What range of reactions have you seen?"

"From someone fainting right then and there." Jerrod felt his chin quiver. "To one man who thanked me and apologized for how difficult this must be for me. Can you believe that shit? This man's son had been away in college, is killed in a car crash, he just learned about it, and he's fucking worried about me."

Sidney waited until he spoke again. "An officer showing up in the middle of the night is never good news."

"We don't ever deliver good news, Sidney, day or night," Jerrod scoffed. "We don't knock on doors and tell people their life is about to change because they just won the lottery. We tell them their life is going to change because someone they love is never coming home again."

CHAPTER 38

Jerrod had closed as many investigations as he could and handed the files to Linda Westphal. The other open cases were divided evenly among his team of detectives -- Beach, Nate, and Zippy. A banker's box rested on the stained carpet next to his desk to collect his personal items.

It was his last day in the Property Crimes Section.

"It's getting hot in here," Jerrod said during a rare quiet moment.

"You assholes," Beach said to the snickers of Nate and Zippy. "You guys left me hanging -- actually pretty much half-hard -- in that room with Sapphire. Another minute in there would have started an Administrative Investigation."

"Most probably for an 'accidental discharge while on-duty,'" Nate said.

"Clean-up in Room 3," Zippy added.

Jerrod was somber. "I'm going to miss you mutts. Please treat Roger as well as you treated me."

It was silent for a few seconds until Nate looked to Beach. "Give it to him now."

Beach reached into the kneehole of his desk, pulled out a wrapped package, and carried it to Jerrod's desk. "We got this for you."

Jerrod pulled the paper off the binder-sized package and dropped his head when he saw what it was.

"Had a hard time finding that, Sarge," Zippy said. "Not many of those out there."

"I love it," Jerrod said.

He held the item up to get a better light. Professionally matted and in a brushed-nickel frame was an autographed photo of the star of the Dragnet series and the unit's designated muse: Jack Webb as Sergeant Joe Friday.

"Don't know what to say, guys," Jerrod said.

"'Thank you,' is the traditional response," Nate said.

"We can hang that up when you get paroled from the slammer and come back over," Beach said.

"'WWJFD?'" Zippy said.

Jerrod nodded. "'What Would Joe Friday Do?'"

CHAPTER 39

NOVEMBER 1991 -- Saturday -- 6:45 PM

It was already dark outside when Sergeant Jerrod Gold parked his pickup in the employee parking lot of the Mesa County Main Jail. He wore a black San Francisco Giants windbreaker over his long-sleeved SO uniform shirt. His green uniform pants had crisp creases and his black boots were shined.

"Sergeant Gold. First night," Jerrod said as he looked up to a CCTV camera after pressing the speaker button in the jail vehicle sallyport. He unzipped and pulled open the front of his "cover coat" to expose his badge.

"Come on in," the flat female voice said through the speaker as its lock buzzed and he pulled open the door. He had to wait a few seconds as the first door locked and a second door lock buzzed. In the jail, no two doors connecting the secure interior portion and the outside could be unlocked at the same time.

Jerrod had seen the red plastic sign near the sallyport door dozens of times before, but never really paid any attention to it. The sign read:

HOSTAGE POLICY

THE MESA COUNTY SHERIFF'S OFFICE HAS A STRICT "NO HOSTAGE" POLICY. THIS MEANS NO INMATE WILL BE ALLOWED TO LEAVE THIS JAIL FACILITY BECAUSE OF TAKING A HOSTAGE. THIS POLICY WILL BE APPLIED IN ALL CASES WITHOUT REGARD TO SEX, AGE, OR STATUS OF ANY HOSTAGE. FORCE MAY BE NECESSARY TO RESCUE HOSTAGES.

Jerrod entered the Booking Area. He had been in the room several dozen times over the years when delivering arrestees to be processed. The overwhelming sinus-stinging smell of the room could be best described as a combination of wet socks and vomit.

A dozen holding rooms with thick, shatterproof windows and heavy metal doors formed three sides of the large room. Several men and one woman stood looking through the windows of their rooms, pounded on the glass, and yelled to get his attention.

The fourth side of the Booking Area was a raised counter with two booking stations.

"Where's the sergeant's office?" Jerrod asked a male booking officer in a SO uniform. The seven-point gold badge pinned to his shirt read: "Sheriff's Detention Officer."

The pale officer glanced up from his computer screen, squinted through oversized glasses, and took a few seconds to study Jerrod. He turned and pointed to an open office door behind the booking counter. "The *Watch Commander's* office is right there."

"Thanks," Jerrod said as he stepped around the counter and onto the platform behind it.

He walked toward the office door and saw an unoccupied desk. When he reached the doorway, he found a pencil-thin man wearing a uniform seated behind a second desk. He was writing into an open black binder.

The man looked up and a satisfied smile spread across his face. He placed his pen down on the page and sat back in his chair. "Welcome to Siberia: Where new sergeants come pay their dues... and disgraced sergeants are sent to pay their penance."

Former Lieutenant Mitchell T. Sullivan watched Jerrod as he peeled off his jacket and hung it on a rack just inside the doorway.

"I guess you're right," Jerrod said as he sat in the chair of the unoccupied desk. "I've been sent over here to 'do my time.'"

"What goes around--,"

"Save it, *Mitch*," Jerrod interrupted -- knowing full-well Sullivan went by "Mitchell," not "Mitch."

"Suit yourself," Sullivan said. The smile had not disappeared from his face as he picked up his pen and continued writing in the binder. "But you are the reason I am sitting here right now."

"You're the reason, dipshit. Want to re-hash Brent Rozman's suicide and the cover-up?"

"That will not be necessary."

Jerrod sighed. "Anything happen today I should know about?"

"Normal day. Booking was busy and we had a few fights in Housing," Sullivan said without looking up. "It is all in here." He raised the binder cover. "This is the Watch Commander's Log. Read it... or do not read it. I do not care."

Jerrod said, "Looks like we're going see each other at least a half-dozen times a week. How about we agree to just be civil on those occasions?"

Sullivan thought for a moment. "Request denied."

"Fine with me."

The doorway to the Watch Commander's office was filled by man in a SO uniform who stood at least six-foot-five with massively wide shoulders, a deep chest, and upper arms the size of a normal-sized man's leg.

"Excuse me, gentlemen," he said in a predicable deep voice. He turned to Jerrod. "Sergeant Gold, I'll be your SDO. Ready for a tour."

"Sure," Jerrod said as he pushed away from the desk.

"Try to stay awake," Sullivan said. "I think it is a full moon tonight. You should have fun."

"Thanks."

Jerrod followed the officer out of the Watch Commander's Office and into Booking. He braced himself for the handshake he was about to receive from the tree-trunk of a man -- who had corporal chevrons sewn to the straining sleeves of his uniform shirt. As he turned, Jerrod noted his name tag read: "Albert Porterfield."

"What's an 'SDO,' Albert?" Jerrod asked.

The booking officer snickered and repeated, "Albert." He as quickly glanced away when the SDO glared at him.

"It stands for 'Supervising Detention Officer,'" he replied. "Everyone here just calls me 'Alpo.'"

"'Alpo?' Like the dog food?"

"Yes, sir."

"AL-bert and PO-terfield. Interesting nickname."

"I'm okay with it. Your tour, sir."

Alpo's speech was accented with the unmistakable drawl of the Deep South. "When an arrestee is brought into the vehicle sallyport," he said as he guided Jerrod to the Intake area, "the transporting officer secures all of his or her weapons in the trunk of their car."

"I've done that a few times," Jerrod said.

"The transporting officer presses the button and one of the DOs -- Detention Officers -- in Central Security can see who they are and let them into the facility."

"The arrestee is searched and their property inventoried," Alpo continued, "the booking charges received from the officer, and we accept the arrestee for processing. The arrestee then sits in these holding rooms until they are booked."

"Where are you from, originally, Alpo?" Jerrod asked. "You weren't raised around here."

"Alabama, sir," Alpo said. "Huntsville, Alabama."

"What brought you to Mesa?"

"The war in Vietnam did, sir. I trained at Fort Ord, you know, down near Monterey."

"I'm familiar," Jerrod said.

"Did my year... over there... and got discharged in San Francisco. Decided I liked California better than Alabama."

"See some action in Vietnam, Alpo?"

Alpo paused. "Sir, I'm not ashamed of my time in the service, but I just don't talk about what happened there."

"Understood. I apologize."

"No problem, sir. Your tour."

"This is Booking," Alpo said. "Arrestees have their identifying information and the charges typed into the computer system. We check for outstanding warrants and prior criminal histories. Everyone is photographed and fingerprinted."

"Then what?"

"If they're here on minor charges, they just get 'OR'd'... uh... released on their 'own recognizance' to appear in court."

"And major charges?" Jerrod asked.

"Bail is set to an amount from a bail schedule. If they can raise the bail -- they get out with a court date. If they can't -- they go to Housing."

"So far, so good," Jerrod said.

Alpo stopped in a long corridor leading away from Booking. "Everything past here is considered 'Housing.'"

Jerrod looked to the left and found two men in white hospital scrubs playing cards in a storage room. The men stopped their game and stared at Jerrod.

"Breaking in another new boss, Alpo?" one of the men asked.

"New 'Watch Commander' and it's none of your fucking business," Alpo said. "Did you two run out of things to do? Need me to find something?"

"Nah. We're good," the other man said. "We've got things to do."

"Get to it," Alpo barked.

Jerrod followed Alpo down a wide corridor. "Are those two guys considered 'trustees?'"

"'Inmate workers,'" Alpo said. "They're sentenced minimum-security inmates doing county time. They get 'work time' off their sentences to deliver meals, clothing exchange, sweep, mop, and other tasks."

"Okay," Jerrod said.

"Inmate workers are still inmates, sir," Alpo added. "So please remember, 'trustees' are not to be trusted."

The corridor ended in a large foyer. Thick wire-reinforced glass panels separated a variety of rooms.

"We call this open area "Times Square,'" Alpo said.

In a room to the left, a male DO and a female DO were seated and concentrating on a sweeping console of lights and switches and a bank of over twenty TV monitors.

"This is Central Security," Alpo said. "All doors and access for the entire building are controlled from here."

Alpo got the attention of the female DO and pointed to the door. She reached for a switch and the door lock buzzed.

Jerrod followed Alpo into the small sallyport. As the door to the hallway closed behind them, Jerrod noted Alpo held the heavy brass doorknob, twisted it, and pulled at the door to make sure it was secure. A second door from the sallyport to the control room was buzzed open.

"This is our new Watch Commander -- Sergeant Gold," Alpo announced. The two DOs looked over at Jerrod, nodded, and resumed their focus on the monitors and console.

"Nice to meet you," Jerrod said -- getting mostly grunts in return.

Alpo said, "This is the most secure room in the building. It's always manned by at least one officer, but usually two. It can get a little crazy in here at times."

"I can imagine that," Jerrod said.

"Let's get some coffee," Alpo said. "It's going to be a long shift."

Jerrod followed Alpo out of Central Security, pulled the hallway door closed, twisted the knob, and rattled the door to make sure it was secure.

"Quick study, sir," Alpo said with a smile. "You've been paying attention."

Back down the corridor near the inmate worker station, Alpo stopped at an unmarked door, punched a four-digit code into the lockset, and pushed open the door.

"This is the staff lounge," Alpo said. "Coffee, tea, soda machine are available 24/7. No charge. Since we can't leave during our shift, we get one free meal as well."

"Delivered or what?" Jerrod asked.

Alpo laughed. "No. Same thing the inmates got for dinner. The kitchen makes extra trays for us of the, well, 'entree du jour.'

"Sounds great."

Jerrod's sarcasm wasn't missed. "I've had worse," Alpo said.

Jerrod reached for a plastic coffee cup.

"Before you do that, sir," Alpo said. "Consider everything in this facility contaminated. You touched that doorknob back in Central Security and we have no idea what nasty creatures are on it."

"Okay," Jerrod said.

"Just a suggestion. Wash your hands good before you touch anything. Coffee cups. Your face. Your eyes. Even when you go to the restroom. Wash your hands first. Do... uh... your business. Then wash them again."

"Thank you," Jerrod said as he stepped to the sink and scrubbed his hands.

Jerrod and Alpo sat in one of the three booths in the otherwise empty lounge.

"Alpo, can I ask you a serious question?"

"Yes, sir."

"And please hear me out," Jerrod said. "I sense a certain... hostility... from the staff here. The DO in Booking and the two in Central Security."

"Hope I'm not giving you that impression, sir."

"No. Not at all."

Alpo sipped his black coffee. "Permission to be candid, sir?"

"Of course."

"Sergeants come and go around here, sir. Six months. A year. Maybe a year-and-a-half. The new sergeants come in because they have to and can't wait to get back out to Patrol or whatever. Others are sent here for a reason. We know why you're here. We know why Lieutenant... excuse me... Sergeant Sullivan is here. But while y'all rotate in and out -- we'll still be here. This is our full-time gig. We just tend to not get too attached to the sergeants here."

"Thank you for being honest. So SDO is the highest rank you can reach?"

"That's it."

"Ever think about testing for a deputy spot? Maybe expanding your promotion opportunities."

"Sir, I'm forty-two years old and have been working in jails and prisons for over twenty years. I'm a little too old to go to another academy and then chase kids on the street. I'm pretty much stuck here in the Detention part of things."

Jerrod nodded. "How long have you been here?"

"Eight years. Before this facility was built. Do you remember the old jail downtown? That place was medieval."

"You worked in prisons as well?"

"Was with CDC... uh... the California Department of Corrections... for just over thirteen years. Folsom. San Quentin. Vacaville. Soledad. Chino. And a few others."

"See some things there, Alpo?"

"Yes, sir. I don't really talk about that either."

Jerrod took a sip or coffee and added more sugar to it. "Alpo, what's the worst thing that can happen in here?"

Alpo thought for a moment. "You not getting payroll in on time, sir."

Jerrod laughed. "Very good."

"Seriously. Not including a staff member getting hurt." He thought some more. "I'd say, either an escape or a death in custody. I've been here for both. Pretty ugly."

"How ugly?"

"Worst kind of ugly. This place goes nuts when it happens. Detectives. Brass. Media. Lots of questions. Then the 'blame game' begins. Who fucked up? Fingers get pointed. The four shifts blame each other. The Brass blames everyone as they look for the scapegoat. Someone eventually gets 'fanged,' you know, suspended, or fired. This can go on for weeks. Like I said... ugly."

"Let's not let that happen. Deal?"

"Deal, sir."

Back down the corridor and past Central Security, Jerrod heard an increasing unpleasant symphony of human noise.

"These are the two main Housing areas," Alpo said. "He pointed left to a sliding door leading to another foyer. "That's West Housing." He then pointed to the sliding door to the right.

"That must be East Housing," Jerrod said.

"That is correct, sir. Let's get a closer look."

They walked past the sliding door into West Housing and the noise became more extreme. Talking. Yelling. Pounding. Slamming. All which caused the stress level to go up several notches.

Two male DOs were at a circular counter at the center of the foyer. Alpo introduced Jerrod to the officers, and they shook hands.

"How do you put up with all this noise?" Jerrod asked the officers.

They looked at each other and back to Jerrod. One then said, "What noise?"

Alpo led Jerrod to a door for one of the housing units and they stood looking in through the thick glass.

"Both East and West Housing have six housing units each," Alpo explained. "West has Unit 'A' through Unit 'F.'"

"And East is 'G' through... um... 'L.'"

"'Smart as a whip,' as my meemaw used to say."

"'Meemaw?'"

"'Grandmother.' Sorry, sir. Forgot we were in California for a minute."

Jerrod walked from door to door and watched the source of the noise -- the inmates -- as they interacted.

"The main open area in there is called the 'dayroom,'" Alpo said. "Inmates have free access to the dayroom when they're not 'racked' -- that is 'locked' -- in their cells. We'll get to that later."

An inmate cupped his hands along the sides of his face and against the window as he peered through them. Alpo walked over and slammed his palm against the window directly in the inmate's face. The inmate recoiled back. Alpo yelled, "Stay off the fucking glass" as the inmate slinked away.

"The windows are mirror-tinted on the inside," Alpo said. "We can see in, but they can't see out until they do that with their hands."

Jerrod walked from unit to unit and watched the inmates. He noticed a pattern: all were male, all were dressed in orange jumpsuits with "Mesa County Jail" stenciled on them, and, mostly, the units were segregated by race. Primarily Latino inmates lived in in three units -- with a few black inmates found in one. Only whites occupied two other units. The last unit, "F," was full integrated and by far the most active of the six units.

Jerrod turned to Alpo. "Do we segregate these units on purpose?"

"We don't, sir. They do."

"Explain, please."

"Sure," Alpo said. "Our official policy is that we intentionally separate only two classes of inmate: Males and Female. Unsentenced and Sentenced."

"Officially?" Jerrod asked.

"Yes, sir. However, the inmates ultimately decide who can -- or can't -- stay in each unit. They have their own politics and power structure in there."

Jerrod looked around into the six units... not noticing that he no longer noticed the noise level. He looked at Alpo. "Explain each unit to me."

"Sure. "A" is almost all Northern California-based Hispanic inmates. Black inmates tend to be okay with the northsiders.

"Okay," Jerrod said.

"B" tends to be more Southern California-based Hispanic -- southsiders if you will. However, the southsiders from Mesa and the ones from Valle Verde don't get along so good. Nothing but problems and fights with them, so we have to keep them apart -- Mesa inmates in "B" and Valle Verde inmates in "C."

"I get the north-south, norteño-sureño, red-blue, 14-13 thing," Jerrod said. "Saw plenty of that in Patrol."

One of the male DOs said, "Tell him about the 'MS-13' guys."

"Shit," Alpo said. "We had these three little dudes in from LA. They were El Salvadorian gangsters. 'MS' stands for '*Mara Salvatruca*.' They were in here for a couple-days as a courtesy house for the Border Patrol."

"Never heard of them," Jerrod said.

"13ers. Southsiders, right," Alpo said. "Dressed 'em out and put 'em in "C." It 'kicked-off' as soon as they stepped in.

"'Kicked-off?'" Jerrod asked.

Alpo showed an annoyed look. "'Kicked-off' means a fight... with everyone involved. Those three MS dudes fought off about twelve others until we got them out."

"Then what?" Jerrod asked.

"Moved the MS guys into "B" and it kicked-off there too. We had to rack those guys down together over in East Housing until they were out of here."

"How about the white units?" Jerrod asked.

"They select their residents more based on... what's the right word... 'sophistication.'"

"Sophistication?'" Jerrod parroted.

"Well," Alpo said, "it's along the lines of those who have done time in prison and those who have not. The ex-cons have very little patience for the younger 'skinheads' and 'peckerwoods.'"

"And that creates friction," Jerrod said.

"To put it mildly, yes," Alpo said. "The good news is the bikers tend to get along with either group."

"Okay," Jerrod said. "'D' and 'E' Unit are covered. What's up with the United Nations that's in 'F.'"

"'F' is... uh... special... needs... ish," Alpo said as they walked to the door. "'F' inmates can't be housed with many other inmates for a variety of reasons."

"Such as?"

"This is where the rapists, those with 'snitch jackets,' the 'Short-Eyes,' and the 'Hot-Med J-Cats' live."

"And Asians," one of the male DOs added.

"And Asians," Alpo repeated.

"'Rapists and snitches, I can understand," Jerrod said. "But I have no idea what 'short-somethings' or a 'hot cats' are.

The two DOs erupted in laughter.

Alpo's face got serious. He glanced at the DOs and they stopped laughing. "The 'J-Cats,' or 'Category J's' as they're known in the prison system, are the seriously mentally disturbed inmates. 'Hot meds' are the ridiculously powerful drugs we give them to keep them from killing each other... or themselves."

The faces of the two DOs had also become serious.

Alpo continued, "'Short-Eyes' are the 'Chomos' or 'Chesters.' The pedophiles. The child molesters. We have to protect them while they are here."

"I see," Jerrod said.

"The inmates in these places have their own form of justice, sir. Anyone who's a snitch and any sex offender, especially if they're accused of violating a child, is automatically 'green-lighted.' That is, they will be instantly attacked on-sight if any inmate can get their hands on him. That's not a great position to be in while in custody."

Alpo leaned his head toward the microphone of the radio to listen. "Problem in Intake," he said to Jerrod. "Let's go."

Alpo walked at a fast clip toward Booking. He looked at Jerrod. "Sir, move quickly, but don't run in here."

"Got it. Thanks."

In the Intake area, the male Booking DO and a young male Mesa police officer had a struggling middle-aged man pinned upright against the padded wall in the intake sallyport. The man screamed obscenities and tried to spit at the police officer. "Fuck you. I'm going to sue your ass."

"What's happened?" Alpo yelled to the DO.

"Came off the wall when I was searching him."

Alpo looked to the Mesa officer. "What's he in for?"

"'Deuce-crash.' Totaled his car into a power pole."

A "deuce-crash" is a drunk driver who is arrested after a traffic collision.

Alpo stepped into the sallyport, grabbed the out-of-control man by his shoulders, and told the Mesa officer, "You can leave the room. We've got it from here."

The Mesa officer hesitated.

Alpo raised his voice. "I said we have this. Get out."

The Mesa officer stepped out and Jerrod moved between the officer and the sallyport doorway.

The man continued yelling and redirected his venom it at the DO.

Alpo pulled the man back and then slammed him forward into the padded wall. The impact caused the man to stop struggling.

Alpo leaned his massive weight against the pinned man and talked directly into his ear. "Listen to me, fuckhead. You're gonna be here awhile, so unless you like getting bounced off of walls -- calm down and go with the program."

The man eked out a barely audible, "Okay," and Alpo moved his weight off him.

The DO finished his search of the now compliant man and he was placed in an adjacent holding room.

The Mesa officer looked at Jerrod and peaked down at the sergeant's chevrons sewn on his sleeves before nodding toward Alpo, "I don't think he got hugged much as a child, Sarge."

Jerrod replied, "Comment noted. Now unless you have any more business here, you're free to leave."

"Coffee, sir," Alpo said.

Jerrod looked at his watch. It was 4:35. "Why not."

In the lounge, Jerrod added more creamer than before to cut the stale bitterness of the staff coffee.

"Not a bad night, I guess," Jerrod said.

"It's not over yet, sir."

"I guess so."

"When I was growing up," Alpo started. "My mama used this big metal kettle with a tight lid to cook meals in. A pressure cooker."

"My mom had one. I'm familiar."

"Well, mama would fill that pot up, twist the lid on, and give it the fire. Once it got cooking, steam would hiss out of top under a little knob that would rock back and forth."

"Sure."

"Mama told all us kids that we should never touch that little knob, because, if we did, the kettle would explode and kill everyone in a four-mile radius."

Jerrod smiled. "Ever mess with it?"

Alpo chuckled. "Hell yeah. Tell a little boy not to touch something. Shit."

"I'm sure this is going somewhere, right?"

"My point... sir... is that this jail is just like that pressure cooker. Always on simmer. Everything can be going on just fine, but if someone touches the knob -- it can kick-off instantly."

"Clever analogy, Alpo. Use that story on all the new sergeants?"

Alpo looked away. "Maybe."

Jerrod sipped the coffee. "I noticed all our officers carry some equipment on their duty belts."

Alpo nodded.

"A radio, a set of handcuffs, and a pouch of some sort. What's in that?"

Alpo unfastened the pouch from his belt and pulled the contents out. "Here you go, sir." He spread out a pair vinyl gloves and a plastic CPR mask."

"Do a lot of CPR in here?" Jerrod asked.

"Once in a while," Alpo said. "The mask makes a better seal and eliminates direct contact during mouth-to-mouth." Alpo grinned. "Ever have to give CPR respiration without a mask?"

"Sadly, yes," Jerrod said. "A drunk guy who got hit by a car in Valle Verde and a young fellow who hanged himself in mid-county."

"Save either of them?"

"To use a baseball term, Alpo, I am '0-for-2.'"

"I'll get you a pouch and mask from the jail nurse. Just in case."

"Thank you. We get a lot of medical emergencies in here?"

"All day and all night," Alpo replied. "Seizures, heart problems, heroin and other-drug withdrawals, and the 'DTs' -- delirium tremens -- in alcoholics."

Jerrod nodded.

"And that's just the staff," Alpo added. "Inmates have it worse."

"You're pretty entertaining, Alpo."

Alpo smiled as he listened to some radio traffic from Housing.

"Since we're on a roll here -- please tell me about our 'Hostage Policy." Jerrod asked. "I've seen that sign out in the prisoner sallyport a hundred times, but never paid any attention to it."

Alpo thought for a second. "'Hostage Policy' should actually read, 'No-Hostage Policy.' Those same red signs are also hanging in the Lobby, Visiting, and inside each housing unit right by the door."

"How does it work?"

"Basically, if any staff, nurse, visitor, attorney, anybody, is taken hostage by inmates -- both the hostage and the inmates know that under no circumstance will we bargain with them or allow them to leave the facility. We'll do everything we can to get the hostage released, but no one leaves the building."

Jerrod thought for a moment. "What if, say, I was taken hostage and ordered you to let the inmate go? Would you have to do it?"

Alpo sipped his coffee. "I'd tell you it's been a pleasure—"

Jerrod interrupted. "I'm serious."

"Okay. Let's up the ante a little: Sheriff Osborn comes in here all the time. Unannounced. He looks around the place and talks to staff."

"Okay."

"Say the sheriff, himself, is taken hostage and orders you and me and everyone else in sight to let an inmate go. What would you do?"

"Say 'no'... and get fired later."

Alpo made a buzzer sound. "Sorry, wrong answer."

Jerrod laughed.

"If any, I repeat *any*, staff is taken hostage -- they immediately lose their authority and are unable, per the policy the sheriff signed -- to give any orders, regardless of rank."

"Good to know. Thank you."

A female Booking DO came to the Watch Commander's office doorway. "Alpo. Everyone we can release are gone, but there's one guy in holding refusing to sign-out. He says he wants to talk to 'whoever's in-charge.'"

"I'll be out in a second," Alpo said.

"Room 2. Only one in there," she added.

"Thanks."

"See what I mean?" Jerrod asked.

"See what? Alpo answered.

"The hostility."

"I don't understand, sir."

"That DO just came into *my* office, ignored *me*, addressed *you*, and said someone wanted to talk to *whoever was in-charge*. Right?"

"Yeah. Sure. So?"

"So, answer me this: Who's *in-charge* of this shift right now, Alpo?"

"You are, sir. Unquestionably."

Jerrod and Alpo went to the door of the holding room, and they found it occupied by the resistive deuce-crash arrestee from earlier in the shift. The man was agitated and banged his hand on the thick window.

"Is this a common thing?" Jerrod asked. "I've always expected people didn't want to come in here -- but would have no problem being let out."

"It's not that uncommon. But if he doesn't sign-out now, he'll have to sit for another hour, or so, and dayshift will have to deal with him."

Alpo reached for the doorknob. "I'll just bounce him off the wall again and see if that works."

"Hang on a second," Jerrod said.

Alpo let go of the knob.

"Fuck you. Fuck you, cops." the man yelled. "Blow me. Come in here and I'll kick your ass."

"How long do we have until he won't be able to sign-out on our shift?"

Alpo looked at his watch. "Twenty minutes."

"Remind me again who's in-charge here."

"You are, sir."

"I'll bet you one dollar I can talk him into signing-out... by six-thirty... and he'll even shake my hand on the way out."

Alpo looked at the man in holding -- now with the middle finger on both hands extended at them. "You have a bet, sir."

Jerrod opened the door, stepped inside the holding room, and eased the door closed -- but not latched. The smell inside was fetid.

"What's your first name, pal," Jerrod asked.

"'Eat Shit,' is my first name." the man yelled. "And 'Go Fuck Yourself' is my last... and I'm not your pal."

"I doubt your name is really "Eat Shit,'" Jerrod said. His voice calm and low. "I'll bet it's 'Andy' or 'Steve' or something like that."

"It's none of your goddamn business," the man screamed.

"Am I yelling at you?" Jerrod asked.

"No. I am just pissed," he said -- his volume having come down a notch.

"Gonna be in a little trouble when you get home?"

"This is my second DUI." His volume dropped again. "And I wrecked our only car. I'll be in more than just trouble."

Jerrod said in nearly a whisper. "I can't fix what's happened already, but I can get you out of this stinky room."

"It does stink in here. You should do something about that."

"I'll do just that, but we need to get you out first. There's an officer waiting for you to sign for your personal items and some other stuff."

"Then I can go?"

"Then you can go." Jerrod pushed open the door. "After you, sir."

The man, now calm and cooperative, walked out of the room and into Booking.

Alpo watched and shook his head as they walked by.

The man signed the booking sheet, a promise-to-appear in court, and collected his personal items.

"Is it cold outside?" the man asked.

Jerrod paused. "I haven't been out all night. I don't know. But I'll walk out with you."

"Thanks," the man said as he stuck out his hand and Jerrod shook it.

"Central Security. Watch Commander," Jerrod radioed. "Booking to Lobby, please." He glanced at his watch as the sallyport door unlocked. It was 6:28.

Jerrod walked back into Booking and Alpo handed him a one-dollar bill.

Jerrod snapped the bill. "Money won is twice as sweet as money earned."

"Sir, I would have taken a hundred dollar bet that you wouldn't be able to talk that guy out."

"Thanks. I'm sure you'll get more opportunities to win your buck back."

Sunday Night

Alpo stepped into the Watch Commander's Office. "I promised you a tour of East Housing, sir. Is now a good time?"

Jerrod looked up from the Detention Bureau Policy binder he had been studying. "Yeah. Sure."

As Jerrod and Alpo passed Central Security on their left and were about to enter Times Square, Jerrod stopped and pointed out a series of four small rooms with a table and two plastic chairs inside them. The walls were, floor to ceiling, made of reinforced glass which allowed an unobstructed view. One of the rooms had a metal cage with a lockable sliding door in it. One chair sat inside the cage. Another sat outside.

"What are those rooms used for, Alpo?"

"Those are attorney visit rooms. Defense attorneys are in there all the time and use those rooms to talk to their clients."

Jerrod nodded.

"Unlike the regular inmate visiting rooms down there." He gestured down a hallway leading to the public lobby. "These attorney rooms are not monitored, and we can't hear what they are talking about."

"And the cage?"

"That's for our maximum-security inmates. They can have no direct contact with anyone in this facility... including their attorney."

"Good to know. Thanks."

They walked to the right through Times Square and into East Housing. It was a mirror image of West Housing and was staffed by two male and one female DOs. Introductions were made and Jerrod wasn't shocked when he received lukewarm greetings.

"Sir, it's set up just like West Housing -- six units -- each identified by a letter designation."

Jerrod nodded.

Alpo led Jerrod to "G" Unit. "This is where the male inmate-workers live. As I mentioned yesterday, all are sentenced, so they have to be segregated from unsentenced inmates."

Jerrod watched inmates in white scrubs watch TV and play cards in the remarkably subdued unit.

"'H'" and 'I' Units are both for unsentenced female inmates waiting for trial, sir. 'J' is for sentenced female inmates doing county time."

They moved to the windows for "I" as women in maroon jumpsuits went about their business.

"A male DO," Alpo added, "can only enter any of these three units when accompanied by a female DO."

"Okay," Jerrod said. "Now I see no one in the dayroom of both 'K' and 'L.' Why is that?"

"Those are both 'rackdown' units,"Alpo answered. "'K' is a disciplinary unit and 'L' is our maximum-security unit."

"What does 'rackdown' mean? And please explain the difference between these units."

"'Rackdown,'" Alpo explained, "means twenty-three hours inside the cell with one hour out to shower, exercise, watch TV, and make phone calls."

Jerrod nodded.

"One inmate at a time,' Alpo continued, "no direct contact with any other inmates."

"And the difference?" Jerrod asked.

"Inmates in 'K' have violated major facility rules -- smuggling contraband, assaulting other inmates or staff, found with a weapon--"

"I get the idea," Jerrod interrupted.

"Those inmates can be placed in disciplinary rackdown for a maximum period of time."

"And 'L?'"

"Those inmates are classified as 'maximum security' due their criminal sophistication, the nature of the crimes they're here on, assaultive behavior, and prior escape attempts. They wear yellow jumpsuits."

Jerrod scanned the "L" Unit's spartan and lifeless interior. "Inmates that are classified by their general badass-ness, Alpo?"

"That's not an official classification, sir," Alpo chuckled. "But pretty accurate."

"Thanks for the tour."

CHAPTER 40

"I see that having Nikki in your life has been a very positive thing," Sidney Yamamoto said.

Jerrod sat on the sofa across from him. They were thirty minutes into their bi-weekly session. "She has," he said. "She tends to get me back to ground when my mind takes off and I get distracted. She sort of protects me from myself."

"You're lucky to have found her," Sidney said. "She sounds to be very strong and compassionate."

"Yes," Jerrod chuckled. "She's strong and kindhearted... to a fault."

"Please explain?"

"Okay. For example. Turns out that that man I shot behind city hall was a regular at the restaurant Nikki manages. I guess he's been going there for years with his son. Nikki makes friends with everyone -- including all her customers."

"Keep going."

"She feels sorry for the son, Kirk. So, she went to the funeral for his father, and they had coffee together after. She suggested I sit down with Kirk and share my feelings about the shooting."

"How *do* you feel about that?" Sidney asked. "You tend to talk in anecdotes and faux humor, but not with much emotion or candor."

"Sidney, I have emotion. Once in a while. Some stuff gets to me. Remember that movie back in the 70s -- *Brian's Song.*"

"I'm talking about real emotion. About real things. And real people."

Jerrod thought. "Sure. I don't know. Sometimes. Not really."

"Was it difficult just admitting that?"

"Not difficult. Just the way it is. We've already had this discussion. Good and bad. Same thing. Remember."

"I remember," Sidney said. "Back to Nikki. Do you confide in her the things you feel and hold inside you?"

"To be honest, I do my best to protect her from those things."

"You are good at compartmentalizing subjects that make you uncomfortable?"

"Yes."

"And I suspect," Sidney continued, "you only talk about those uncomfortable things with those who will understand... mostly other policemen."

"Sometimes. Not always," Jerrod said while staring at the carpet. "We tend to get it out of our systems over beer at the end of a shift."

"A party?" Sidney asked.

"Kind of. We call it a 'CP.'" Jerrod corrected. "Anyone can call for a 'CP' after a bad shift."

"What's a 'CP?'"

"'Choir Practice.'"

"Do you sing there?"

"No." Jerrod laughed. "We drink and bullshit and go home and sleep for a few hours and do it again the next night."

"Why do you call it a 'Choir Practice?'"

"That term came from a Joseph Wambaugh novel -- *The Choirboys*. Get it? Choirboys? Choir Practice?"

"I think so. Do you drink a lot now, Jerrod?"

"Not like I used to."

"That's all relative, I suppose."

"I can quantify it for you." Jerrod sat upright. "I will have a beer or two when I get home after work. Maybe some beer and a cocktail on weekends. If I'm going to be driving, I have only one drink. I don't drink before work, and I don't drink during work. I never drink if I'm driving a 'G-ride.'"

"A 'G-ride?' I'm afraid I don't know what that is."

Jerrod chuckled. "A 'G-ride' is an unmarked county-issued car. We also call it a 'take-home car.' The 'G' stands for 'Government.'"

Sidney nodded, took a note, and a long pause followed.

"Are we making progress?" Jerrod asked.

Sidney scoffed. "We haven't scratched the surface yet. You were very brave coming here to talk with me. It shows you understand the trauma you have experienced."

"I'm not a fucking victim, Sidney. I just need help sorting things out. Like the reason I came here in the first place: how I can kill a man and not react to it? Have I become that callous? Is there going to be some type of delayed reaction? I need some answers."

"You're talking about it now. The answers will come."

CHAPTER 41

Saturday Night -- Mesa County Jail

"What do you do for fun, Alpo?" Jerrod asked. "Sports? Music? Hunt? Fish?"

"Oh, I hunt, sir. Squirrels mostly."

"Squirrels?"

"Sure." Alpo looked off to a corner of the room. "I love to go up into the redwoods with my .22 and bring home a whole mess of squirrels. Good eatin', sir. Yum."

"Squirrels." Jerrod curled his nose. "Please don't tell me they taste like chicken."

"Not like chicken, sir." He thought for a second. "More like possum."

"Different strokes, I guess," Jerrod said.

"Just pulling your leg, sir. I'm from Alabama, not Louisiana. I buy my food at the store like most other people. What kind of redneck do you think I am?

"I... uh... hope that question is rhetorical."

"What does that mean?"

"Never mind."

"I'll tell you what I like to do, but it may sound silly," Alpo said. "I like to go down to the beach at the break of dawn with my metal detector and scan for treasure."

"Any luck?"

"You'd be surprised, sir." Alpo smiled. "Lots of junk. Mostly bottle caps, foil, and other garbage. But also plenty of coins and jewelry and watches and sunglasses and other valuables. The 'towel line' is especially lucrative."

"The 'towel line?'"

"The area right above high tide where people put their towels down. Sunscreen and slippery fingers make for a very successful bounty for me."

"Fascinating."

Jerrod was in the Watch Commander's Office when Alpo walked in and plopped a stack of pink forms in the in-basket. Jerrod picked up the stack. "What are these?"

169

"Inmate Grievance Forms. If inmates have a problem with a rule, or request, or really any kind of complaint, they fill out the form and it goes to the Watch Commander for review."

"What do I do with them?"

"Typically, you review 'em, deny 'em, sign 'em, and return a copy to the inmate. The original goes into their C-File."

"What's a "C-File, Alpo?"

"'Central File' or 'Custody File.' The file we keep on all inmates here. Booking information, property inventory, bail records, court papers, disciplinary reports, and... inmate grievances. The file is kept in Booking while the inmate is here and goes to Records when they leave."

"To make it easier for you," Alpo continued. "Medical stuff just goes to Medical. The jail nurses and contract doctors handle that. Minor discipline punishment can't be appealed. Major discipline can be appealed, but we really don't have a way to do that. We kind of have to wing it."

"Okay," Jerrod said. "Let's take a look."

"Sir, I took the liberty of reviewing them, uh, already. To keep you from being... how to say this... from being overwhelmed tonight."

"Very thoughtful, Alpo. Thank you."

"Anytime, sir."

Jerrod thumbed through the complaint forms handwritten in thick felt pen. "Do the inmates use Magic Markers to write these things?"

Alpo smiled. "No pencils or ball-point pens are allowed in the housing units -- they're too easy to make into weapons. We issue felt pens."

Alpo left the office and Jerrod started reading the complaints. Each one listed the inmate's name, the date, their assigned identification number, and the housing unit they reside. Most contained slang, spelling errors, and an overall in-cohesiveness that made them difficult to read: One was a request for a second mattress, another was to arrange a contact visit with a family member, and a third said the inmate had a toothache, the fourth was written in Spanish, and a fifth he simply could not make out what the inmate was asking for.

One grievance was different: Handwritten in perfect block letters, the well-drafted document articulated a complaint regarding a major infraction after a "shakedown" in his housing unit. The three-page grievance was structured like a legal brief -- with a clearly defined introduction, a table of contents, a persuasive statement of facts, an argument stating legal authorities, and a compelling summary.

Jerrod noted the inmate's name to be "Bradley Sean Stapleton" and he resided in "F" Unit -- the "special needs-ish" housing.

Jerrod went into Booking and got the attention of a female DO. "May I have the C-file for an inmate named "Bradley Stapleton."

"Sure," the DO said as she grabbed the handle of a wide metal filing cabinet under the booking counter. She pulled the thickest file from the cabinet and used two hands to lift the file to Jerrod.

"Thank you," Jerrod said.

"Stapleton's a piece of work, Sarge" the DO said. "He never stops moving. He's as smart as they get and pretty hard to talk to."

Jerrod thumbed through Stapleton's file and noted he had been charged with multiple felony counts involving financial fraud. His bail had been set at five-hundred-thousand dollars and the court papers listed his attorney as being "pro per" or as representing himself.

Jerrod went to West Housing and asked the male DO to pull Bradley Sean Stapleton out of "F" Unit.

"He's already out, Sarge. He's in the law library. Been there about an hour."

The law library was located just off Times Square. Large windows allowed an open view into the room. A shelf contained a variety of California and Federal law books, there was a single table, a locked storage cabinet, and a manual typewriter.

Bradley Sean Stapleton -- around forty, skinny, pale, clean shaven, orange jumpsuit buttoned to the top -- sat alone at the table. He had a book open and was taking notes onto a legal pad.

"Mr. Stapleton?" Jerrod asked as he stepped through the doorway.

"Bradley Sean Stapleton" is my name and that's how I wish to be addressed."

"That's a lot of name," Jerrod replied. "Can't we just use 'Bradley' or 'Brad?'"

Stapleton looked at him but didn't respond. He was a ball of quirky energy. Hands gestured. Legs bounced.

"Have it your way," Jerrod said. "What are you working on?"

Stapleton turned the legal pad over. "My defense."

"I noted in you file you were 'pro per.' Do you have some legal background?"

"I've been to law school."

"Get your JD? Your 'Juris Doctor,' sir."

"Didn't complete my studies."

"That serial killer -- Theodore Bundy -- didn't complete his studies and was *pro per* too. Didn't work out so well for him."

"I'll take my chances. It's not like I'm getting any help--"

"Help from who?"

"I've said too much already."

"Okay." Jerrod raised the pink grievance form Stapleton had prepared. "Too bad you didn't finish school, I read your brief on the matter and am truly impressed."

"Thank you. So, you must concur with my assessment. A major infraction is not warranted."

"Well, it's not that easy," Jerrod said. "A piece of carbon paper was found in your cell. I'm still new at this assignment and just learned that carbon paper must remain in the law library. It's considered contraband in Housing. Apparently, inmates in the past have extracted ink from the paper to make tattoos."

Stapleton pulled up the sleeves of his jumpsuit. "I have no tattoos, Sergeant."

"I trust that to be true, but the rule exists all the same," Jerrod said. "However, I do know pro per inmates get priority use of the law library and its supplies."

"At least someone in this facility finally understands that," Stapleton said. "I have a hard time getting access on a regular basis."

"I've reduced the offense from a major to a minor infraction," Jerrod said, "and the penalty will be the loss of one commissary. "

"As you wish," Stapleton resigned. "That's a fair compromise."

"Be warned," Jerrod added. "A future violation will not be treated as generously."

"Understood."

"And I'll ensure you get as much time in here as you need to prepare your defense."

"Thank you, Sergeant, for your time on this matter. If I may get back to my case?"

"Of course. Have a good evening."

"What's happening here, Alpo?"

Jerrod watched a group of inmate workers with large rolling hampers and a single-file line of inmates at the open door of "B" Unit. The group of Latino inmates wore only brownish-colored towels around their waists.

"Clothing exchange, sir," Alpo said. "Each unit. Twice a week. Two sheets. One towel. One jumpsuit. One set of underwear."

Jerrod watched the inmates toss the sheets, jumpsuit, a second towel, and their t-shirts, briefs, and socks into a hamper. Each inmate was then given the same fresh items in return.

Jerrod asked. "Alpo, why are the sheets white, but the underwear and towels brown?"

"Skid marks, sir." He smiled. "Shit stains. The replacements are clean, but... uh... previously used. Inmates would fistfight to get a brand-new pair of tighty-whiteys."

"Where does one buy brown underwear?"

"We buy the white ones," Alpo said. "But we dye them that color. It was an inmate worker's idea. There's one washing machine in laundry we use to do the dying."

"Brilliant," Jerrod said.

"It's quite an art, sir. It took a few tries to get the color just right. Those dyes can be a little tricky. Little brown. Little green. Little yellow."

"So, everyone now just gets clean, but shit-stain-colored underclothes?"

"Bras and panties too, sir," Alpo added. "Lady inmates get equal treatment around here."

Jerrod went to one of the large windows and looked into "B" Unit. Male and female DOs were busy searching the cells and Jerrod saw various contraband items being tossed from the cells into a common pile.

"'Shakedowns,' sir," Alpo said as he moved beside Jerrod. "We search -- 'shakedown' -- the units at clothing exchange. Extra clothing. Extra food. Extra razors. Extra toothbrushes. Pictures pasted on the walls. And we're always looking for anything that can become a weapon."

"Such as?"

"Any piece of loose metal will become a 'shank'... uh... a stabbing weapon," Alpo said. "Razors taken out of the handle are obvious, but extra toothbrushes can be melted down made into a shank. That's why we cut the handles off. Extra little pieces of soap can be pressed into a

173

ball, placed in a sock, and that can make a pretty effective blunt-force weapon."

Jerrod chuckled. "'Shank' means something completely different on the golf course. Neither one is good."

"I wouldn't know, sir," Alpo said.

"Do these inmates get written-up for all this contraband?" Jerrod asked.

"Nah. We just take it and ruin their day."

"So, what deters these inmates from just accumulating more contraband if there are no consequences for having it?"

"Nothing, sir."

"Let's make this the last 'freebee' inmates get," Jerrod said. "Next time we shakedown a unit for any reason, every inmate found with contraband gets written-up."

"Copy that, sir."

Sunday Morning

"Question for you, Alpo" Jerrod asked. "And please don't laugh. I'm serious."

"Can't promise I won't laugh until I hear it, sir."

"Okay. In the movies, they always play up the... uh... sex that happens in jails and prison. You know. Men making men do things against their will. 'Don't drop the soap.' How true is that?

Alpo let a chuckle out. "Happens all the time, sir. Like bunnies back there. Day and night."

"I should have asked someone else. I knew I wouldn't get a straight answer. Shooting squirrel. 'Tastes like opossum.' Remember?

"It's not near as bad as depicted on TV and in movies," Alpo said. "Does it happen here? Occasionally. But it's actually pretty rare. Most of the sexual contact here is consensual."

"You worked in the prison system," Jerrod said. "Bigger problem there?"

"Yes and no."

"Explain."

"I need to set this up: When an inmate gets to prison -- any prison -- they go through a classification process with both the prison itself and with the other inmates."

"Okay," Jerrod said.

"The prison tries to place an inmate in a facility and at a level that matches their age, conviction charges, criminal sophistication, violence potential, prior prison incidents, and other factors. They get assigned a security level based on a points system. High. Medium. Low.

"So far. So good."

"Then the inmates classify each other by race and gang affiliation. Just like the inmates in this jail does. They call it 'being in your car.'"

"Fascinating," Jerrod said.

"Whites ride with whites. Blacks ride with blacks. Latinos ride in their own 'car' -- but it's either with northerners or southsiders."

Jerrod asked, "How about, say, Asians and Native-Americans and Middle-Easterners. Do they have a 'car?'"

Those groups are considered "Others,'" Alpo said. "And they don't have a 'car.' They take the bus."

"Very funny. Back to the sex thing."

"Getting there, sir," Alpo said. "The weaker inmates -- physically smaller or new to prison or mentally not-all-there -- can get 'turned-out' when they get inside. Often that means being a 'punk' for a more respected senior inmate -- an 'OG,' or 'Original Gangster.' They run errands, clean cells, prepare food, and, often, perform sexual services in exchange for not getting beaten or extorted or forced to do... well... worse things."

"Kind of an involuntary consent deal?"

"There's no consent involved, sir. It's predator or prey inside those facilities. It's more like an act of pure survival."

"Fight in holding," a DO yelled as he and two other male DOs ran to the largest holding room near Booking.

Jerrod heard the commotion and followed from his office.

The holding room contained seven detainees. One Latino man cowered in the fetal position on the floor as a white man assailed shoeless kicks at him. The DOs pulled open the door, team-grabbed the white man, and body-slammed him to the floor. The three DOs piled on top the detainee, wrestled with him -- and each other in the process -- until they had him under control and placed him in handcuffs.

Alpo appeared, slightly out-of-breath, from his dash from Housing to Booking. "Take him to a safety cell," he directed the three DOs.

The handcuffed detainee quit struggling as he was carted, with most of his body weight suspended off the ground, by the three DOs. He was dumped, literally, into a secure and padded safety room nearby.

One of the DOs was holding his left wrist as he exited the room. It appeared he had injured it in the struggle.

The Latino detainee was helped to his feet and had no obvious injuries. The other detainees all said the white man had made the unprovoked attack after yelling some racial epitaphs.

Jerrod pointed to the safety cell. "Add '242' to that asshole's charges and get this other inmate to Medical."

"242" referred to California Penal Code section 242 -- Misdemeanor Battery.

Alpo held his palms out. "Hang on a second, Sarge."

"'Hang on,' Alpo. Are you serious? In my office. Now."

"With respect," Alpo started, "this crap happens here every night."

Jerrod plopped into his desk chair.

"Several times every night, sir. We can't arrest everyone, and it wouldn't go anywhere if we did. Unless staff gets assaulted, an inmate gets hospitalized, or someone dies -- no one outside these walls gives a shit."

Jerrod could still feel the heat of anger in his face. "That guy was getting pummeled by the other one. Unprovoked. With witnesses. And we do nothing? That's bullshit."

"Separate the combatants," Alpo said. "Check for injuries. Cut an incident report. No harm. No foul. Play the down over."

"Unbelievable," Jerrod scoffed.

"Sir, you're welcome to write up a crime report, add the 242, and see what happens for yourself." Alpo shrugged. "But you'll find it'll all be wasted time. It's different in here."

"'Different in here?'" Jerrod repeated. "It's a third-world country in here."

"Yes, sir." Alpo agreed. "Add *Lord of The Flies* too. It's all about survival. Inmates and staff."

Jerrod took in a few deep breaths. "How is our officer? He was holding his wrist after that... that... cluster-fuck... sloppy use of force in there."

"He's fine, sir. And those are called 'pig-piles.'"

"What?" Jerrod asked.

"'Pig-piles.' Alpo said. "When we use shear body weight to get control of someone until the 'cuffs go on. It's not pretty but is effective all the same."

"There's got to be a better way?"

"Only if you come up with it, sir."

"Challenge accepted."

"Anything happening back in Housing, Alpo?" Jerrod asked from the Watch Commander's desk. He was still fuming from the incident in Holding.

"Nah. Normal BS. Had a fight in 'B" Unit."

"Anyone hurt?"

"No, sir. Broke up when we got to the door. A-V-A. N-H-I."

Jerrod felt his face flush. "Close the door and sit down."

"What?" Alpo asked as he closed the door.

"Animal-Versus-Animal. No-Humans-Involved?" Jerrod asked. "Alpo, if I hear you, or any of our people, use those terms again, I'm going to take immediate action and it's going to leave a permanent scar."

"Uh... sorry... I thought...."

"The inmates in here are people. Just like you and me. They are not animals. They are not sub-human. They are not some foreign threat our government intentionally dehumanizes to make easier to destroy."

"But sir--"

Jerrod held up his palm. "Most of the inmates in here haven't been convicted of a damn thing. Nearly all are sitting around waiting for trial because they just don't have the resources to post bail. How fair is that?

"It's not."

"Alpo, do we have a lot of doctors and dentists and lawyers and CPAs -- or any of their kids -- housed back there wearing orange?"

"No."

"Please remember that we control everything in their world here and we will treat them with the same human respect we would demand if the tables were turned."

"Sir--"

"Pass the word," Jerrod interrupted as he stood up. "Do you copy?"

"Copy that, sir."

CHAPTER 42

Tuesday Afternoon

"He was in the restaurant today," Nikki said.

"That's nice," Jerrod said from his La-Z-Boy. He turned a page on the Lescroart novel -- *Dead Irish*.

"Did you hear me?"

"Yes," Jerrod said without looking up from the book. "President Bush was in the restaurant today. He had a Reuben sandwich and a Dr. Pepper. The Secret Service guys were cute."

She shook her head. "Where the hell did that come from?

"My distracted mind. That's where." He looked at her. "Who, dear, was in your fine establishment today?"

"Kirk."

"I'm just shocked by that."

"He congratulated us on getting engaged. He said he heard another customer talk about it."

Jerrod marked the spot in the book. "That's fantastic. Gonna send him an invitation?"

"Don't be silly."

Jerrod thought for a long moment. "How can I say this without pissing you off?"

"If you think it's going to piss me off -- don't say it." Her hands went to her hips.

He picked up the book and started reading again.

"Say what's on your mind, Jerrod?"

"I think you should find another job."

"Another job. What, a 'real' job?" she asked. "Managing a restaurant isn't 'real' enough?"

"I don't like that Kirk comes in there. 'Kirk,' like I've ever met the guy. Forget I said anything." He went back to the book.

"Put the damn book down. And, by the way, I don't forget anything you say."

"Yes. I'm aware of that." He motioned to the sofa. "Please sit down."

She sat.

"We're going to have two mortgages right after the wedding. I'm looking for someone to rent this house now. We're going to need as much income as we can get and be careful how we spend what we do have."

"'House poor,'" she said. "I just had this conversation with my mom."

"What did Bernice have to say?" He was looking for an ally... any ally.

"Same thing you did." She looked out the front window. "I've been at that restaurant since high school. Lilly and Marty were practically raised there. I have so many friends from that place."

Jerrod nodded.

"Mom offered me a job at the roofing company. Full time. Managing the office. Billing. Payroll. She wants to slow down a little."

Jerrod scooted forward in his chair. "You'd be helping her out. Sounds like that has some potential."

"I met Blake there." Tears formed. "I'll be reminded of him every day."

"I never want you to forget him, Nikki. Or for the kids to forget, either. He was a great man who got a bad break."

She pushed a tear away. "I'll think about it."

"Jerrod," Nikki asked. "I need to go to the restaurant for a couple hours."

Jerrod was watching a movie from his recliner. "Have a wonderful time."

"The girls will be home about three-thirty. Can you make sure their homework is done before they go back out?"

Jerrod didn't look away from the screen. "Homework before play. Copy that."

"Thank you."

"Want us to make dinner?" he asked.

She hesitated. "That's a very nice offer... but I don't want to clean the kitchen after you're done in there."

"Ouch."

"Seriously. I'll make dinner when I get home. Should be between five and five thirty."

"We'll find something to do."

"I'm afraid of that too."

"And I have a session with Sidney tonight."

"Of course, Sidney," she said as she closed the door.

At three thirty, Lilly and Marty walked into the house.

"Where's mom?" Lilly asked.

"Yeah, where's mom?" Marty parroted.

"She had to go to the restaurant. It's you girls and me for a couple hours... after homework gets done."

"No homework," both girls said in unison.

"Want to go to a park or something?"

"Nah," Lilly said.

"Nah," Marty said.

"Fine. You're going to miss me when I'm gone."

"Where are you going?" Marty asked.

"Figure of speech, honey. Figure of speech."

The girls changed out of their school clothes and headed for the front door.

"Bye, Jerrod," Lilly said. "Going to Grama Laura's."

"Bye," Marty said. "Going to my friend's down the street."

"Fine. Be home by five."

After the front door closed behind the girls, Jerrod turned off the television and found himself alone in a very quiet place. He had become used to the constant level of chaos and noise and energy and life the two young girls and their mother had brought to the house.

His face drew dour as he recalled the time he lived alone in the house after the shooting of Armando Mendoza. He shook his head as he recalled the private hell he created for himself by using prescription medications and alcohol to dull the pain and how he came so close to walking in front a moving truck to end it all.

A smile spread across his face as he counted the blessings he had enjoyed since Nikki and the girls entered his life. He was, indeed, a very lucky man.

Jerrod saw Lilly through the window as she walked back to the house. Always punctual, it was a few minutes to five. He hid behind the front door and as it closed behind her, said in a gravelly voice, "Thanks for coming home on time."

Lilly jumped and flailed her arms before falling to the carpet. He thought she had fainted.

"Don't do that!" she scolded.

"I'm sorry, honey," Jerrod said as he helped her to her feet. "I didn't mean to scare you. Well, I did... but not that much."

"I don't like being scared." Tears appeared in her eyes.

"I said I was sorry. But what would you do if a stranger had been behind the door instead of me?"

"I don't know."

Jerrod thought for a second. "You should know."

Marty walked into the house at three minutes past five -- close enough to "on-time" for that child. "What're you guys doing?"

"Jerrod scared me," Lilly said. "I almost peed my pants."

Marty giggled.

"And she freaked out," Jerrod added. "You girls need to know how to defend yourself if someone attacks you."

"Like the boogeyman?" Marty asked.

"Sure. Like anyone who touches you or scares you or tries to take you. You have to fight back and get away."

Lilly asked, "How do I do that?"

"I'll show you."

They moved the coffee table and met in the middle of the living room.

Jerrod said to Lilly, "Turn and face the TV." He then walked behind her a placed her in a bear hug.

"If someone grabs you from behind like this, you yell as loud as you can and hit them in as many vital areas as possible."

Marty asked, "What's a 'vital area?'"

"Glad you asked, child. A vital area is anyplace that hurts really bad when it gets struck or scratched or stomped."

"Such as?" Lilly asked.

"The face -- eyes, nose, and mouth. The throat." He pointed to the area of his abdomen midway between his sternum and navel. "This is the solar plexus. The shins and the feet. And the ... uh--." He searched for the proper wording. "The groin area on men. Especially the groin area."

"The 'balls,'" Lilly said. "I heard that at school. Boys don't like getting hit in the 'balls.'"

"That is correct," he said. "But we need to come up with a better term for that... area."

"Let's try again," Lilly said.

"Mom's home," Marty announced.

Nikki walked in as Jerrod grabbed Lilly from behind again.

"Yell and fight back. Stomp down on my shin and the top of my foot and..."

Lilly raised her foot and slammed down Jerrod's leg and foot. Jerrod felt the impact.

"... and don't hurt me," he said. "Little late now. Now try to break away and scratch at my face and--"

"Mom," Marty said. "Jerrod's the boogeyman and Lilly is 'pretending' herself and she's gonna kick him in the balls."

"What the hell?" Nikki said. "Stop. No ball kicking." She looked at Marty. "And you can't say that."

"Sorry Mom," Marty said.

"Now let's try again," Jerrod said to Lilly. "Scream and fight. Use any weapon in reach. Careful on the stomping and kicking... what do we call hitting the groin... how about we call it the 'Nuclear Option.'"

Lilly had new confidence. "Ready."

Jerrod grabbed her again. She let out a blood-curdling scream, stomped down on his foot, broke out of his clinch, swiped her fingernails near his face, and kicked at his groin.

"Yeah," Jerrod said. "Just like that."

Marty clapped her hands and cheered. "In the balls. In the balls."

Nikki shook her head. "What have you done to my children?"

Jerrod shrugged.

She added, "I pity anyone who attacks either one of these girls."

Jerrod smiled. "Me too."

CHAPTER 43

"I got an EOB in the mail from my health insurance," Jerrod said as he sat on the sofa facing Sidney Yamamoto. He pulled the explanation of benefits from his pocket.

"My fees are well within the normal range for this area," Sidney said.

"I'm not concerned about the fees," Jerrod said. "I'm sure they're fair." He held up the form. "I want to know what these codes are."

Sidney studied the form for a moment and handed it back. "Those are Current Procedural Terminology or 'CPT' codes. It's a standardized way we bill for treatment."

Jerrod pointed to a specific area on the EOB. "What do these two codes mean?"

"The first is the code for 'post-traumatic stress disorder' and the second is for 'depression.'"

"PTSD and depression?" Jerrod asked. "I came to see you because I didn't have PTSD. And, for your information, I'm not depressed."

"Jerrod," Sidney said. "You, my friend, have both. And I'm here to help you with them."

Jerrod scoffed and thought for a flash to just get up and leave. "Explain, please."

"Okay," Sidney said. "During our sessions, I let you talk freely, and I ask questions here or there. Correct?"

"Yes."

"I also watch what you do -- how you answer and how you move -- in addition to what you tell me and your responses to the questions I pose. Although you hide it well in public, you give clear indicators you are suffering from both PTSD and depression. Want an example?"

"Yes."

"When we talk, you typically cross one leg over the other knee and your foot doesn't stop moving for much of our session."

Jerrod looked at his bouncing foot and stopped it.

"That is an indicator of agitation -- as does your rubbing of that scar on the back of your right hand."

Jerrod took his hand off the scar.

"With the tumultuous family history you have described -- the divorce, your mother's remarriage, the disappearance of your brother, and others -- coupled with your choice of professions and the violence you have both seen and been a part of -- all indicate you have many unresolved issues. PTSD and depression have resulted."

Jerrod puffed his cheeks as Sidney's words sunk in. "Are you saying not having symptoms *is* a symptom."

"But you *do* have symptoms," Sidney said. "I have a question for you."

"Go ahead."

"I've never been to your home," he continued, "but I've listened to you reference these things a few times."

"Okay," Jerrod said.

"You do all of your own landscaping? You detail your own cars?"

"Of course."

"Ever thought to hire that work out? Pay a landscaper or take your vehicle to a car wash?"

"No."

"Why?"

"Because they couldn't do as good a job--" Jerrod had just listened to his own words.

"Precisely," Sidney said. "They couldn't do as good of a job as you can. No one can. You see that as a source of pride. I see hypervigilance as a symptom. You are doing everything you can to control the world around you because, deep down, you feel you have no control."

Jerrod shook his head. "Well, fuck me."

"We'll continue to peel the onion one layer at a time," Sidney offered.

"The 'onion' being my brain?"

"Your *mind*. But the same general area. Yes."

"Sidney. None of this can get back to the sheriff's office. I beg you. I'd be ruined."

"Our sessions are confidential. You already know that."

"Thank you."

CHAPTER 44

Willowmere Police Chief Doreen Salt had a good job. Resort town. Small department. Big budget. Affluent residents. A very good job.

The twenty-two-year law enforcement professional had earned every commendation and promotion she had received in the otherwise male-dominated profession.

She had moved up the ranks of a large Northern California sheriff's office through the winning combination of smarts, courage, and stamina. She went to college while working unpredictable shifts, earned both an undergraduate and a graduate degree, and rose to the rank of undersheriff.

Tough and affable. Demanding and cordial. Fit and feminine. No one had ever questioned Doreen Salt's qualifications or ability to do the job. Any job.

She had married a California Highway Patrol officer ten years her senior. Their careers leapfrogged as they moved up the ranks of their respective departments. When he retired in 1989, they escaped California's Central Valley heat and traveled to the ocean-cooled beach community of Willowmere to celebrate.

While in Willowmere, she learned the police department's longtime chief was retiring and the city was looking for candidates from outside the area to replace him. She mulled a decision, applied for the position, and six-months later was sworn in as the Willowmere Chief of Police.

"Chief," the young, uniformed desk officer said. "There's a man in the lobby who says he has an appointment to see you."

"His name?" Chief Salt asked.

The young officer looked at the note he had written on the palm of his hand. "Yes, ma'am. Mr. Sullivan... uh... Mr. General Michael Sullivan, ma'am."

"Would you escort him to my office, please."

"Sure... ma'am... Chief."

Retired General Michael T. Sullivan had a swagger. Shoulders back. Head straight. Hair cropped. Eyes clear. Even to someone who didn't know anything about men's fashion -- his tailored suit, crisp white shirt, silk tie, and high-polished shoes meant business and commanded respect.

"Please have a seat... General... I guess," the chief said after she stood and shook hands.

"I'm retired, Chief. Please just call me 'Michael.'"

"How many stars did you wear, *Michael?*"

"I was a Brigadier General. So, one star." He looked down at her uniform. "Just like you."

Doreen Salt had opted to wear just one star on her uniform collar instead of the traditional four stars most male police chiefs and sheriffs sported. She felt the excessive brass was mostly decoration intended to compensate for a lack of penis size. She didn't have that cross to bear.

"Very well," she said. "Your phone call was intriguing, but pretty vague. Please elaborate... but stay concise. I have a department to run."

Sullivan unbuttoned his suit coat and looked around the small office. "Very well. Okay. We think you should be the next Mesa County sheriff and we want to help you do that."

Chief Salt leaned back in her chair. "I've got the best job in the world here. Why would I want to be sheriff?"

"Because the Mesa sheriff has a history of not promoting females," Sullivan said. "In the entire 100-year history of the agency, only one female has been promoted up to the rank of sergeant. And that was just last year. We want to change that."

The chief was listening.

"The current sheriff, Wayne Osborn, and I have been friends since high school. We entered the Army together. I stayed in and made it a career while he came home and got into law enforcement."

"Okay, Michael. Wayne's had a good, long career and is ready to relax a little. I'm sure there are some very qualified people who will run to replace him."

"We're pretty sure Eric Blanchard is going to run. But there it is -- we don't think another white male should continue leading the sheriff's office."

"You're a *white male,* Michael," her eyebrows rose as she spoke. "And who the hell are the 'we' you keep referring to?"

"Sorry. 'We' are a group of local business... uh... people who just care about our community. We have a long history here in Mesa County and access to funding and other resources."

"A group of local business... uh... *men,* I presume?"

"Yes. But--"

"I'm not interested," Chief Salt interrupted. "Find someone else for your cause. I'm fine right here. Thank you for your time."

General Michael Sullivan was not used to being told no. "There's another issue we're very concerned about."

The chief stood up. "What's that?"

"That sheriff's sergeant who struck your officer with that shotgun. Jerrod Gold. We all saw what happened on TV and were upset he wasn't fired and charged criminally for that unprovoked attack. We think he got off too light for what he did."

Chief Doreen Salt sat back down. "Tell me more."

CHAPTER 45

"Hey Alpo," Jerrod said. "Check this out."

"What's up, Sarge?"

"We have a new tool in our arsenal. You challenged me a few weeks ago to come up with a solution to the 'pig-pile' problem. Here it is."

"Okay"

"I convinced The Brass we needed a new use of force option, and your sergeant always gets what he needs."

"Impressive, sir. What is it?"

"'Oleoresin Capsicum,' or just 'OC,'" Jerrod said as he examined one of the two black and red spray-top cylinders on his desk. "It's better known as 'pepper spray.'"

"Why do we need that, sir? "

"Violent inmate situations. I've never been a fan of the old chemical mace -- CN and CS tear gas. But I heard this stuff actually works."

"We take care of 'violent inmate situations' just fine without chemicals, sir." Alpo scoffed. "We just use superior violence."

"That may work great for you, Alpo. But not everyone is 250 pounds of manly-man with hands the size of catcher's mitts."

Alpo looked down at his hands and back at Jerrod. "245, sir."

"Regardless. It's a new dawn and the days of the pig-pile are coming to an end."

There was a memo and a VHS cassette accompanying the OC canisters. Jerrod read the memo to Alpo: "All Detention Bureau Watch Commanders, SDOs, and DOs were to view the California Peace Officer Standard and Training tape -- "POST Oleoresin Capsicum" -- and were then authorized to use OC pursuant to the Escalation and Use of Force Policy. No actual test exposure to the chemical agent was required by personnel."

"Let's go watch a movie," Jerrod said.

Off the Lobby were the Reception desk and the private offices of the lieutenant assigned as the Jail Commander and the Chief Deputy assigned as the head of the Detention Bureau. Between their offices was a conference room which housed a large wooden table and enough chairs for twelve people. On a portable stand in the corner was a 35-inch TV attached to a VHS player.

189

The nineteen-minute POST tape was slightly comical, but educational all the same. They learned that OC was a resin made from ground chili peppers mixed in a solvent. When sprayed directly into the face of a violent subject; it should have immediate effects. The OC attacked the eyes, nose, throat, lungs, and skin of the subject. The subject's eyes would involuntarily close and he would experience difficulty breathing, which, in theory, would make the subject unable to fight.

It was recommended officers avoid cross-contaminating themselves and let the OC take affect before approaching and handcuffing the subject.

The tape also recommended decontaminating the subject's face and other effected areas with cool, plain water. Full recovery from exposure would be within forty-five minutes and there were no known long-term health concerns to be considered.

"Simple enough," Alpo said. "Glad we don't have to be exposed to OC as part of the training. I did that with regular tear gas in the Army and it was no fun."

"Me too," Jerrod said. "I did the same at the police academy. We called it "The Gas Chamber." I threw away the clothes I was wearing after that."

Alpo nodded. "How about we wheel this TV into the staff lounge and have all of our people watch it tonight?"

"Good idea," Jerrod said. "I'm sure we'll get to see how this stuff works. In due time."

CHAPTER 46

"Just hand me The Watchtower and have a blessed rest of your day," retired US Army Lieutenant Colonel Charles Horvath said. The spoke through the front door screen of his home to the man wearing a dark suit, white shirt, and conservative tie. "I promise to read it cover-to-cover before disposing of it with proper reverence."

"Colonel Horvath," the man replied, "I don't represent the Jehovah's Witness. But I do have an important matter to discuss with you."

"My mistake," the colonel said as he moved the door to close it. "Must be selling insurance then. I'm taken care of in that respect. Nice talking to you."

"Colonel," the man said as he moved closer. "My name is Michael Sullivan, Brigadier General, US Army, Retired. I have a few questions for you."

Jerrod had just got up after a decent six-hour sleep and was mentally preparing for another fun-filled night at the Mesa County Jail. As he sipped his second cup of coffee, Nikki, Lilly, and Marty stormed in through the front door.

"Mr. Horvath just asked me to check if you were up yet. He said he has something important to discuss... at his house."

"He came to see me," the Colonel said as he flopped into his recliner. A tall glass containing his infamous gin and grapefruit juice cocktail -- The Fat Burner -- rested half-consumed on the console table beside him.

"Who, sir?" Jerrod asked.

"Michael Sullivan. General Michael Fucking Sullivan," he said before taking a large gulp of the cocktail.

"You're kidding me?" Jerrod said. "He showed up here?"

"He knew who I was and, obviously, where I live. He knows who you are too, Jerrod, and where you live. He knew everything about us."

"How? What?"

"I had made those calls to St. Louis. You know, looking into Sullivan's service record and such. Like you asked me to."

Jerrod nodded.

"He must have been tipped-off," the Colonel said. "Someone told him I was snooping around, and he showed up here to find out why."

"That son-of-a-bitch," Jerrod said. "What did you tell him?"

"I said I was trying to find an officer I had served with the last few years of my career. 'Michael Sullivan' is, fortunately, a fairly common name."

"Did he buy it?"

"Not for a minute." The Colonel scratched his short beard. "I warned you about these former high-ranking officers being dangerous. He knew my whole record, every assignment, every promotion, every citation, and even the circumstances around that Bronze Star over there." He lifted his hand toward the shadowbox on a wall which contained his military rank devices and service ribbons.

"I'll take care of this, Colonel. You were doing me a favor. He'll never bother you again."

"Jerrod. He scared the shit out of me... and I don't scare easy." He leaned forward. "Be very careful around that man."

Before leaving the house for work a half-hour earlier than usual, Jerrod checked the Pacific Telephone White Pages under the letter "S". He dragged his finger down the pages until he found it.

Sole.

Sturm.

Sulk.

Sullivan.

Brian.

Daniel.

John.

Michael.

Sullivan, Michael&Monica, 1120 StandishCt Wil

"Michael and Monica Sullivan," Jerrod jotted onto the spiral notepad he kept in his uniform breast pocket. "1120 Standish Court, Willowmere."

Jerrod made a quick detour off the PCH on his way to the jail. He did a slow drive past a gated, winding driveway leading through lush landscape to the Mediterranean-style mansion perched on a hill. He was on Standish Court and the mailbox read: "1120."

"Bruce Witt," the voice on the phone answered.

"Jerrod Gold here. Remember what an asshole Mitchell Sullivan was -- and still is -- for that matter."

"Sure."

"Well, his father is an even bigger asshole."

"So," Bruce said.

"Want to make some quick cash from some breaking news?"

"Always."

"Okay then. Get something to write on."

10:10 PM

"Watch Commander. SDO." Alpo radioed. His tone got Jerrod's attention.

"Watch Commander. Go ahead."

"Inmate refusing to rackdown in "A" Unit. Let's test the 'hot sauce.'"

"Copy that," Jerrod said as he removed a canister of OC spray from his desk and headed to West Housing.

In the middle of the "A" Unit dayroom were Alpo, three male DOs, a female DO, and a single Latino inmate in a tense standoff. The inmate was in his mid-twenties and had the top of his orange jumpsuit tied around his waist. Jerrod noticed numerous norteño gang tattoos on his skinny arms and neck. The inmate bounced on the balls of his feet like a prize fighter.

"Inmate got pissed when we broke up their card game, Sarge," one of the DOs said. "Says he we'll have to make him rackdown."

"I was winning, asshole," the inmate yelled as he launched spittle from his mouth.

"Oh, you're gonna rackdown," Alpo warned.

"Alright. I'm ready. Come and get some," the inmate screamed. He raised his hands and took a fighting stance.

As a few of the DOs moved toward the inmate, the other inmates yelled encouragement to their comrade... from the safety of their cells.

"Stand by guys," Jerrod ordered. He was shaking the canister of OC as he turned to the inmate. "What's your name, son?"

"You don't need to know my name, *puto*," the inmate shouted.

"Puto" was Spanish slang for a male prostitute, or also used to mean "coward" or "traitor."

"Guess not," Jerrod said with a quiet, confident voice. "Well, young man, you have a decision to make. I suspect you kind of have to go down hard now. You're a little peer-committed with your friends watching and all."

The inmate looked around and saw several inmate faces pressed to their cell door windows watching the events develop.

"Kind of. Yeah," the inmate said. "Can't just give-up now."

Jerrod nodded and used a low voice. "Let's give 'em a good show."

The inmate nodded back and screamed. "Bring it, puto."

Jerrod used his most official voice. "Inmate. You have five seconds to cuff up... or we use this stuff." Jerrod held up the OC canister for the inmate and everyone else to see.

"Fuck you," the inmate said. "I've been maced before. It don't do nothing."

Jerrod sighed. "Oh, but this ain't mace, babe."

"Let's go," the inmate said.

Jerrod waited five seconds, aimed the canister, announced "OC," and delivered a one-second stream of oleoresin capsicum. The spray impacted the inmate square in the chest of his jail-issued shit-color-stained t-shirt. Jerrod launched a second spray, and it struck the inmate in the face. The chemical agent had immediate effect as the inmate yelled in pain and covered his face with his hands before falling to his knees.

Before Jerrod could say anything, the four DOs rushed the screaming and coughing inmate, tackled him to the ground, and wrestled his arms behind his back to be handcuffed. Just as quickly, each of the officers started to cough as they attempted to control the inmate. As they jerked the red-faced and tear-streaked inmate to his feet, all the DOs were red-faced and tear-streaked as well.

The pig-pile had happened anyway.

As the inmate stood upright, eyes closed tight and still screaming, a stream of clear mucus originated from his nostrils. The stream slowly grew longer and longer until it connected his nose to the floor. This was the first time anyone in the room had witnessed what would later officially be named: an "OC-induced snot rope."

The air in the dayroom was thick with the smell of OC and, as Jerrod tried to speak on the radio to advise Central Security the situation was

"Code Four," he found he was unable to take a full breath without coughing himself.

Alpo seemed unaffected by the chemical spray as he spoke to Jerrod. "'L' Unit, sir?"

"Straight to 'L,'" Jerrod said.

"That's some nasty shit, sir," Alpo said.

"Love it. But we need to work on what we do after we use it."

2:50 AM

"SDO. Watch Commander," Jerrod radioed. "Meet me in East Housing."

"SDO copy."

At the doorway to "L" Unit, Jerrod asked Alpo. "How's our OC'd inmate doing?"

"He asked to be let out for a shower and some fresh clothing a couple hours ago," Alpo replied.

Jerrod looked at his watch. "It's three o'clock straight-up, so he's been 'marinating' for about five hours now."

"That's about right," Alpo said.

Jerrod radioed, "Central Security. Watch Commander. Open the door to 'L.'"

Alpo unlocked the heavy cell door and Jerrod stepped inside to greet the inmate. "I suspect you won't pull that stunt again."

The inmate looked up with bloodshot eyes. "No. I'm sorry. I had to do it... you know."

"Understood," Jerrod said. "Alpo tells me you asked for a shower and new clothes."

"Yes. Please."

"Request granted," Jerrod said. "Come on out and jump in the shower."

The inmate rushed past Jerrod as he stripped off his jumpsuit and underclothes. "Thank you," the inmate yelled to Jerrod as he pulled the vinyl curtain on the shower and started the shower spray.

Fifteen seconds later, a high-pitched scream came from the shower. Alpo pulled the curtain open and found the inmate pressed into a corner.

"The water makes it worse," the inmate screamed. "My face... and my balls are on fire."

"Use only cold water," Jerrod said to the inmate. "Hot water must have opened your pores and reactivated the OC."

The inmate glared back at him.

Jerrod turned to Alpo. "I guess we have a bit of a learning curve on this stuff."

3:00 AM

"Mesa Comm," dispatcher Tammie Moyer said to the 9-1-1 caller. "What's your emergency?"

"My grandparents. They're being robbed," the muffled male voice said.

"Where are they now?"

"They're at home. Two men broke in. I think they have knives. I got away by the pool. I'm so scared."

"Where are they?" Tammie directed. "What's the street address?"

"I'm not sure. Standish Court," the caller said. "The foothills above Willowmere."

"Standish Court. Good." Tammie said. "I'm starting deputies that way now."

"I hope they don't kill my grandparents," the caller said. "They said they wanted their money and jewelry and prescription drugs."

"What are your grandparent's names?"

"Uh... Michael and Monica... uh... Sullivan."

"Stand-by and don't hang up," Tammie said as she typed "Michael Sullivan" into the DMV database.

"Found it," Tammie said. "1120 Standish Court."

"'1120. That's it," the caller said. "It's a big house. There's a gate at the driveway. Please hurry."

"I have four deputies enroute now," Tammie said. "Where are you?"

"Pay phone. Near... I don't know where this is. Down the street. I'm just visiting."

"What's your name, son?" Tammie asked.

"Jeremy. Jeremy Sullivan. Please help them."

"Stay right by that phone, Jeremy."

"I hear them. I hear the sirens. They're coming. Thank you. Thank you." The caller hung up.

Bruce Witt peeled the vinyl gloves from his hands and pulled the wads of tissue from his cheeks as he walked back to his car. He checked the battery level on his video camera and made sure it had a fresh tape.

Then he waited for the cavalry to arrive.

6:55 AM

"You look like shit, Mitch," Jerrod said as Mitchell Sullivan shuffled into the Watch Commander's Office. "Lose track of time at the strip club last night? Proper restorative sleep is very important for a healthy lifestyle."

"I do not go to... just save it, please," Sullivan said.

"What's going on? You can talk to me."

"At three o'clock--" Sullivan started to say before cocking his head to compose himself. "At three o'clock this morning, someone called 9-1-1 and reported that my parents were being robbed at their house. Two men with knives."

"Oh, my God," Jerrod said with an exaggerated gasp.

Sullivan continued. "There were no robbers with knives. It was a prank call from a pay phone down the street."

Alpo walked into the office.

"That's not a very funny prank," Jerrod said.

"The caller said he was their grandson, 'Jeremy,'" Sullivan said. "Their only grandson is named Maddox and he is stationed at an Army base in Germany."

"Someone could have been hurt," Jerrod said.

"To say the least," Sullivan added. "The deputies broke the gate to the driveway. Drove a patrol car through it. They searched the house and knocked over one my mother's vases."

"But your folks are both okay?" Jerrod asked.

"Yes. They are okay. Shook up. Embarrassed. Humiliated. All the neighbors were out gawking. The deputies asked my mother if she had been sexually assaulted."

"But I hope she's fine?" Jerrod asked. "Mitch, do you need a hug right now?"

"Yes. No. No hug. Nothing happened to my mother. But that video reporter -- Bruce Witt -- was there. Big camera. Bright light. It will probably be all over the news today."

"Bruce does have a nose for those things," Jerrod said. "Listens to the scanner. Out all night. I don't think he sleeps at all. That's going to catch up to him some day."

"Sheriff's gonna be pissed," Alpo said.

"He is already angry," Sullivan said. "The sheriff was there at my parent's house. My father called him... right after he called me."

Jerrod shook his head.

"Your name came up, Jerrod," Sullivan said. "My father thinks you were behind this. Where were you at three o'clock?"

"Here at work, but...," Jerrod stopped to think. He placed a finger to his chin and turned to Alpo. "I pretty sure we were dealing with that OC-soaked inmate in 'L' at three."

"That was right at three o'clock," Alpo added. "Shower and clothing change. That was definitely three o'clock, sir."

Jerrod turned back to Sullivan. "Sorry, Mitch. Gonna have to look elsewhere. I was pretty busy back in Housing... with witnesses."

Mitchell Sullivan nodded.

"But please, Mitch," Jerrod said. "From the bottom of my heart, let your father know that I understand the overwhelming and powerless feeling a man gets when his home -- his very castle -- is violated by an unexpected and uninvited visitor. He'll understand what I mean."

CHAPTER 47

"Watch Commander. Central Security," the male DO radioed.

"Watch Commander. Go ahead," Jerrod radioed.

"There's a visitor in the lobby," the DO radioed. "He said you were expecting him."

"Watch Commander, copy. I'll go get him."

Jerrod passed through the Lobby sallyport and found a small man with long white hair pulled back in a ponytail seated on a bench.

"Been a while, Dewey," Jerrod said.

Duane "Dewey" Mazurek stood up and walked to Jerrod. Jerrod stuck out his right hand and Dewey grabbed it with both of his.

"How are you doing, brother?" Dewey asked in his familiar soft, calming voice.

"Every day above ground, you know."

Indeed, brother. Indeed." the ruddy-faced and bearded Vietnam veteran and PTSD counselor said. "Why am I here?"

"Let's have a seat. I have a big favor to ask."

Ten minutes later, Jerrod buzzed Central Security from the lobby door and Dewey followed him into the secure portion of the jail.

"This is Booking here," Jerrod said as he pointed areas out to Dewey. "Intake is over there. Housing is down there to the right."

"What's that smell?" Dewey asked. "It's like wet dog in here."

"What smell?" Jerrod said. "Let's get some coffee."

Jerrod led Dewey to the staff lounge and punched in the lock code. Dewey followed him into the vacant room.

"Help yourself to some coffee -- regular or unleaded -- as you prefer."

As Dewey grabbed a cup, Jerrod radioed, "SDO. Watch Commander."

"SDO. Go ahead." Alpo radioed.

"Meet me in the lounge."

"SDO copy. From East Housing,"

A few minutes later, Alpo entered the room and paused in the doorway when he saw Dewey seated with Jerrod at a table.

"Sorry to interrupt," Alpo said. "Uh... you called me, sir."

Jerrod said, "This is a friend of mine. In for a little jail tour. Alpo, this is Dewey."

"Nice to meet you, sir," Alpo said as he stepped toward the table and shook Dewey's tiny hand with his massive one.

Jerrod said to Alpo, "Grab a cup and sit down."

Jerrod sat next to Dewey and Alpo sat across the table.

"Dewey and I go back a few years," Jerrod said. "Helped me when I needed some help."

"Okaaaaay," Alpo said.

"Dewey spent some time in Vietnam," Jerrod continued. "Army. Like you. Thought maybe you two might have a chat or something."

"Yeah, Sarge...um...," Alpo stuttered.

Jerrod stood up. "Turn off your radio. Talk with Dewey. I'll cover the jail for a while."

"You know... fuck... sorry... sir... I don't talk about--" Alpo looked around for an escape route.

"Do I need to make it an order, Alpo?

"No, sir." Alpo's anxiety level was visible on his face.

"If Dewey starts to tell you a story about an ingrown hair," Jerrod said. "Listen carefully."

Yes, sir," Alpo said.

Jerrod nodded to Dewey and left them alone in the lounge.

"Central Security. Watch Commander," Jerrod radioed.

"Central Security. Go ahead."

"Staff lounge is off-limits until further notice. SDO is busy. Direct any issues to me."

"That was pretty uncomfortable, sir," Alpo said.

"It was intended to be just that," Jerrod responded. "Facing uncomfortable things is, by definition, uncomfortable. Dewey works with a lot of other vets... and cops... when asked. He helped me get through a bad one."

"He didn't say anything about an 'ingrown hair,' though."

"What analogy did he use?"

"'Rucksacks,'" Alpo said. " You know, the backpacks we used on patrols in... there... Vietnam."

"How does that work?" Jerrod asked.

"He said our brains are like rucksacks. They get full of stuff. Junk we don't need. He said we have to clean 'em out once in a while and get rid of the useless stuff and lighten the load we're carrying."

"Does that make sense to you, Alpo? Has your rucksack been full of bad stuff since you came back from war?"

"Yes, sir."

"Going to see Dewey again?"

"We're meeting for a beer next week. Gonna meet some of the other vets he knows."

"Promise you'll go."

"Promise, sir."

CHAPTER 48

Friday -- Midnight

Jerrod lay alone and restless and staring at the ceiling.

It was the night before the wedding, and he had been booted from his home by some odd tradition that groom and bride could not sleep under the same roof the night before -- even if they had done so for the five previous years.

Nine months of planning had culminated in the events of that weekend. The list of tasks had been completed. Venue and invitations and caterers and beverage and flowers and music and bridesmaids and groomsmen and dresses and tuxedos and rings and cakes and flowers and accommodations and a rehearsal with a dinner that followed. He couldn't wait for it to just be over.

Laura and Don had offered their guest room -- his former bedroom -- for the night. He had firm instructions from Nikki to behave himself and not drink too much the night before. Jerrod had had but one Heineken all night, but he could have finished many more. Now he needed sleep.

Wedding Day -- Saturday Afternoon -- The Redwood Center

"Are you ready, son?" whispered Gabriel Ferreira -- Nikki's uncle and the official who would performing the ceremony.

They stood together in the kitchen of the Center. Jerrod's stomach was in knots as he watched the caterers scurry to prepare the meal they would enjoy after the ceremony. Months of preparation had been built into this very moment.

Jerrod checked his black bow tie. "Ready as I'll ever be, sir."

Gabriel smiled and opened the black binder he was carrying. "You wrote these vows?"

"We did. Yes, sir."

"Nice. Now walk with me."

Jerrod and Gabriel left the kitchen and walked the length of the aisle to the river rock fireplace where the vows would be exchanged. Jerrod anxiety was at a fever pitch as he scanned the blur of smiling faces of the family and friends who had given their time to attend.

The three groomsmen were in place. Craig Wallace and Willie Sanchez and Marko Otero. They looked sharp in their black tuxedos and red bow ties. A single red rose graced their lapels. Jerrod nodded to them. All beamed back with pride.

The bridesmaids were stationed. Beautiful all.

Jerrod and Gabriel took their places in front of the huge rock fireplace.

As they waited for Nikki to come down the aisle, Jerrod looked into the crowd. Laura and Don sat together in the front row. Jerry Gold sat next to Laura with his mother -- Jenne -- beside him. Aunts and uncles and cousins were there. Colonel Charles Horvatz, waved from his seat.

Jerrod saw friends from the Valle Verde PD sitting together. Pete Hanson. Rusty and Katy Browne with their son Jimmy. Dave Yamamoto and Allison "AJ" Jenkins. The Kevins -- "Big" Kevin Arneta and "Tall" Kevin Holcomb. And Al Kees.

The wives of Roger Collins, Beach Sutton, Nate Boxley, and the girlfriend of Zippy Zippich were seated together, but the four detectives were not with them. He could not find Ben Zaff or Eric Blanchard or Shroom Mingus or Ted Lindsey in the crowd either.

This got his attention: VVPD personnel were there and MCSO personnel were not. So, he surmised, something very bad had happened in an unincorporated portion of the county and the guys were still at work.

Lilly appeared and walked down the aisle carrying the rings. Marty followed and scattered rose petals along the way.

The DJ started the bridal march and Nikki appeared from the private room. Her mother -- Bernice -- walked with her. Nikki's brunette hair was up in a style that must have taken three hours to set. The veil was down.

And the queen's shoes matched her intricate off-the-shoulder dress.

Gabriel conducted the wedding like a stern judge ran a courtroom. Everything in place and everyone on time. He looked to the guests. "Please be seated." He returned to Jerrod and Nikki. "Please hold hands."

Nikki gave her bouquet to Lilly and placed her hands in Jerrod's. Her eyes were clear. Her smile perfect. This was their time.

"Friends," Gabriel began, "we have gathered here today to witness and celebrate the coming together of two separate lives. We are here to join this man, Jerrod, and this woman, Nikki, in marriage and to be with them in the making of this important and lifelong commitment."

Jerrod heard Craig try to stifle a cough. Willie shook his metal watch band.

"The essence of this commitment is the taking of another person in his or her entirety, as lover, companion, and friend. It is therefore a decision which is not to be entered into lightly, but rather undertaken with great consideration and respect for both the other person and oneself."

Nikki's hands started to shake. Jerrod winked and she smiled back.

"Love is one of the highest experiences that we humans can have, and it can add depth to our lives. The sensual part of love is one of life's greatest joys -- and when it is combined with real friendship -- both are infinitely enhanced. The day-to-day companionship -- the pleasure of doing things together or in doing separate things but in delighting to exchange experiences -- is a continuous and central part of what a man and a woman who love each other can share."

Jerrod glanced a Marty. Her eyes were moist. He smiled and nodded to her.

"Marriage symbolizes," Gabriel continued, "the intimate sharing of two lives, yet this sharing must not diminish but enhance the individuality of each partner. A marriage which lasts is one which is continuously developing and in which each person is individually developing, while growing in understanding of each other. Deep knowledge of another is not something that can be achieved in a short time., and real understanding of each other's feelings can develop only with years of intimacy.

"This wonderful knowledge of another person grows out of deep caring for the other -- so much that one wants to understand as completely as possible what the other is feeling. Thus, it is possible to share not only joys and successes, but also the burden of sorrows and failures.

"Jerrod and Nikki, as you enter married life, I would like to express some of the wishes that your family and friends have for you. First, we would wish for you a love that makes both of you the best that you can possibly be, that continues to grow and give you joy and abundant living, and that provides you with energy to face the responsibilities of life.

"We wish for you a home made by you together -- not just a place of wood and stone, but a haven of comfort and serenity in a frenzied world. We wish to give you a blessing on this special day, for long and happy lives together and for a strong, warm, and abiding love throughout all the days of your lives. Be patient with each other, work on understanding each other, and know that we who join in this celebration are always there to support and rejoice in your love."

Gabriel spoke to the guests, "Now for the fun part." He turned back to the couple. "Jerrod. Do you take Nikki to be your wife? To have and to hold from this day forward. For better or for worse. For richer or for poorer. In sickness and in health. And to love and cherish her as long as you both shall live?"

Jerrod held Nikki's hands a little tighter and looked deep into her emerald eyes.

"Anytime, mister," Nikki whispered.

"I do."

"Nikki. Do you take Jerrod..."

"I do."

"Now as an outward sign of their love for each other and the vows they have just taken, Jerrod will give a ring to Nikki and Nikki will give a ring to Jerrod.

Nikki looked to Lilly, and she walked toward them -- a gold ring in each hand.

After the rings were exchanged, the judge added: "May these circles of gold forever be a symbol of lasting faith, constant hope, and abiding love. May your love and affection for each other be like these rings -- without end."

Gabriel turned to the guests again. "But wait... there's more. This gathering marks not only a celebration of the love and union of Jerrod and Nikki, but the creation of an entire new family to include two very special children -- Lilly and Martina."

Nikki motioned for the girls to join them, and they all held hands.

Gabriel said, "Jerrod. Do you promise to love, support, counsel, and protect Lilly and Martina as if they were your very own?"

Jerrod looked at the tears streaming down the face of the youngest child. "Yes, sir. I do."

Gabriel added, "We who are present, and those who are absent thinking about these two people, hope that the inspiration of this hour will not be forgotten. May this family continue to love one another forever.

"Now, by the power vested in me by the State of California -- but most of all by the power of your own love -- I pronounce you man and wife."

He smiled at the couple. "Jerrod. You may kiss the bride."

They kissed and embraced with the kids.

"Ladies and gentlemen," Gabriel said, "it is with great joy I present to you Mr. and Mrs. Jerrod and Nikki Gold... and family."

Jerrod didn't hear the applause as they walked together down the aisle for the first time as a true family.

As the after-ceremony photos were being taken, the drinking and schmoozing had begun without them.

The disk jockey was spinning Paula Abdul's song "Rush Rush" when Jerrod and Nikki joined the in-progress reception. The newlyweds made the rounds and found the group of mates for the sheriff's office detectives seated around a table together.

"The boys out on a big one?" Jerrod asked.

The ladies all looked at each other. Kim Collins, Roger Collins' wife, was the first to speak. "Something happened yesterday afternoon. They've been working ever since."

"What is it?" Jerrod asked. "Haven't seen anything in the paper or news. Kidnapping? Homicide?"

"Jerrod. Nikki," Kim started, "Roger asked us not to ruin your day. But... uh... yeah, someone was killed."

Jerrod nodded.

Kim added, "They said they would try to come by the reception if they finished with some warrants they needed to serve."

"Okay," Jerrod said. "I'm sure the details will come out at some point." He looked around the table. "You all look lovely and thanks for being at our wedding."

Jerrod walked away with Nikki. "No one from Investigations is here. That case must be a doozy."

"Thank you both for coming all this way," Jerrod said to Craig and Sandi Wallace.

After some small-talk, Jerrod asked, "How far is Winnemucca from your place in Nevada?"

"Couple hours," Craig said. "It's on Interstate 80 between Reno and Elko. What's in Winnemucca?"

"I'm not sure," Jerrod answered.

Jerrod saw Beach Sutton, Nate Boxley, and Zippy Zippich walk into the reception and look around for their mates. They found the ladies at the table and just as quickly headed to the bar. All three detectives looked like they had been up all night... because they had.

Jerrod greeted them as they ordered drinks. "Glad you could make it. What the hell have you guys been working on?"

The three men glanced at each other until Nate spoke. "Bad one, Sarge. Real bad."

Let's go outside," Beach suggested. "No one else can hear this. And you didn't hear it from us."

Alone by the tree swing, Beach spoke first. "All the other guys: Ben, Roger, Shroom, Ted, Jeff and Calvin are still working on this thing. Chief Blanchard too. "

"They cut us loose to get here before it was over," Zippy said. "They all send their regards."

"What the hell happened?" Jerrod asked.

Nate asked Jerrod, "Do you know who Bryan McCrane is?"

"Sure. Met him once. "Bryan 'Shredder' McCrane. President of the Fer-de-Lance Motorcycle Club."

"That's him," Zippy said. "He's in-custody right now for first-degree murder."

"Who'd he kill?" Jerrod asked.

"One of his members," Nate said.

"Former member," Beach corrected. "The guy tried to drop-out of the gang and, to put it mildly, that didn't go so well."

"Sorry I missed it," Jerrod said. "Sounds like a great case."

"Be very glad you missed it," Zippy said. "I don't care if that guy was a biker; no human being should suffer a death like that."

"How?" Jerrod asked.

None of the detective wanted to describe the scene.

"No problem, boys," Jerrod said. "Probably best not to know."

"It's not so much we don't want to tell you, Sarge," Nate said. "It's more like we don't want to see it in our heads again. It was way past 'torture' and so far out into another world we will never comprehend."

"I understand." Jerrod looked at his three traumatized friends. "Can I buy you guys a drink? In case you haven't heard, I got married today."

They drove away from The Redwood Center at nearly 8 PM. A string of aluminum cans clattered from the rear bumper of his truck until they got to freeway speed on the PCH.

Nikki let out a relieved sigh.

Jerrod reached over and held her hand. "I love you, 'Wife.'"

"I like the way that sounds. I love you too, 'Husband.'"

"Those are our official names now. Your uncle just pronounced us exactly that," Jerrod added. "'Husband and Wife.'"

The Mesa hotel wasn't fancy, but it was conveniently close after a hectic day. Jerrod checked in at the office.

"I have your reservation right here, Mr. Gold," the young female night clerk said. "Two guests. One night."

Jerrod handed her a credit card.

She glanced at his tuxedo and smiled. "Get married today?"

"Oh. No," he said. "Junior prom."

The clerk narrowed her eyes but choose not to respond and just handed him back the card with the room key.

"I need to get out of this dress and into the shower," Nikki said. "It took at least two cans of spray to get this hair in place and there must be a hundred bobby pins in there too."

"Shower away, dear," he said. "I'll find something to do."

She closed the door and started the shower. He stripped and hung his clothes on chairs, turned on the clock radio to KHJB for some classic rock, got his copy of *Dead Irish* out of his bag, and flopped into the bed.

He had read an entire chapter by the time the shower water stopped. "Pretty sure we're gonna get a surcharge for all the hot water you just used," he shouted at the closed door.

He got no response.

Five minutes later, Nikki opened the door and stood in silhouette wearing only her wedding veil.

The book lay open on his chest. He was sound asleep.

Sunday Afternoon

"The Golds," the concierge said. "Very good. Honeymoon couple. Congratulations. Your bungalow is ready."

"'Our bungalow is ready,'" Nikki repeated in a whisper.

Located at the end of a narrow curving in the oak tree-covered foothills off the Silverado Trail was the exclusive resort named simply: The Napa Valley Ranch.

"I heard about this place from a friend," Jerrod said. "It used to be a trailer park. Is that correct?"

The concierge chuckled. "Still is... technically. It has quite the history."

"Now we must hear it," Nikki said.

"Long story longer," the man started. "This had been a trailer park for many years. The current owners bought the property with grand visions of creating a luxury resort right here in the heart of the Napa Valley."

Jerrod nodded.

"The existing trailers were moved out. Plans were drawn and submitted to the county for approval. All were denied. The county refused to rezone the property and stated it must remain a trailer park."

"Ruh roh," Jerrod said in his best Scooby Doo voice.

"Indeed," the man said. "The owners, undeterred, created a new plan using only modular buildings strategically placed to form our private bungalows. Every building on the property arrived on wheels. Plan approved. Problem solved. Here we are."

"Brilliant," Nikki said.

The concierge looked at a computer screen. "I have your reservation confirmed for dinner tonight at seven o'clock. Honeymooners have a very special menu I am certain you will enjoy."

Jerrod nodded as he noted a young man standing outside the office next to an over-sized golf cart.

"You can leave your vehicle right where it's parked. Oscar will get your bags and shuttle you anywhere you wish. Just call the desk for a ride. The spa is open. And we will have some very nice wines available for tasting in about an hour."

Oscar loaded their bags and took them to their home for the next two nights.

A redwood deck connected three modular buildings set in a horseshoe shape: A living area with a stereo and large television screen on the left side. A dining area with a gourmet kitchen to the back. And a master suite with a glass-enclosed two-head shower to the right.

Lush trees and hedges made the entire space private.

After Oscar had delivered their bags and showed them the features of the bungalow, Jerrod -- having learned his lesson on under-tipping at the Willowmere Golf Club -- handed the young man a crisp ten-dollar bill. It was received with a broad smile and a handshake.

Nikki walked into the dining area and found a note next to a bottle of champagne in a bucket of ice. The note read, "To the new couple. With our congratulations. The staff of The Napa Valley Ranch."

Jerrod walked into the room and held her around the waist. "Spa or wine tasting?" he asked.

"Bedroom," she said.

Tuesday

The drive home from the Napa Valley was bittersweet.

"I loved that place," Nikki said. "The wine. That dinner the first night. The other things we did."

Jerrod grinned. "Back to our real life."

"I've never been away from the girls this long," she said before going quiet.

They started crossing the Benicia-Martinez Bridge and he peeked out at the mothballed ships moored in neat rows in the Suisun Bay. He knew she hated bridges and decided the lingering subject on his mind could wait until they were back on firm ground.

Near the petroleum refineries at Mococo, he finally spoke. "Do you know why Nate and Beach and Zippy were late to the reception and a bunch of the guys from the SO didn't make the wedding at all."

"Kim Collins told me they all got called out on a homicide," she said. "She didn't give any details."

"Know who's being charged with that homicide?"

"No."

"Bryan 'Shredder' McCrane."

"Bryan the Biker? The regular from the restaurant?

210

"That's the one."

"No way," she said. "He's super nice."

"Not to the guy he killed."

"I find that hard to believe. Seriously. He's been coming in for years. You've seen him in there."

"I know. But this homicide was so bad, that the guys -- all experienced detectives -- wouldn't even describe how the victim died."

"Good," she said. "Then you can't describe it to me."

"Not that I would," he said. "They did tell me they served a search warrant at his home. Big modern house on a bluff way up off Mesa Road."

She nodded.

"They arrested McCrane there. He has a snake for a pet. A huge venomous snake."

"Loose?" she gasped. "In the house?"

"No. In a big glass terrarium."

"Good."

"They called Fish and Game wardens out and they said it was a bad-ass snake from some Caribbean island. They ended up calling handlers from the zoo in San Francisco to move it somewhere safe. Nate's terrified of snakes and was still freaking out when he told me about it."

Nikki was quiet for several miles. "He asked me out."

"Nate?"

"No. Bryan."

"Shredder asked you out?"

"I don't call him that," she said. "But yeah. A few months after Blake died. Before I met you."

"Did you go?"

"We had coffee."

"At Sophie's?"

"No. On the pier."

"Willowmere Pier?"

"That's the only pier around, Jerrod."

"Just coffee?"

"Just coffee."

211

"That's too bad," he said not taking his eyes off the road. "You could have met his pet snake for yourself."

"Very funny."

A few miles later near San Ramon, Jerrod said. "You realize he's sitting in my jail right now? I'll no doubt be dealing with him at some point."

"I suppose so."

"Yes," Jerrod said before shaking his head and thinking: *Sophie's Diner -- Crossroads of The Fucking Universe.*

"Mommy," Marty yelled as Nikki and Jerrod entered the house on Rochester Avenue.

"Glad your home, Mom," Lilly said. "You too, Jerrod."

Nikki received long hugs from her daughters, and they stayed close to her as they moved to the kitchen to join Laura and Don.

"We baked cookies and painted and sewed," Marty recounted. "And I love my new room."

Her new room, Jerrod thought. *Tommy's old room.*

"How was the honeymoon?" Laura said.

"Fantastic," Nikki said.

"Too short," Jerrod added.

"Were the girls good?" Nikki asked Laura.

"Absolute joy," Laura said.

Don spread his arms wide as he looked at Jerrod and Nikki. "Are you two ready for this to be yours?"

Jerrod looked around the house. "Sure."

Don suggested, "Let's talk about timing."

They all sat in the dining room and Don led the meeting. "The paperwork has been drawn up and is at the attorney's office."

"Excuse me," Nikki said. "I'm still not sure what we'll be signing."

Don said, "I'd be happy to explain."

"Please," Nikki said.

"Basically," Don started. "We are selling the house to you and Jerrod, and we will hold the note. We act as the bank. Once the sale is recorded with the county, the house becomes yours.

"Okay, so far," Nikki said.

"There is a mortgage," Don said, "both principal and interest which is paid to us each month. We declare the interest paid as income and you write-off that same interest on your taxes."

"Why not just sell us the house?" Nikki asked.

"We are," Don continued, "but Laura and I get the advantage of spreading the taxes over many years rather just this year. The capital gains hit on this place would be significant."

"And how about the property taxes?" Jerrod asked.

Don said, "Since the property is being passed down from parent to child, we'll file a form with the county and keep the property assessment at the same level it is now. Normally it would be reassessed at sale and the new property tax would be based on the actual sale price. This is one of the exceptions."

Laura said, "The movers will be here on Friday. We're having a farewell party at a friend's home on Friday night and we're driving to Arizona on Saturday. You can move in any time after that. You already have a key."

Don looked to Jerrod and then to Nikki. "Is there a day this week that works for both of you?"

"And all of this is legal, right?" Nikki asked. "It sounds a little sketchy."

"I can assure you this is all very legal." Don chuckled. "People with money make these laws so people with money can keep their money."

Jerrod looked to Nikki, and she nodded back. "See if the attorney is available on Thursday."

Saturday Evening -- Mesa County Jail

"Okay, Alpo," Jerrod said. "Please explain to me why Bryan McCrane is classified as maximum security."

"Welcome back from your honeymoon, sir," Alpo said.

"Thank you very much. Please answer my question."

"It came down straight from Sheriff Osborn," Alpo said. "'Based on the severity of the crime' was the wording on the memo I saw."

"I checked his C-File and didn't see any memo. There's just a note saying he would be kept in 'L" Unit for his duration here."

"Yes, sir."

"So, they just bypassed the entire classification process and ordered it be done?"

"Yes, sir."

"I checked his RAP sheet and found McCrane has a number of arrests, but not a single prior conviction."

"I know," Alpo replied. "With all due respect, sir, why are you sticking up for this guy? He's charged with mutilating and killing a man. Are you two friends or something?"

"Not friends." Jerrod rubbed the side of his face. "I've been working with the Jail Commander on a new classification and discipline policy. I'm trying to build an impartial system for inmates that also keeps us within the law. This thing with McCrane goes against all of that."

Alpo nodded.

Jerrod dropped his chin to his chest. "Maybe I'm too fair."

CHAPTER 49

Kirk LaMahieu couldn't believe it was true when he studied the announcement in the newspaper. Nikki -- his Nikki -- had married the very man who killed his father.

He knew she drove a blue Pontiac and had waited for her to leave Sophie's Diner after her shift. He followed her as she headed south on the PCH toward Valle Verde. She stopped at a supermarket, loaded some groceries into the trunk, and he followed her through town. He watched her pull into the inclined driveway of a house on Rochester Avenue as the swing-up garage door opened remotely and the blue car disappeared with the closing door.

He studied the house from his car for a few minutes. He wondered out loud how a cop and a waitress could afford a house that size in such an upscale neighborhood. He prayed to see a glimpse of her through the huge front plate glass windows. He fantasized she must be putting groceries away or changing her clothes or taking a nice relaxing bath.

He opened the door to the glove box and looked at the chrome revolver. He studied the house and glanced back to the revolver.

I wonder if he's home now. Kirk thought. *I could just knock on the door and shoot him when he answers. He'd never see it coming. How about if Nikki answers? That's better. I'll just shoot her and let him find her. He killed my dad. I killed his wife. Fair is fair. He'd understand. We could just call it even. And, besides, if I can't have her... he shouldn't have her either.*

He heard some talking and giggling behind him on the sidewalk and glanced in the rearview mirror. Four girls. Elementary and junior high school age. He closed the glove box door just as they walked past. Two girls split from the group and crossed the street. They raced each other up the driveway and into the unlocked front door of the big house.

Kirk LaMahieu recognized the girls. He had seen them in Sophie's many times. They were pretty... just like their mother.

CHAPTER 50

"I turned in my two-week notice at the restaurant," Nikki said.

Jerrod put down his copy of *Dead Irish*. "How do you feel about that?"

"Mixed emotions. Happy and sad at the same time."

"I've never really understood that saying, 'mixed emotions.'"

"Let me give you an example and you tell me how you would take it."

"Fire away."

"How would you react if I told you, 'Of all your cop friends -- you are the best lover?'"

"Uh," he said as he resisted the visuals attached to that statement and searched his entire vocabulary. "Conflicted."

"Precisely," she said. "My last day is Saturday. March 14. They're having a little going-away party the next Monday. It's your day-off, so, maybe, my husband can show-up and help me say goodbye."

"I'll be there."

"I take over at the roofing company the following Monday," she said. "I'm taking the whole next week off before I start there."

"Congratulations," Jerrod said.

"I'm not feeling too excited about it." She paused for a long moment. "I've spent most of my life in and out of that restaurant."

"I bet Bernice is pleased you'll be helping her," he said -- looking for a bright spot.

"She's tickled and I'll have plenty to do. Regular hours will be nice. But..."

"What, honey?" Jerrod said.

"Nothing."

CHAPTER 51

Saturday Night

"Sarge," the male DO yelled from Booking. "Patrol deputy here to see you."

"Thank you," Jerrod yelled. "Enter."

Deputy Scott Jackson ambled into the Watch Commander's office. He had his black "Tuffy" duty jacket zipped to the top and faux-fur collar pulled up on his neck.

"Scott. A pleasure. Little cold out there?"

"Frigging freezing."

"Want some coffee? Little warm-up."

"No, thanks. Gotta get back out."

"What's up?"

"I wanted you to know I've been accepted to law school. Over in San Jose. I've decided to be a lawyer."

Jerrod stood up and extended his hand. "Congratulations."

"I'm going to bailiff in Court Security for a while and Judge Kohnke has offered me a clerkship."

"I suspect Sam's pretty happy. You getting off the road and having a normal schedule."

"Yes, sir. She's dreaded every day since I went back to work."

Jerrod nodded.

Scott chuckled. "She didn't ask me to get out of law enforcement..."

"But she didn't put up a fuss either."

"No, sir. She did not."

There was an awkward silence.

"Sarge," he stammered and looked down. "I'm glad you were there with me both of those times. You know."

"I know, Scott. I'm glad you were there with me too."

Sunday Night

Jerrod was in the law library discussing the most recent inmate grievance from Bradley Sean Stapleton when he was startled by a loud bang on the door behind him. He turned and saw a screaming orange jumpsuited inmate through the window.

"What the hell?" Jerrod muttered.

Jerrod pulled open the door as the inmate -- mid-thirties, stringy long blond hair, goatee, with a swastika and SS lightning bolts tattooed on his neck -- yelled past him at Stapleton.

"Careful who you talk to, motherfucker," the inmate bellowed. "Fucking snitch. You fucking snitch."

"Sorry, Sarge," the male DO who had been escorting the inmate said.

"Cuff him and put him in an attorney visiting room," Jerrod directed.

"Let's go," the DO said as he shuffled the inmate across Times Square.

"What the hell was that commotion all about?" Alpo asked as he came charging out of West Housing.

"Our little Nazi over there thinks Stapleton is a snitch."

"So?" Alpo asked.

"So. Stapleton wasn't snitching. I was talking to him about this." Jerrod held up a pink Inmate Grievance Form.

"What are you going to do about it?" Alpo challenged.

Jerrod thought for a second. "Thanks for asking. I think Adolph needs a crash course in the dangers of false perceptions. That's what I'm going to do about it."

Alpo didn't respond

"Get McCrane out for an attorney visit," Jerrod directed.

"Copy that, sir. It'll take a few minutes to get him ready and clear the area."

"No problem."

Jerrod walked across Times Square and entered the room holding the white supremacist inmate. He stood over him as he spoke.

"That was pretty rude," Jerrod said.

"I hate snitches," the inmate replied.

"What makes you think he was snitching? We were having a conversation about this," Jerrod said as he shook the pink form at the inmate. "We were discussing a 'beef' he had about some discipline. That's all."

"Oh,' the inmate said. "I didn't... uh... fuck him anyway. Snitch. Bitch. Punk-ass J-Cat motherfucker."

Jerrod said nothing as he folded the grievance form in half, unfastened a button on his uniform shirt, and slid the page from sight against his belly.

Alpo came out from East Housing. Jerrod gave him a thumbs-up.

"What are you doing?" the inmate asked. "Just take me back to my unit."

Jerrod sat down across from the inmate, leaned forward, and said in a near whisper. "Now watch this."

Ten seconds later, Inmate Bryan "Shredder" McCrane was escorted past the room. Even in a yellow jumpsuit -- with his ankles shackled and his hands secured to a thick chain around his waist -- McCrane projected the cool body language and confident saunter of a natural leader.

McCrane glanced to his left and made eye contact with the inmate.

"Know who that is?" Jerrod asked.

The inmate didn't immediately respond as he watched McCrane being secured in the locked cage two interview rooms away from him. "That's Shredder McCrane," he eventually said.

"Know what he's in here for?"

"Yep," the inmate said as his eyes kept focus on McCrane.

"Is he staring at you right now?" Jerrod asked.

"Yep."

"Think he knows what we're talking about?" Jerrod asked.

"Nope."

"Maybe he thinks *you're* snitching right now?"

"I hope not."

With his back toward McCrane, Jerrod pulled a corner of the pink form from under his shirt. The inmate glanced down at the form and then back to McCrane.

"Ready to go back to your unit now?"

"Hang on a second." Beads of sweat appeared on the inmate's brow. "Let him see the form. Maybe he'll think we're just talking about that."

Jerrod tucked the form back under his shirt and fastened the button. "I have a question: Who's the most dangerous person in this facility at this very moment?"

The inmate lifted his chin toward McCrane. "He is."

"Think again," Jerrod suggested.

The inmate looked at Jerrod's face, down to the buttoned shirt, and then snapped back up when he had the epiphany. "You are... sir."

"That's right. Now give me something."

"What?"

"Give me something," Jerrod repeated. "You have five seconds to give one piece of information. Drugs. Weapons. Escape plans. Something. Clock starts now. Five."

"I can't snitch."

"You must snitch. Four."

"Don't do this, man. Please."

"Option A: Give me something." Jerrod leaned forward. "Or Option B: I smile, say 'thank you' loud enough for McCrane to hear, pat you on the shoulder, and send you back to your unit. Three."

"You... you wouldn't do that?"

"And you can dream about Shredder McCrane tonight... if you dare even falling asleep. Two."

"Fuck. I can't--"

"But you can." Jerrod interrupted as he peeked a corner of the pink page from under his shirt. "One."

"Okay... uh... shit... the southsiders in 'C' have a tray."

"Zero. Now elaborate."

"A tray. A steel serving tray from chow. Got left inside a few days ago." The inmate glanced at McCrane. "They've been taking the tray apart and making shanks. Sharpening the pieces on the floor. Gonna hit the northerners from 'A' or any of the 'rats' or molesters from 'F' first chance they get."

"Now we're getting somewhere."

"That's all I know, sir." Tears appeared in the inmate's eyes. "I swear. Please."

Jerrod pulled the pink page out and pretended to discuss the merits of the grievance.

"Thank you, sir."

"Are you gonna kick my door again? Jerrod asked.

"No, sir."

"Still feel the same way about 'rats?'"

"No, sir."

"We'll keep this conversation between us. Okay?" Jerrod suggested.

"Just fine with me, sir."

"We're done here." Jerrod stood up. "Let's get you home."

"Mr. McCrane," Jerrod said. "There seems to have been a bit of a mix-up. Your attorney isn't here. My apologies for the inconvenience."

"Call me 'Shredder,'" he said. "But that's alright. It's kind of nice getting out of that cell for a while."

"I'm sure it is," Jerrod said. "How about a cup of coffee? A little token... for wasting your time."

His chains rattled as McCrane pulled his hands up and they lifted only a couple inches.

Jerrod grinned. "Gonna need a straw."

"Can't drink coffee with a straw," McCrane chuckled. "Especially out here in the open."

"I'll take one cuff off," Jerrod offered.

"Make mine black."

"What was up with that peckerwood in the other room?" McCrane asked as he sipped hot staff coffee from a plastic inmate cup. "Little prick's face looked like he saw a ghost when I walked by."

Jerrod nodded. "Just a little disagreement over an inmate grievance thing. New baby. Lost visit. All worked out now."

"Whiny bitch," McCrane said. "But thanks for the coffee."

"You're welcome," Jerrod said. "I can't talk to you at all about your case, but I am fascinated by your choice of pets."

"What? My snake? He's more of a mascot. Had that terrarium built especially for him. Hope he's okay wherever they took him."

"What kind of snake was it? Jerrod asked.

"'*Bothrops Caribbaeus*' is the scientific name," McCrane said. "The 'Lancehead' or 'Fer-De-Lance' are the more common names. It's the most aggressive and venomous pit viper in the Caribbean and South America. Got him in St. Lucia. Makes a rattlesnake strike look like a mosquito bite. Understand it now?"

"Sure. 'Fer-De-Lance.'" Hence the name of your... well... social group."

"'Motorcycle Club,'" McCrane corrected. "The 'Fer-De-Lance Motorcycle Club.'"

"Not 'OMG?' Jerrod asked. "As in, 'Outlaw Motorcycle Gang.'"

McCrane scoffed. "We prefer, 'Club.'"

"So, back to the snake, Mr. McCrane. Do you have to have a special license or something to keep a snake like that?"

"I don't know," McCrane dismissed. "Probably. I don't really care. And please call me 'Shredder.'"

"No. I won't call you that," Jerrod said.

"Suit yourself. A man with standards. Rare these days," McCrane chuckled.

"I suppose so."

"You and I have met before," McCrane said. "At Sophie's Diner. Do you remember?"

"I remember. You left so fast, I never got to thank you." Jerrod paused. "Finish your coffee. I need to get you back to your unit."

"No problem," McCrane said. "And, by the way, congratulations on your recent wedding. I apologize for not sending a gift."

"You weren't invited, so no gift was anticipated. But thank you for the gesture."

McCrane drained the last sip. "Please give my regards to Nikki. She's a fine catch."

"I'll be sure to do that."

"What the hell did you two talk about back there?" Alpo asked.

"Let's get a cup," Jerrod said.

After they settled in a staff lounge booth, Jerrod said, "Me and McCrane talked about a few things: our white power inmate, grievances, snakes, nicknames, men with standards, and he congratulated me and Nikki, by name, mind you, on getting married."

"Fuck me," Alpo said. "He knows Nikki?"

"From the restaurant. Sophie's Diner. He was a regular there."

"So, you've met him before?" Alpo asked.

"We talked just one time. It was kind of friendly."

"I need to hear this."

222

"Okay. I was working dayshift in Patrol. Nikki was working at Sophie's, so I went there to meet my beat partner, Roger Collins, for a late breakfast or early lunch."

"Brunch?"

"Yes. No. Not brunch," Jerrod continued. "You eat when you can in Patrol. And you eat fast."

"The Army was like that too."

"Who's telling the story here?"

"Please, sir. Carry on."

"Anyway, I pull into the lot and Roger's patrol car is already there. I park next to it and walk toward the front door."

"This is really exciting," Alpo snarked.

"It gets better," Jerrod said. "In the parking lot was this absolutely gorgeous motorcycle. More than a motorcycle. A piece of art made of metal and rubber and leather."

"Okay."

"My dad was, still is, a mechanic and he worked on all kinds of cars and motorcycles. I'd help him sometimes when I was a kid, but it really wasn't my thing."

"This story leads somewhere, right?" Alpo asked.

"Yes. Fine. This Harley-Davidson had a hardtail frame, a nice 'shovelhead' motor with lots of chrome and was painted a crazy deep green metallic with hand-painted pin stripes. The forks were raked. Highball handlebars. Electric start. Hand-tooled custom single leather seat. Just beautiful."

"But?"

"The headlight was still on," Jerrod said. "I didn't want to mess with the bike, so I went into the restaurant and looked for the owner."

"Great story, Sarge. Not sure Mark Twain could tell it better."

Jerrod ignored him. "I see this guy eating alone. The motorcycle had only one seat, so, you know, I used to be a detective. Powers of deduction and all."

"Used to be one, sir."

The guy is Bryan "Shredder" McCrane. But I had no idea who he was then. He has a big omelet in front of him and is pouring Tabasco sauce on it like syrup on a short-stack."

Alpo checked to make sure his radio was turned-on.

"I walk over to McCrane and ask him if that was his 'hardtail' in the lot. He tells me it was none of my business." Then I tell him, 'Okay. Headlight's on. I don't care if you don't care. Have a great day... or a really bad day. Your call."

"Did he go check his bike?"

"I sat down with Roger, and we watched him. McCrane had a decision to make: Stay in his seat and hope his battery would still start the bike or go out and turn the light off. It had no kick start, so he'd be stranded in the lot if the battery went dead. Shovelheads are hard to fire up with a kick start and impossible to roll start -- even if the engine's already warm."

"This is getting better," Alpo said.

"Roger tells me who he is -- the president of the Fer-De-Lance OMG -- and asked what me and McCrane were chatting about. I told him the headlight was on. Roger said he noticed the headlight too and didn't say a damn thing to McCrane about it."

Alpo nodded. "I wouldn't have either."

"Whatever. So, we're watching McCrane, and he heads to the men's room right near the front door. He's in the restroom for a few seconds and then walks out the front door. He comes back a minute later and sits back down to his cooling Tabasco-soaked omelet. No eye contact."

Alpo started a slow clap. "Great story, sir."

"Wait. There's more. Roger and me order coffee and breakfast. McCrane finishes his plate, pays his check, and walks out. Again, no eye contact. I hear the Harley start up and he tears out of the lot."

"Can I share this story with all my friends, sir?"

"When we're done, Nikki tells me McCrane picked up the tab for both of us. How cool is that?"

"Very cool. Please excuse me, sir. I think they need me in Housing."

"You asked. Smart ass."

Alpo's laugh ended as he studied the expression on Jerrod's face.

"Alpo." Jerrod sipped his coffee. "There's a metal serving tray in 'C' Unit right now. It's being broken down to make shanks."

Alpo stood up. "Let's go get it."

"Hang on a second. Sit. Please."

Alpo sat back down.

"What time is 'lights-out' tonight?" Jerrod asked.

"Ten o'clock."

"Have our people rack everyone down in 'C' as usual," Jerrod said. "Then we go in and find the tray while everyone is in their cells."

"So, we can tell exactly who has the weapons."

"Exactly. And we don't leave until the entire tray is recovered."

"Copy that, sir."

"You didn't mention this," Nikki said as she held up that afternoon's *Valle Verde Sun*.

Jerrod poured his first cup of coffee after a daytime sleep. "What?"

The newspaper headline read:

SIX COUNTY JAIL INMATES ARRESTED WITH IMPROVISED KNIVES

"Just another night at the office, honey. We got our tray back... in pieces.... but we got it back."

"So, the prisoners have weapons?"

"'Inmates,'" Jerrod corrected. "And we call them 'shanks.' Anything in the jail can become a shank... especially pieces of metal. I'm learning inmates have very creative arts and crafts skills."

"I thought Patrol was dangerous. I have to worry about you there too."

"It's not *that* dangerous. I have really good people and they tend to find the weapons *before* they get used."

"I'm not liking this assignment much."

"I didn't ask for this assignment. I was sentenced there by the sheriff."

"For something you did."

Jerrod stared at his coffee cup. "I'm doing my time. Just like those inmates. I might even get an early release for good behavior."

Nikki shook her head.

"Maybe you'd like me to quit and go sell cars or something."

"That's not what I meant."

"Oh, damn, I forgot. We now have two mortgages and two property tax bills. Can't quit. Sorry."

She looked away. "I hate you like this."

"And I hate me like this."

Wednesday Night

"On your feet, McCrane. Shakedown," Alpo barked from the cell doorway. "Strip down to your shorts."

Inmate Bryan "Shredder" McCrane marked the page of the paperback he had been reading and took his time standing up from the thin mattress pad on a concrete bed platform -- known as a "rack."

"Is Gold on-duty tonight?" McCrane asked. "I want to talk to him."

"Right here," Jerrod said as he stepped to the door. "This shakedown was my idea. You're not the only one. Please go with Alpo."

"This is bullshit," McCrane said as he walked to within a foot of Jerrod. "Was just getting to a good part of that book."

"I understand your frustration," Jerrod assured him.

"And don't trash my 'house' like last time," McCrane said as Alpo applied handcuffs and led him away to be strip searched. "There's nothing in here I can't have."

Jerrod supervised the two experienced DOs who entered the cell and started a methodical search for weapons and contraband. All clothing, bedding, and towels were removed. All potential hiding areas were inspected with flashlights and small mirrors on telescoping handles.

Jerrod picked up the novel McCrane had been reading -- *52 Pick-up* by Elmore Leonard -- and nodded. He had enjoyed the book... back when he had time to read without interruption.

"It's clear, Sarge," one of the DOs said.

"I'm disappointed," Jerrod said. "Would expect an outlaw like him to break all of the rules here."

The second DO shrugged.

"Bring in McCrane's replacement clothing and bedding while I tidy up," Jerrod directed as he lifted the jail-issue mattress from the floor and placed it on the rack.

"Told you there was nothing," McCrane said as he looked around his cell. "Looks like a tornado came through here. You guys are assholes."

"No," Jerrod said. "We just have standards."

McCrane chuckled.

"Sweet dreams," Jerrod said as the cell door closed. "I think it's scrambled eggs with bacon and toast in the morning."

"Oh, yum," McCrane replied. "More like boring eggs, fake bacon, and burned toast. I can't wait."

McCrane grumbled as he collected his meager possessions and re-made the bed. He stretched the new bottom sheet over the mattress and lifted a corner to tuck it in. "I'll be a son-of-a bitch" he muttered as he stopped, dropped the pad, stood upright, and started to laugh. He pulled the pad up again, shook his head, and continued to laugh as he stared at the six single-serve packets of Tabasco Sauce that had not been there ten minutes earlier.

CHAPTER 52

Willowmere Golf and Country Club

"Thank you for meeting with us, Chief," Michael Sullivan said as Police Chief Doreen Salt arrived at the table.

The club dining room was quiet for a Thursday night. A few couples were finishing a dinner and a handful of golfers lingered at the bar. Their table was situated in a corner near a huge window looking out to the 18th green. No others sat near them.

The four men, all wearing conservative suits, stood and buttoned their coats as she arrived.

Sullivan said, "Let me introduce you to my partners." He swept his hand. "This is Pirro Espiritu. Importer and exporter... mostly."

"'Mostly,'" Pirro Espiritu repeated as he extended his right hand. "Pleasure to meet you, Chief."

Sullivan used his other hand and introduced the second man. "And this is Gaspar De Perras. He deals in computers."

Gaspar De Perras and Doreen shook hands.

Sullivan gestured across the table. "And, finally, this is Fenris Cernv. He buys and sells wine."

"Pleasure's mine," the chief said as she sat.

The men then sat as well.

A male server came to the table. "Would you like to order any drinks?"

Gaspar De Perras looked to Doreen Salt. "Ladies first."

She shook her head, then turned to the server. "Iced tea, please."

The server looked to the men. "Usual cocktails, gentlemen?"

"No," Sullivan said. "Iced tea... everyone... sound good."

The other men nodded.

"Five iced teas it is. Thank you."

"Again," Sullivan said to Doreen, "thank you for meeting us. We're running out of time and need to get this moving."

"I haven't committed to anything," Doreen said. "I'm still on the fence about this whole sheriff thing. I'm not sure I even want to be sheriff."

Pirro Espiritu asked, "Have you discussed this opportunity with your husband?"

Sullivan shot a side glance at him.

Doreen canted her head to one side. "I don't need my husband's permission to do anything."

"Oh... sorry... I didn't intend--"

Fenris Cernv interjected, "We think you are the perfect candidate for sheriff. With the good you have done here in Willowmere. Perfect."

Sullivan said, "We're concerned about diversity and opportunity at the sheriff's office. It's a big job. You know this area and are the most qualified person we can think of for that position."

Gaspar De Perras said, "A friend in the county elections department told us Eric Blanchard has already filed for the position. We thought there would be more interest, but he is the only one so far."

Sullivan began to speak as the server returned with a full tray.

"Five iced teas. Here you go," the server said as he distributed the drinks and then walked away.

"As I started to say," Sullivan continued, "the primary is Tuesday, June 2. We'll need your decision soon because the last possible filing date is Friday, March 13 at 5 PM. If only two candidates run, the election will be decided in June. There will be no run-off in the November general election."

Doreen scanned the faces of the four men seated with her. "You, gentlemen, are up to something. Every instinct I have tells me you are trying to use me for some other purpose. I'm pretty sure I'm going to pass."

The men looked at each other around the table.

"Jerrod Gold is still working for the sheriff," Cernv said. "We were appalled when we saw him assault your officer and get away with just a hand slap."

Espiritu followed. "Wayne Osborn should have terminated him. Good 'ol boys club. He didn't even demote that bastard. Assigned him to the jail. Big deal."

"The media has a short memory," De Perras said. "But we don't."

Sullivan added, "If... correct that... when you become sheriff, Jerrod Gold will be working for you."

Chief Doreen Salt sipped her tea and looked at Sullivan. "I'll think about it. I have your number."

CHAPTER 53

"Watch Commander. Central Security," a male DO radioed.

"Watch Commander. Go ahead," Jerrod answered.

"Attorney and another man in the lobby. Asked specifically to see you."

"Copy that. Enroute."

"Sergeant Gold?" the dapper gray-haired man asked.

"That's me."

"My name is Julius Rodman." He reached under his custom-tailored pinstriped suit coat and pulled a business card from his shirt pocket. "I am Bryan McCrane's criminal defense attorney."

Behind Rodman was a huge, bearded man wearing a black leather vest. He stood next to two brown leather duffel bags and a cardboard box.

Jerrod studied the business card. "Yes, sir. I've seen you in here before."

"As you may be aware," Rodman said. "Mr. McCrane's bail on his current charge has been set at one million dollars."

"He's in here for first-degree murder," Jerrod said. "That bail amount wouldn't surprise me."

"Alleged murder," Rodman said. "At the most recent bail hearing, the judge stipulated that Mr. McCrane would have to post that bail in cash. No services of a bail bond agent could be used."

"I'll take your word for it," Jerrod said. "Subject to verification, of course."

"Of course," Rodman repeated. "My associate has exactly one million dollars in United States currency in one of those bags. I would like to post Mr. McCrane's bail... immediately."

Jerrod caught himself without words for a moment. "A million dollars? In a bag? You're not serious?"

"I am absolutely serious," Rodman said. "Mr. McCrane directed me specifically to bring this cash in when you were on-duty. He informed me you were a man of honor and would ensure his timely release."

"How did you know I'd be working tonight?" Jerrod asked.

Rodman scoffed. "We know your schedule... and your silver Ford F-150 is out in the jail parking lot right now."

Jerrod nodded.

Rodman motioned to the man holding the bags. He placed the larger duffel on the Reception counter and unzipped it. Jerrod looked in and saw stacks of half-inch thick bundles of crisp hundred-dollar bills with money bands showing the amount of ten thousand dollars each.

"One hundred bundles of ten thousand. One million dollars," Rodman said. "You will need to count it."

Jerrod rubbed his chin. "Mr. Rodman, this is very unusual. That amount of cash... I not sure I can... I need to make a few calls."

"Please make your calls. We are not leaving until Mr. McCrane is released. We'll be right here in the lobby awaiting his arrival."

"SDO. Watch Commander," Jerrod radioed.

"SDO. Go ahead," Alpo said.

"Meet me in Booking. Code Three."

"A million in cash?" Alpo repeated.

"I only looked at the top layer. But they have a bag full. What do we do now?"

Alpo thought for a moment. "Inmates can post cash bail here anytime. I've seen it up to a couple thousand dollars before. But not a million."

"Do we have to accept it? Can it wait until morning? I don't want that much just sitting around all night."

"Before we do anything," Alpo said. "We have to verify the bail set in his court papers."

Alpo pulled McCrane's in-custody C-File and thumbed through the green "jail" copies of the court records.

"Yep. Right here," Alpo said. "Bail set at one million. No bond allowed. Must be cash only."

"We have to accept it?" Jerrod asked.

"I'd say so," Alpo said.

"I need to call The Brass on this one."

"I called the Jail Commander at home," Jerrod said to Alpo. "He called the Chief Deputy. He called Sheriff Osborn."

"And?"

"They're not happy about. But we have to take the cash and release McCrane... tonight."

Alpo scoffed. "Money talks... and a killer walks."

"Alleged killer," Jerrod added.

"Yeah. Right."   .

In the lobby, Jerrod asked Rodman, "Aren't you afraid someone would walk in here and try to take that cash."

Rodman glanced over to the menacing man guarding the duffels. "Not really."

Jerrod nodded. "It's going to take some time to count this and I'm not going to do it out here. Please follow me."

Jerrod led Rodman and the man into the conference room.

"What's in the other bag, big man?" Alpo asked.

Rodman answered for him. "A fresh change of clothes for Mr. McCrane."

"And the box?" Jerrod asked.

"A brand-new banknote counting machine," Rodman said.

"You thought of everything, didn't you?" Jerrod said.

"'Everything,'" Rodman replied without hesitation. "I typically do."

The cash was stacked on the conference table and the counting machine was plugged into a floor socket.

Rodman slid the band off one of the bundles and placed the loose bills into a hopper on top of the machine. He set the machine to the one-hundred-dollar denomination and pushed a start button. The bills cycled rapidly through the machine and into array of flat, spinning arms. After the last bill had passed, the display read "$10,000."

"I need to do a test run, Mr. Rodman," Jerrod said.

"Be my guest."

Jerrod took a random bundle from the stack and ran it through the machine. It counted "$10,000." He tested a second bundle and removed three bills from it. "$9,700" the display read.

It took forty minutes for Jerrod to count the cash with the use of the machine. At the same time, Alpo placed the bundles into a plain

232

cardboard inmate property box. There was a total of precisely one million dollars.

Jerrod looked at Rodman, "To the penny, sir." He then nodded to Alpo. "Go ahead and roll McCrane up."

Alpo took an unusually long time to respond. "Yes... sir," he said as he headed out of the room.

"Mr. McCrane's change of clothes, Sergeant," Rodman said. "The clothes he had been wearing at the time of his arrest were seized by the detectives."

"He can walk out of here naked," Alpo said.

"I think not," Rodman shot back at Alpo.

"Let's see what you brought him," Jerrod suggested.

Rodman nodded to his associate, who pulled opened the smaller duffel and took out a pair of jeans, a black henley-collar long-sleeved shirt, a pair of boxer shorts, socks, and black biker boots.

Jerrod looked to Alpo. "McCrane can wear those out."

Alpo sneered at the man as he collected the clothing. "This is bullshit."

The burly associate remained silent as a broad smile spread across his face.

"Mr. Rodman," Jerrod asked. "How is it you could come up with a million in hundred-dollar bills in a single day?"

Rodman pondered for a few moments and answered with a question of his own. "Sergeant, you belong to a law enforcement labor union of some sort. Yes?"

"I do."

"And you pay dues to become, and remain, a member of said labor union? Those dues are pooled for use by all members?"

"Yes."

"And this labor union also has a Legal Defense Fund? They provide business agents and attorneys to represent you if needed?"

"Yes. We have an LDF. I have to pay extra for that."

"Mr. McCrane does as well. However, it is through his association with many other, shall we say, like-minded motorcycle enthusiasts."

"I'm pretty sure I understand now."

As the associate took the empty duffels and the counting machine outside, Jerrod prepared a handwritten receipt for the cash. He used a

233

two-copy pad generally used in Reception to accept commissary money for inmates.

> To: Julius Rodman, Esq.
> Receipt of: One Million Dollars.
> Reason: Cash Bail for Bryan McCrane.
> Signed: Sgt. Jerrod Gold.

Rodman studied the receipt for a moment before folding it and placing in his shirt pocket. "Pleasure doing business, Sergeant."

"Of course," Jerrod replied.

Jerrod heard the sliding door from Booking to Lobby and Alpo appeared escorting McCrane.

Rodman walked to McCrane, and they shook hands.

The associate walked in through the front Lobby doors with an item on a clothing hanger.

"Oh, fuck this," Alpo said.

McCrane took the item off the hanger and slipped it on. It was a black leather jacket with a cloth patch saying "President" on the left side of the chest. On the back was a large snake-head patch in the center with a curved upper "rocker" reading "Fer-De-Lance," a square patch with "MC" below and to the right that, and a lower rocker which read "Mesa, Cali."

After McCrane zipped the jacket, he looked at Jerrod and wagged his finger. "Now be sure not to help yourself to any of that cash."

Jerrod nodded. "Everyone has a price, pal. That's not quite enough."

"My man with standards," McCrane chuckled. "Send my best to your gorgeous wife."

"Let's go," Rodman said. "Your ride awaits."

"First round's on me," McCrane replied as the three men walked from the lobby into the cool evening coastal fog... and newfound freedom.

CHAPTER 54

Saturday -- 5:55 PM -- Mesa County Jail

Jerrod stripped off his San Francisco Giants cover coat as he walked into the Watch Commander's office. Mitchell Sullivan was seated at one of the desks and had the telephone receiver pinned to his ear with his shoulder as he wrote with a ball-point pen onto a page of the Watch Commander's Log. He gasped surprise to see Jerrod walk into the room.

"I will call you back," Sullivan said into the phone before slamming the receiver on the cradle. He pulled the piece of lined binder paper he had been writing on, folded it into quarters, and tucked it into his uniform pocket.

"Sorry to interrupt, Mitch. Were you planning a rendezvous with your girlfriend or something?"

"I was talking to my father. And I am married."

"Tell your daddy I can show him where his golf ball is if he still wants it back. He'll know what I'm talking about."

Sullivan appeared perplexed. "Why are you reporting to work an hour early?"

"An hour early? Shit. My bad. I'll leave and come back. No, seriously, it's daylight savings tomorrow at 0200 hours. You're familiar with that concept, right? 'Spring ahead. Fall back.'"

"Yes. So what?"

"When we 'spring ahead' one hour, my shift loses an hour of work. My people don't like to lose their pay for an hour of work. So, I planned a special activity for them."

"Such as?"

"Shakedowns. I love doing shakedowns. The Jail Commander loves when I do shakedowns. Inmates fucking hate when I do shakedowns. In about five minutes, my people are going to walk into three housing units -- selected by me -- and are going to search high and low and all places in between for all items of contraband they can find. I suspect there is going to be more than a few losses of visits and commissary for a week or two. Maybe we'll find something real exciting."

"I was not briefed on this."

Jerrod scoffed. "Briefed? This has nothing to do with you, Mitch. You're an irrelevant little shit. I cleared it with my boss -- who's also your boss -- and I don't need your permission to do a goddamned thing."

"Suit yourself," Sullivan said.

"Consider it suited, dickhead."

Jerrod returned to the Watch Commander's office and reveled in the haul of contraband his competent staff had collected. Extra food, extra clothing, extra razors, pornography, tobacco, and a few crude improvised weapons were found and seized. He expected an avalanche of pink inmate grievances and looked forward to responding to each one.

Mitchell Sullivan had since left the jail and Jerrod sat at the desk he had occupied earlier. He opened the Watch Commander's Log to make some notes about the shakedowns and noticed the blank page had imprinted words on it.

He recalled Sullivan having been writing into the log when he startled him by coming in early. He had ended the call with his father and subtly removed the page from the binder.

Jerrod picked up the binder and moved it around in the light to see if he could make out any of the words. They were impossible to read.

Alpo walked into the office. "Good call, sir. The inmates will be grumbling for days about those shakedowns. I suspect the other units already know and they'll be expecting the same. We may have to call the plumbers out tonight with all the contraband being flushed down the toilets right now."

Jerrod heard bits and pieces of what Alpo said.

"Do you have a pencil?" Jerrod asked.

"No pencils in here, sir. I told you months ago. They can be used as weapons."

"I might have one in my truck."

Jerrod rooted around in the center console of his truck and found a short red pencil he had liberated as a souvenir from the Willowmere Country Club. Its eraser was unused.

In the Watch Commander's Office, Jerrod held the pencil at an angle and lightly rubbed the graphite over the page under the one Sullivan had written on. Words began to appear: "Surf." "Operative." "Salt." "Kelly." "Accident." "Unaware." and other random words which, without some context, made no sense.

Next to the word "Kelly" was what appeared to be a telephone number: "904 555 8723."

"What do you make of this Alpo?"

"That's Sergeant Sullivan's handwriting, sir. I recognize that. But the words don't mean anything to me. Maybe he's planning a beach party or something. If I'm not mistaken, '904' is the area code for Jacksonville, Florida. I have friends there."

"Jacksonville," Jerrod repeated. "He's up to something."

"Jerrod," Nikki said.

He was curled up in his La-Z-Boy reading a crucial scene from *Dead Irish*. "One second, please."

"One thousand one," she said.

He marked the spot. "Ready. Full attention now."

"Reminder they're having a going-away party for me on Monday. I'd like you to attend."

"Is your boyfriend going to be there?"

"Kirk?"

"Yes.

"I'm think I got something going on that day. I'll have my people contact your people."

Hand to hip. "It's your day-off and you're going to be there."

"Yes, dear."

Friday Evening

"She's running for sheriff, Jerrod," Chief Deputy Eric Blanchard said as he slumped into a chair in the Watch Commander's Office.

"Who's that, sir?" Jerrod asked.

"Doreen Salt. Willowmere Chief of Police Doreen Salt."

"I know of her, sir. Never met her though."

"She had the courtesy of coming to see me before," Eric said. "But she filed papers with the County Clerk an hour before the five o'clock deadline."

"I though the final deadline for candidates was last Friday?" Jerrod asked.

"So, did I. At first," Eric said. "Sheriff Osborn reminded me that since he, as the incumbent, was not running for reelection, the filing period gets extended one week. Today was the last day."

"Well, that makes things exciting."

"Sure does. Although 'exciting' isn't the term I'd use." Eric let out a small laugh. "She's good, Jerrod. She's real good."

"Of course, you have reason to be concerned, sir. But you have all the qualities--"

Eric raised his palm. "It's a new world now. Law enforcement isn't the 'good-old-boys-club' it used to be. Don't get me wrong, we have great female deputies now."

"And secretaries, and records clerks, and DOs," Jerrod added. "But just one female deputy has been promoted to sergeant in the history of the office. Think Chief Salt's going to play that card?"

"I'm certain she will." Eric scratched his face. "She'll argue that the sheriff's office -- that is, the sheriff -- has somehow discouraged or discriminated against women being in sworn positions and has kept them in more traditional roles."

"And she plans to change that," Jerrod said. "Think she's right?"

"Maybe," Eric said. "How long ago did you attend your police academy?

Jerrod thought for a few seconds. "Twelve years ago. Spring of 1980."

"How many recruits were in that class?"

"About forty guys."

"'Forty guys?' No women?"

"Not one, sir."

"My point exactly," Eric said. "It took you, what, ten years to make sergeant. There are plenty of very competent women in sworn positions in our office. Smart. Doing the work. Paying their dues. And their time is coming."

"But?" Jerrod asked.

"But not fast enough." Eric said. "That's the perception Doreen Salt is going to create. The politics in this county has changed. More liberal. More inclusive. More and more every day."

"That's not a bad thing, sir," Jerrod said. "But, regardless, you'll still be the most qualified candidate."

"You may be right," Eric said. "But that very well may be an anchor around my neck when running against a woman for that office at this time."

Saturday Evening

"Inmate Stapleton was convicted today. All counts," Mitchell Sullivan said as Jerrod walked into the Watch Commander's office.

"Today?" Jerrod asked. "It's Saturday."

"The jury came back today," Sullivan said. "That is all I know."

"Have you talked to him?" Jerrod asked.

Sullivan looked up from his entry in the Log. "Why would I? Inmates get convicted all the time here."

"Guess you don't know him," Jerrod said.

"Feel free to talk to him all you wish."

"You're a great humanitarian, Mitch."

Bradley Sean Stapleton was where Jerrod expected to find him -- the law library.

Jerrod said, "I heard the jury didn't quite go your way."

"Understatement, Sergeant," Stapleton said as he turned over the legal pad he had been writing on.

"When's your sentencing?"

"Sixty days. Middle of May."

Jerrod nodded.

239

"I've already started my appeal. There were many errors made at trial and I think there is a good chance this conviction will be overturned."

"I wish you luck," Jerrod said. "Are you going to be okay? Not going to hurt yourself?"

"I'll be fine. Thank you." Stapleton paused. "But I would like to share with you some things about some very bad people I have dealings with. They're planning a major move right now."

"I'm intrigued," Jerrod said as he pulled out a chair. "And I'm available. All ears."

"Not now," Stapleton scoffed. "But soon. I promise."

"Deal."

"West Housing. Central Security," a male DO radioed. "Panic alarm. Fight. Man down in 'F' Unit."

"'F' Unit," Jerrod said to Alpo. "No, no, no."

The dayroom floor of the "special needs-ish" housing unit was covered in blood. An inmate dressed in a red-soaked jumpsuit lay on his side facing away in the middle of the floor. DOs ordered the other inmates away from the man and to their cells.

"We've got the down inmate," Alpo yelled to the three DOs who entered the dayroom with them. "Check every inmate in here for injuries and bloody clothing."

Jerrod found no mess-free path to the man and just walked through the muck. He grabbed the man by the shoulder and gently rolled him to his back. He braced himself for what he was about to see.

"Oh, my God," Jerrod said. "It's Stapleton."

Bradley Sean Stapleton's face was almost unrecognizable. Blood poured from multiple gashes on his forehead and cheeks and chin. His nose was broken, and several teeth had been knocked out. He struggled to take in quick, raspy breaths.

A female DO yelled from a cell door. "Inmate here is covered in blood."

"'Cuff him," Jerrod directed. "Leave the clothes on him. Take him straight to an interview room. And secure that cell."

Jerrod turned to Alpo. "I'll stay here. Get an ambulance rolling. Shutdown the entire jail. Everyone in their cells. Get all patrol cars out of the sallyport. And I need the jail nurse back here too. Code Three."

As the handcuffed inmate was escorted from the unit, a male DO reported, "All the other inmates are clear, Sarge."

"Rack 'em down and come help me."

Jerrod checked Stapleton and found he had stopped breathing. He tilted Stapleton's head back and established an airway, but the bloodied man took no breaths.

"Keep his airway open," Jerrod directed the male DO.

Jerrod took the CPR mask from the pouch on his belt and placed it over the unconscious man's nose and mouth. He pushed three deep breaths into Stapleton's lungs and watched his chest rise and fall.

"Breathe, you son-of-a-bitch. Breathe," Jerrod pleaded as Stapleton remained unconscious.

Jerrod gave three more breaths and saw no change.

The DO checked Stapleton's neck for a pulse. "Nothing there, Sarge,"

"Start chest compressions," Jerrod directed. "Twenty compressions and then I'll give two breaths."

The DO knelt along Stapleton's torso, pulled the front of his jumpsuit open, used his fingers to locate the proper position to place his hands on his sternum, and began pressing down on the lifeless man's chest.

"Good. Good," Jerrod said as he counted the compressions. "Six... seven...keep... that... heart... pumping... twelve... thirteen...."

At "twenty," Jerrod placed two more deep breaths into Stapleton's lungs. He felt for a pulse and found no change.

The jail nurse arrived and attached a football-shaped resuscitation bag to the CPR mask. She squeezed the bag and pumped more air into Stapleton's chest.

"Resume compressions," Jerrod directed. "One... two... don't... you... fucking... die... seven... eight...."

"Stop CPR," the nurse said. "She placed a stethoscope against his chest. "No heartbeat. Resume CPR."

Jerrod added. "Don't stop until the paramedics arrive."

As the DO compressed Stapleton's chest and the nurse squeezed air into the fallen man's lungs, Jerrod studied Stapleton's injuries and looked around the dayroom. It quickly became obvious that repeated impacts with an immovable blood-smeared stainless-steel seat attached to a nearby table had been the cause of Stapleton's head injuries.

"Stop CPR," the nurse directed. She checked for a heartbeat again. "Resume CPR."

The DO who had been performing chest compressions hesitated. "What... the hell?" With huge eyes, he pointed to Stapleton's belly. Although covered by a jail-issue t-shirt, the abdomen of the skinny man had become distended like he had been pumped full of air.

"Oh, shit," the nurse said. "Major internal bleed."

"It's no use, Sarge," the DO said as he moved away from Stapleton. "I think he's dead."

"It's okay. Just relax," Jerrod said to the DO as he moved over Stapleton and a started compressions himself. With all the strength he could muster, he pushed his weight against the man's chest in a steady rhythm and prayed for a miracle to happen.

At four minutes, a trickle of sweat rolled off Jerrod's nose. "Come... back... you son... of... a... bitch... Open... your... eyes... I... need... to... know."

At seven minutes, a male and a female paramedic arrived in "F" Unit. Two plastic cases containing medical supplies and a green oxygen bottle were carried in on a rolling gurney. The male took over compressions as the female replaced the CPR mask and twisted the valve on the oxygen to full flow. The mask didn't fog.

The female paramedic attached the leads for a heart monitor and ordered CPR stopped. "Nothing. No rhythm," she said as she looked up at Jerrod, "How long has he been down?"

Jerrod was still catching his breath. "Eight... or nine... minutes... since we... got here."

The male paramedic shook his head. "We'll keep trying," he said as he resumed compressions.

"You have to... save him," Jerrod sputtered. "You... have to. Please. Zap him or something."

The female paramedic placed the paddles of a portable defibrillator device on Stapleton's chest. "Everyone stand clear," she ordered before the device delivered a violent electric shock. Stapleton's torso jolted upward.

Jerrod watched and hoped.

"No rhythm," the female reported.

"Hit him again," Jerrod pleaded.

A second electric shock was sent. Same result.

Jerrod hung his head.

The male paramedic looked up. "We'll get him to the ER, Sergeant. But don't get any hopes up."

Jerrod thought of his very first night as a Jail Watch Commander: Over coffee, he had asked Alpo what the worst things that could happen in the jail. Alpo said either an escape or a death-in-custody were the worst. "Ugly," was the term he used.

Jerrod prepared for "ugly."

The moment Bradley Sean Stapleton's battered body was discovered, West Housing "F" Unit became a crime scene.

The Mesa County Sheriff's Office Major Incident Policy was implemented, and all notifications were immediately made: The on-call detective and Crime Scene Unit were summoned to conduct the investigation. The on-call Deputy District Attorney, the Jail Commander, and Sheriff Wayne Osborn were notified at home and advised of the situation.

A patrol deputy was assigned to go to the emergency room at St. Michael's Hospital and to stay with Stapleton -- alive or dead.

All involved staff wrote reports documenting their involvement. The Jail Commander made an appearance and disappeared to update the chief and sheriff.

Four detectives arrived. All "F" unit inmates were interviewed. Photographs were snapped. Measurements were taken and diagrams prepared. Clothing and all of Stapleton's personal items and paperwork were collected. The bloody mess was cleaned and disinfected by inmate workers. The remaining inmates were released from their cells.

And then it was over. One by one, the responding personnel drifted away. In a mere few hours, the Mesa County Main Jail was back in operation like nothing had occurred there.

Except that Bradley Sean Stapleton -- the keeper of the secrets -- was gone and his vital information was gone with him.

Jerrod stirred half-and-half into his coffee. "Alpo, I'd much rather be swirling three olives in a 'perfect' martini right now."

"Understood, sir," Alpo said.

"Here's the story I got about what happen tonight," Jerrod paused. "Okay. Stapleton was returned from the law library about a half-hour after I talked to him. He goes straight to his cell, puts his legal papers on his bunk, and walks back into the dayroom."

Jerrod winced as he took a sip of the stale coffee.

"Stapleton then walks up right behind that other inmate -- who was seated and watching television. You saw that other dude. He was huge. And he's in here on violent sex charges."

Alpo nodded.

"Anyway, Stapleton just pushes this inmate off the seat and sits down on it. The big inmate jumps to his feet and flips-out. He punches Stapleton in the face and knocks him to the floor. The inmate then kicks Stapleton numerous times in the gut before grabbing him by the hair and bashing his face into the steel seat. Repeatedly."

"I don't get it," Alpo said. "Stapleton was wacky, but not violent. Did he have some prior 'beef' with that other inmate?"

"No. Not a hint of that. It seems he got along with everyone in the unit before this."

Alpo sipped his coffee.

"And," Jerrod added. "This is really weird. At no time did Stapleton attempt to protect himself or resist the attack."

"This all doesn't make sense, sir," Alpo said.

"Maybe it does, Alpo? Stapleton was no fool. Maybe it does make sense."

Sunday Morning --12:30 AM

"Call for you, Sarge," the female DO yelled from Booking.

"Send it," Jerrod yelled back.

"Sergeant Gold," said into the receiver.

"Jerrod, this is Ted Lindsey."

"I guess I know why you're calling."

"Yeah... well... yes it's about Stapleton. He was pretty much DOA when he got to the ER. I just picked him up."

"Ted, that guy teased me earlier with... I don't know... a 'revelation' about some shit about to go down in this county. He wouldn't get into detail. Now he's gone."

"Maybe not," Ted said.

"What do you mean?"

"At the ER, they cut Stapleton's jumpsuit off, and an envelope fell out. I'm looking at it now."

244

"You're kidding."

"Nope," Ted said. "The envelope is sealed and addressed: "Sergeant Jerrod Gold. For his eyes only."

"I don't believe this. Did you open it?"

"'For his eyes only,' means *your eyes only*. Can you get away and meet me at the morgue?"

"Ten minutes."

When the door to the morgue was opened for him, Jerrod was not only greeted by Ted Lindsey, but by the sensory overwhelming smell of formalin -- the formaldehyde-based solution used to preserve human tissue -- that he had learned to tolerate each time he visited the unmarked facility.

Ted led him to the autopsy suite where Jerrod found the body of Bradley Sean Stapleton laying naked on a stainless-steel gurney. His blood-covered head was propped up with a black plastic block. A respiration tube hung from his mouth and EKG leads dangled from his chest. The pale body of the formerly hyperactive man appeared calm and relaxed -- most probably for the first time in many years. It took his death for it to happen.

"Did you know him well?" Ted asked.

"Not really. We had a few conversations in the law library. I talked to him right before... you know. The guy was a ball of energy when he was alive. Nonstop. It's weird seeing him like this."

"This is going to be classified as a 'homicide,' Ted said, "But it's really a suicide. Kind of like 'suicide-by-cop' when someone puts an officer in a situation and they have to shoot them."

Jerrod's gaze had not left Stapleton. "Suicide-by-inmate."

"Exactly," Ted said. "Any indication he was suicidal when you talked to him last?"

"None. He was upset about his conviction but was already planning his appeal. I didn't pick up any vibe he would hurt himself... or cause it."

Ted nodded.

Jerrod looked at Ted. "I came here to see that envelope."

"Sure." Ted walked to a counter, opened a folder, and handed Jerrod a white letter-sized envelope. Its bulk felt like there were several folded pages inside.

Jerrod went into the adjacent office and used a pair of scissors to carefully trim off an end of the envelope. He pulled out the pages and unfolded them to reveal a five-page letter. He instantly recognized the precise block print which had been used by Stapleton.

The letter read:

Dear Sgt. Gold

As you read this letter, you already know I am dead. No appeals for me. It is unlikely I'd make it out of prison alive and I'm too much of a coward to take my own life. So, as you now know, I found someone to do it for me. I'll just have to make a convincing closing argument to Our Maker I am worthy of a pain-free afterlife.

I am sorry I did this on your shift, but I could take no chance this letter would not reach you. You have been fair and honest with me. I appreciate your respect for the rights of the inmates in your custody. You are a gentleman and truly the protector of all.

I previously alluded to some information I would be sharing with you. I suspect you had an extended conversation in mind, but, nevertheless, here it is:

I worked for four wealthy and powerful men who, in the most literal sense, run the County of Mesa. This group is collectively known as "The Tetrad." The four men comprising The Tetrad are: Gaspar De Perras, Fenris Cernv, Pirro Espiritu, and they are led by Michael T. Sullivan. Their criminal activities include...

The letter went on to describe in extreme detail the various crimes and schemes and influence and connections The Tetrad had gained and controlled for over the previous twenty years. Stapleton specifically described how he had helped The Tetrad launder the money they earned from their unlawful endeavors. He listed a dozen shell companies and named a series of bankers and politicians who both knew about and enriched themselves by helping The Tetrad.

Jerrod was not sure he took in a single breath as he finished reading the last page -- which outlined a violent scheme by The Tetrad to install their handpicked candidate for sheriff and exactly how they planned to accomplish it.

"Are you okay, Jerrod?" Ted asked. "You don't look well."

"No, Ted. I'm not okay. I have some calls to make."

CHAPTER 55

"Watch Commander. Central Security," the female DO radioed.

"Watch Commander. Go ahead," Jerrod radioed.

"Dayshift sergeant is in the Intake sallyport," she radioed.

"Copy that," Jerrod radioed as he looked at his watch. It was 6:50 AM.

Mitchell Sullivan walked through Booking and into the vacant Watch Commander's office. He peeled off his cover coat and hung it neatly on the rack.

Before Sullivan could sit down, Alpo walked in and filled the office doorway.

"Sergeant Gold has a situation out front, " Alpo said with a tone of urgency. "Please come with me."

"Fine," Sullivan said as he followed Alpo through the sallyport to the Lobby.

"What is going on here?" Sullivan asked as Jerrod met him.

"Thanks, Alpo," Jerrod said. He turned to Sullivan. "It's in the conference room. After you."

"I do not have time for this," Sullivan said.

"Go with the sergeant," Alpo said -- now standing directly behind Sullivan.

Jerrod followed Sullivan into the conference room and had to give him a shove when he stopped at the doorway.

"Inside, Mitch," Jerrod said. "I think you know everyone here."

Seated at the conference table were: Chief Deputy Eric Blanchard, Investigations Lieutenant Ben Zaff, DA Inspector Stan Walsh, FBI Special Agent Romero Diaz, and Sheriff Wayne Osborn.

"Sit down, Mitchell," Ben Zaff directed. "We have a few questions for you."

Sullivan slammed his palms down on the oak table. "You want me to implicate my own father in a conspiracy to commit murder. I will not do that."

"Suit yourself, Mitchell," Ben Zaff said. "Anyone got a *Miranda* card handy."

"You are going to arrest me?" Sullivan asked the group.

"That's a strong consideration," Stan Walsh said.

Jerrod unfolded the graphite-smeared piece of binder paper and placed it on the table. "Watch Commander's Log, Mitch. Your handwriting."

"You have some explaining to do," Eric Blanchard said.

Sullivan made eye contact with every man in the room -- settling on Sheriff Osborn.

"Your law enforcement career is over, Mitchell," the sheriff said. "But you can do the right thing now and save your dignity."

"Wait. Wait. Wait," Sullivan said as he paused to collect himself. His voice trembled as he spoke. "This was not my idea. I will tell you what I know."

Sergeant Mitchell Sullivan started the session slowly. He was vague and evasive with his answers at first but was no match for the assembled group of experienced investigators. For the next hour, he was peppered with questions from all angles. His ambiguities and inconsistencies were exposed. His answers became more consistent as the conspiracy by the four members of The Tetrad to assassinate Chief Deputy Eric Blanchard -- a declared candidate for the office of Mesa County Sheriff -- became clearer and more focused: They had planned to eliminate Eric by making it look like he died in a surfing accident. His death would clear the way for Doreen Salt to become the next sheriff.

But there was one missing piece -- the identity of the assassin who had been hired to kill Eric Blanchard. Sullivan only knew him as "Kelly" -- a proficient surfer from Jacksonville, Florida. He had already been paid ten thousand dollars and would receive another ten thousand when the deputy chief was found to have died in "a tragic accident while surfing."

Sullivan sat at the end of the long conference room table. Defeated. Elbows rested on the tabletop. Chin in hands. Eyes wet.

Sheriff Osborn had been silent during the questioning. He stood and walked around the table until he towered over Sullivan.

Sullivan turned his head and peered up at him.

"I should have fired you after the Brent Rozman fiasco," the sheriff said -- his voice calm and quiet. "I had the chance to do it then; I won't pass on the opportunity now. I'll need that badge, Mitchell. Consider yourself suspended pending termination."

Sullivan nodded and reached to unclasp the badge.

"Put your hand down," the sheriff directed.

Sullivan froze.

The sheriff reached down, wrapped the fingers of his beefy hand around the seven-point gold star and yanked it -- along with a piece of khaki fabric -- from Sullivan's uniform shirt.

"Hey," Sullivan yelled -- having nearly been pulled up from his seat. "You ripped my shirt."

"No, Mitchell, that's *my* shirt," the sheriff said. "And I'll take it too."

Before Sullivan had arrived for work, Jerrod assigned Alpo to cover the dayshift crew. Jerrod met Alpo in the Watch Commander's office.

"Anything happening?" Jerrod asked.

"Quiet as church," Alpo said. "Shift change went without a hitch."

"Good," Jerrod said. "Here's what we're going to do."

Fifteen minutes later, Jerrod and Alpo went back to the conference room. Alpo was carrying a yellow jumpsuit, a shit-stain-dyed jail towel, and a pair of PVC inmate slippers.

"Are we done with *Mr*. Sullivan here?" Jerrod asked.

"We may have some more questions later," Stan Walsh said. "But we're done for now."

"You can come with us, Mitch," Jerrod said as he reached under his t-shirted upper arm.

Sullivan shrugged his hand off. "Do not touch me... and I want to make a telephone call."

"Request denied," Jerrod said. "Let's go."

Jerrod pulled Sullivan by the arm into the Jail Commander's office and Alpo followed.

"Strip down to your underwear and socks," Jerrod directed.

"I am entitled to a telephone call," Sullivan replied.

"Strip... or I'll help you strip," Alpo said as he moved a step closer.

Sullivan paused, shook his head, and then sat down to remove his boots and pants.

Now wearing an over-sized bright yellow jumpsuit and shuffling along in the loose slippers, Sullivan stepped out of the Jail Commander's office and into the lobby.

"Put this towel over your head and cover your face," Jerrod directed.

Alpo handed Sullivan the towel. Sullivan stared at it. "Don't panic, it's fresh. Right out of laundry," Alpo said.

Sullivan put the towel over his head and covered his face. Jerrod and Alpo each took an arm.

They escorted Sullivan along the visiting corridor to Times Square. No inmates occupied the law library or visiting rooms. Inmate workers had been returned to "G" Unit. They led Sullivan into an eerily quiet East Housing. All the dayrooms were empty with the inmates secured in their cells.

As Alpo opened the door to "L" Unit, shouts came from the occupied isolation cells -- all with sheets of copy paper covering the small windows on each cell door.

"What the fuck?" one inmate yelled.

"Who's coming into our 'house?'" another yelled.

Sullivan was walked to the open door of a floor-level cell. Paper covered the inside of that cell door window.

"Get in," Jerrod said. "There's a toothbrush there for you. Not much else. You might want to leave that window covered when the others get their hour-out."

Without comment, Mitchell T. Sullivan walked into the cell, looked around his new confined quarters, removed the towel from his head, and turned to face the open doorway. He and Jerrod locked eyes. As Alpo started to swing the door closed, Jerrod raised his right hand to chest height and extended his middle finger.

"Who is that Sarge?" the female East Housing DO asked.

"Protective custody," Jerrod said. "'John Doe' for now."

"Ooh," the DO said. "Mysterious."

"We have a problem," Ben Zaff said as Jerrod walked back into the conference room.

"What's that?" Jerrod asked -- before noticing Assistant DA Lorena Delgado had joined the group.

"Hello, Jerrod," she said. "I think I understand what's happened so far."

Jerrod studied Lorena for a moment. She wore the same crewneck long-sleeve University of Southern California sweatshirt she had worn the first time they met -- at the scene of the horrific Cardinal Lane murder-suicide two years earlier. "Cardinal and Gold" she had said at the time. Cardinal and gold were the USC school colors.

"Ma'am...uh... Lorena," Jerrod said as he sat at the conference table.

"I thought we were missing something," Ben continued. "Ms. Delgado was kind enough to come in this morning and confirmed that."

"The 'overt act,'" Jerrod said.

"Exactly," Lorena said.

Eric Blanchard said to Lorena, "Please go over the elements of the conspiracy laws again so we're all on the same page."

Lorena cleared her throat. "Sure. Penal Code section 182 lays out the basic elements we will need to prove: Two or more person have conspired, that is, jointly agreed, to commit a crime -- in this case a premeditated first-degree murder of a peace officer -- and then committed one or more 'overt acts' toward completing the crime, whether the actual crime is carried out or not. An overt act can be any actual, tangible step or steps made by any of the conspirators toward the completion of the crime."

Jerrod asked, "What's the sentence for murder... uh... conspiracy?"

"Same as the actual crime," Lorena said. "Life, or worse."

"So, hypothetically," Ben scoffed, "four rich guys can sit around together drinking scotch and smoking cigars while agreeing to contract a hitman to follow the Chief Deputy out into the surf, bash his head with a club, and guarantee their handpicked candidate for sheriff wins the June primary... but unless they make some tiny provable step toward actually doing it, there is no crime?"

"Not entirely correct," Stan said. "Hiring the hitman -- 'Kelly' -- would be an overt act. But we'd have to catch him--"

"I have an idea," Jerrod interrupted and looked around the table. "WWJFD."

"Pardon me?" Lorena asked.

"What Would Joe Friday Do?"

Ben Zaff said, "We need to get a better handle on this "Kelly" character." He turned to Special Agent Diaz. "Romero, would contacting a hitman across the country and making a trip over state lines to complete an assassination violate any federal statutes?"

"Most likely," Romero said.

"We need to ID that guy," Jerrod said. "All we have is a phone number."

"Let me see what I can come up with," Romero promised. "Can I use one of those offices?"

"Use the Jail Commander's office," Eric said

Stan smirked. "And I thought the *new* FBI-thing was just a joke."

Romero winked and headed to the office.

"We need to decide on a beach to do this," Jerrod looked to Eric Blanchard. "Chief. Suggestions?"

"Depends," Eric said.

"Where do you usually surf?" Jerrod asked.

"'Two Trees' or 'Picnic Table' are my favorites. But they're both locals only. An outsider wouldn't last in the water very long before getting challenged."

"Little territorial, aren't we?" Jerrod asked.

Eric chuckled. "I suppose. But it's more about skill and respect. You have to earn your spot in those places."

Jerrod asked, "How about someplace less... exclusive? Preferably with some vantage point so we can monitor the situation in the water."

"The only place that fits that bill is Willowmere Pier," Eric said. "It has okay surf. Lots of tourists. Unobstructed view from the wharf itself."

"Perfect. I know the place," Jerrod said. "We're gonna need some people in the water with you. Any surf buddies you can trust... with your life?"

"Already got that covered. Three guys I served with in the Navy are on their way here from SoCal right now. All good surfers. They'll be here tonight."

"Four versus one," Jerrod scoffed. "Not a very fair fight."

"Fights are never 'fair,'" Eric warned. "We've got the numbers, but 'Kelly" will have the advantage of surprise."

Romero Diaz emerged from the office. "Officially, the FBI is not allowed to do this."

"But?" Stan Walsh said. "Unofficially is pretty okay with us."

Romero smiled. "I learned the phone number is to a cell phone. It was activated in Jacksonville a few weeks ago and the subscribers name is: 'Kelly Machado."

"He wouldn't use his real name?" Ben Zaff suggested.

"It's an alias," Eric Blanchard announced. "Clever though. Kelly Slater and Rob Machado are, without question, the two best surfers on this planet at the moment. He's using a combination of their names as an AKA."

"Didn't know that Chief," Romero said. "But it makes sense. 'Kelly Machado' has a valid Florida driver's license with an address that's to an abandoned hurricane-damaged beach house."

"What does he look like?" Jerrod asked.

Romero looked at his notes and gave a generic physical description.

"Can we get a picture?" Ben Zaff asked.

"Working on that," Romero said. "But there's more. 'Kelly Machado' boarded a flight -- red-eye business class -- from Jacksonville last night."

"He's on his way," Stan Walsh added.

"He's already here," Romero corrected. "He had a layover in Salt Lake City and then continued on to San Jose. He got in at 6 o'clock this morning."

"Carry-on only. No checked bag?" Stan asked.

"Yep," Romero said. "Looking into rental cars from San Jose now."

"Nice job," Eric said.

Sunday – 10:00 AM

"Hey, Alpo," Jerrod said. "Want to do some police work tomorrow morning."

"Sure."

"Good. Bring your metal detector."

"Bruce Witt," he answered into the telephone receiver.

"You still owe me, asshole," the voice on the other end said.

"Jerrod Gold: The gift that keeps giving."

"Want some exclusive video?"

"Is the pope...? Do bears...? Hell yeah. Want to know how much I made off that Michael Sullivan 'men-with-knives' video."

"No," Jerrod said.

"Well, it was a lot. Not as much as the city hall thing. But still a lot."

"I'm happy for you," Jerrod said in the flattest tone he could muster. "Meet me at four o'clock tomorrow morning at Tomei's Restaurant on Willowmere Pier."

"They're not open at four o'clock," Bruce said. "Tomei's is a dinner place."

"They're opening for us."

"Okay."

"Bring your camera and a tripod," Jerrod said. "Do you have a remote monitor for that big-ass camera?"

"I have every piece of video equipment there is. Thanks to you, dude."

"Just those three items."

"What's this all about?" Bruce asked.

"Just gonna film some surfers. You'll find out the rest in the morning."

Jerrod hung up the phone on the Watch Commander's desk, opened a drawer, and placed one of the black and red canisters of oleoresin capsicum into his jacket pocket.

Monday 12:35 AM -- Beachcomber Inn, Willowmere

The five men stood in the chilly fog of the luxury hotel parking lot next to a red Ford Bronco. Three surfboards were secured to the roof rack.

"Chief Blanchard is at home right now," Jerrod said. "We suspect his house is under surveillance and we need to keep appearances as normal as possible."

The men nodded.

"Thanks for driving all this way to be a part of these festivities. I'm Jerrod Gold and I'll be your contact here in Mesa. Introductions, please."

The three men summoned on short notice from Southern California were all -- much like the chief deputy himself -- suntanned, in-shape, clean-cut, and carried themselves in a quiet and confident manner.

"Gregorio Barajas," the first introduced himself. "From Dana Point. Everyone calls me 'Goyo.'"

"'Goyo,'" Jerrod repeated as they shook hands.

"Michael Rouché from Oceanside." They shook hands. "'Roach,'" is fine. Glad we could help."

"Roach,'" Jerrod said. "Thank you."

The third introduced himself. "Joseph McDonough from La Jolla. 'Joey' is cool. Been meaning to surf a little in Mesa. Just wanted to do it at a little more relaxed pace."

"'Joey.' It's my pleasure," Jerrod said.

"Who's the big man?" Roach asked.

"Let me introduce you to my partner here," Jerrod said. "Albert Porterfield."

"Just call me 'Alpo,'" he said.

"'Alpo?' Like the dog food?" Goyo asked.

"I'm okay with it," Alpo answered.

Joey smiled after hearing Alpo speak. "Alabama?"

"Roll Tide," Alpo said -- the rallying cry of the University of Alabama Crimson Tide sports teams. He had noticed Joey's accent too. "Huntsville."

"Roll Tide," Joey said. "Montgomery."

"We've set you guys up with a suite here," Jerrod said. "Two queen beds and a roll-away. Hope that's okay."

"That's way more than we need," Goyo said. "We'll be fine."

"Is Eric paying?" Roach asked.

"He is," Jerrod answered.

"In that case," Roach said. "Hope they have room service. I'm starting a tab."

"Willowmere Pier is within walking distance from here," Jerrod said. "I suggest we take a look and go over the plan. Hope you guys brought wetsuits."

"We brought everything we'll need," Goyo said. "Let's go."

CHAPTER 56

Monday -- 4:00 AM -- Tomei's Restaurant

"Bruce Witt. This is Detective Nate Boxley," Jerrod said. "He'll be with you this morning."

"I remember you from behind the city hall," Bruce said. "You were with Jerrod back there."

"Sadly, I was." Nate said.

"I should probably shut up about that, huh?" Bruce asked.

Nate gave him a cold nod.

"All-righty then," Bruce said. He turned to Jerrod. "Why am I here?"

"Do you have your cellphone, Bruce?" Jerrod asked.

"Always."

"Give it to Nate and bring your gear inside."

"Mr. Tomei," Jerrod said, "the restaurant owner, is a friend of my mother-in-law and is letting us use his place for this operation."

"'Operation,'" Bruce repeated with a smile. "How intriguing."

"Shut-up and listen, Bruce," Jerrod said. "This is serious."

"Two humorless cops. Okay. This should be fun."

"We've cleared the tables and chairs from that picture window," Jerrod said. "You'll set your camera up there."

"Fine," Bruce said.

The three men stood at the window and took in the unobstructed view of the surf line. Lights danced on the waves as they rolled into the beach

"Little 'flat' out there," Bruce commented without looking away from the glass. "Waves are kind of small for surfing."

"As long as there are waves," Jerrod said. "We'll be fine."

Bruce turned to Jerrod. "Why did you take my phone?"

"Here's why," Jerrod said as he described the events that brought them to that point and the plan he had developed.

Bruce held the sides of his head with his hands. "A letter from a dead inmate. Michael Sullivan. The Tetrad. A fucking contract killer from Florida. A murder staged to look like an accident to get Eric Blanchard out of the way so Doreen Salt will be the next sheriff. This shit is like a novel. A really bad spy novel."

"Bruce. Focus," Jerrod said. "Your job is to follow the action in the surf. Nate will watch on the monitor and with binoculars. He'll communicate with me. I'll be on the beach with another guy and will coordinate events there."

Bruce nodded.

Jerrod added. "The chief deputy is going to leave his house and get here at dawn -- about six o'clock. We expect he will be followed here by the hitman -- 'Kelly Machado.'"

"That's clever," Bruce said. "'Kelly' and 'Machado' are the names of the two--"

"We know already," both Jerrod and Nate interrupted.

"Oh. Sorry. Just trying to help."

"There will be three of Eric Blanchard's friends in the water already. Nate will help point them out to you."

"Okay," Bruce said.

"We have a rough description of the hitman from a bogus ID," Jerrod added. "But since everyone will be in black wetsuits and on white boards, we'll have to wait until he makes his move."

Bruce asked. "Do you know how he's going to attack?"

"We don't... exactly," Jerrod said. "The Tetrad wants it to look like an accident. A drowning while surfing was a logical way to do that. So maybe a bash to the head? A syringe full of drugs? We just don't know."

Alpo joined the group.

"Bring your stuff?" Jerrod asked.

"Good-to-go, sir," Alpo said.

"Who's this gorilla?" Bruce asked as he looked up at Alpo.

Jerrod smiled. "'Like a bad spy novel,' right, Bruce?"

"It is."

"Meet Code Name: 'Towel Line.'"

CHAPTER 57

"Kelly Machado" was not his real name, and he didn't grow up aspiring to be a contract killer.

The Jacksonville native grew up surfing the waves up and down both of Florida's coasts. His dreams were to hone his skills until he got a sponsorship deal and could then travel the world as a professional surfer.

He was hired, and, usually abruptly, either quit or got fired from thirty different menial jobs in the few years after he dropped out of high school. Dishwasher. Stock boy. Car detailer. Toy-part assembly. Night clerk. Forklift driver. Messenger. He found that if the waves were good; work could always wait.

At a dismal entry-level job at a slaughterhouse near Tampa, his role was to herd cattle off delivery trailers into the plant. To expedite that transfer, he was issued a portable livestock prod -- a handheld battery-operated waterproof device with two metal electrodes and a thumb switch. He found he enjoyed sadistically tormenting the doomed cattle with the prod. A poke on the rump got a 1,200-pound steer moving; a poke to the neck made it fall to its knees. He relished the power it gave him and managed to swipe one of the devices before being fired for his callous animal abuse.

He killed his first human during an affair with a bored married woman near Brunswick, Georgia. In exchange for two thousand dollars in cash, he made sure the husband left for work in the morning and did not return that evening. The livestock prod was used to subdue the man and he made the crime look like a robbery gone bad.

For the next four years, he found he could satisfy his appetite for the finer things and have plenty of time for surfing by arranging the untimely deaths of others. His underworld reputation -- as well as his retainer fee -- grew with his body count. .The livestock prod played a role in every murder he engineered.

In March 1992, "Kelly Machado" received a telephone call from a man who asked him if he would be interested in some work in California.

CHAPTER 58

Willowmere Beach

"So, you do this for fun?" Jerrod asked Alpo. "This is a good time to you?"

Alpo glided his state-of-the-art metal detector in sweeping arcs across the sand as Jerrod used a mesh scoop attached to a broom handle to dig in and recover whatever metallic item lay underneath.

"Yes, sir. It relaxes me after a night at work," Alpo said. "Crisp salt air. Waves crashing. I get home, sort my treasure, and sleep like a baby."

Jerrod shook his head as Alpo tightened the arc to a single spot.

"Yeah. Right there, Sarge," Alpo said as Jerrod scooped his third bottle cap of the morning.

"You know we really don't have to be looking for stuff," Jerrod said.

"Then what's the point of bringing the metal detector?" Alpo asked. "You want us to look realistic, right?"

"Fine. Whatever," Jerrod said as he was surprised by finding a quarter in the bottom of the scoop.

"Comm check," Nate radioed from the window at Tomei's.

Jerrod heard the broadcast on his hidden portable radio through an earpiece. Since Jerrod and Nate had both once been baseball players, they had worked out a simple set of hand signals. He gave the signal -- swiping his right hand down the center of his chest -- to signal he could hear him.

A second signal -- a pull of the left ear -- had identified the three Southern California friends as they entered the water at different times on various parts of the beach. Roach was first in. Goyo two minutes later. Joey a minute after that.

Nate watched Jerrod's signals through binoculars and pointed the three men out to Bruce.

Chief Deputy Eric Blanchard arrived at precisely six o'clock. Jerrod used the third signal -- his right hand to his belt buckle -- when he stepped into the surf.

"We've got them all in sight," Nate radioed. "Would be nice if there were some colors for wetsuits other than black."

Jerrod swiped his chest.

Two high school aged boys carried their surfboards across the beach. One stopped and looked at Jerrod. "How about you two bums find real jobs?"

Alpo growled and made a sudden charge at the boy. His eyes got big as he turned a made a frantic run into the surf.

"'Method acting,' sir," Alpo said. "I think that little smart-ass peed himself a little."

"'Bums?'" Jerrod asked. "Who says 'bums' these days?"

Jerrod dug in the sand and watched a variety of surfers -- all male, all ages -- enter the water. "Kelly Machado" could have been any of them.

The surfers all paddled out through unbroken water and away from others riding breaking waves. They waited in a loose queue -- "the line-up" -- until it was their turn to catch the next wave.

Nate shifted the view through his binoculars to Eric Blanchard. He closely followed the chief deputy as he straddled his board and bobbed in the surf moving closer to a rideable wave. It was nearly his turn when Eric allowed a surfer to go before him. Another surfer farther back in the queue -- black neoprene hood covering his head -- laid flat on his board, pointed the nose at Eric, and paddled frantically directly toward him.

"Someone's moving on the chief," Nate radioed. "This didn't take long. Going right at him. Head's up."

Eric saw the surfer heading for him and prepared himself. "Come on, asshole," he muttered to himself. "Come on."

Roach, Goyo, and Joey saw the move and inched closer to Eric.

The wild paddling stopped when the surfer slammed broadside into Eric and pulled his hood back.

"Gonna fucking sit or surf, kook?" the teen-aged boy yelled. "You new in the water or something?"

"Yeah. Pretty new at this," Eric said. "Go on ahead of me, kid."

"Learn to surf somewhere else, Barney," the kid said as he pulled his hood back up and paddled away.

"False alarm. False alarm," Nate radioed. "The chief's fine. Standby."

Eric caught the next wave and had a decent forty second ride until he bailed out. Joey and Roach caught the next two waves. Goyo stayed in the line-up and followed Eric's progress as he paddled back around. Roach and Joey paddled together at a distance behind Eric.

As Eric got back into the line-up and sat up on his board, another surfer got Goyo's attention. He thought he saw a glimpse of an object -- something dark -- in his right hand.

Goyo pointed the nose of his board toward Eric and moved slowly toward him.

"Something's happening," Nate radioed with the binoculars to his eyes. "Our guy is watching someone."

Jerrod swiped his chest.

While still straddling his board, the surfer inched closer and moved behind Eric. Goyo paddled toward them. The surfer laid on his board and paddled without his hands breaking the surface of the water. He got to within six feet behind Eric when Goyo yelled his name.

Eric turned as the surfer reached his right hand out of the water and pushed the livestock prod at him. Eric fell to the right off his board as the prod struck his left shoulder. He felt the jolt and lost sensation in his arm. Goyo paddled directly to them as the surfer plunged the prod into the water and stunned Eric two more times.

"The chief's down. He's off his board," Nate screamed into the radio.

"Kelly Machado" knew he had fallen into a trap and paddled toward shore. Goyo helped Eric -- stunned, but conscious -- cling to his board and stay above water. Joey and Roach paddled with all their energy to catch the escaping attacker. The hitman pushed past the others in line, caught a wave, and body surfed toward the beach.

"That guy," Nate radioed. "That guy body surfing just attacked the chief."

Jerrod swiped his chest to signal Nate and watched the waves. He spotted one, then a second, then a third surfer in on their bellies riding waves toward shore.

"The first one," Nate yelled into the radio. "The first one. Our guys are behind him."

Jerrod gave the signal to Nate and looked for the first one to touch the beach. It became obvious when the surfer jumped off, abandoned his board, and started running across the wet sand.

"That's him," Nate screamed. "He's running. Get that bastard."

Goyo helped Eric back onto his board.

Jerrod ran in the dry sand -- parallel with both the shore and the sprinting surfer -- hoping to cut off his escape route from the beach. Alpo struggled to keep up, then tripped and took a fall. The surfer made a hard

261

right turn and ran directly toward Jerrod. There was a black object in his right hand.

"That's him," Nate yelled on the radio. "Right in front of you. Take him. Take that son-of-a-bitch."

Jerrod pulled the Glock from its holster and pointed the muzzle at the man. "Sheriff's office," he screamed at the hitman. "Freeze right there." He was unsure what the black object was but could see that it wasn't a handgun. The hitman slowed to a deliberate march but gave no hint he intended to stop.

Goyo helped Eric paddle toward the beach. Joggers and dog owners fled to safety under the pier. Oblivious surfers lingered in the water behind the hitman and stayed in danger of being struck if Jerrod fired the 9mm and missed his target. The killer continued walking directly toward Jerrod.

"Stop," Jerrod warned. "Stop right there."

The killer advanced and raised the black object to waist height. He came within twenty feet. Jerrod focused the front sight of the Glock the exact location he would shoot the man -- the center of the most vital area available -- the middle of his chest.

"Stop," Jerrod yelled as the man moved forward.

The killer got to within twelve feet. Jerrod applied pressure to the trigger. "Stop. Stop."

"Take him. Take him." Nate pleaded on the radio. "Dump his ass."

Jerrod then remembered he had the OC he had taken from the Watch Commander's desk. He pulled the canister from his left jacket pocket and aimed it alongside the Glock as the killer moved another step closer. He still could not make out what the black object was. Surfers were in the background. Roach and Joey were now running directly behind the hitman and were in the line of fire.

"Marinate on this, motherfucker," Jerrod said as he launched a three second burst of OC which struck the killer directly in the face.

Now blinded, the killer slapped his hands to his face. The black object fell to the sand.

Then it happened.

Much like an unsuspecting pedestrian in a crosswalk being struck by a speeding car, Albert "Alpo" Porterfield -- now moving his great mass at maximum velocity -- dropped his shoulder at the last moment and drove it into the unprotected side of the hitman's torso. The impact lifted both men off their feet until they tumbled into the sand.

"Tell me you got this, Bruce," Nate said.

"I got it, dude. I got it all."

Alpo held his body weight on the killer as Jerrod and Roach and Joey jumped onto the pig-pile. They pulled the hitman's arms behind his back and secured them with handcuffs before jerking him to his feet.

The hitman's face was fully coated in pepper spray and sand. As he tried to open his eyes, a sand-crusted snot rope emerged from his nose. Joey and Roach had to be physically restrained by Alpo to keep them from tearing the man apart. Goyo helped Eric trudge through the sand to see the hitman up close. Three sheriff's patrol cars -- lights flashing and sirens blaring -- skidded into the beach's parking area.

Alpo picked up the black livestock prod and recognized what it was immediately. He found a discarded aluminum can nearby and pressed the electrodes of the device against it. As he depressed the trigger, the can jumped from an intense arc of electricity.

Deputy Chief Eric Blanchard walked up to confront the would-be-assassin. He cradled his limp left arm in his right hand and paused for a moment as he gathered his thoughts.

"Hey, what the hell?" Bruce said as Nate pushed the camera to the side so his view became that of the open Pacific Ocean and away from the developing drama on the beach.

Nate said, "You're experiencing some 'technical difficulties' at the moment."

Bruce nodded.

On the beach, Jerrod braced for whatever was about to happen.

The chief deputy looked "Kelly Machado" up and down before speaking. "I don't know who you are, asshole. But you came to the wrong beach. This one's for locals and invited guests only."

Eric turned to Jerrod. "Get him to the office."

Jerrod and Alpo grabbed the hitman by the upper arms and led him to the parking area. Just as he was being handed-off to a patrol deputy, Jerrod spoke directly into the man's ear: "Don't worry, dipshit. We'll have a nice hot shower waiting for you at the jail."

CHAPTER 59

Noon -- Investigations Division Commander's Office

"We didn't get a single word out of him, Chief," Jerrod said. "He just glared at us. Nate tried. I tried. This guy's a pro and isn't going to give anyone up. He's on his way over to the jail right now."

Sorry, sir," Nate added. "Good cop. Bad cop. Nice cop. Worse cop. Nothing worked."

Jerrod added, "He just sat there and looked at whoever was talking through his beady little red-rimmed eyes. Not even a hint of expression."

Chief Deputy Blanchard sat across the table from them. He rubbed his left arm and wriggled his fingers. Two raised welts had developed around his shoulder from the charge of the prod. Two more sets of marks were on his back. "Not surprised," he said.

Jerrod nodded.

"Thank you," the chief said.

"Yes, sir," Jerrod said. You're okay and one hitman is off the street. I'd say it been a rather good day."

"Yes, it's been a good day, but that's not what I meant," the chief said. "You probably saved my life today. If we hadn't known this attack was coming--"

"You're welcome, sir."

Lieutenant Ben Zaff entered the office. "Romero Diaz has the FBI looking into this guy," he said as he sat at his desk. "He's requesting agents in Florida get involved and he'll make sure this guy's fingerprint card gets expedited to see if we can find out who he is."

"The new FBI," Nate said.

Jerrod smiled and turned to Eric. "How are your boys? Goyo and Joey and Roach?"

"They're probably down at the hotel bar flirting with some local hotties and running up a well-deserved tab."

"They were great, sir," Jerrod said.

"They are great," Eric said.

"Did Alpo play football somewhere? Eric asked. "That tackle would have gotten the attention of an NFL scout. How long has he been over at the jail?"

"Eight years, sir." Jerrod answered. "He's my SDO,"

Eric looked to Ben. "Do you know him? This SDO? Alpo?"

"No, sir."

"How about you, Nate?"

"No, sir."

"The staff over there," Jerrod said, "are pretty much invisible to the rest of the office."

"That can't be true," Eric said.

"I didn't know him either -- until my first night there. He could take over my job tomorrow and the shift would run just fine. Our Detention staff do a hell of a job."

"I'll have to look into that," Eric said.

Jerrod yawned and stretched.

"When was the last time you got some sleep?" the chief asked.

Jerrod thought back. "Real sleep. Pillow and blanket sleep. Cuddle with the wife sleep. Probably a few days ago. Had a couple naps.

"Get some tonight, Jerrod. You earned it."

"Yes, sir."

Ben's desk phone rang and he reached to answer it.

Jerrod stretched again. "I'm going to grab some coffee and start writing this case up now. Bruce Witt caught the whole thing on video, but the Ms. Delgado is going to want at least a summary on paper by tomorrow morning."

"You do that," Eric said.

Jerrod went to the empty break room and poured a cup. He stared into his reflection in the coffee and relived the manic events of the last few days. His sleep deprivation had peaked and the adrenaline-dump from the beach scene had left him drained. He realized he hadn't had anything to eat in over twenty-four hours. The first sip of coffee caused a sudden wave of nausea that caught him off guard.

CHAPTER 60

Jerrod walked from the restroom back into Ben Zaff's office five minutes later and found only Nate Boxley there.

Standing.

Waiting.

"Sarge. There's something happening right now."

"Damn right there's something happening," Jerrod said. "I just need to write it up."

Nate grabbed him by the shoulders. "Listen to me."

"Okay," Jerrod said. "Ruin my day. What's so damn important?"

"The L-T and the chief are on their way there now," Nate said.

"Where? What?"

"It's Nikki. She's at the restaurant... Sophie's--"

"I know," Jerrod interrupted. "She went there to get her last check and have a little going-away party. I was gonna go, but this thing--"

"Sarge, listen, please," Nate interrupted back. "There's a man there. With a gun. He's holding Nikki and says he'll kill her if you don't come to the restaurant right now. I need to get you to Sophie's. Code Three."

Nate sped Jerrod in his unmarked sedan through ridiculous traffic to Sophie's -- somehow getting there without killing them or someone else. Jerrod learned the man went into the diner during the party, got next to Nikki, pulled out a handgun, and told everyone else to leave or they would be shot.

When Jerrod arrived at the restaurant, he didn't know if Nikki was alive or dead.

The scene at Sophie's Diner was bedlam: Marked Willowmere PD, Mesa SO, and CHP patrol cars -- with overhead lights activated -- created a haphazard perimeter around the building. Uniformed and plainclothes officers with handguns and shotguns trained their muzzles at the diner. Camouflage-uniformed members of Mesa SO SWAT donned their gear, checked their weapons, and planned an assault. Citizens stood behind yellow crime scene tape and gawked from all angles. News crews with their vans and antennas and cameras arrived and set up -- all hoping to catch some gore for the evening's lead story.

"Jerrod. Sergeant Gold," a familiar male voice yelled.

Jerrod looked toward the voice and found Bruce Witt behind the tape line. Camera ready. He nodded to Bruce but kept walking.

Nate led Jerrod to an improvised Command Post that had been set up in a nearby car dealership. Ben Zaff, Eric Blanchard, and a woman wearing a Willowmere PD uniform with single gold stars on her collar were talking on their cell phones and to each other as Jerrod arrived.

"Sergeant Gold," Ben said. "Do you know Chief Salt?"

"Yes, of course. But we've never met." Jerrod turned to her and extended his hand.

She held her phone in her right hand and made it obvious she had no intentions of shaking his.

"Whatever," Jerrod said to the chief before he turned back to Ben. "Is Nikki okay?"

"She's alive," Eric Blanchard said. "Hostage negotiators have been talking to the guy in the diner on the phone. The officers on the perimeter can see inside and we can hear everything on the cell phone. He has a chrome revolver pointed at her most of the time."

Jerrod asked, "Do we know who he is?"

Doreen Salt spoke. "His name is 'Kirk LaMahieu.' Ring a bell?"

"'LaMahieu,' sure," Jerrod said. "The son of the guy from the city hall thing."

"That's him," Doreen said. "And he has it in for you."

"Nikki has talked about him," Jerrod said. "She described as a real nice guy."

"Not anymore," Ben said.

Eric said, "The negotiators tell us LaMahieu is pretty animated, but said he won't hurt Nikki on one condition."

"Her... for me," Jerrod said.

"Exactly," Doreen said.

Jerrod turned to Eric. "Tell the negotiators I'm going in."

"We can't let you do that," Ben said. "That'd be suicidal. And we'd have two hostages instead of one to negotiate for. "

"You are not going in that building," Eric directed. "That's an order."

"Sarge," Nate pleaded. "Don't do it."

"This isn't going to happen," Doreen ordered. "I forbid it."

Jerrod addressed Doreen. "Chief, you and I are probably never going to be friends. So, ma'am, with all due respect, I don't take orders from you."

Nate gave an audible gasp.

Jerrod looked to Eric. "Sir, who has tactical command here?

"The sheriff authorized SWAT, so I have tactical command."

"Eric," Doreen said. "You can't approve this. You can't."

Chief Deputy Eric Blanchard was a decisive man. But he took an exceptionally long time to respond.

"Sir," Jerrod continued. "How was my plan this morning? How did that work?"

"Brilliantly."

"I can't stand here with my thumb up my ass and watch something happen to Nikki. I have a plan for this too. I need you to trust me."

"No, Jerrod," Eric said, "there's just too much risk. I would be responsible--"

Jerrod interrupted. "Chief, remember that conversation we had a couple years ago: 'I like people who take charge, can make decisions, and get results.' Remember that?

"Yes. Sure. How many times are you going to use that comment against me?"

"Sir, I'm the only one who can walk into that restaurant without that guy hurting Nikki. He's expecting me. Just me. And I have a plan. Please let me go in."

"What if it goes wrong?" Ben asked.

Jerrod ignored Ben's comment. "Chief, that's my wife in there. We have two daughters, and they need their mom. They did just fine before me, and they'll be just fine without me. But it won't go wrong."

Eric paused again.

"Eric," Doreen said. "You're not considering this. I won't allow it. This violates every standard and protocol. I won't let you do it."

"Doreen," Eric snapped, "Our SWAT team. Our sniper teams. Our negotiators. My command."

He looked for a reaction and got a blank stare.

"Or perhaps," he added, "you'd prefer we just stand-down so you can send a couple of your patrol officers in to save the day... again. How did that work out the last time?" He didn't wait for a response. "And, by the way, I don't take orders from you either."

Doreen glanced at Eric, then to Jerrod, and back to Eric. Her mouth opened, but no words came out.

"Guess that's settled." Eric turned and looked at Jerrod. "Tell me your plan. WWJFD?"

"Sir, this plan is one even Joe Friday could never come up with."

CHAPTER 61

Jerrod drew the 9mm pistol from his holster, lifted the left pant leg of his jeans, and tucked the Glock into his sock on the inside of his ankle. He looked at Nate Boxley, Ben Zaff, Eric Blanchard, and to Doreen Salt.

Jerrod asked, "Are the snipers in place?"

"Two teams," Ben said. "Alpha and Bravo teams have good vantage and comms directly to us."

"They understand the signal?" Jerrod asked.

"If you tap the top of your head with your hand... they fire," Eric said.

"Good," Jerrod said.

"What if LaMahieu locked the door?" Ben asked.

"The front door has no lock," Jerrod said as he looked toward the restaurant. "Tell everyone I'm going in."

The police radio crackled: "All units. All units at the hostage situation. A plainclothes officer is going into the building. He's wearing a black jacket, gray shirt, blue jeans. Allow him through the perimeter."

Jerrod walked from the Command Post in a straight line toward Sophie's Diner. The eyes of every officer, member of the media, and citizen looky loo at the scene followed his deliberate steps. He acknowledged none of them. As he stood at the front entrance and reached to pull the door open, he took in a deep breath, puffed his cheeks, and muttered, "This better fucking work."

"Your buddies told me you were coming in," Kirk LaMahieu said. "We finally get to meet. I've been waiting for this moment."

LaMahieu was seated at a booth in the center of the restaurant. Nikki sat next and on the other side of him. Jerrod could only see part of her. A boxy cellular flip-phone rested on the tabletop next to a half-eaten cake and some used plates. A short-barreled chrome revolver was in his right hand.

"Nikki, are you alright?"

"I'm okay. You shouldn't have come in here."

"Enough," LaMahieu said. He looked at Jerrod. "Do you have a gun?"

"Left it out there."

"Take off your jacket and throw it on the floor."

"Fine," Jerrod said. His voice quiet and calm. He peeled off the jacket and hung it on a chair.

LaMahieu screamed, "You don't follow directions very well."

"I've been told that before," Jerrod said.

"You have to do what I tell you," LaMahieu bellowed.

"Kirk, am I yelling at you?" Jerrod asked in a barely audible voice.

"No," LaMahieu replied. His tension relaxed at little. "Now pull up your shirt and let me see your waistband."

Jerrod pulled up his shirt and turned slowly so LaMahieu could see his empty holster and waistband.

"Good," LaMahieu said. "How do you want to do this?"

"It's your show. You tell me."

LaMahieu swung the revolver away from Nikki and pointed it at Jerrod. "Maybe I can just shoot you now and it'll all be over."

"Yep," Jerrod said. "But before you do, I'd like you to know how sorry I am about your father. I think about that every day and have nightmares about it... when I *can* sleep. I wonder how that could have ended differently. I take full responsibility for what happened."

"Too little. Too late."

"Your right. But, again, man-to-man, I am sorry. You'll be doing me a favor by killing me. I just can't live with the guilt anymore."

LaMahieu shook the handgun at Jerrod. "Fuck you and your sorry."

"I'm ready to die," Jerrod said.

"You were supposed to die in a restaurant full of people," LaMahieu said. "But you missed your own wife's going-away party. What kind of a jerk does that?" Kirk snickered. "I had planned for it to be your 'going-away' party too."

"Something came up. Can Nikki leave now?"

LaMahieu grabbed Nikki by the arm and yanked her to her feet. He put his arm around her neck and the revolver to her temple.

Nikki shrieked. "Kirk, please. No."

"You said you'd trade Nikki for me. Here I am. I don't want her to see me die, so please just let her go. I'm ready."

"Fair enough," LaMahieu said as he pointed the handgun back at Jerrod.

Nikki started to cry. "Jerrod. Don't do this."

He looked at LaMahieu. "Can I say a few words to her before she leaves?"

"Sure. Make it quick."

Jerrod looked directly into Nikki's eyes. Tears welled in his. "You are my life and my soul. I love you and I treasure every moment we've been together. I love the girls and will miss them too. I'll miss all the fun we had together. Our wedding. Our honeymoon. Our trips. Our bike rides. And the games we played in the living room."

Tears trickled down Nikki's face and she looked perplexed at what he was saying.

"Those games... with the girls. You know, like the 'Nuclear Option' game." Jerrod cracked a smile. "That was a lot of fun."

Nikki's perplexed look faded as it was replaced by familiarization.

LaMahieu rolled his eyes.

Jerrod chuckled. "Remember that game: '1-2-3. Nuclear Option.'"

"'Nuclear Option.' This is dumb," LaMahieu said as he rotated the revolver in a let's-move-this-along-already motion.

"That was fun. I do remember," Nikki said with a nod.

"Best game ever," Jerrod said. "1-2-"

On "3," Nikki raised her right foot, slammed it down along LaMahieu's shin and impacted the top of his foot. The muzzle of the chrome handgun raised to the ceiling. When he pulled his arm off her neck, Nikki spun and drove her knee into LaMahieu's groin.

"You bitch," LaMahieu yelled as he doubled over in pain.

Also, on the count of "3," Jerrod had crouched and removed the pistol from his sock. He stayed kneeling as he raised the Glock to his line-of-sight.

Nikki grabbed a dinner fork from the nearby tabletop and drove it into LaMahieu neck. As LaMahieu reeled back upright, Jerrod fired two rapid rounds -- one missing completely, but the second hitting LaMahieu in the right upper chest near the shoulder. The revolver clattered to the floor near LaMahieu's feet.

Jerrod stepped onto the revolver and kept the muzzle of the Glock focused on the center of LaMahieu's chest. "If you move, I'll empty all thirteen rounds I have left into you."

"Fuck you," LaMahieu said.

"Nikki," Jerrod said, "toss me that phone."

Nikki took the flip-phone off the table and handed it to Jerrod.

"This is Sergeant Gold. We have shots fired. Suspect is hit, but not down. It is not Code Four. Repeat. Not Code Four. The female hostage is unharmed and coming out the front door. Do you copy?"

A male voice replied, "We copy. Suspect hit. Not Code Four inside. Female hostage coming out."

Jerrod spoke into the phone. "Do not make entry until I advise."

Jerrod looked briefly at Nikki. "When you go outside, just keep your hands up, and follow the directions of the officers. You'll be fine."

She headed for the door. "I love you, Husband."

"Love you too, Wife. Forgetting something?"

"What?" Nikki asked.

"Kiss."

She ran over and kissed him on the cheek before going back to the door.

"Leave me," Jerrod said. "Go now."

He watched her run outside to an officer and knew she was safe.

Jerrod glanced at LaMahieu then back to the phone.

He placed his thumb on the display and pressed the "off" button.

"We've lost communication inside the diner, Chief," the Willowmere patrol sergeant said to Doreen Salt. "The phone went dead."

"What the hell?" she muttered to herself. "What's that idiot up to?"

"You're leaking pretty bad, Kirk," Jerrod said. "Shot in the shoulder and 'forked' in the neck. Wish I could help you, but I'm not really in a position to render first aid right now. So, I'll just stand here and watch you bleed out."

LaMahieu touched his shirt and pulled away a hand covered in blood. "I guess so."

"If you pull that fork out; you'll bleed faster," Jerrod offered.

LaMahieu pulled the bloodied fork from his neck and dropped it on the table. "Aren't you supposed to arrest me or something?"

"Technically... yeah... I guess."

"'Technically?'" he scoffed. "Didn't you swear to protect the public and save people and shit like that?"

"Sure." Jerrod thought for a moment. "But I tend to make up my own rules as I go along."

LaMahieu snickered. "Great."

"I really am sorry about your dad. I was getting him to surrender, and he had just let the lady hostage go--"

"Save it," LaMahieu interrupted. "Save your bullshit. I don't need it."

"Fine with me. But I'm telling you the truth."

"So, what happens now?" LaMahieu asked.

"Well, I see just two options," Jerrod said. "You die here... or you go to prison and die there."

"Probably so."

"Ever been to jail?"

"No."

"They've got me working at the county jail now. I wouldn't want to live there."

LaMahieu looked at him with a blank stare.

"Prison's worse. So I hear. Never been. Just rumors."

LaMahieu swiped his index finger into his blood-soaked shirt and drew a small "X" in the center of his chest. "Here you go. Marked the spot. Just shoot me now and get it over with."

"Nope," Jerrod said. "You, my friend, held my wife against her will and pointed a gun at her and threatened to kill her and made her cry and ruined her party and then you called her a 'bitch.' Thinking about you spending the rest of your miserable life in prison gives me a certain sense of satisfaction."

"What happens now?" LaMahieu asked.

"Do you follow baseball, Kirk?"

"No."

"So, you don't know the signal a batter makes when an umpire is standing in his line-of-sight and he wants the umpire to move."

"No."

"The batter pats the top of his head with his hand. That's all. The umpire moves a few steps to the side and play resumes."

"What the hell does that have to do with us?"

"Two sniper teams are set up right now. The crosshairs of the shooters' scopes are focused on you. Their partner scouts are watching me. If I pat the top of my head, you get at least one .308 caliber high-velocity round inserted into your brain."

"What are you waiting for? Pat your fucking head."

"I told you. I want you to rot in prison."

LaMahieu shook his head. "I'm not going to prison."

Jerrod nodded. "So, let's discuss that, Kirk."

"What the hell is he doing in there?" Doreen Salt demanded of the Willowmere officer peering into the restaurant through binoculars.

"Chief, they've been having a conversation. For a few minutes. Both are talking. Calmly. The officer has still got his handgun pointed right at the bad guy. Uh... Chief... somethings happening. Officer's moving closer. Finger is on the trigger. Wait. More conversation. Officer has his hand... kind of... hovering over his head. Hang-on."

Every person at the scene flinched when they heard the report of a single gunshot.

A male voice radioed: "Suspect is down. Repeat. Suspect is down. Plainclothes officer is heading to the front door now."

Jerrod walked out with his arms extended. The Glock was in its holster. His jacket was in one hand and he extended four fingers with the other. "Code Four. Suspect is deceased. The scene is secure. Where's my wife?"

As uniformed officers ran into the diner, Jerrod scanned the perimeter for Nikki. He found her standing with Nate. He ran to her, and they hugged. Tears flowed.

"You're okay?" Nikki asked as she held him away and looked for injuries. "There was another gunshot."

"It's all over. He won't be a problem again."

A pudgy uniformed Willowmere PD officer walked up to them. He was the same officer he had struck with the shotgun.

"Excuse me," the officer said. "That was the dumbest fucking stunt I've ever seen. But I'm glad you're both okay."

"Second dumbest stunt... but thanks," Jerrod said. "Hey, I'm sorry about that... thing... behind city hall. Are we good?"

The officer nodded and stuck out his right hand. Jerrod shook it.

"We're good," the officer said. He turned to Nikki. "Ma'am, I'll need to get a statement from you."

As Nikki gave her account of the incident and the officer scribbled notes, Jerrod walked a few steps away and talked with Nate.

Nate looked around to see if anyone was listening. "Can you hear that?"

"Hear what?" Jerrod asked.

"The deep clanging sound of solid brass balls every time you move."

"My wife was in there. What would you have done?"

Nate pondered a moment. "I don't know. Ask you to handle it, I guess."

Jerrod scoffed.

"You realize that *was* the number-one dumbest fucking stunt. Don't you?"

"Yeah. Probably."

"I can't believe the chief deputy give the okay to do that." Nate shook his head. "You know what that would have done to his career. He'd be finished."

"Do you mean if I'd been killed?

"Yeah."

"Nate. Do realize what that would have done to *my* career?"

Nate couldn't contain his laughter.

"In a few minutes, I'm gonna have to go do the shooting thing... again. I don't know how long that's going to take. Can you make sure Nikki gets home okay?"

Nate smiled. "I'll get her home just fine."

"Where's Chief Salt?" Jerrod asked Eric Blanchard and Ben Zaff at the command post.

"She had enough," Ben said. "We treated her pretty bad."

"We've got some fences to mend with her," Eric said. "Lots of fences. We were disrespectful. In her own city."

"I bet she secretly wanted me to die in there. It would give her some good ammo against you in the election."

"She's dropping out of the election," Ben said.

"She... what?" Jerrod said.

Eric picked up. "We told her about The Tetrad and their plan to eliminate me so she would win. She's withdrawing. She's an honorable person and said she wouldn't want to win that way. So, unless a very popular write-in candidate appears in the next few months, I'll be elected the next sheriff."

"Excellent news, sir. Congratulations."

Investigations Interview Room

"The following is a tape-recorded interview with Mesa SO Sergeant Jerrod Gold regarding an officer-involved shooting. Today's date is Monday, March 16, 1992, and the present time is 1923 hours. My name is Inspector Stanley Walsh with the Mesa County DA's Office..."

"... and we'll conclude this interview at 2006 hours," Stan said before pressing the "stop" button on the tape recorder.

"This is now the third time we've done this in six... seven years?" Stan asked.

"That's about right," Jerrod said.

"Did you know the cell phone was 'on' in that diner during the entire incident? Right until Nikki was about to walk outside."

Jerrod shrugged. "Battery go dead or something?"

"Battery was fine. It was 'off' when they recovered it."

"It was a little crazy in there, Stan. I don't know what happened to the phone."

"Off-the-record," Stan said as he leaned closer to Jerrod. "What the hell did you two talk about before... you know?"

Jerrod looked around the room and leaned toward Stan. "Same thing I told you on-the-record: He was despondent over me shooting his father, planned his revenge, wanted to kill me, and he took Nikki hostage to get me there."

Stan snickered. "That's the part we already know. All the officers at the scene could see you and LaMahieu talking. Two, three minutes."

"What do you want to hear, Stan? That guy was bleeding pretty bad and probably knew he was going to die anyway. I was hoping he would just pass-out or something."

"Yeah, right after you shot him, and your wife stabbed him in the neck with a fork." Stan snickered. "By the way, I'd suggest not complaining about anything she cooks in the future."

"Very funny. She was scared and reacted the way we practiced."

277

"You practiced for a situation like this?"

"Yes. No. Not for this, exactly. The kids. Never mind."

"But what did you two talk about?"

"Baseball. Customs and traditions. Couple other topics." Jerrod shifted in his seat. "We didn't have some deep philosophical conversation or anything."

Stan shook his head. "I know you too well by now. I just don't buy it."

"Buy or don't buy, Stan." Jerrod scoffed and looked away. "I was there -- you were not."

CHAPTER 62

Jerrod walked into the living room of his house and found Nate Boxley laid-back with feet up in the La-Z-Boy. Heineken in hand.

"Welcome home, brother," Nate said. "Got Nikki home fine... just like you asked."

Nikki came out from the kitchen and looked at Jerrod. "Are you alright?"

"Yeah. Fine. You?"

"Not fine."

Jerrod nodded. "Where are the kids?"

"With my mom."

"Got another beer in the 'fridge."

"Of course."

Nate moved to the sofa and Jerrod claimed his chair.

"I'm exhausted," Jerrod said. "Hitman surfer dude in the morning and hostage-taking revenge-seeking lunatic in the afternoon. No sleep for three days. I shouldn't have even driven home tonight. Surprised the CHP didn't pull me over thinking I was DUI."

"I'll drink to that," Nate said.

"Cheers, man." Jerrod tipped his bottle. "All I wanted to do was finish my jail sentence and work my way back into Investigations. I miss you mutts."

Nate sipped his beer. "Don't take this the wrong way, Sarge. Roger Collins is a great guy and all, but--"

"'But' what?"

"We miss you too, man."

Nikki and Jerrod held each other under the stream of a comforting warm shower.

"We never get to do this," she said over the noise of the water. "Not since that resort in Napa."

"We should make this a 'thing," he responded as he rubbed soap on her back and shoulders. He avoided the darkening bruises on her upper arms. "Those look tender."

She glanced at the bruises. "He grabbed me pretty hard. I don't think he intended to hurt me."

Jerrod had a few instant responses pop into this head, decided it best not to comment.

"I'm a mess," she said."

"No. You're beautiful."

"I hope you can get some sleep tonight," Jerrod said as they cuddled in bed. "At least you don't have to go to work again for a few days."

"I don't know," Nikki answered. "How do you do it? How do you sleep after a day like this?"

"Exhaustion and alcohol seem to help."

She kissed him.

"Now close your eyes," he whispered. "You're safe here with me."

CHAPTER 63

Thursday Morning -- Chief Deputy's Office

"Does the address of '626 Tamsen Lane' in Valle Verde mean anything to you?" Eric Blanchard asked.

Jerrod sat in the chair across from his desk. "Sure. That's the house next to my rental. It belongs to my neighbor, Colonel Horvatz."

"How about '630 Tamsen?'"

"That *is* my rental. I used to live there."

"Where do you live now?"

"A few blocks away. Rochester Avenue."

"How long ago did you move there?"

"A month ago," Jerrod said. "Mind telling me why you're asking me this, sir?"

"We found some items in the van that that hitman -- 'Kelly Machado' -- stole in San Jose: A backpack full of clothes. His bogus driver's license. An open return airline ticket to Jacksonville. His cell phone. A .22 caliber pistol with a silencer. And a map of Valle Verde with the addresses of 226 and 230 Tamsen Lane circled on it."

Jerrod let the news sink in. "He was gonna take us out too."

"Killing you I can understand."

"Thanks, Chief."

"Not what I meant." He stifled a laugh. "This isn't funny."

Jerrod's eyes drifted away in thought. "He was going to kill the colonel and me. Maybe Nikki and the kids too."

"My earlier point was simply: Why Colonel Horvatz?"

"Michael Sullivan visited him, sir. Went right up to his house. Scared the shit out of the old guy."

"Why?"

"Because he did me a favor." Jerrod looked at the floor. "He did some checking on Sullivan's military background."

"At your request?"

"Yes."

"Jerrod. Were you behind that prank call at Sullivan's house? The men with knives? The broken gate? All of that?"

"Sir. I did not place that emergency call into 9-1-1."

"But were you behind that call? Did you put that scheme together?"

"Do you actually want to hear the answer to that question? I won't lie to you, sir."

"I fucking knew it." The chief slapped his hand to the desk. "That had your fingerprints all over it."

"Metaphorically, sir?"

"Yes, metaphorically. Smart-ass."

Jerrod grinned.

"Now," the chief said, "I need to know what you and Kirk LaMahieu talked about in that restaurant."

"I gave my statement to Stan Walsh."

"I read your statement to Stan Walsh. It's total bullshit." He took a calming deep breath. "I want to know from you, off-the-record, what happened in there."

Jerrod leaned forward and made direct eye contact. "No, you don't, Chief." His voice moved to a hushed tone. "Again, sir, I won't lie to you. But please trust me -- you don't want to know."

"Perhaps I don't." Eric Blanchard said as he sat back and took in the moment. "I understand you, Jerrod. I get how you think."

"Sir, if I ever feel the need to see someone to help figure out how I think, I'll come to you first." He had no intention of letting anyone in his law enforcement family -- especially the next sheriff -- know about his bi-weekly visits with Sidney Yamamoto.

The chief gave a quick laugh. "I mean, I understand your mentality. You have a warrior mentality."

Jerrod shrugged.

Eric took a sip from an over-sized blue coffee cup with "Navy" stenciled on it. "You met my buddies -- Joey and Roach and Goyo. In case you were wondering, we didn't meet waiting for a wave in Malibu."

"Kind of figured that, sir."

"It was more like getting 'wet and sandy' on a beach at Coronado. We're the last four from that class."

Jerrod nodded.

"We served our country by doing things we can never talk about... even to each other. Are you following?"

"Yes, sir. Much like the ninja."

"I see you know your warrior history too," the chief deputy said. "Yes. Very much like the ninja. Driven. Mission critical. Stealthy. Innovative. Effective. Discrete."

"Deadly, sir?"

"And often deadly."

"What happens now?"

Eric Blanchard leaned back again in his chair. "You most probably saved my life, and perhaps that of your family and neighbor in the process. I am grateful. Thank you."

"You're welcome, sir."

"I will be the next sheriff. Sheriff Osborn is going to finish his term as planned but is also going to use up a chunk of accrued time-off before he retires in January. He'll be absent from the office quite a bit until then."

"Yes," Jerrod said.

"He has left me in charge. I'll be putting together next year's budget and making all assignments."

Jerrod nodded.

"Write your own ticket. Just tell me where you want to work and I'll make sure you get there."

"Is this my 'get out of jail free' card, sir?"

"It is. But with a caveat. I may be tasking you -- and I'll word this carefully -- with 'special projects' from time to time."

"'Special,' sir?"

"Yes. Any ideas about your next assignment?"

"I have a few, sir. They involve moving around some positions."

"Let's hear them."

Saturday Evening -- Mesa County Jail

"What the hell are you doing here?" Alpo asked.

Jerrod, dressed in civilian clothes, had just stepped into the Watch Commander's Office. "You told me on my first night the worst thing that could happen in here was me not getting payroll in on time. I'm here to do payroll."

"But you're on suspension," Alpo said.

"More like 'administrative leave,' so that's kind of a gray area."

"I heard about that thing in the restaurant, sir. The military hands out medals when soldiers do shit like that."

"My wife was in there. I just wanted to get her out."

Alpo nodded.

"And, by the way," Jerrod said. "You owe me a Coke."

"Why?"

"I saw you on TV. If someone mentions they saw you on TV, you have to buy them a Coke... or an ice cream. I forget."

"Are you talking about the Bruce Witt video? You were in that too. So, I guess we're even."

"Thank you for all you did helping catch that guy, Alpo."

"That was fun." Alpo laughed as he saluted. "'Code Name: Towel Line' at your service."

"And that hit you put on him. Holy shit. Like a wide receiver going up for a high pass and getting creamed by a linebacker whether he caught the ball or not."

"I was a little pumped up, sir."

Jerrod said, "The FBI is looking into that guy for a series of unsolved homicides in Florida and Georgia. They say an electric prod device like he had may have been used in those cases. We'll see."

"What happened to Sergeant Sullivan?

"He's now in federal custody -- along with Daddy Sullivan and his business partners. I would have loved to have been there when the FBI and the DEA and the ATF -- and I'm sure, a few other federal acronyms -- swooped in, kicked doors, searched mansions, and took 'em all away in handcuffs. Human trafficking. Drugs. Illegal weapon sales. Computer fraud. Money laundering. You name a crime, and they were in on it."

Alpo nodded.

Jerrod continued, "Sullivan apparently thought he could get his lieutenant bars back after Doreen Salt became sheriff. Mitch actually called that hitman's cell phone from his home. There's a long-distance toll record. For an educated man, that was not a very smart move."

There was a pause and Jerrod's face got serious. "Have you been meeting with Dewey?"

"Yes, sir. We had beers with some guys who were, you know, over there. We understand each other. Saw the same things. Did the same things. It's not as awkward talking about... uh... issues with them."

"I'm glad. You're a good man, Alpo."

"Thank you, sir."

Jerrod said, "I'm going to get these payroll sheets submitted and call it a night."

"I've got things under control otherwise."

"I have no doubt. Thank you."

CHAPTER 64

"You've had some week, Jerrod," Sidney Yamamoto said. "I saw the news reports and feared you might not show up this evening."

"I had to do the shooting interview and write up that hitman thing and meet with the chief deputy. And I'm suspended... again.... but *with* pay this time."

"How are you feeling?"

"Pretty okay. Got caught up on rest. Finished the novel I've been reading... *finally.*"

"Do you want to talk about the incident at the cafe? You saw a man die."

"Sir, I have a question," Jerrod said as he pulled a side pillow onto his lap. "The first time we met, you said that our conversations are private and confidential, right?"

"That's correct. To clarify, unless you tell me you intend to hurt yourself or commit a crime against someone else -- patient-therapist confidentially exists."

"How about a crime that's already happened?"

"That would remain between us."

Jerrod paused for nearly a minute as he chose his words carefully. "You're not gonna hear this on the news." He paused again. "I watched that man in the diner die because I talked him into killing himself."

"You... what?"

"You heard me. I, Jerrod Gold, used all my powers of persuasion and manipulation -- my blessing and my curse -- against the man who threatened to hurt my wife. I talked that poor bastard into putting the muzzle of a .44 magnum revolver against his chest and pull the trigger."

"I... uh...," Sidney started to speak.

"How's that for a sales job, Sidney? The ultimate sale. One day only. While supplies last. All sales are final... make that *fatal.*" Jerrod leaned back. "Ever see what a .44 does point-blank? Little hole in front. Big hole in back. "Messy' doesn't quite describe it. And loud... fucking deafening loud. Ears are still ringing."

Sidney stammered. "I'm not sure what to say."

"Did you know it's a crime in California -- a felony, in fact -- to aid or encourage someone to commit suicide?"

"I'm aware of that."

"*You* helped me do it."

"How did *I* help you?"

"After Nikki left the restaurant and I turned off the cell phone, I told that guy that if he lived, he was going to prison for a long time."

"He most probably was... considering the crime."

"No doubt," Jerrod said. "But I painted a very colorful picture -- Bob Ross-would-be-proud-colorful -- for him on what hard-time was going to be like and how miserable his life was going to be."

"Most people understand prison can be dangerous and violent," Sidney said.

"Oh, I went way beyond 'dangerous and violent.' I described to him the most graphic ways imaginable how he would be 'turned-out' within ten minutes of passing through the gates at San Quentin. I detailed all the sexual abuse a fair-haired innocent 'punk' like him would undoubtedly have to endure at the hands -- and other body parts -- of the big, hairy, tattooed hardcore convicts he would be housed with."

"Why?"

"That was my plan when I walked into the restaurant," Jerrod explained. "That's my Hostage Policy and it's simple: End it there. Kill him. Or have him killed. Or, as it turned out, get him to kill himself. Finish it right in the middle of Sophie's Diner."

Sidney searched again for words.

"I gave him the option of how he was going to die," Jerrod continued, "but I made it abundantly clear he was going to die. He told me he'd do it. I kicked the revolver over to him and he took it from there."

Sidney shifted in his chair.

"I suspect it was his plan all along to kill himself -- but only after he shot me first." Jerrod paused. "I didn't know this at the time, but LaMahieu only had two cartridges in that six-shot revolver. Presumably one for me and one for himself. He just needed a little shove."

"But... again... how did I help?"

"You, sir, gave me the tools to do it. I took something you said to me, an otherwise innocent comment, and reshaped it into a weapon. Just like those creative inmates in my jail can make a 'shank' from nearly anything. I gave that guy a way out. Honorably. Just like the samurai. Death before dishonor or defeat. *Hara-kiri. Seppuku.* You know. Like we discussed."

"That's not... that wasn't my intention. We were talking about you."

"*You* were talking about me. *I* used it against *him*. Just like I always do. Please remember good and bad are the same thing to me... if it serves a purpose. My purpose. At that particular moment."

Sidney shook his head but didn't speak.

Jerrod tossed the pillow against the armrest and scooted forward. Their knees touched briefly. "I'll understand if you want me to leave now and don't want to see me as a patient anymore."

Sidney paused. "I want you to leave now."

Jerrod started to stand. "Understood."

"And I want to see you again in two weeks."

CHAPTER 65

"How was your session?" Nikki asked when Jerrod got home from Sidney's office.

"Good," he said. "He wants to see me again. It's nice to have someone to confide in."

"You can't confide in me?"

"Of course, I can. It's different with Sidney. He gives me inspiration and advice I can use to make clear decisions."

Nikki placed a hand on her hip. "Such as?"

"Such as... let me think... how about... I'm hungry and should eat something before my blood-sugar falls too low."

"Escape and evade. Classic Jerrod."

Nikki rested her head on Jerrod's bare chest and listened to his heartbeat.

"Is this going to be our life?" she asked.

"Is what?"

"This. Being taken hostage by a crazed man bent on revenge. Being rescued in dramatic fashion. Making love with the hero and then laying with him in the afterglow."

"No, on the hostage and rescue part. Yes, on in the lovemaking and afterglow part." He paused. "And I'm no 'hero.'"

She looked up it his face. "You walked into that restaurant and were willing trade your life for mine. I think that qualifies as 'heroic.'"

"It was a little more calculated than that."

She looked away. Silence. A sniffle. Then a tear. "I was so scared. I've already lost one husband and was sure I was going to lose you too."

"I can't bring Blake back. But I swear to you, I'll be here with you and the girls for as long as we both shall live."

CHAPTER 66

"Jerrod," Nikki yelled from the front door. "Phone's for you."

'I'm washing the truck. Tell them I'll call back. Who is it?"

Nikki spoke on the phone. "Sergeant... uh...something." She listened for a few seconds. "'Pez.' He says his name is 'Pez' from Las Vegas."

Jerrod dropped the sudsy wash mitt into a bucket and dried his hands on his t-shirt as he jogged to take the phone from Nikki.

"This is Jerrod."

"Roy Bloomstrom, Las Vegas Metro."

"How are you, sir?" Jerrod said. "Is this about my dad or something? Is he alright?"

"No. No," Pez said. "In fact, I just talked to your dad. He's fine."

"What's this about?"

"Well... uh... we found some bones. Human bones. Been there awhile. Down along the Colorado River near Laughlin."

"You think it might be Tommy?" Jerrod asked.

"We don't know, and I don't want to get hopes up. Coroner thinks it, or they, uh, based on the shape of the pelvis mostly, may be from an adolescent boy. I recalled this case and so on."

"You have dental records, right? My mom furnished those right after he disappeared. Just compare 'em."

"We have the records alright, but...," Pez paused, "we, uh, don't have the skull, or hands, or feet--"

"I get the picture," Jerrod interrupted. "Keep looking."

"We did. It was at a construction site. They were digging footings for some new apartments and found the bones. Big search. Homicide Unit and CSI. K-9s. Police Cadets. In fact, Kid remembered you and went down to help out. They spent a couple days digging and sifting dirt and such."

Jerrod's mind raced.

"Coroner says there were some marks on the wrist bones. Radius. Ulna. Both. I forget," Pez said. "They were possibly made from a fine-tooth saw or something. Not from animals gnawing. You know."

"That kind of rules out 'natural,' 'suicide,' and 'accidental' as the manner of death," Jerrod said. "Only leaves one."

"Pretty much. Want me to call your mom?"

"No, her number has changed since we met. Let's keep this from her until we know a little more."

"Okay," Pez said. "How about you come down here the next chance you get, and we'll go over what we have so far. The guys in Homicide are handling the case, but I'm working with them. The bones aren't going anywhere."

"You just ruined my day, Pez. My stomach's doing flip-flops right now. I want it to be Tommy... and I don't want it to be Tommy."

"Understood," Pez said. "'Closure' is an overused word in our profession. But I've found, most times, knowing is better than not knowing."

"I'll call you before I fly down, Jerrod said. "I need to make sure my dad is in town. We'll deal with this together."

"That'll be fine."

"You're not gonna understand what I'm about to say, Pez."

"I'm listening."

"But my 'ol man has a chess game he needs to finish."

ABOUT THE AUTHOR

James C. Gray is a retired twenty-five year
California law enforcement officer.

He lives with his wife, Cindy, in Northern Nevada.

Made in the USA
Middletown, DE
01 November 2021